MW01137535

# SILENT SUN

Hard Science Fiction

## BRANDON Q. MORRIS

BRANDON Q.
MORRIS
HARD SCIENCE FICTION

# Contents

# Silent Sun

## October 15, 2071, 1866 Sisyphus

"STOP SQUIRMING AROUND!"

Sobachka hung her head in acknowledgment of the reproach. Finally her muscles relaxed, allowing him to slide the suit over her front paws. It was a familiar procedure, yet the anticipation of an upcoming excursion inevitably got the better of her.

"Good girl!" said Artem encouragingly, stroking her head softly. The suit's soft material hardly restricted her movements. Just the diaper at her rear end bulged outward. He wore one, too. The excursion would only last a short time, but in space one never knew, and as always, 'better safe than sorry.'

"Hold still, now!" Here was the tricky part. Sobachka never liked him closing her helmet. She couldn't understand, of course, that vacuum was lethal.

He would probably react the same if someone was to interfere with his primary senses in the same way. With the helmet closed, the dog could only smell herself. He stabilized the back of her head with his right hand and shoved the helmet over her head with his left, until the helmet snapped into place at the middle of her neck. Then Artem activated the comms. "Great job!" he told her.

Sobachka shook her head and tried to lick his hand, but the helmet cut the effort short. She yapped in a sound kind of like growling and howling all mixed up.

"Sure, sure. I don't like that myself." Artem had tried to leave her on board during a spacewalk but the dog liked that even less. Besides, he needed her to do her thing later on.

He put on his own helmet, leaving the visor open.

He queried the helmet radio: "Current position?"

A small, transparent heads-up panel moved before his left eye. He focused on it and recognized their destination: Asteroid 1866 Sisyphus. Stats on the side indicated 1,500 meters distance from his ship. The object, the term 'egg-shaped' probably coming closest to an accurate description, wasn't more than a grain of sand in the sea of the universe. From this close, however, its eight-kilometer length was pretty impressive.

"Exit in ten minutes," the system intoned in a monotone voice. He had intentionally opted out of an AI-sounding voice. While he considered the decision some-what silly, he hadn't wanted the ship to sound more intelli-gent than himself. After all, he had Sobachka, who was brushing around his legs right now, for company during the months of solitude in space. Sometimes he couldn't help thinking she'd have preferred to be a cat. The dog, a mongrel, had gotten used to space nearly as quickly as a cat, and to the lack of up and down in space, too.

"Come along then," he said. Artem opened the inside hatch of the airlock. Sobachka knew what he expected and followed by his side as he entered the chamber. He broke a smile despite himself as he saw her giving just the tiniest push with her rear paws to sail in alongside.

He closed the inside hatch and locked it with the rotary wheel.

"Hatch closed," he said aloud. Then he flipped his helmet shut. Beside the hatch there was a panel with several buttons. He pressed the blue one.

The system confirmed: "Evacuating airlock." It was heavenly. A lovely silence built during the evacuation. He lifted his feet to cut that last path of transmission and relished the brief moment of complete silence.

"Three minutes."

Things were getting serious. Artem checked whether Sobachka was breathing regularly. He bent down, made eye contact, and stroked her back. She was doing well. She had been a professional cosmonaut for a long time now.

"Shall we, Sobachka?"

She tried to bark upon hearing her name, which didn't work well inside her helmet. Artem held her with one arm and attached the short lifeline between his spacesuit and the hook at the back of her suit. Then he clipped his own lifeline to the hook next to the outside hatch. This line was quite long, being his means of returning to the ship with Sobachka. His right hand grabbed the rotary wheel and he opened the hatch.

The moment had come. He couldn't help his heart beating faster just before launching himself downward. He pressed the hatch out, aided by the last remnants of air.

Far below he saw brightly-lit rocks with hard-cut edges and deep black shadows. Now that he viewed the asteroid first-hand, rather than on a display, it felt like the gateway to hell—and fearfully far at the same time.

But the display claimed only 300 meters to go. Artem jumped with the dog in his arms. A brief moment of panic, then experience kicked in and let him reorient his senses. The destination was ahead, not below. With his ship in orbit, he slowly drifted toward the asteroid. Every meter yielded more detail.

A tourist would not notice, but the expert quickly noted that Sisyphus had been being mined for a long time already. The visible lines were too straight to be natural. And the residual waste filling craters was out of place, too. But that was what Artem was here for. His money came from being quicker than the rightful owner. Others would call him a thief.

Early on he had aspired higher, maybe a kind of Robin Hood, but more recently he had admitted to himself that it was all about the money. Sisyphus was going to reach its closest orbital point from Earth in about a month, the perfect opportunity for its owner, the Russian conglomerate, RB, to send specialized transport ships to pick up the results of two-and-a-half years of mining.

He was going to be quicker. He didn't need special transport since he was only here for the rare earths that the machines of the RB Group had extracted from the rock of the asteroid. A ton and a half of his bounty would pay for the next three years—plus add a sweet little sum to his bank account. The risk was minimal, the core operation would take about half an hour, and his small ship could accelerate faster than those plump transporters.

Only 50 meters to go. The distance indicator started blinking on the display. He needed to concentrate. The asteroid rotated by in slow motion. At the moment, the dome where the two guards spent their time was passing under him. They posed no threat since their pay was terrible. The RB Group only employed them to meet legal requirements to keep the mining license on Sisyphus. At one point, trade unions had been able to ban staff-free mining. Even if these guys tried to interfere, he'd have his weapon to keep them in check. And before that, one of them would have to look up into the sky and notice his ship. Normally they would rely on their radar to detect visitors more reliably than any video cam. But his ship was protected against radar by expensive meta-materials. So far he'd had eight successful raids and everything had gone well.

At ten meters he ignited the braking jets. There was a big rock between himself and the dome so that his activity would go unnoticed. The dome was of no interest to him. It housed the guards and he'd avoid them anyway. The resources he was after were stocked about 500 meters away from the dome.

Artem checked directions on the eye display and carefully released Sobachka. The dog noticed at once that she was free. At first she struggled with her legs, but then she remembered how things worked in space. Her suit had its own jets that she controlled by pressing her front paws to her body. The harder she pressed, the more she would accelerate. Sobachka was perfectly in control. She showed him artistic pirouettes. Artem smiled and was deeply pleased to see her enjoying the performance. He'd have loved to be able to sit on a rock and keep watching, but they had work to do.

He pointed in the direction of the stockpile with his right arm, and the dog followed along obediently. Halfway there the sun rose; a cold, white fireball. It appeared over the near horizon, with the rapid rotation of the asteroid speeding the process along. Rocks glistened where they were flooded with light while hard-edged, pitch-black shadows spread behind objects. Then the stockpile came into sight. It was easy to spot by the rectangular shapes of the containers. They stood out like paper cutouts.

He had worked on an asteroid as a contractor before going independent, so he knew the processes here quite well. The containers were hard steel all around. Opening them in space was not part of the procedure. To fill them, they had docking ports on all sides for tubes with a diameter of half a meter. Flat robots that looked like many-legged cockroaches transported the resources that had been previously mined and separated into specific raw materials. Extending the length of the tubes was all that was required as the mining process moved along.

To avoid inefficiencies due to long distances, the guards had to add a new 'roach' to the system every three or four weeks. That was where the maintenance hatches in the tubing came in. Artem was heading there.

"Come!" he called out to Sobachka. The dog responded immediately. Ahead of them a tube snaked across the scraggy surface. Artem pointed forward with his headlamp. He only needed to move ten meters toward the container to find an entry. He was able to remove the cover, secured by eight large screws, with the toolkit he had brought. He set the screws aside. He'd put them back in place later. The guards wouldn't even guess that he'd moved through. Later, back on Earth, some manager would notice an unusually low yield of rare earths.

Now it was his companion's turn. He knelt before the dark opening, stroked her, and removed the safety line. Sobachka didn't flinch. She knew what he expected of her. On his first trip he had tried a drone but it proved impossible to maneuver through the dark tubes. Artem lit up the helmet lamp for the dog, put his hand in the tube, and knocked on the floor there. That was her signal. The dog had an infallible instinct for her surroundings. He wouldn't need to guide her around obstacles. If he spotted anything on her camera he'd let her know via helmet radio.

"Search!" he commanded. Sobachka turned toward him for a last look and disappeared into the dark. Artem followed her progress on the display. Where each raw material was stored was different from asteroid to asteroid. The dog entered the first container. It was nearly full, so it couldn't be anything valuable. Artem activated the gamma spectrometer on Sobachka's back anyway. It detected some iron mineral, complete junk. No need to say anything, the dog was already looking for the next tube onward. The containers were interconnected so the roaches could store any raw material as needed.

Half an hour later they finally came across something. The gamma spectrometer indicated the stuff he was looking for, starting phase two. He encouraged Sobachka via radio, prompting her to remember the container. Then he called her back. He was glad to see her crawl out of the hole after another five minutes. Unimaginable, if something were to happen to her!

He loaded her with a bundle weighing about a kilogram on Earth. Training her with this pack bag had been the most difficult part. Sobachka carried the bundle straight to the right container, unrolled it, and spread it roughly over the desired material. Then Artem activated the fibers at the edge of the textile. They dug into the pile and enclosed part of it in the pack bag. That was the first load of bounty. He praised the dog again, and she started the return journey carrying the full but nearly weightless bag. Artem checked the clock: 47 minutes for the first bag.

To meet his expenses, Sobachka needed to fill eight bags. His goal was twenty. Thirty would be a personal record. The longer they took, the higher the risk that one of the guards would see the bright speck that didn't belong up there in the sky, and wasn't detected by radar.

He heard a noise on the helmet radio. *That can only be Sobachka*, he thought. Artem quickly knelt before the tube entrance. But the camera in her suit showed no image.

Had something happened to her? His heart raced. He tried to peer into the tube in the direction from which she would be coming. Right then something knocked into his visor. She was back. *Phew, first transport done.* Artem stood up. Even as he rose he noticed a shadow next to him that hadn't been there before. He pulled the weapon from his suit pocket, blinked while working out where the origin of the shadow would be, and shot. The recoil made him feel the projectile leaving the barrel, vacuum preventing the sound from reaching his ears. There was a dull groan on the helmet radio. *Hit!* Artem lifted his head and saw a person holding the side of his spacesuit.

"He hit me! Shit, shit!" came through the radio in Russian, a male voice. That had to be one of the guards. How had they noticed him?

"Your own bloody fault, idiot, I told you not to approach from that side," said a second voice. *Was that the other guard? Wouldn't he run to help his colleague? The first man would die otherwise, no doubt,* Artem thought.

But the second guard wasn't so stupid. He probably figured out he would be shot then, too. Or not? Indeed, there was a second person showing up next to the shot guard. Artem was lifting his arm to take aim when he got a hard kick against his elbow. He managed not to drop the weapon. At the same time somebody grabbed him around the neck. *Couldn't be the kicker, so I must be up against four. Has RB been ramping up security? And I haven't noticed anything?*

"My partner is aiming at your head," said a new voice. It didn't sound like a bluff, but he wasn't intimidated and kept aiming at the second man. His suit ramped up the ventilation as he was sweating profusely now. His mind raced. *What are my options? Should I give up? I don't think they'll let me live. Shouldn't I at least take one of them along with me?*

"Don't you dare," said the last voice, "or we'll take the helmet off your little pet here."

A man in a brand-new RB spacesuit stepped into his view and brushed Artem's weapon hand aside in a careless move. He had Sobachka stuck under his arm.

"Should I? She would probably look real sweet yapping for air."

Artem released the weapon. It sailed away in slow motion.

"I give up!" he yelled.

"That's very wise. Maybe we let your dog live that way. However," the guard said in an ominous tone, "the Chinese cook on board has asked us for fresh meat so many times now…"

"You son of a bitch! You thug!" burst out of Artem.

"Hey, take it easy, Artjom. The villain here is you."

"Artem, you Russian asshole, it's Artem. I am Ukrainian."

"Isn't that the same, Artjom? I'll call you what I choose. Be glad I don't call you a piece of shit—I am well educated after all."

Artem tried to twist out of the grip of the man who was holding him from behind, but with no luck. The other guy, who still was holding Sobachka and seemed to be the boss here, kept coming closer and closer until their helmets met. He had blue eyes, a receding forehead, and the oft-broken nose of a boxer.

"Nobody steals from RB. That should be clear to you!" he hissed over the radio.

Suddenly an incredible pain seared through him. *Sobachka* was his last thought as he lost consciousness.

## October 16, 2071, SS Lenin

"FOR THE LAST TIME, who have you been working with?"
The blue-eyed guy waved pliers in front of Artem's face
without getting any reaction.

"I asked you something!" The man opened the pliers
and adjusted them to Artem's little finger. Then he started
to squeeze. Artem tried to pull his hand away, his muscles
twitching, but he was strapped down.

"Alone. I am alone," burst out of him. He tried not to
show it, but the pain was so excruciating tears were
running down his face.

"Indeed you are, Artjom, but that doesn't answer my
question." The pliers moved to his ring finger. He saw in
slow motion how its jaws closed. Then, after a brief delay,
pain flashed. The room on board the Russian ship with the
outdated name began to waver. Maybe he'd be lucky and
lose consciousness. Then somebody poured cold water over
him from behind, and that hope vanished. The torture was
set to continue.

"You know, Artjom," the boxer-guy said in a preten-
tiously jovial manner, "you must think I am a sadist. But

torture is as strenuous for me as it is for you. Really. Can't we meet halfway? You tell me who buys your wares and I… I let your dog live."

*Sobachka—they haven't killed her.* The first good news since waking up only to be tortured by this sadist. Warm feelings welled up as he thought about Sobachka. Suddenly the deal didn't sound bad. He'd give the name of the Chinese trader to whom he sold the rare earths, and Sobachka could join him. The trader wouldn't be in immediate danger since Russia couldn't afford trouble with China.

Artem gave the name.

"That's the way!" said the man who was torturing him. He came closer and stroked Artem's forehead. "You are a good boy, after all, Artjom."

"I want a real trial."

The man stepped back and looked at him with genuine surprise. "You want to be shot? After all, you killed an innocent man."

"I want a fair trial," said Artem.

"But we have a far better offer for you. You really impressed the big boss, Artjom. He digs creative work. We need people like you. You work for us in the future. We pay quite well, right guys?"

The two men left and right of him nodded in unison.

"And Sobachka?"

"You can keep the bitch. Where else do you have that option, pets on spacecraft? Only with us."

"And if I refuse?"

"Then you get the trial that you wish for so much. I can assure you that you will end up with a bullet in the head. Our unbribable courts show no mercy for villains of your kind."

The man with the blue eyes laughed out loud and the other two chimed in obediently.

## March 24, 2074, Paris

"DAMN DOORSTEP!" Alain Petit held on to the doorframe and complained loudly. Not in spite of being alone in his apartment, but because of it. If his wife were here—instead of resting at the Passy Cemetery—she'd reprimand him. She would tell him to lower his voice because of the neighbors, and because loud rants are improper in the first place. Alain smiled. It had been hard losing her a year and a half ago, but by now he was starting to appreciate his new-found freedom.

That included fried noodles from the Asian fast-food place, which he had just eaten with a healthy appetite. And it included his hobby, astronomy, for which he no longer had to endure cold nights. He owned a good telescope that had been on the expensive side, and he had even gotten the permission of the landlord to position it under a skylight, but the nights in Paris had become too bright to see any useful details.

Last year his son had shown him how to move his hobby to the computer. Professional astronomers world-wide had too much on their plates with millions of high-res pictures streaming in from probes all across the solar system. Astronomers were often still busy with a given set of pictures years after the particular probe had already shut down. They had tried to train AIs but the results were far from perfect, especially when it was not clear what one was looking for in the first place. So, astronomers were glad to have the help of hobbyist-researchers.

Alain dedicated every afternoon to this task, starting after lunch and continuing until it got dark. He would only interrupt his routine for visitors, and grudgingly at that. The software he was using had awarded him with a virtual prize—apparently he was the participant who had analyzed the most images to date.

His computer greeted him with the familiar startup chime while he settled down. He launched the app developed by an American university and followed the instructions. Some scientists were trying to learn how small sunspots moved across the surface of the sun. To that end, the app kept showing him time-lapsed photography of a particular location.

His task was to track a specific spot with the mouse. The spot was defined in a first shot of the series at hand. The same set was also shown to other users since the spot was not always clearly defined. Although Alain knew that others were repeating his work, and that he worked on photos others had already processed, his work felt rewarding. In a few months, once the voluntary scientific aides finished their processing, the professional astronomers would use their results in a research report and his work would be part of that. Humanity would have learned something new about the sun.

Alain leaned back after 30 minutes. It was time to close the curtains a bit to avoid glare on his screen from the afternoon sun. This particular spring was unusually warm, necessitating extra trips to the cemetery to water the flowers he had planted on his wife's grave. But today he had a day off. He shrugged his shoulders, feeling the pain of rusty joints. Fortunately his eyes were still good except that he needed reading glasses.

Then he pressed 'Start.' Some youngster's stats had been catching up on him over the past weeks so he couldn't afford long breaks. His daughter had given him an odd look when he had explained why he could not take his bothersome grandchildren over the weekend. His competitor had to be young judging by the smiley and newfangled codes in his alias. Alain wondered where he might be from. Was it a man, or a woman? A Frenchman like himself? Or maybe an Australian, or even from China or India? Since India had overtaken China in population, that was the most likely answer, he mused.

*Wait. Where did the spot go?* Alain squinted. A moment ago it was all clear. To keep conditions constant it was not permitted to zoom into the picture. But his son had installed a software loupe. "So you can read the fine print!" he had said. Alain had laughed at that. He didn't think he needed a loupe. Now he was glad it was there since he could zoom even though the software lacked the function. He was cheating, that was clear enough, but he felt comfortable because his competitor certainly was at least 30 years younger and so much more efficient.

The spot remained lost. Alain checked the picture line-by-line and sector-by-sector. He tried to picture how the spot would look under the loupe, but there wasn't anything even remotely like it. What he did notice was a fine line. He moved the entire window with the picture just to make sure it wasn't something on his monitor—the line moved along just fine. Was there a scale somewhere? He didn't find anything on the solar image itself. He rummaged

BRANDON Q. MORRIS

around for the instructions that he had printed out for moments like this. It was in the drawer of his desk. And the number was right there: Every pixel of the image corresponded to ten kilometers in reality. Alain stared at the screen again. Then he used the loupe one more time. It was crystal clear—the line was exactly one pixel thick and if he zoomed in it grew into little blocks.

Alain had been an engineer all his life. Sometimes, he knew, there were faults in pictures, so-called artifacts, especially if computers had processed the image. Was this an artifact? He flipped forward a few times and stopped at a different picture of the series. He zoomed in again. Any thin lines? He concentrated, squinting again. Nothing. He was disappointed.

But he wouldn't give up so quickly. He randomly selected yet another image from the series, enlarged it as far as possible, and then scrutinized it for lines. Nothing. Alain straightened his back, which was letting him know his age once again. One more photo, quick! If he didn't find anything now he would return to his actual task, the solar spots. No lines in that photo either. It was time to give up. *On the other hand...* he thought. *No.* He... had been reasonable all his life. Today he'd give in to folly and look at one more picture. Just one!

And, there it was—a line, one pixel strong, parallel to the sun's equator! He had two hits now. That might not be enough to bother a scientist, but it was enough to nudge him to keep looking for more evidence. The sunspots would have to wait, even if his smiley-faced competitor would be overtaking his spot in the rankings.

THREE HOURS later Alain noticed that he was cold. Small surprise with the window open all that time. He got up and closed it. Night was falling outside so he closed the curtain, too. Then he turned around and looked at his desk, dimly lit by the pale screen light. His wife would have called him to dinner around this time. They would sit opposite each other, facing each other and exchanging thoughts in silence. Alain missed her.

He shook his head to drive out the memories and returned to his desk. Twelve pictures with lines—a dozen out of maybe 300 pictures he had assessed. That should be enough to get a scientist interested. He opened his email account and dropped a note to the lead scientist of the sunspot project. Before shutting down he quickly checked the leaderboard. His competitor now led him by one point. Alain smiled in recognition of good work. Someday he wanted to meet that man—or was it a woman?

He powered down his computer. It was time for his evening walk around the block.

LITTLE COULD he imagine how that one-pixel-wide line would change his life.

## March 31, 2074, Mercury

ARTEM CAREFULLY OPENED the heavy lid of the hatch and climbed up the ladder. Helmet comms transmitted a bark. Sobachka was being lazy. She had turned into an old lady. He climbed back down to fetch her. The short ladder shouldn't have been a problem with gravity at just a third of Earth's pull. Artem stepped out onto the dusty Mercury soil and set Sobachka down. They wore matching garb— spacesuits with a special silvery coating to reflect the sunlight.

However, the sun wasn't visible despite Artem climbing to the surface to see it. The sun had yet to creep over the steep walls of the Kandinsky Crater. The station was on the edge of the formation that measured about 60 kilometers in diameter, torn into the planetary crust by a meteorite some three billion years ago. The reason for the station was some two kilometers south. Artem put a hand to his visor as though he had to shield himself from too much light, but of course that didn't help him to see the ice reserves on the crater walls. They formed where the sun never shone—obviously not in the 88 earth days of night, but neither in the equally long mercurial day.

Sobachka prodded her helmet against his knee in lieu of her nose, then ran off. She returned just to run away once more. She seemed to enjoy their stay on the surface a great deal despite having had to squeeze into the spacesuit first. Space inside the station was cramped, and the wide landscape let Artem breathe more freely, too, despite the air being compressed inside a bottle on his back.

They had a few kilometers to walk. On the right there were two space vessels—a fast courier ship, and a transporter to ferry the resources extracted here. Extracting metals alone would be far too expensive, but there was a side benefit. Helium-3, still one of the most expensive resources of all, changed the game. It was easier to obtain on the moon, but those licenses had been sold out for a long time.

Where had Sobachka gone? He didn't see her anymore. She had probably run ahead. Artem activated the searchlight. The horizon was bright enough but the atmosphere was too thin to illuminate the shadows from pitch black. Suddenly Sobachka leapt at him from behind. Artem got a shock—and laughed. Sobachka whined. She had probably scared herself, too, by jumping higher than expected in the light gravity.

He called out, "With me!" and his companion came alongside.

They slowly strolled by the spaceships. Sobachka lifted her head as if to sniff. Of course, she couldn't sniff anything. There was no danger on Mercury. No food, no other animal to mark its territory. This world was incredibly old and just as dead. As long as one didn't stay in the sunlight—at 430 degrees Celsius—so long that cooling failed, or take off one's helmet on the surface, nothing could happen.

As chief of security, it was Artem's job to inspect the spacecraft regularly. If ever there was an emergency of the kind that nobody wanted to imagine, or that nobody was able to imagine, the ships had to be ready for take-off. But today was his day off. The stroll was solely to satisfy his curiosity. He had wanted to see one of the rare sights that Mercury had to offer: the moment when the sun moved backward. He had been on Mercury for more than two years now but he had missed the moment every time so far.

"Boring," the others had warned him.

Even station chief Vladislav had opined, "Less than spectacular!" and he had studied astronomy in an earlier life. He had also explained how the phenomenon came about. Every so often there was a time when Mercury would move faster along its trajectory around the sun than the speed of its rotation around its own axis. During those times the sun appeared to move backward in the mercurial sky.

He was going to form his own opinion, but for that he and Sobachka would have to leave the shadows.

AN HOUR and a half later they were looking at an unbearably bright stone desert ahead. Shadows perfectly traced the crater walls. There was no transition, just hard lines. The thermometer jumped from minus 160 degrees to 430 degrees in twenty seconds. Life support droned in Artem's ears. Sobachka returned of her own accord. Presumably the noise was bothering her, too. He checked the watch on his wrist display. Ten minutes to go. Artem decided to step back into the shadows to ease the load on life support. Sobachka joined him.

13:55 UTC. Another minute to go. He motioned to Sobachka. Then he looked at the sun. The visor darkened instantly. The glaring white disk was impressive. It appeared twice as large as on Earth and it moved on a backdrop of deepest black. Artem concentrated. Was it moving forward or had the reverse motion started already? He tapped on his wrist display and guiding lines appeared inside his visor while the sun was darkened out. Now it became obvious: The sun was moving backward. Artem looked down on the ground. The long shadows cast by the sun now moved forward, the reverse of their just-previous direction. The sun would now stay on this course for a few Earth days before resuming the journey to her highest point. Simple celestial mechanics, but he was awed just the same.

"Come, Sobachka," he called out. "Let's walk back to the station."

He bent down to pick up a stone. Then he reached out and hurled it into the night.

## April 2, 2074, Paris

"Dear Alain Petit," began the email that he had just opened. "We appreciate your great interest in our Citizen-Science-Project. Congratulations on reaching the top rank once again. I would like to comment on your questions as follows."

Alain nudged his glasses back in place.

"Topic 1. You are not our oldest participant. This title goes to a lady from New Zealand whose name I can't provide for privacy reasons. If you would like to get in touch, I'll be more than happy to pass along your message."

No way. A woman from New Zealand! He certainly did not plan to exchange emails.

"Topic 2. We have done lengthy investigations into the anomalies you submitted. We concluded that they were formed when stitching individual exposures. The images taken with different cameras at different wavelengths are superimposed with specialized software. As the various instruments sit at slightly different angles, their perspective on the target is not fully identical. You can get a feeling for the issue by covering your eyes alternately while looking at the same picture. The composing issue grows more significant toward the edges, like the linear artifacts you observed."

Okay, so they believed he had seen artifacts—technical errors.

"Based on your message we have checked our processes. Unfortunately the primary processing can't be reversed with a reasonable amount of work. You will therefore keep finding such lines. We have no reason to change methods, as the primary mission goal is to catalog sunspot movement."

*I got that,* he thought, *you were busy enough and didn't want any additional work. Publishing deadlines were bad enough already.*

"Regardless, we are proud to have such attentive volunteers in our team and thank you in advance for your continued support. Best regards…"

Alain sat up to stretch. The back of his seat squeaked. Spring smells wafted through the window, which he had opened halfway again. A little walk was due. His tube of toothpaste was empty, and if he passed by the convenience store on the corner he would save a trip to the supermarket. On the other hand… Alain drummed on the table with his fingers. That message had left him with an odd feeling, one he had almost forgotten. It felt like getting turned down by a beautiful woman. *I really seem to be getting quaint now.*

Should he resign himself to that answer? That had never been his way. He never would have married Marie if he had given up on her first refusal. Later it had turned out that she liked him very much, but her best friend warned her about this 'weird guy.' Alain smiled. Eventually that friend had married his brother. They, too, had died…

But he was alive, and he would not let the rejection stand.

His computer had just crashed for the third time. Alain was prepared for that. He had taken notes of all he had found. In Hawaii, or—to be more precise—on the Haleakalā volcano on the island of Maui, was the DKIST, the Daniel K. Inouye Solar Telescope. It had been put into service more than 50 years ago, but its 4-meter mirror was still the worldwide leader. If anybody could help with his problem it would be somebody on their team. He had also found the source for the raw data of his probe, the very data that shaped the images he was investigating for sunspot movement. If he followed the official message, the lines would not be in the raw data. Unfortunately the raw data was inaccessible, protected by the login/password of some large astronomical research organization. He had to find a scientist who would give him access, or at least provide him with the relevant part of the raw data. Ideally he could get someone from DKIST to help.

It was the middle of the night in Hawaii, so a call wouldn't work. Besides, scientists there had better things to do than to chat about lines on the sun. So he started to prepare the evidence. He pulled together the twelve snap-shots with the lines, zoomed in, and took screenshots of the critical areas. Alain was proud of himself for remembering the keyboard shortcut for doing this. His daughter had taught him two or three years ago, and he had not forgotten despite that much time having passed.

Then he typed out his message. As an engineer, he was used to reading foreign literature, so laying things out in English came together readily. He had looked up the addresses of three scientists who didn't have staff of their own. Heads of teams rarely had time for such issues—people doing real work were more likely to be sympathetic.

"Dear Mr. XYZ," he started out. He would paste in the surname later on.

"While studying images from the NASA sun probe, I came across thin lines parallel to the solar equator. Their width is close to image resolution itself. I must add that the project lead considers them artifacts secondary to the combination of data sources."

Would that ruin his chances? On the other hand, the probe team would be their first stop if he did get their attention. He was going to save everyone time by laying out all the facts.

"However, the argument did not convince me. This is why I am asking you for a second opinion, in best scientific tradition."

That sounded good. He hadn't mentioned anywhere that he was a retired mechanical engineer.

"The original probe images are available at... Unfortunately I do not have access due to my external status. I would appreciate it very much if you could make object numbers," he'd insert the list of images here later, "available to me as digital files. I am attaching the results of my research for your reference."

He tried adding his screenshots to the message but he was unable to add any after the sixth one. Alain counted the attachments and noted six screenshots were indicated. That had to be enough to illustrate the issue. Images were too easily manipulated to prove anything, anyway.

"I hope to hear from you soon. With best regards, Alain Petit."

He checked the message. Maybe it was better to fly to

Hawaii straight away? That was crazy, his wife would have been right about that. He inserted names and addresses and sent the messages off one after the other. Then he stood up, donned a light jacket, and set out on his evening walk.

## April 3, 2074, Maui

HEATHER CLOSED the metal door behind her. Sunlight overwhelmed her to the point of teary eyes. She held her hand up to her brow. She had forgotten her cap in the car once again, but she couldn't be bothered to walk back to the parking lot for it. The plastic bag in her hand began to collect condensation after coming out of the refrigerator. Her daughter had prepared a sandwich, wrapped in a paper napkin. That would serve as lunch. She was going to look through the thesis of her postgraduate student, Tetsu. He clearly hadn't pulled it together yet. She had been poring over his work for three hours and desperately needed a break. There was an air-conditioned common room over at the Pan-STARRS but she wouldn't go there unless it rained.

HER PREFERRED SPOT was on the wall in front of the DKIST, with the view out to the north. She crossed the narrow tarmac, scaled the demarcation that felt so primitive compared to the high tech behind her, and let her legs dangle. The breathtaking view never failed to relax her. The sweeping, volcanic landscape in shades of gray and brown had an alien touch, like a landscape on Mars or Mercury, perhaps. Small and large lava blocks were scattered over the hillside, just as the shield volcano Haleakalā had dropped them. In the distance the ocean sometimes shimmered, forming a deep blue backdrop. Today the sea of clouds was close. White and gray fleecy clouds stretched out to the horizon. A fresh wind carried the salty scent of the sea. From 3,000 meters altitude, it seemed like the world was a peaceful place.

She unpacked the sandwich. It was her favorite, lots of European cheese. Her daughter, a vegan, would be disgusted. She was deeply grateful that her daughter had prepared the sandwich anyway. The events two years ago had really turned their lives upside down, but slowly things had been calming down. If it hadn't been for that black hole out of nowhere she would have been on the successor of the DKIST for some time already, but priorities had been radically changed. At least that near-catastrophic event had produced the nice result of returning her daughter from the distant mainland to the island where she had been born.

The wind freshened up and she shivered. She had worn nothing over her T-shirt and was without sun protection so she couldn't stay around for long. She was good for a few more minutes though. The clouds showed some movement. Maybe a thunderstorm somewhere down below. Suddenly steps came up from behind and to her right. She tried to guess who it might be. It was two people neatly in sync. *That could only be*—she turned and yes, it was Steve and José hand in hand walking toward her. The two young men had been an official couple for several years now and still acted as though they had just fallen in love. Heather was a bit envious, although she couldn't stand Steve at all. She hadn't yet formed an opinion on José.

"Hi Heather, how's it going?" asked Steve.

"Good, thanks, and how about you?"

She kept her demeanor professional, hoping they would move along.

"We're doing great, right José?"

Steve looked at José and cracked a wide smile.

"Yeah, I think so," replied José.

"Can we sit down for a bit?" asked Steve. *No more solitude.* "The weather is so refreshing right now," he added.

"Sure—the wall isn't mine," answered Heather.

"Thanks, that's so kind of you!"

Steve and José sat down. Now they were three, looking out to the north. Conversation died and Heather was glad for that.

"Did you also get that email?" asked Steve after a while. Heather wasn't sure whether five minutes or fifteen had passed. The skin on her arm felt warm, so it was probably more like fifteen. Where was her head? She needed to get back into the shade. She burned easily, a legacy of her Irish ancestors.

"What email?" she asked back.

"Some Frenchman. Maurice Petit or something like that. He emailed José and me separately. Probably thought it would improve his chances."

"I didn't have a chance to check my mail yet. What does he want?"

"He thinks he discovered some lines on the sun. And that we should help him confirm his discovery."

Heather sighed. Such messages were frequent. People who proved Einstein wrong somewhere and asked her to verify the proof. These people seemed to be writing to thousands of scientists and stealing their time.

"And how does he expect you to help?"

"He'd like access to the original imagery from the last solar probe."

"Well, at least you won't need to debunk some alternative quantum theory."

Steve laughed. "Anyway," he said, "my time is too precious for something like that. *Our* time." He caressed the knee of his friend. The gesture did not appear tender, it bordered on the possessive.

Heather was reminded why she did not like Steve. She stood up. "I am getting pretty red, guys," she said, pointing to her arm. "See you around."

"See you later," replied Steve.

*Hopefully not,* thought Heather. An electric car honked at her as she crossed the road.

"Sorry!" she called out. Those things were so quiet, she thought, so hard to notice. She continued across the road and disappeared into the lab of the solar telescope.

IT WAS EVEN COLDER in the lab than it was outside. Tetsuyo had turned up the air conditioning yet again, and he wasn't even in the lab. She looked at the clock. Her scope time didn't start for another half hour. She'd relieve her colleague then. She switched off the air conditioning and opened the door, hoping for some warmer air.

Then Heather sat down at her desk. She shifted the picture of her daughter Mariela back to its spot while the computer started up. The janitor had probably moved it.

Next to Mariela was an older man, Heather's ex. He had disappeared two years ago without a word and never contacted her again. Heather had sworn to never look for him.

She had 53 new messages waiting, the perfect way to pass the time until her shift on the sun scope came up. Half of them came from a worldwide mailing list for solar physicists and astronomers. A couple of spams, too, of course. *How long, and still humanity hasn't been able to solve that problem?* Heather remembered her grandfather nattering about this pest back in the 2030s. But even quantum cryptography didn't stop her from getting promotions for breast enlargements. Or the one from a British widow whose husband died in a '72 explosion, soliciting help in managing her 7-figure inheritance.

Heather looked down at herself. She was quite comfortable with her breasts. Hips and belly were a different matter. And her bank account would do much better with a million or two more in it.

Then she saw the message that Steve had mentioned. The man was named Alain, not Maurice. His message was very nice, but he clearly was an amateur. She deleted the message and promptly had second thoughts. Shouldn't she be glad that amateurs were interested in their work? Steve was right though—such correspondence could turn into a real drag. Active amateurs especially—the ones who were so convinced of themselves that they wouldn't be stopped by evidence to the contrary. She had experienced such a case herself. That man had even taken to calling her at home.

Maurice Petit—she corrected that thought. *Alain* Petit didn't seem to be that single-minded. She undeleted the message. It conveyed true interest. She looked up his name. He seemed to have lots of time, helping out with projects that made use of amateurs. He even had the top rank in the sunspot project. She pictured him as a spotty 17-year-old with thick glasses. But maybe she was wrong. His style was pretty mature despite not writing in his first language.

The project lead of the Citizen Science Project had considered his findings irrelevant. Perseverance was considered to be an important asset for every scientist. Shouldn't she be rewarding him for that? She hesitated. Then she remembered Steve's haughty remarks. That was why she needed to respond to this Frenchman. She reminded herself not to enter any discussions and just send out the files he had requested. That would not take too long. She entered her credentials on the database, loaded the images, and forwarded them to Alain Petit in several messages.

"Your turn now," said Tetsuyo. Her colleague closed the door and went straight to the air conditioner. "It's warm in here, isn't it?" He turned the dial all the way to the left. A cold stream of air hit Heather's forehead. *Time to get out!*

"Okay, I'm heading to the scope. See you tomorrow," she said as she got up and left the room through the door that Tetsuyo had just come through.

## April 4, 2074, Paris

IT HAD WORKED! He had the files, in duplicate! Alain rubbed his hands in anticipation. A kind astronomer had responded. Heather Marshall. And shortly after her mail came a second one from someone named José Marino. Both wished him good luck with his work and asked him to kindly refrain from further discussion. That was perfect for Alain. He expected the scientists got lots of emails from crazy people who just wasted their time.

He quickly retrieved the attachments. Opening the files was another matter, though. All his apps refused the files. He should have thought of that. The probe cameras obviously had a special file format. Now he was unable to use the original files. Should he ask the two kind astronomers for a pointer? *Probably not.* He might have more specific questions later. This problem was his own to solve.

He was an engineer, after all. While he had spent his life treating sewage, the basic engineering work process was applicable everywhere. So what was the problem? He had some original files in an unknown format. And he had photos derived from those files. So he was looking for the process that turned the originals into photos. That was a well-defined problem for which there could only be a single solution—very reassuring. He started searching for image-processing algorithms but quickly noticed that the math was too complex for him. He would not be able to find the solution himself. But if someone provided the solution he would be able to verify it by comparison with the photos he already had in hand.

Problem-solving experts abounded on the net. He checked relevant marketplaces and registered on the biggest one. Quickly he typed up his problem and deposited the money he was ready to offer for the solution. He felt generous and invested half his monthly pension. That yielded instant offers. Experts seemed to have been waiting for an offer like that.

Somebody from India wrote back. "Hello Alain, I must tell you honestly that there is a free software product for your problem. It is not easy to use but you will manage. I can do that for you if you like, but the money you offer is far too much for this job."

Alain was impressed by such honesty. The man was not out to empty his pockets. He decided to give him more than just an hourly wage. He awarded half the promised amount. He could easily do without the money. He didn't need much anymore.

He sent the material to the Indian. "When joining the component spectral images," he wrote, "I am mainly inter-ested in the edges of the result. I am told that artifacts can appear. Please check if that can be avoided. Many thanks!"

Alain leaned back after sending the message on its way. It was just before 1 p.m. He had just saved a quarter of his pension so he decided to celebrate by going out for lunch. The bar on the corner offered snacks at noon, prepared by the cook—the wife of the owner. He had always enjoyed a bit of innocent flirting with Geraldine.

THE AFTERNOON SUN shone into his sitting room. Dust glittered in the rays of light. Alain fetched a moist rag from the kitchen and wiped the big round table. The layer of dust surprised him. Nobody had spent time in this room since his wife had died. He really needed to clean more frequently or he would turn into one of those old men suffocating in their dirt. The good food made him drowsy, and he was not used to a lunchtime glass of red wine anymore. Should he rest for a while? Instead, the computer tickled his curiosity. A quick glance at the screen revealed a new message. The Indian had responded already. Alain sat down. The results were in the attachment, photos just like those he had been checking for the sunspot project. Apparently his hired expert had been successful.

Alain used the loupe to zoom in on the photos. Would he find any lines? He pushed the image back and forth on the screen, squinting in an effort to concentrate. There they were! He had been right, hadn't he?

He skimmed the text message from India. "I have combined the spectral images as requested. To test the hypothesis of artifact formation, I have used different clipping magnifications than were used before. If the lines are technical issues they would now appear elsewhere. See for yourself."

Alain excitedly opened an original image, looked for a line and jotted down its coordinates. Then he repeated the process with the corresponding new image. The coordinates were identical. The lines appeared in the same locations. Clearly no artifact involvement. There was something in that location that nobody else had discovered! Alain clutched his chest because his heart was beating so rapidly. If he had a heart attack now, nobody would hear about his discovery. He laughed. The idea was ridiculous. He was over 70 but his heart had never given him any trouble. He just needed to calm himself, and find someone to talk to about his discovery.

## April 12, 2074, Paris

PETIT. There it was. The name was engraved in a bell plate that must have been screwed to the entrance wall many years ago. Arthur Eigenbrod pressed the button. He was disappointed. Instead of the hoped-for melodic ringtone of olden days, he heard a modern buzz. If there was still a residence standing that had a real old-fashioned doorbell, surely it would have been this ancient apartment block. It had to be at least 250 years old. He leaned on the door and it opened.

He was met by cool air on the other side of the door. April was giving them a preview of the hot Parisian summer ahead, so Arthur was glad for the cooler air, even if it was a bit stale. In the corner there was a pram. *A family with a child can afford an apartment in this area?* To the right he saw an elevator that looked as old as the house. It sported iron bars instead of a door. He decided to distrust technology and give his body something to do after all the sedentary hours at his editing terminal. Arthur was overweight. There was no overlooking that fact as he wheezed his way up the granite staircase. Fortunately the handrail was sturdy and Petit only lived on the second floor.

He spotted the old man from the previous landing. Monsieur Petit smiled and waved him on. He had to be over 70. He looked a bit dried up. Maybe he was a strong smoker. Arthur conquered the last steps, wiped his hand on his pants, and shook the hand offered by Petit.

"I am glad you found time for me," said the old man.

In reality, Arthur would have preferred to stay in the office and give the young apprentice important writing tips. Instead, it was his colleague Michel who carried the burden of passing on his knowledge about the W-questions. After all he, Arthur, had lost the wager about which of the two new colleagues in sales would be pregnant first. As a result, he was now working on the assignment the boss had given to his colleague.

"Bonjour, Monsieur Petit. My colleague Lemaire sends his excuses, he had another assignment on short notice."

"I'm glad you have come."

He was curious what Petit had used to pressure their boss who had insisted Michel was to make the visit within a week—probably some old favor or a common skeleton in a basement.

"And it is my pleasure," said Arthur.

The man asked him into his apartment. He feigned taking off his shoes, but Petit signaled him not to, just as expected. *Just as well,* he thought. On warm days his feet tended to develop their own 'special aroma.'

"Shall we talk in the living room?" Petit pointed to a large round table with old-fashioned embroidered linen. Two coffee cups and two plates awaited them, along with the pleasant scent of real coffee. This meeting didn't look to be that bad. The message had sounded much more eccentric—so maybe it was too early to relax.

Petit pulled a chair out from under the table for him. Arthur sat down.

"What was your name again?" inquired his host.

"Eigenbrod, Arthur Eigenbrod."

"An uncommon name."

"Indeed." Arthur sighed. He had been teased about it all through school.

"You probably got teased all the time in…" The old man slapped a hand to his mouth to keep it shut. "Sorry," he said.

"No problem. You are so right. Did you know that the German word translates to something like individualist?"

"Oh, I could live with that."

"Me too, Monsieur Petit."

"That's okay then." Alain Petit shuffled toward the kitchen.

Arthur looked around. His wife would say the place missed the hand of a woman. But he had seen old people in worse conditions. He himself only had 15 years to go to be a pensioner and sometimes he wondered how retired life would be.

"Coffee?" asked Petit.

Arthur jumped, as he had not noticed the man approaching. "Yes, please. Neither milk nor sugar."

"That is how I drink it, too." Petit served Arthur and then himself and sat down on the other chair.

"Have you lived here for a long time?"

"Since my birth. My grandparents bought this apartment."

"Congratulations, you must be a millionaire then."

"If I sell, maybe. Over my dead body."

Arthur laughed out loud. "I like that. I wish you a long life," he said.

"Let's look at why you are here," Petit said. "Wait a

minute, I forgot the cookies." He got up and brought a bowl of cookies to the table. Arthur couldn't help himself and stuffed two chocolate ones into his mouth. His wife would have admonished him. She wanted him to lose weight for better health. Alain Petit crossed the room and returned with a laptop. "This is what I wanted to show you, Monsieur Eigenbrod."

There were red, orange, and yellow spots on the screen. It could be a snippet from an expressionist painting.

"What is that?"

Petit tapped the keyboard, zooming into the image.

"That is the surface of the sun—its photosphere, to be precise."

"The sun has a surface? I always had thought of it more like a ball of gas."

"Very good. But all that energy created by nuclear fusion is trapped inside. All we can see comes from a relatively thin outer layer."

"The photosphere," added Arthur.

"Exactly. But I don't want to show you the photosphere. Rather, it is about this right here." Petit pointed to something on the lower edge of the screen. Arthur craned his neck to see a very thin dark line.

"I see a line," he offered.

"Excellent. But it does not belong there." Petit enlarged it further.

"And it isn't a mistake? Something technical?"

"I checked that already. There really seems to be something there."

Lines on the sun? Arthur scratched his head. Approximately 150 years ago Parisian papers had record print runs with the channels on Mars, despite later proof that it was an optical illusion. Space secrets still drew attention, especially with the drama two years ago.

"Could that be dangerous, somehow?" he asked. Lines were all well and good but they needed some significance to be newsworthy.

"Well. Since they can't have appeared naturally in that location, they would have to be of extraterrestrial construction…" Petit thought out loud.

*This man knows what journalists need,* Eigenbrod thought to himself. "Aliens—now that would be news, especially if they still are there!" he said.

"That is quite possible."

"And you say that you have verified that it can't be a technical issue?"

"Definitely not a technical issue, no."

He would have to double-check that. Arthur had an idea. He knew a professor at the Sorbonne who owed him a favor.

"Okay, we buy your story."

"I don't want any money for this."

"What I am saying is that we will report on this."

"That was quick," Petit replied.

"All or nothing, that's how it goes for us."

"Would you like a Calvados to celebrate?"

"With pleasure, Monsieur Petit!"

The old man walked over to the kitchen and returned with two glasses and a dusty, nearly-full bottle. He served, sat down, and they raised their glasses. The brandy was excellent.

"To the page one story," said Arthur.

"Do you think so?"

"No, it is more likely to appear somewhere in the science section. I need to discuss that with my colleagues. I am from the local news. Maybe it runs in our part. After all, you live here."

"The main thing is that you print it. Another one?"

Petit pointed to the bottle. Eigenbrod had come via Metro underground and didn't need to return to the office, so he nodded in reply.

"Monsieur Petit, please tell me how come our editor-in-chief was so insistent about checking out your story?"

"I worked in the sewage industry. Should I tell you the story?"

"Oh, yes, please!"

"But first we have another one."

"With pleasure."

Two hours later the bottle was empty. Arthur Eigenbrod had laughed more than in a very long time, and he had learned something about his boss that was so embarrassing that it would secure his job until retirement, for sure.

## April 18, 2074, Maui

"Did you see that?" Steve held his smartphone up, right in her face.

"Ominous lines on the sun—created by aliens?" she read under her breath. It was an online piece by the New York Times.

"Sounds solid," she said, looking out to the horizon again. Steve had sat down beside her without asking. She just wanted to eat her sandwich in peace.

"That Frenchman is behind this. Maurice Petit," said Steve.

"Alain," corrected José.

Heather looked at Steve's friend.

"Somebody must have fallen for him and answered his message," said Steve.

"Looks like it," offered José. He noticed her look and shot a secret smile. Apparently he wasn't an idiot like Steve. What on earth did he like about Steve? But she had fallen for an exceptional idiot herself. He would notice that Steve was not worthy of him, eventually. She didn't need to feel sorry for him.

Heather paused briefly. Tetsuyo had called in sick this morning. That meant more time on the telescope than she needed for her tasks. Should she risk a look at those ominous lines?

"Got to go, guys," she said, standing up. She made sure, this time, to check left and right before crossing the road.

THE ROOF RATTLED to the side while the dome rotated into position. Heather pointed the solar telescope at the target area. Once locked in, it would follow the solar trajectory automatically. The news piece didn't provide much detail, unfortunately. That included the French original she had looked up and translated. A pity that it wasn't a scientific publication, but Alain Petit obviously couldn't get published in those magazines. This way he made headlines and got attention from astronomers, too. And even if most astronomers would smile condescendingly, there would be some who would be curious enough to take a closer look— just like she was doing right now.

But where was she to start the search? The various online articles didn't offer any clues at all. She remembered the images she had sent to the Frenchman. But if she followed the hypothesis of an artificial object, then the lines had to be all over the surface. It wouldn't even matter where she looked.

Heather let the telescope focus on its last position. Probably Tetsuyo had looked for something there, or maybe one of the astronomers who used DKIST via remote access. The screen display changed in breathtaking speed. It was out of focus but that was normal. The main mirror, more than 4 meters across, had a special feature—

on its rear side there were 144 little helpers that could modify the mirror surface to a certain degree to compensate for the atmospheric situation over Maui. Optically, that made DKIST operate as though it was located in space.

The software signal locked on the desired position. Recording kicked in automatically. Heather zoomed right in to the resolution limit. But there were no lines to be seen. She leaned back, somewhat disappointed. Alain deserved to be right, just for being so tenacious.

On the other hand, her failure to see anything was not conclusive. Her telescope showed any object larger than 15 kilometers. If the object was smaller it would go unnoticed. Heather searched for the specifications of the solar probe. Indeed, it had been able to show much more detail because it had operated so close to the sun.

That created an issue for Alain Petit: Nobody would be able to verify his discovery. The probe had evaporated long ago and would not send images anymore. And there was no telescope on Earth more advanced than her DKIST.

## April 20, 2074, Mercury

ICE SCRUNCHED UNDER HIS FEET. Artem looked upward.
The beam of a spotlight showed a cliff with loose debris
collecting at its base. Sobachka stood beside him, watching,
waiting for his command. He wasn't so convinced of the
decision anymore, now that he stood right in front of this
wall that towered 800 meters high. It was some hare-
brained idea out of the conglomerate's research department back on Earth. They wanted to set up solar radar on
Mercury. A technician had told him that the parts had
been collecting dust in some storage room. But suddenly
the orders came; that radar needed to start operating
tomorrow! No word why, and lots of pressure from those
armchair captains instead. Artem clenched his fists as far
as his gloves allowed.

He couldn't fault them with the stupid idea to climb
this mountain, though. That was his alone. The radar
system required the setup of fifty receivers, about 100 kilograms each, across an area of 100 square kilometers. From
their current location near the North Pole, the view of the
sun would not be good enough. So they first had to move

all those receivers 100 km due south. This cliff stood in the way of that project. A rover could drive around alright but that cost three hours extra on each leg, if not more. Back and forth, fifty times. So, it meant 300 hours—or about two weeks—a bit less if they worked around the clock. Impossible, especially with mining having priority, so they kind of expected him to do it all alone. *What a rotten plan!*

His first idea had been quite reasonable. They would build a funicular to cross the edge of the crater. Those receivers only weighed a third of their weight on Earth. And the cable length would not exceed 2 kilometers by much. Of course the cable had to be anchored safely up there. It would have been easy by rover, going the long way around. That was when he had been stupid enough to prefer climbing up the wall. On screen it had been so much less intimidating.

"Your very own fault, Artem," he said out loud. Sobachka looked up. She was used to him talking to himself.

"Alright, let's go then." He secured the dog with a life-line between their suits.

The first meters were a strenuous uphill battle against a mixture of loose dust and frozen water on a steep patch in this realm of eternal ice. Artem quickly started to perspire despite ventilation gearing up and a solid minus 160 degrees outside. He heard Sobachka panting. *The poor dog.* He would have preferred to leave her in the bunker but she had complained loudly. It had been very much unlike her.

Now it was time to start using climbing gear. Artem had climbed a lot in his youth, mainly in the Caucasus Mountains. His muscles remembered all the movements and he quickly established his old routine. This wall however was so different from anything he had encountered on Earth.

Mercury had no atmosphere, so there was none of the degradation produced by rain and ice. Over billions of years, solar wind had produced similar effects. Rock turned brittle and crumbled. But there was no sleet and no surface wind to send loose bits downhill. Only when gravity overcame the holding forces would anything move. For Artem that meant he couldn't trust the cliff at all. Not only was it hard to see a crack in the spotlight, but it was also quite possible that parts of the wall would fall apart even if there wasn't any crack to be spotted. And if that was the place where he placed his hold or sank a hook…

Artem shrugged the thought away. Pessimism was not helpful, ever. Besides, it had been his own choice.

After half an hour of hard work he reached a ledge. Artem sat down and reviewed their progress. It had to be about 200 meters. Sobachka didn't seem to have any issues with the height. He patted her. She was a great space dog. But if he didn't gain speed he would probably take longer than with the rover. Should he return instead?

"Should we go back?" he asked Sobachka. The dog didn't seem to understand.

"Okay," he decided, "let's continue our climb."

Artem decided to speed things up. Not enough to be less secure, but enough to save time in the end. He regained his rhythm quickly, enjoying the subsequent flow. It almost felt like levitating up the cliff. Only the sweat running down his back reminded him of the effort involved. He was proud of himself. That also went for his backpack, perfectly packed with the lead rope for the funicular line and the material for the clifftop support. He nearly forgot that Mercury was helping him a great deal by way of its low gravity.

An overhang was looming above. Artem thought about working his way around it, but the challenge got the better of him. He took a hook, set it tentatively, and pressed against it. Then he noticed that the rock forming the overhang was just loosely connected, and now his arms were all that prevented its fall. Artem quickly reckoned its volume and came up with 1,500 kilograms on Earth. Here on Mercury, that still worked out to 500 kilograms. He could never hold that. He needed to get to safety without delay. He had one arm's length head start. Oddly enough that old question about a pound of feathers or a pound of iron falling faster sprang to his mind. Of course both of them would speed up by 13 km/h every second as dictated by Mercury gravity. If Artem didn't slow himself down using his safety line he wouldn't have contact until ground zero, and that would be the end of it. He risked a quick look down. He had about 20 meters of rope to get out of the way of the deadly chunk.

He kicked off sideways with his feet, trying hard not to slow his fall. He hoped Sobachka was safe while clasping her paws on his backpack. He was unable to do anything for her right now. The first second of falling sent him down by 3.7 meters. *Kick, kick, and hold.* The safety line went taut and held up. His back hit the wall, hard. *Ouch! Is Sobachka okay?* Then he wondered about the contents of the backpack.

He was in luck. The rock brushed his arm and continued downward in silence. Shortly after he sensed a dull impact at his back. That probably was the only effect of the crash below that would reach him. Artem avoided looking up in case smaller debris was following the rock but nothing happened. The entire incident took less than five seconds, but to him it seemed like several minutes.

"Sobachka?"

The dog growled. She was well. What a relief! She did

seem to be quite scared, though. Artem turned around and started to climb again.

Two hours later he reached the top of the ridge. He lifted his head over the edge of the cliff. Instantly he went from absolute darkness into full light. The sun stood as low in the sky as he remembered it from an Indian summer evening back on Earth. He clambered onto the level ground. The sun was so cold and brutal here that Artem had to remind himself that it was the same star.

"Artem calling base camp, do you hear me?"

"Loud and clear. Did you get up there in one piece?"

"Of course. Nothing to report."

"We measured what looked like a miniature earthquake."

"I didn't notice that. No time for a chat, I am ready to set up the post with the diverting pulley now."

"Confirmed."

Artem took the drill out of his backpack. He needed a hole that was half a meter deep. He set the drill in position near the edge of the cliff and started it. The machine operated in complete silence. Thirty minutes later the drill had made enough headway. Artem set up the pre-assembled post, attached the diverting pulley at its top, and completed things by connecting the leader line for the cable. The base of the post went into the prepared hole. He filled in the space around it with special paste out of a tube. One end of the leader line had a special ball with an emitter. Using a compressed-air gun, he fired that end down to the base of the cliff.

"Leader line coming your way," he said.

"Starting search now," answered somebody from the base camp.

At the same time the radio channel started beeping. He turned around to see the rover arriving on autopilot.

"Hey, are you joining us finally?"

No answer from the rover.

"Look, I've prepared everything."

He wished he could have left with the rover right away. The rover carried the first receiver plate, due for installation today. But first he had to wait for his colleagues to find the other end of the leader line. Artem turned around. Sobachka looked at him expectantly.

"Ah, I see," he said. Artem bent down and plucked a stone, throwing it far into the plains. Sobachka ran off in pursuit.

"Sorry, no sticks here."

But that was no issue for the dog. She imitated picking up the stone with her jaws, ran back, and mocked laying down the stone in front of him.

"Good girl, Sobachka," he said. She was an excellent actress.

"We have the capsule," came in from base camp.

"Are you attaching the line?"

"On the job. Detaching the capsule first."

He waited.

"Done. Start pulling."

He used a crank on the pulley to slowly wind up the real line. This one, a cable thick enough to carry the receivers, had been tied to the lead line. After twenty minutes of cranking, the thick transport line had made it into his hands. He fed it through the pulley. Now it just had to make its way back down again, pulling the lead line alongside. Another twenty minutes later and that was done, too. He opened the safety knot on the lead line.

"Will you pull in the lead line? It would be a pity to lose it. I need to move on."

"Okay," confirmed base camp.

Artem turned around. He had no time to lose with 100 kilometers through the hot Mercury desert ahead of him.

"Sobachka!" He pointed to the rover and the dog obliged him by jumping on board. The rover had two seats, and a cargo pad in the back that held the shiny black receiver. If he had it right, he was to add its 49 siblings to create a distributed radio telescope that would scan the solar surface in unprecedented resolution. But first he had to set them up in the desert according to the predetermined pattern.

Artem entered the destination and started the vehicle. He let the rover drive autonomously in the hope of getting some sleep. He turned around and pulled up a tent-like shade that was made of semi-transparent material. If it blocked all light it would be far too cold, and if too much light came through, his cooling system would eventually be overloaded. Now all he was missing was a pair of shades. Artem let his arm pad play music, a classic Johnny Cash song, as he rode his convertible through the desert, into the sunset. His copilot was the only female he loved. The sky was black, not blue, but that was easy to ignore.

## April 21, 2074, Mercury

THE DRIVE TOOK LONGER than five hours because they ended up driving around a crater that looked flatter on satellite imagery than it actually was. It was way past midnight, Earth time, when they finally arrived at the setup site. The sun stood higher now, due to them being further south.

Artem decided to take a longer break before setup. He had to get Sobachka out of her suit. The passenger cabin of the Rover supported an atmosphere when sealed. The vehicle had enough oxygen in its tanks to create a breathable atmosphere. Artem removed his helmet and took a few deep breaths. Everything seemed to be okay. Next he freed the dog of her packaging. Her fur was completely damp. He made a mental note to check her cooling status more regularly. Thankfully she did not seem the worse for it, jumping around happily and shaking herself from head to tail. He played with her for a good while, fed her, and finally ate something himself.

Then he lay down on his back and looked up into the sky. The dome over the rover was darkened and the sun was reduced to a pale spot. Here on Mercury he was three times closer to the sun than on Earth, but that didn't make this star any friendlier. Here the sun wasn't the life-giving mother, it was searing and hot like death. He was glad that the RB base camp was mostly underground.

SOBACHKA'S WHINING woke him in the morning. He sensed her need, but unfortunately there was no way to take her for a walk. He had to relieve himself into a container inside the rover, too. For the dog, he spread one of the canine diapers she normally wore in the spacesuit. After breakfast they put in playtime. She kept looking at him with those brown eyes. There was such an unconditional love in them that it pricked his conscience that he was unable to return it just as unconditionally. But it went without saying he would give his life for Sobachka.

Then it was time to suit up. First he prepared the dog for vacuum, then himself. He let the pumps suck up the atmosphere and the last remaining air hissed out as he retracted the dome. Now all that remained was to return the seats to their upright positions to restore the convertible look.

He had to install the receiver prior to their return. First he examined the surface. According to the technician, no special care was necessary—make certain it wasn't near a fissure, and clear of major rubble. The receiver would determine its position and inclination automatically, and software would calibrate things accordingly. The unit wasn't even a typical dish, making it easier to manufacture and transport. A solar panel provided energy. At night it could not operate, simply because the necessary batteries had not been available on the short notice allowed by the scheduling of this project. Setup was to happen as quickly as possible since the sun would set in 70 days, and it would not rise again for another 88 days.

Artem wired up the components. His arm pad told him which plug went into which socket. The technician had prepared that amazingly well, especially considering that he was working just as alone as Artem. He made a mental note to ask the technician where he had learned all that. The receiver would communicate with all the other receivers in a distributed wireless network. The results would be aggregated across all the stations and then sent to base camp together.

Done.

"Sobachka, come, we're leaving," he called out. Nothing happened. He swiveled an anxious three-sixty, looking all around. The dog was nowhere to be seen.

"Sobachka!" His voice betrayed a touch of panic. He needed to keep his wits together. Then a stone rolled into sight from behind the rover, followed by Sobachka. She was busily moving the stone toward him with her front paws. He went to meet her, picked up the stone, and showed it to her.

"Good job, Sobachka," he commended her while patting her back. He calmed down, his racing heart slowly normalizing.

THE RETURN to the crater went a little quicker. Artem thought about driving all the way around but then he would miss an experience he had been excited about since yesterday. He stepped up to the crater wall and looked down. He only could see the very first part of the cliff where the post with the pulley sent the carbon nanotube line out and over the edge and down to base camp.

"Base camp, do you read me?"

"Artem, are you back?"

"Looks like it. Just to make sure, you don't have anything on the line yet?"

"Nope. We have been waiting for you."

"Great, see you real soon then."

"What do you mean? The rover will take at least two hours."

"Yes, the rover will take that long. Artem over and out."

His plans, however, were not the business of anyone at base camp. They would just try to forbid them. But what should he do with Sobachka?

"Sobachka, come to the rover." He tried to call her to the vehicle but today she refused despite loving to sit on the passenger seat.

"Okay, so you want to come along?"

She started turning in circles like crazy. That seemed to be a 'yes.' Artem grabbed her suit and attached her to his spacesuit with a lifeline. Then he lifted her onto his backpack where she was comfortable holding on with her paws. He used a second line to secure her just to avoid trouble from any exuberance on her part. Then he attached a short lifeline to his own suit. He added a carabiner to the other end and moved up to the post with the pulley. Next, he hitched the carabiner onto the transport line that went down to the base camp. He took a couple steps for run-up and then jumped over the cliff into the darkness, like diving into a deep lake. Everything was eerily silent but not for long, as he shouted out loud and Sobachka added her howling to his.

## April 23, 2074, Pasadena

"HEATHER MARSHALL?" The man in uniform gave her a friendly smile.

"That's me." She handed over her ID. He looked at the picture and compared it to her.

"You look much younger in reality," he stated matter-of-factly, no trace of a compliment. He'd made her day, but she didn't say anything.

"Welcome to the JPL," said the guard. "Your vehicle knows where your host is expecting you?"

"Yes, all is perfectly prepped."

"Have a nice stay then and please sign out with me. If you need a guide to Hollywood my shift ends at six."

She laughed out loud. The guy had to be at least fifteen years younger than she was.

"Sure," she said, and quickly pressed the button to bring the window up.

She could hardly believe she was in California so suddenly. The day before yesterday her boss had gotten in touch about that odd story, asking for her part in it. She had readily admitted sending the Frenchman the data instead of leaving José to take the blame. That had gotten her the assignment to visit the Jet Propulsion Laboratory headquarters to find out whether the JPL solar probe could have been sending false data.

Her contact, a certain Callis John, was the overall project manager for the solar probe. Callis was his first name—she had asked about that to make sure. The car knew the location of his office. She lowered the window again as soon as the guard post was out of sight, and enjoyed the pleasant breeze. JPL headquarters was nicely arranged. The office buildings weren't new anymore, but they spread across a park-like area with old trees and green spaces.

"You have reached your destination," the car informed her. "I will inform our client. Would you like to leave feedback about your experience?"

"No."

"Have a productive day. Use the code 'NEXT' for a 15% discount on your next ride with our fleet."

Heather unfastened the safety belt and the door took the cue to open automatically. She got out in front of a flat building that reminded her of a bungalow. She noticed big boxes on the roof, probably air conditioning units. The door closed behind her and the car started beeping to inform her of its imminent departure. A moment later a longhaired man stepped out of the building and walked to meet her. He was dark-skinned with a neatly trimmed beard.

"I'm Callis. It's nice to have you here, Heather," he said, holding out his hand. His handshake was firm but comfortable.

"My pleasure to be here."

"Would you like to freshen up, or should we get to work right away?"

Heather started thinking. She would have preferred to go straight to the hotel where her luggage was waiting. No hunger yet, she was still recovering from the airline sandwich that had ballooned by about 500 percent while chewing and still felt like a stone in her stomach.

"Work first," she decided.

Callis cocked his head ever so slightly. "Great attitude," he said, but his voice didn't fully match the statement. It was only yesterday that Steve had warned her that Californians had a laid-back work attitude.

"Not sure how long I'll be able to keep going, but I'd rather just get started."

"Understood. I thought somebody might be coming soon. But I was expecting NASA administration to send someone over."

"I hope I am not getting in your way."

"No. We are in a transition phase right now, no pressure. The next big project won't start for about six months. But let's talk inside."

Callis went ahead to open the door for her. It was cold in the building and she put on the cardigan she had been carrying draped over her arm.

"I've gotten used to that by now," said her companion, who wore only a white T-shirt with his jeans. He was in front of her so she could admire the muscles standing out on his back.

Now that she was inside, the building seemed much larger than it had appeared from the outside. They walked for several minutes along hallways lined with posters and scientific works. Very obviously, work related to space travel had been going on in this place for more than a century.

"I'll show you the clean room first," said Callis as they entered a small locker room. "We need to change here." Callis grabbed a one-piece white lab coverall out of a locker and handed it over to her. "I guess 'change' is the wrong word—just put this on over your street clothes." He went over to another locker, picked out a suit, and got into it under ten seconds.

Meanwhile she was having a hard time finding the right sequence to the zippers.

"May I help you?" he asked.

"Please."

He pulled the edges of the material together in a few places and suddenly the zippers worked as they were supposed to.

"Please come along," he said. Moving to a door at the back of the locker room, he pressed a button. The door opened and they entered some kind of an airlock.

"Do we get disinfected here?" she asked.

Callis smiled. "No, this isn't a biological lab. The airlock helps us keep the clean room under higher pressure. That keeps out the dust."

Another door opened into a room the size of a gym, except the ceiling was not quite that high. It was somewhat colder. The floor had stripes of different colors. The room contained desks that held space-tech items in varying conditions, silver and gold glittering everywhere. Callis strode forward with purpose and she had to make an effort to keep up.

"Here we are."

They stood in front of one of the many desks. *Is this supposed to be the solar probe?* Heather had checked photos before she left on the trip. The thing in front of her didn't look anything like the photos.

"Everybody is disappointed at this point," said Callis. He had read her expression correctly. "You see, in those pictures you mostly see the heat shield. That shielding is way too expensive to keep it around our copy of the probe. This desk only has the probe itself."

"This probe is no different from the probe that fell into the sun?"

"No different at all. That is critical to such a mission. Every command sent to the original must be tested on this one first. And the copy needs to be perfect for that."

"That also goes for all the instruments, I guess?"

"Of course. You are probably interested in the telescope, mostly?"

"Sure. Do you think it is possible that it might produce artifacts in the recorded images?"

"Anything is possible. The instrument went through rigorous testing before launch and nobody noticed any artifacts, but that doesn't mean anything."

"What does that mean for our problem, Callis? We have recorded images with odd lines on them. How do we find out if they are real?"

"I could detach the recording module from the probe, but that won't help much. The telescope was built for use outside Earth's atmosphere."

"Could we test it in a vacuum chamber?"

"All the electronics around will give you so many emissions that you will be buried under artifacts. There is only one real solution, as far as I know."

Suddenly Heather wasn't so sure she wanted to hear the next sentence. She had an odd feeling come over her, a sense those words would have something to do with the future—and not just her future, but that of mankind. She shivered. She really needed to collect herself. She had never had anything weird like this happen to her before. As though saying a few words out loud could change the future!

"And that would be?" she asked.

"You need to take the probe into space and have it take pictures of the sun."

"Ha-ha." Heather imitated a laugh. That was the best she could do because it wasn't funny, it was downright crazy.

Callis gently laid his hand on her shoulder. "You'll handle that alright," he said.

"We'll talk about that later," she answered, "once we have tried everything we possibly can do on Earth."

"Okay," said Callis. "The full routine?"

"The vacuum chamber, that's the least we can do."

"Got it. Yes, a space trip is expensive. You don't get that until you have exhausted all other possibilities."

"Um, there is a misunderstanding. I am not doing a space trip."

Callis put his hand over his mouth.

What could be so amusing? She just had a simple assignment. She'd take care of it and then it would be back to Hawaii.

"I am sorry. No offense intended, but I know how things like this play out. You don't want to see it, but those artifacts have been stuck on you. You aren't going to get rid of them until the issue is solved."

"We'll see about that." She crossed her arms decisively. She never did anything she didn't want to do. *Well, mostly… Okay, only sometimes, to be honest.*

"We'll do the chamber test now. Do you want to be part of it?"

"Do you need me? If not, I wouldn't mind driving to the hotel."

"I'll handle that on my own. No problem, Heather. It will take me three or maybe four hours. We'll have the results by morning."

"I am sorry to burden you with the extra work."

"No problem. As I said, we don't have that much going on right now. It's perfect timing."

"Great, see you tomorrow then?"

"If you could make it here at nine?"

"Perfect."

"I'll leave you now, Heather. Have a good night. The building will guide you out."

"See you tomorrow, Callis."

Her host entered something into his phone. A green arrow popped up in the flooring.

"Just follow the arrow," said Callis.

Heather started walking. She was somewhat excited and not sure why. At the exit of the clean room she turned around, but Callis was busy detaching the telescope from the probe.

## April 24, 2074, Pasadena

"Do you have any idea how late it is here?" Heather looked out of the window. The sky was dark, as dark as it possibly would get over Los Angeles. She put the call on speakerphone and laid down the phone.

"Very sorry about that, Heather," said her boss, "but I am getting a lot of pressure from above. You got our institute involved in this. The media wants to know what we have to do with it, and the community of astronomers isn't sure whether to pity us or envy us. I need your confirmation that there is nothing to this story."

"I am working on it. When you call me in the middle of the night, it doesn't make it go any quicker."

"But we need clarification as quickly as possible. Speculation is running rampant in the media. Have you seen the online editions yet?"

"I had work to do, and that didn't give me any time for reading."

"When will I get an update from you?"

"I can't tell yet. Right now we are testing the camera of

the duplicate probe." *We?* she mused. Heather felt a twinge of guilt because she had left Callis to do the work.

"That's good. I am expecting you to stay on top of this all the time. There is no room for failure. When do we get results?"

"Tomorrow, well, that is today."

"Ahh, that's better." Her boss sounded relieved. "I can work with that."

"Boss, one more thing."

Best to brief him now.

"It is possible that the results won't be decisive."

"Whaaaat? What does that mean?"

"The solar telescope is built to operate in space. Down here it could be flooded by interferences."

"Could be?"

"That is what we are looking into."

"I am hoping that it is a non-issue."

"The project leader of the solar probe thinks it is unlikely to work here."

She heard nothing but breathing from the other side for an entire minute. She hoped her boss wasn't having a heart attack.

"Heather?" he finally asked in a surprisingly soft voice, "I'm relying on you. If the test on Earth doesn't work out, you will need to take it into space. I will get you the next available spot."

"Boss!" Now it was her turn to be speechless. "You can't do that! I am an astronomer!"

"There will be no discussion. You got us into this mess. Either you solve the problem or you can pick up your papers tomorrow. And I will have you investigated for misuse of public funds. You had no authorization to pass on those pictures. Now go back to sleep."

The line clicked as her boss hung up. Suddenly the

room felt hot to her, though she hadn't thought so before. Heather stood up, went over to open the window, and stood there enjoying the fresh air. Absent any miracles to save her she would have to fly to space. Once there she would be breathing air that others had had in their lungs dozens of times already.

She went back to bed. It was 3 a.m. She needed more sleep or she would not make it through the day.

HER PHONE WOKE HER. The sun lit up the room. It was Callis.

"Weren't we meeting at nine?" he asked.

She jumped up. *Damn. It's 9:30 already.*

"Sorry about that, it must be the jet lag. And my boss who called me in the middle of the night."

"No problem. I was thinking you might not want to see me anymore."

Had he just made a pass? She couldn't be hearing right. "I'm on my way," she said. "Just a quick shower."

"I can't offer breakfast here. But just outside the JPL there is an excellent German bakery on the left."

"But I am running late already."

"No rush, please. I know how to keep busy. Go get something at the bakery. Our coffee machine is quite good. If you don't mind, please bring me a salted pretzel. It's the only place one can get them."

"Okay, see you in about an hour then."

"I look forward to that," said Callis, and then he hung up.

Heather pulled off her pajamas and hurried over to the bathroom. She managed to shower, dry and dress in under twelve minutes, complete with makeup. She was proud of herself. She left the housekeeper a dollar on the desk and left the room. At the reception desk she extended her stay by a night. She wouldn't make the flight at noon anyway. A robotaxi was waiting in front of the hotel. She waved and the door opened for her.

"Next," she said into the car.

"I am very sorry," answered the car "but this code is only valid between 11 and 3 o'clock. Where may I drive you?"

She provided the address, belted up, and relaxed into the soft seat cushion. She had nearly dropped off to sleep when she remembered the bakery.

"Stop at the German bakery near my destination," she said.

"New destination confirmed," answered the car.

AN HOUR and a half later she sat on a camping chair opposite Callis John, a small round table between them. Behind them was a truck-sized rolling gate. She was looking out onto sandy terrain with rusty machines lining the edges.

"This is our Mars yard," said Callis, "where we test our Mars rovers. I like to hang out here."

"It is… unusual," she replied.

Callis laughed. "Yup, not green here, true. But it is nice and quiet. We are right on the edge of the JPL campus."

He handed her an insulated cup. The scent of hot black coffee wafted up while she took a sip. Callis bit into his pretzel. She saw grains of salt dropping to the ground. Her cake was sitting on the table. She had chosen a piece of spice cake with raisins, because the raisins made her think of sunspots. She took a bite—moist and sweet, but not too sweet.

"Did you get a good rest?" her host asked.

"Not sure," she responded. "I guess it depends on what you will be telling me."

"Really? Why is that so important?"

"I gave the Frenchman the original data. Nobody could have imagined how that would blow up. He made such a good impression, wrote a nicely phrased email."

"I would have done that, too. It's great when the public gets interested in our work."

"My boss doesn't see it that way."

"Then the Frenchman was lucky to have contacted you instead of your boss."

"One of my colleagues also sent him the same data."

She was not sure why she was providing him with such detail. It had nothing to do with her assignment. But she wanted him to understand her. It was bad enough that she didn't understand herself.

"And you took responsibility? That was brave."

"My colleague isn't as senior as I am. And I felt sorry for him because he has such an idiot for a partner." Talking about it this way things felt completely logical and comprehensible.

"You did everything right, Heather."

She felt better for the praise. "Thank you," she said. "It would be even nicer to hear that you managed to find artifacts coming from the camera."

"I have to disappoint you on that. On the images there are so many technical artifacts that it does not prove anything. Do you want to see them?"

Heather dismissed the idea. "I trust you." She bent forward, supported her head on her arms, and fell silent.

"What's up, Heather, what is the problem?"

"My boss insists on me finding proof for the artifacts."

"That is great. I would have never met you otherwise."

Heather had to smile despite herself. He really was making a pass—her impression on the phone had been correct. She was grateful for it even if she didn't want to open that box right now.

"That means I need to go sit on a pile of explosives and have myself blasted into space."

"That is amazing. I envy you. I really do!"

"It is horrible. Space is disease and danger wrapped in darkness and silence."

"I hate to tell you, but the Starfleet operates in space."

Heather laughed out loud—he had caught on to her Star Trek reference! How crazy was that? The episode was more than 60 years old!

"Star Trek 11," said Callis.

"I know."

"Five times," he offered.

"Seven times, I win!"

"Congratulations!"

She went serious again. "It is really nice to chat with you here, but it looks like I need to get ready for a space flight." She got up and stood straight as though Scotty would beam her up to the Enterprise in the next second. That would be really nice, as it would save her the rocket episode.

"If I can help you…" Callis stood up as well. He went around his chair and stood directly in front of her. Why did her stomach go into a tight knot, and what made her heart suddenly beat so quickly?

"Great," she said while taking a step back. "Yes, I could use some help. The probe needs to get to the launch pad somehow."

"Leave that up to me. It would be perfect if we could start from Vandenberg."

"We?"

"You, of course. A lapse." He took a step back now, too. Heather was glad things had relaxed, but she felt a bit sorry, too.

"First and foremost I need to update my boss," she said.

"Good luck with that. Please wait a moment."

He entered the storage space behind them and returned to give her his business card.

"Here are all my contacts. Feel free to call me if you need anything at all. That also goes for tonight, if you are bored."

She didn't look at him, concentrating on his hands instead. On his left hand she discovered a ring. Something stabbed her heart.

"Is your wife out of town?"

"My wife went missing in the upheaval two years ago."

Heather bit her tongue. That had been too stupid on her part. Why did she have to go and remind him that way?

"It's okay," said Callis. "I only wear the ring for senti-mental reasons."

## April 26, 2074, Mercury

NUMBER SIX. What a stupid job he had gotten himself into. Another 44 receivers to set up, 44 trips back and forth, 44 times twelve hours on the track, only interrupted by twelve hours rest. He knew the route from memory already. He had considered camping out at the destination, but he could not do that to Sobachka. The dog needed to get out of her suit regularly. Base camp under the surface wasn't huge, but it was sufficient to give her room to tire out. Several days on the rover just to make his life easier, that would not be fair.

But maybe he did not need to carry things to the bitter end. He had chatted with the technician yesterday. Fortunately, 50 individual receivers was the maximum setup. The improvised radio telescope could be sufficiently sensitive well before that. It sounded like they were trying to verify certain information, but the technician had been very tight-lipped about what exactly that was.

Maybe it had something to do with those odd lines that Frenchman had claimed he discovered on the sun. The online media sources he was receiving here were censored by the RB administration, but by now several large Russian channels had been reporting the so-called discovery. Whatever it might be, it would hardly affect him. Mercury was three times closer to the sun than the Earth, but it was still very far to travel.

HE STAYED calm for that very reason when base camp informed him about an impending coronal mass ejection, or CME. A huge batch of plasma, mainly hydrogen kernels—protons—and electrons, was moving outward from the corona into space. Mercury would be hit in ten hours.

Artem looked at the sun. It behaved just as always. The star that was responsible for life on Earth ignored him just like it ignored everybody else. CMEs were invisible to the eye and to light-based telescopes. The invisible cloud had a mass of about one billion metric tons. It would engulf Mercury for two or three seconds and be off on its way again. Only the satellites in orbit were in danger—or would have been had RB not been clever enough to protect them against most effects of the solar weather. Maybe the radio link to base camp would be interrupted briefly, but before he would notice that, the CME would already be thousands of kilometers away.

It was a pity that Mercury didn't have an atmosphere. That would have given a purpose to the CME—he would have been able to admire spectacular polar lights tonight. Well, he would play with Sobachka instead. That was the better evening entertainment anyway. Artem sat down and gripped the wheel. He needed some distraction now. First he hooked up Sobachka with the safety belt, and next he double-checked the receiver on the cargo pad. Then he hit the accelerator, and the rover went speeding ahead through the stony desert.

## April 28, 2074, Vandenberg Air Force Base

"I GUESS IT'S A SMALL WORLD!"

She recognized the voice. Heather turned around. The project leader from JPL walked briskly toward her.

"What are you doing here, Callis?"

"Bringing you my baby." He held something almost hidden in his hands.

She pointed to his hands. "Do you mean that?" she asked.

"No, the probe, of course." Callis laughed. "Treat it well, as it is the last of its kind."

Sure. The probe. What was she thinking? The probe would be flying to space in the hold of the rocket that she was going to be entering in a short while. She was on her way to the Ark, the international space station that had circled the Earth since the incident two years earlier. Up there she would get the opportunity to test the probe under proper conditions.

"I promise to take good care of it," she said.

"Thanks. By the way, why didn't you get in touch with me the other day? I was hoping for your call."

Heather felt a wave of embarrassment. Why did Callis have to bring this up now, when she was on the way to the launch?

"I… it seemed inappropriate. You don't know anything about me. I am just a lowly astronomer and live six flight-hours away from you." The words just tumbled out. That had not happened to her in a long time.

"No problem," said Callis. "Here. I wanted to bring you this in person." He handed her a flat object. It was wrapped in elegant paper with a decorative ribbon looped around it.

"Thank you," she said. What would he be handing her? His phone number again? She took the package in her left hand.

"Please don't open it until after the launch," said Callis, interrupting her thoughts. "See you later."

"Good bye," she answered, instantly more than a little angry with herself for such a formal response.

Callis turned around and walked back to the main building. One of her company tapped her shoulder.

"We need to be moving on."

"Of course, sir."

They crossed the hot tarmac to the launch pad. Heather looked up. The rocket was surprisingly small, especially in comparison to the huge Mars rockets she had seen on live video. They stopped in front of the elevator that would bring her up to the actual capsule. One of the aides, dressed in a blue coverall, touched her elbow.

"I am very sorry Ms. Marshall, but this object can't go on board. It hasn't been through the check."

"It is a gift from a friend."

"No exceptions allowed. Please hand it to me or I can't let you board."

Heather sighed and quickly untied the ribbon,

removing the paper in the process. A flat metal case appeared. She found the catch and flipped the lid to find an expensive card inside. 'Invitation' was embossed on the front. She opened the card. Callis was inviting her to a restaurant, three weeks from today—she should certainly be back by then. She didn't know the restaurant, but the package looked upscale and expensive. She shoved the card inside her overall and handed the rest to the blue suit beside her. He nodded appreciatively and opened the door for her.

HEATHER HAD USED the diaper for the second time already, but the launch still was not happening. The four of them were laid out like herrings on flat loungers that were slightly elevated on the head end, staring upward in unison. She did not know the other passengers, two women and a man. They seemed to be lay people, as she had been labeled. *Maybe medical or technical personnel for the Ark?* The horrible incident two years ago certainly had escalated the importance of the space directly surrounding Earth. There were regular shuttles between the Ark and the surface, making both launches and zero-gravity research much more accessible.

*How about starting the countdown, finally? Shouldn't we have been on our way already? Something must be wrong with the rocket,* thought Heather. She didn't trust the recycling concept that most companies were using these days.

"CapCom here," said a male voice. "Ladies and gentlemen, I am responsible for your launch until Ark Control takes over your flight. If you have questions, please go ahead."

"When do we lift off?" asked Heather.

"In exactly sixty seconds, starting... now," CapCom replied. The loud ticking of the final countdown kicked in and she counted along.

At zero an earthquake started to grumble deep down below her. She closed her eyes. The explosion that would tear them to bits, no, vaporize them, would be upon them in an instant. A slight pressure pushed her onto the lounger. It was not a big deal, much like the feeling she remembered from her father accelerating their car back in the days when one was able to set the speed manually.

"So when are we taking off, CapCom?"

"All is peachy. You are at 300 meters... at 400, 500, and counting."

"We are flying? And all is going well?"

"Yeah, sure. What were you thinking?"

The man was right. Her fellow passengers probably thought her hysterical. Of course she had been informed that space flight launches with commercial rockets weren't so exciting anymore, and that real astronauts looked down on so-called vacation rockets. I *can't believe it would be so smooth. Even my standard civilian flight out of Honolulu was more exciting at takeoff.*

She relaxed, slowly. Unfortunately she had to pee again. What was wrong with her bladder? The good news was the diapers seemed to be made of some sort of magic substance, very good, because they had another 14 hours until rendezvous with the Ark.

The ceiling of the capsule, where they would be looking for some time to come, had a large screen built in. So far it had been showing the logo of the carrier company. Now it switched to images that seemed to come from a camera in the tip of the rocket. They flew straight into the sky, no clouds to be seen anywhere. The blue was getting darker by the minute. Soon Heather wasn't able to tell it from black.

"Are we in space now, CapCom?" asked the man, who was on the lounge next to hers.

"Nearly so. Won't be long until we cross the 'Kármán line.' Then you will be astronauts, officially."

Heather concentrated on the display. She was expecting to see stars appear. And… *Yes, right there! There they are!*

"CapCom here. You are now 100 kilometers above ground. Space starts there, according to the official definition. Congratulations!"

Heather silently congratulated herself, too. *Maybe it isn't so bad, after all, that I sent Alain Petit that data,* she thought. *I'll have to remember to drop him a note from orbit.*

"CapCom again. For your comfort I am darkening the cabin now. The current burn phase will last another 90 minutes."

THE LIGHTS CAME BACK UP. Heather blinked. She had actually been able to sleep. The screen showed pitch black— and the moon. She thought it had come closer, but that couldn't be.

"CapCom here. Burn phase is ending now. Your vessel will attain orbit at 400 kilometers altitude, take a couple of turns around Earth, and initiate the coupling process with the Ark. I am afraid this may take a while, as all docking ports are full at this time."

*Caught up in a traffic jam, in space of all places,* she thought with a wry smile.

Suddenly Heather's stomach contents rose into her throat. She shut her mouth and swallowed a few times, and she managed to send those horribly sour bits back down. Zero gravity!

"Micro gravitation. You may carefully release the belts now," said CapCom. "Please watch out for nausea or space sickness."

Heather quickly released her belts as though zero gravity would be over soon. Then she noticed herself levitate, her body no longer pressing onto the lounger. It was a very odd feeling, incomparable to anything she had experienced before. She shrieked involuntarily. The man gave her an odd look. Somebody had said it was like floating neutrally during a dive but it wasn't. It was completely different. Heather gave a small push with one hand and slowly floated across the capsule.

## April 29, 2074, Earth Orbit

THE ARK WAS A LABYRINTH. The ship that had been the hope for a small part of humanity to survive just two years ago had now become the largest space station to orbit Earth. In addition to the four newcomers, there were already 221 people on board, as had been explained to them before changing spacecraft. That was twice the number originally planned for. She had somehow received a single cabin despite the obvious limitations. Nobody was available to guide her—everybody was busy with assigned duties. Instead she had been assigned a drone to show her around and to explain the Ark.

Heather had christened her drone with the name 'Mike.' It was the size of a grapefruit, with a screen on one side that usually displayed a symbolic face. Mike spoke with a male voice but she could have chosen a female one instead. He always sounded friendly, no matter what she said to him.

It didn't take half an hour for her to feel stalked in his company. Mike really did not let off for even a second. Technically it seemed quite logical. They were in space, and mistakes had consequences here. Somebody had to watch out that she didn't go and open a hatch leading outside.

But she wasn't alone anywhere. Not even on the toilet, which had been the first place she went after the boarding process was completed. She had to admit that she could not have found the toilet without Mike. A space toilet really did not look anything like what one would have expected. All toilets were public, and they were spread throughout the station wherever other requirements had left some space. The one Mike had shown her was no more than a niche in the wall. At hip level there was a small seat with an even smaller hole in the middle. That hole was the target for feces. For her current need, there was a hose that had to be placed between her legs. A good aim was vital for this, too.

Heather pulled a screen closed behind her. The taut textile protected her from onlookers—all but one. "Can't you look the other way, Mike?"

"So sorry, Heather, but I need to check whether you are handling things according to my explanations."

She pulled down her pants and panties. Finally she was able to get rid of the diaper. "What do I do with this?"

"There is a special container for such waste. Please wrap up the diaper and later I will show you where the disposal unit is."

Heather sat down with the special shape of the seat guiding her into the right position. "This works surprisingly well," she noted.

"The design has been optimized over eighty years of space travel," replied Mike. "Careful now, I am starting ventilation."

A cold blast of air hit the middle of her backside.

"Please place the hose now," said Mike.

"One moment."

"Should I check the correct position?"

"Don't you dare!" She noticed things were correct through the airflow and tried to relax. "Not working for me."

"Closing one's eyes works for some people."

"How many people have you instructed in this?"

"One thousand, six hundred, and sixty four."

"How many successes?"

"Eventually, all of them. It is impossible to stay on the Ark without mastering this."

"How comforting." She closed her eyes and recalled the view from her mountain into the distance. "Doesn't work," she stated after three minutes.

"Should I play some music?"

"No, no way."

"I could turn off the light in the niche."

"That's a good idea. Then I would not feel watched. Don't contradict that!"

"Understood."

The indirect lighting of the toilet niche went off. Light still came through the screen but her brain was content. Finally she was able to relax sufficiently. "Phew," she said as she heaved a sigh of relief.

"One gets used to it," Mike consoled her. Then he switched off the ventilation. Heather cleaned herself with moist wipes she found in a labeled cubby beside the toilet, and then disposed of the wipes in the designated receptacle.

"Can you show me my room now?"

"No, Heather, we have a meeting first."

"Can't we pass by my room first? I would love to change clothes."

"I am so sorry, but we are late already."

"Why did you not say so before?"

"I just did. Before, I did not want to add to your stress."

"That was very considerate of you."

Mike didn't answer. He activated several green lights on his rear and flew ahead.

"By the way, how does your engine work?"

"Little blasts of air," said Mike. "I have an electric compressor."

"And power?"

"Wireless. There are charging pads everywhere so I can recharge as required."

Heather started to sweat despite being weightless. It was probably from the level of concentration she had to maintain to avoid bumping into walls. The fact that there was no up or down hardly bothered her at all. Perhaps her diving trips in the Pacific had sorted that out.

"How big is the Ark?"

"The core, the original Mars shuttle, is just over 100 meters, but many constructions have been added around it since. The passageways and hallways with human access total more than 3.5 kilometers."

"That is more than enough for a morning run."

"Indeed. There is a 700-meter patch that is specially reserved for that purpose."

"I guess one needs to take extra care around there."

"Only in the time around shift changes, between 7 and 9 am, 3 and 5 pm, and from 11 pm to 1 am."

"That is good to know. And where do all these people stay?"

"They share cabins. One works while the other sleeps."

"That sounds a bit taxing."

"I understand that cabins are so cramped that one does not want to stay there for any longer than necessary."

"I see."

"By the way, we will arrive in a moment."

Mike stopped in front of an innocuous door. 'Head of Security' was printed on it. Suddenly the door swept aside. Presumably Mike had communicated with the electronics in the door. The drone went ahead and Heather followed it.

The room was small, sterile-feeling. Walls were bare metal, and there was a small desk with a computer. Behind it was a lean, almost ascetic-looking man who was just opening the belt that held him down on the seat.

"Don't bother getting up," said Heather. "I am Heather Marshall."

The man looked at her, smiled, and floated back down onto his chair.

"Okay," he said while closing his belt again. "My name is Karl Freitag, and I am the head of security for the Ark." He leaned forward, stretching out his hand. Heather took it. Freitag had bony hands that matched his skinny frame. He had pronounced his first name a little oddly. He was probably German or Scandinavian.

"You are from Germany?" she tried.

"Yes," he answered, "but that was a long time ago."

She looked at his desk. There was no decoration, just a small photo showing a middle-aged man with crew-cut hair.

Freitag caught her glance. "My partner," he said.

"Is he on Earth?"

"Yes, but he'll visit in two weeks' time."

The smile playing around his lips told Heather that he was looking forward to the visit. *How sweet,* she thought. Other than that, Freitag appeared a bit tense, but maybe it was part of his job description.

"Great that you found your way here," he said.

"Without Mike I would have been lost." She pointed to

the drone. Then she leaned forward. "Is there anyone looking at what Mike records?"

"No worries," answered Karl. "The onboard AI goes through the material for security-related incidents. We don't want you to take a walk in space by accident."

"And if I don't react to Mike's warnings?"

"The drones are equipped with miniature tasers. If you happen to endanger yourself or others, Mike will you give you a little blast. You have anything planned?"

"No, never had the guts for open rebellion." Heather laughed. *Hopefully he doesn't take my talk too seriously. I probably shouldn't be having such a conversation with the head of security.*

"If you run into any trouble," said Karl, "please get through to me directly. Mike is authorized to put you through instantly, at any time."

Heather was surprised. "I don't merit such attention."

"If you only knew! Those instructions came from all the way up. This so-called discovery has stirred up quite some attention."

"I hope I am not too much of a burden, then, Karl." She tried to pronounce the name correctly.

The head of security leaned back. "That's my job," he said, "and it makes for a welcome change."

"So what's next?"

"A technician is busy fastening the probe on the outside hull right now. I hope you can start with the measurements very soon."

"Today?"

Karl looked at the clock on his computer. "In three hours, at the latest."

MIKE HAD NOT EXAGGERATED. The cabins were minuscule. Heather sat on her bed. When she leaned forward to put on her socks she had to pay attention so she wouldn't hit her head against the wall.

The drone was waiting outside. Mike had initially insisted on monitoring her sleep, but she had been able to convince it with logical arguments. The cabin really didn't have any potential for stupid actions. And she had been able to get some quality sleep. She looked at her phone. The field strength was at 100%. *Should I call Callis and thank him for the invitation?*

But then the door moved to the side. She hadn't put on her top yet! Heather jumped and held the sheets in front of her body.

"Apologies," said Mike. "Had you tolerated my presence, this would not have happened."

"Of course, you little voyeur. You could have knocked."

"I was assuming you were asleep. The installation of the probe completed early. Your presence is required."

"Thanks. Get out now so I can get dressed."

"Of course."

She got into her clothes and stood up, holding her knees slightly bent and her head low to avoid bumping into the cabin ceiling. It was cramped indeed, she thought as she pressed the square button that opened the door.

MIKE LED her to a room that was equipped like a repair shop. A man in a white lab coat was waiting for her.

"I am Dr. Johannsson. This is one of our labs. I am on duty during this shift, but I'm a biologist so I won't be of much help. Besides, I have a ton of work to do. If you would excuse me…"

*Sure, good man, I understand that you have to put up with me on orders from above. Still, you could be a bit more civil,* thought Heather.

"I am Heather Marshall," she said as pleasantly as she could. "If you would just show me my work area."

"Surely your guide up there could do that," Johansson replied, pointing at the drone.

His attitude made her angry. "Dr. Johansson," she said, putting her hands on her hips, "I don't know what put you in this mood, but you are being rather unfriendly. In case you hadn't noticed." Her arm movement had pushed her body into a slow rotation. Heather started to laugh at the situation, and she put a hand on the wall to stop her movement. Now she was looking away from Johansson. "Mike, can you tell me where to go so I can control the probe?"

"Of course, Heather. Please follow me," said the drone in his ever-pleasant voice.

Mike led her to a workplace that consisted of a terminal with a keyboard that was attached to the wall. Below there was a horizontal bar with a kind of bicycle saddle, designed to be flipped away from the wall to be used as a seat.

"Ms. Marshall," she heard the biologist say, "my apologies. You are right. If you need anything, please do come and see me."

"Thank you, Dr. Johansson. Apologies accepted," she replied without turning around. She did not want him to spot her triumphant smile. Then she pulled herself onto the saddle. She looked around but there was no belt. Apparently one was supposed to hold on with one's legs.

The computer had the same software she knew from DKIST, already launched.

"Did you do that, Mike?"

"No, that must have been the technician."

The man must have had good instructions. She wondered briefly whether Callis had been involved with that. She checked the connection to the probe. The link was good, and she could use her regular software to manipulate the telescope in the probe. Heather felt almost as though she was at home on the DKIST—except that she couldn't float around there. And her chair was comfortable.

She slowly moved the telescope into the sun. A regular space telescope would be fried, but this one had been built for the purpose. Its mirror diameter was much smaller than the DKIST, so she didn't expect any spectacular results. Just having lines on the images would not mean anything. The lines would only indicate something real if the photos were also free of any clear artifacts.

Regardless, it was exciting to look at the sun. Heather had wondered many times why other astronomers took to looking at remote stars. Those were essentially permanent lights in the sky, while the sun changed on a daily basis. Depending on the spectrum used for viewing, one could come across some very impressive sights. Huge arcs, larger than Earth, bulged out of the surface. And dark and light spots showed where magnetic fields came through. The sun was made of degenerate gas—plasma—which had very special properties, and she was lucky to be able to look at the ensuing wonders on a daily basis.

She kept taking pictures as the telescope moved along. She could have stopped already, but she had not been able to view her favorite star for two days. It was quiet today. Just a few days ago there had been a huge coronal mass ejection into space. Apparently things were settling down again.

*Okay,* she decided, *that is enough.* Her main task was still waiting. She cut the link to the telescope. The image files were already downloaded, a direct cable link being so convenient. When the original probe was traveling through space, transmission had easily taken a few days. Heather started the analysis application.

The disappointment took 20 seconds to manifest on screen and another 20 seconds to cut through to her thoughts. There were lines, yes, but also loops and other artifacts. The glitches were not visible when viewing the full solar disk, but when she zoomed into the original files they were obvious. *What a shame. These artifacts really do seem to be pursuing me...*

Heather leaned back without thinking about being seated on the saddle. The lack of gravity prevented her from falling, but she startled herself thanks to the missing support. The scare restored her focus—she knew that she needed help. She had thrown away Callis' card after her first visit to the JPL, but his number was on her phone. She had no idea what time it was in California, but she also knew he would not get angry at her even if she should wake him in the middle of the night.

"Give me a minute, I'm in a meeting," he answered. "I'll call right back."

Okay, patience she had. That was her biggest asset. Heather laughed quietly. Unfortunately, quite the opposite was true. But she did not have to wait for long.

"What's up?" asked Callis. "Is it what I was expecting?"

"Those artifacts," responded Heather. "They are still around, loads of them."

"I feared as much."

"But you didn't say anything?"

"I didn't want to influence you. You might have canceled your trip, Heather."

"You bet."

"There is a solution, but I'm sure you don't want to hear it."

"If you say so, Callis, that must be true."

"I'll tell you anyway."

"Please don't."

"Not a chance of that. So—you need to fly out with the probe, a couple kilometers away from the Ark, away from the influence of all that technology there. The probe was built to operate far away from any man-made signals. We never took into account that one might test it this close to its performance limits."

Callis paused for a few seconds, then resumed. "You want the files. If you don't get your data now, it will take a few days. You could try to convince your boss to wait…"

"Forget that. The day after tomorrow is the Congress of the Astronomical Union. He wants results before then."

"Well, you know what to do."

"Can't you come up here and do it for me? You know the probe much better than I do."

"You won't get me into space, Heather."

"You wanna bet?"

"It's nice talking to you, but I need to go back to the meeting."

"Sure, see you later."

"HAVE YOU BEEN ON AN EVA YET?"

Heather squatted in mid air in front of Karl Freitag's desk. *Zero gravity is starting to be fun,* she admitted.

"EVA? What's that mean?"

"Extravehicular Activity. Most people would call it a walk in space."

"A walk in space sounds much better, Karl."

"I can assure you it is anything but that. It's a piece of hard work, even before you get started."

She shrugged her shoulders. "I understand. But I have no choice whatsoever. We need the results fast. And we need to be sure. So I need to do it myself. Believe me, I'd love to delegate it."

"Well, if it is that important I'll organize it for you, Heather. Fortunately the probe is still intact."

"Except for the heat shield, but we don't need that in Earth orbit."

"I'll have an engineer prepare everything. Please be at airlock 23 tomorrow at 0800. Unit A17 will show you the way."

"'A17?'"

"Your drone."

"Oh, I'm calling him Mike. Thanks, Karl," she said. The German seemed a bit reserved, but she sensed intuitively that he was reliable. She looked at the picture of his partner with the soft smile. "When will I leave the Ark?"

"Not before noon. We will need to prep you thoroughly. Best if you come in athletic dress. And I recommend skipping breakfast. Will you be able to last twelve hours without food?"

"I think so."

"Don't forget to wear a diaper. That will spare us both any embarrassing moments."

"Will do. Anything else you can tell me?"

"Don't expect to get everything right. You'll be safe regardless. I will watch over you."

"Thank you, Karl."

"U~ɴɪᴛ~ A17?" she said quizzically to Mike when they were back in the corridor.

"That is my designation."

"Doesn't it bother you when I call you Mike?"

"Not at all, Heather. I like it."

The programmers had put some real effort into designing the personality of the drone. Heather almost believed that it could like being called Mike.

## April 30, 2074, Earth Orbit

HEATHER WAS SWEATING FROM EXERTION. She had been cycling for two hours now. A mask fed her oxygen. She was wearing the Liquid Cooling and Ventilation Garment, or LCVG, but she hadn't noticed any cooling coming out of this high-tech, thermo-reactive underwear.

"How long to go?"

Karl Freitag was back. He had instructed her personally and started her working on the bike before leaving for his regular tasks. A medic was watching her parameters all the time.

"You'll be done soon," said Freitag. "I'm sorry, but it is necessary."

"Yes, I know the issue from diving," she replied.

"We also have more modern suits," said Freitag, "that cling to the skin. Pre-breathing is much shorter with them."

"You didn't give me a choice."

"No. For very long EVAs our experience is better with the old models. Plus they are better for beginners. They have more padding and are easier to control remotely."

"In case I go berserk."

"Which we do not expect, but we do need to be prepared for anything and everything. What we are doing in your case is against all the rules."

"Because you are letting me out without training?"

"Mostly because we're letting you go out alone."

"We've been through that. As few interferences as possible."

"I understand that," said Freitag. "We will keep an eye on you at all times. Nothing can go wrong. But I am a bit nervous, regardless."

*Thank you for that, Karl Freitag,* she thought. *You just made me feel so much better.*

"I am very sorry, Heather, I didn't intend to bother you with this. It is my job to find and to discipline those who break rules, and now I am doing just that myself."

"Tell me about your partner. What does he do?"

Now it was she who distracted the head of security and tried to calm him down. Wasn't it meant to be the other way around? Curiously enough, her own fears seemed rather remote right now.

"He works in administration, a pretty boring job if you ask me, but it is his life. I offered to get him something up here twice already, but he won't bite."

"Perhaps he is afraid. I've heard of people who don't love flying into space."

"According to him it is not fear, he simply loves Earth so much more."

"He could be right about that. The sea, mountains, all the green…"

"Speaking of green…" said Freitag. "You are green now, good to go. Okay, poor joke."

Heather opened the restraining belts and kicked off

from the cycle. Karl pointed to the right. She saw a pile of textile, metal, and glass there.

"Your suit," said Karl.

"Interesting."

"I'll help you."

KARL SHUT Heather's helmet exactly 23 minutes later. A helper had already opened the airlock and she floated inside. She was completely calm. It reminded her of the moment many years ago when she knew she had gone into labor. She'd had no prior experience, then just like now, but it had been crystal clear that there was only one option. She had to go through it—and she would go through this unknown process, too. Helmet radio provided instructions that she followed to the letter. She attached the safety line, opened the outside hatch, pulled herself outside, and discovered the probe that was parked right next to the hatch. The probe looked minuscule and very vulnerable beside the huge Ark.

Karl Freitag had explained how she would connect to the probe. She would essentially be riding it. She just had to stay clear of the slim propulsion unit. It wasn't particularly powerful, since its only job was to keep the probe in orbit. But the ejected mass that delivered the forward momentum was so hot that it would cut right through her spacesuit.

She took a deep breath, moved the safety line from beside the hatch to the probe, and climbed aboard.

"Starting the probe now," said Karl. "Enjoy your flight!"

"Thanks and see you soon."

The probe started moving. The propulsion jet was

invisible. Heather had nothing to do now but to wait until she had put a few kilometers between the probe and the Ark. The probe moved perpendicular to the Ark orbit to avoid losing height. Changing orbit height would be a bad idea.

"Flight status is perfect," announced Karl Freitag. "Well, almost."

"Almost?"

"Don't worry, we will correct the minor deviation later. I know how already."

"Deviation? That doesn't sound good."

"Stay calm and trust me."

*Couldn't he have kept it to himself if it wasn't really an issue? The Ark is disappearing into the night and I am supposed to stay calm?* She consulted the pad on her arm. The probe was losing height but it only amounted to a centimeter every so often. It sounded as though Karl was right. Heather looked up from the pad. Earth was below and it was huge. They currently were over the dayside and crossing a huge ocean. Was it the Pacific? She would be visible to one of the telescopes on Hawaii. That would be one funny view—a human in a spacesuit doing the solitary 'ride into the sunset' on a probe through space.

"HEATHER?"

It was the voice of the head of security. Heather opened her eyes. *I've fallen asleep out here. Unbelievable!*

"Why did you not wake me up?"

"Sleeping is what we like most. You use fewer resources."

"And I can't make any mistakes."

"And there's that."

"Are we there yet?" she asked with a playful whine in her voice.

"Yes, kid," said Karl, playing along, "almost. Another five minutes. You play with your probe in the meantime. That's serious, by the way. You can get started with your preparations now."

Heather opened up the diagnostic kit that a technician had attached to the probe. It contained a computer with the analysis software. Once she ran the cable from it to the probe, the data would be dumped into the computer automatically, starting the analysis right away. Three minutes later they would know whether it was lines or artifacts.

"Ready," said Heather.

"Go ahead," replied Karl.

She pointed the telescope into the sun. Several layers of glass covered the viewing screen, making it less readable than the device inside the Ark. That made the sun much less impressive. But the real work ran in the background anyway. Heather forced herself not to watch the clock.

"Results available," reported the system. "Would you like a full analysis?"

"Answer just one question: Are there any artifacts in the recordings?"

"I did not find any artifacts."

"Did you hear that?" Heather nearly shouted into the microphone.

"Yes," responded the head of security.

"Do you know what that means?"

"Do you?"

Excellent question. She had to admit, she did not know. It could mean anything.

"I would like to fetch you back now," said Karl.

"Glad to hear that."

Earth started turning. Of course it was the probe—and her—making a U-turn.

"There is just a minor issue."

"You mentioned that before, Karl."

"I need you to solve the problem."

"Not sure I understand you?"

"The probe was slightly imbalanced by the payload, that is, by you. That let it drift down a tiny bit. The jet won't suffice to bring you back up."

"You call that a minor issue?"

"Yes, because we just need to help the probe a little bit."

"You want me to push?"

"That won't work in space."

"I know, Karl, it was a figure of speech."

"I see. No, I want you to open the valve of your oxygen bottle a bit. The gas jet will give you the push you need. Well, if you sit in the right place."

"And I won't be needing the oxygen used for this?"

"We have given you triple the amount needed for the trip. One never knows in space."

"Very prescient of you."

"Standard operating procedure. It's the rules."

"Just as good. So tell me what I need to do and how I need to sit."

"Of course, Heather. Let's get started."

THE FLIGHT BACK WAS UNCOMFORTABLE. Karl Freitag kept telling her to change positions, a little bit this way or a little back that way. She felt like a model posing for a demanding painter. The moment she relaxed the push from her oxygen bottle on the probe would change. There was no sound due to the vacuum and nothing to be seen. And no sleep, either. The pad told her that Karl's strategy was working out fine, she would get back safely to the Ark. She was almost afraid of arriving there. She knew that the real work would begin when she got back.

## May 1, 2074, Paris

A LITTLE BIRD had told him a secret: Today his name,
Alain Petit, would be mentioned at an international
convention. Astronomers from around the world were
meeting in Mexico City. Better still, the little bird, a certain
Callis John at the JPL in California, had sent him a VR
ticket to the convention. Fortunately the event took place in
Central America so there was a time offset.

That had given him the chance to grab the necessary
equipment at the nearest Fnac branch that morning. That
had been his idea, anyway. But as he stood before the
closed doors of the store he noticed his calendar showed
the first of May. A public holiday called the Day of Work,
ironically enough. So he had gone out to see his son, who
never took part in the worker's rallies. Alain was sure he
would find him at home.

ALAIN WAS NOW WEARING a headset that, as soon as he
brought it down to cover his eyes, completely cut him off

from his environment. His son had helped him install it in his home. Alain was sure he could have coped himself, but since his schedule was tight he had been glad for the help. Soon afterwards, his son left, and now Alain was waiting for the convention to start. The online program revealed a last minute update, pushing his discovery into the keynote that kicked off the convention. The speech was to be given by a certain Shashwat Agarwal, the director of DKIST, the solar observatory.

Alain was getting restless at his sitting room table. The convention was scheduled to start at 9 am Mexico City time, 4 pm Paris time. It had been less than three weeks ago that he had been sitting here, chatting with the local news editor, Arthur Eigenbrod. He would never forget that name. He had been no more than a nerd with a crazy idea, but Eigenbrod had taken him seriously. Was Arthur following up on the story?

Ten minutes to go. He took a final sip of coffee. The beverage was bitter, the way he preferred it. Then he stood up and carried the cup to the sink. The VR glasses were too tight already, but maybe that was due to him wearing them on his forehead. Today he wouldn't have time to count sunspots, and his unrelenting competitor would overtake him again. Would his 'opponent' know that he was up against Alain Petit, the discoverer of the sun lines? *Old man, you are getting a little full of yourself,* he thought to himself. But it was sad that his wife could not share the moment. She had always supported his hobbies.

The computer signaled a new message. Alain checked his inbox. It was the entry link for the VR participants. He had to click the link. That would launch the special app that would connect him to the event location in Mexico City.

"Please put on your glasses now," requested the app.

He followed the instructions, but pushed the glasses back up immediately. He first needed to seat himself in the chair. The glasses made everything around him disappear completely, and he was afraid of hurting himself. Once seated, he lowered the VR glasses into position. It was impressive. He had moved from his dreamy Parisian apartment to a brim-full convention hall in the blink of an eye. He seemed to be sitting in the walkway between two rows of chairs. The impression was so realistic that he wanted to get up to let the people arriving from behind pass him more easily.

It appeared that the hall doors had opened just a short while ago, and people were milling about to find seats. A mutter of voices filled the hall. Most attendees seemed to be scientists. At least they wore suits and carried briefcases. But there also were journalists in more functional clothes busily unloading their gear from backpacks. Alain's location gave him an excellent view of the stage, as though he was three meters tall. He was able to turn around any way he wanted but he could not leave his position.

A bell rang. The muttering subsided immediately. Those who were still standing looked around quickly for vacant seats. Not everyone was lucky. Some had to sit on the steps of the stairways that led from each of the five entrances down to the stage.

Then a second bell. A man in a dark suit entered the stage. Some people clapped their hands, but the man on the stage just deposited something onto the speaker's desk and left again.

They waited. Finally, a third bell sounded. The hall went quiet. Alain looked around. There were at least a thousand people seated, and another hundred journalists. A lady in a business suit came on stage. She was unexpectedly young, looking almost like a student. General applause came up. Then Alain realized he recognized the woman. He had seen her picture on the news two years ago. She had discovered the black hole that was then threatening the solar system.

"Good morning, ladies and gentlemen, my name is Maribel Pedreira. It is an honor to open your, no, *our* convention."

The applause grew louder. The woman waited until it ebbed off.

"Thank you for your kind welcome. I do not want to bore you with a look into the past. Especially since we have so many topics that concern the future of all of mankind. The greatest potential for this, in my opinion, comes from a somewhat fortuitous discovery by an amateur researcher from France. If I am informed correctly, Monsieur Alain Petit is attending today in VR mode. Please give him a strong round of applause."

People around him clapped their hands enthusiastically. *This is for me!* Alain was getting hot. Good thing he had decided to sit down earlier.

"The discovery and its implications will be detailed by Professor Shashwat Agarwal in his keynote. He leads the efforts at the solar telescope that we all know as DKIST. Please welcome the professor!"

A new round of applause came up. A lean man in a blue suit entered the stage from the side. He held a few papers in his left hand and came to stand beside Pedreira. She shook hands with him.

"Shashwat, if we may ask you, please explain to the global astronomical community what surprises our mother star holds in store for us."

The woman nodded toward the audience. *She looks like she would be glad to be able to leave the stage at this point,* thought Alain. He probably would have felt no different. Shashwat

Agarwal on the other hand looked very confident. It was obviously not his first keynote address.

"Many important discoveries," he began, "started with a coincidence. Just remember the cosmic background radiation. Arno Penzias and Robert Wilson—110 years ago—were experimenting with a new and especially sensitive radio antenna designed to pick up weak radio echoes from balloon satellites of Project Echo. For this they had to eliminate the influence of every other source. They accomplished their goal, but were stuck with deep random noise that was a hundred times stronger than what their antenna should have generated. It came from everywhere in the sky and was constant throughout the day and the night. The two scientists were baffled until they hit a publication that linked radiation like they had discovered to the Big Bang. Eventually this discovery yielded a Nobel Prize for Penzias and Wilson. The story I will be telling today started in a similar fashion."

Agarwal proceeded to give a chronological report of the events of the past few weeks. Alain felt his face turning red again when his name came up for the second time. *Good thing that nobody is able to see me.* He was riveted by the account of the events surrounding the duplicate of the solar probe, first on Earth and later in space. What incredible consequences had come from his dabbling with the magnification of the software loupe!

"So what did we find out there?" Agarwal paused for effect. Alain turned around. Some scientists sat there gaping. Journalists were fidgeting, eager to not miss the next words.

"To be honest… we don't know. So I will stick to the facts. Whatever forms the lines first seen by Alain Petit must be less than ten kilometers in diameter, or else our instruments on Earth would be able to detect them. The lines are distributed across the entire sun. Their origin must be in the photosphere or just below. There is no known physical process that would cause such patterns. Therefore we conclude that it is some form of construction or building. Since we couldn't have failed to notice someone building this, we believe it is older than mankind."

Several arms shot up. The hall filled with noise. Everyone was in discussion.

"Ladies and gentlemen, I am available to take your questions. Kindly log in your request electronically and I will call on you."

The arms went back down. Many in the audience studied the displays in the armrests instead.

The first question came from a journalist who introduced herself and her employer. "Professor Agarwal, what purpose could this construction have?"

"We don't know that."

"It does have a purpose?"

"It must have been incredibly difficult to set up. Whoever accomplished that must have had some kind of justification for doing so."

"Professor Agarwal," came from a Japanese scientist whose name Alain had missed, "in our opinion it is likely that the construction influences solar activity. What do you think?"

"That is an obvious conclusion. The sun has activity patterns that are quite different from other stars of similar size. One could also say that mankind was lucky to have started out in the orbit of this particular star. Elsewhere a planet would have much less time in the habitable zone of a class G star, which means there would be much less time to develop life. Maybe this is no coincidence."

"We are talking about extended periods of time," said

the Japanese astronomer. "If there was a motivation to support Earth in the development of life, the constructor must have been thinking in eons."

"Absolutely," replied Agarwal. "I must add that this is pure speculation. Our scientific observation of the sun does not date back long enough to be able to prove atypical behavior."

"Could it be a weapon of some kind, Professor?" asked an American reporter.

"There isn't much of anything that someone could not also use as a weapon. Human history has ample proof of that. But we can exclude the possibility of humans having constructed this. Our technology will need several thousand years to achieve the necessary level."

"Other civilizations may be as belligerent as humans," the reporter followed up.

"We don't know anything about that. Personally I believe that civilization, the more it progresses, understands more and more that force does not solve problems. To get to the bottom of your question, I'll admit that anybody who controls solar activity also controls Earth. A reduction of just one percent in the solar energy received by our planet would provoke a new Ice Age. Such action would always be directed against all of mankind as it is impossible to impact a single nation or region."

"Michael Cunningham, NASA." The man looked more the administrative type than a researcher. "How do you plan to proceed with researching this discovery? What do you think makes sense?"

"I am glad that you are asking that, Mr. Cunningham," responded the DKIST director with a broad smile. "Right now we have nothing on Earth with which to investigate the phenomenon. While we have telescopes with sufficient resolution, they are unsuitable for observing the sun. It would make sense to pack a solar telescope in a spaceship and check out the construction, or whatever it is, from nearby."

"Could we utilize the duplicate of the solar probe that made the original imagery?"

"Unfortunately, not if we want to obtain new knowledge, Mr. Cunningham. We got what we could out of that probe. We need a new mission, preferably a manned mission. We need to take into account that someone might have to enter the construction."

"What is the rush about?"

The hall got restless, probably because the NASA administrator was on his third question. Cunningham sensed the dissatisfaction and turned around apologetically.

"Last question," he said.

"As a civilization, we simply can't afford not to investigate a huge construction of unknown origin that was built around the very star that makes our planet habitable."

A few people broke into applause. The NASA representative sat down.

A young lady from a Nigerian University was next to be handed the microphone. "Could you explain the algorithms that were used to process the probe recordings?"

Agarwal launched into a technical explanation that Alain could not follow. He decided to log out of the event. The world was turning at breakneck speed. The other day he was talking to Arthur Eigenbrod about his suspicions, and now scientists were rooting for an expedition to the sun. Could things like this really happen in his lifetime? He took off the VR glasses and returned to the safety of his apartment.

The phone rang. It was a Paris number. Alain accepted the call.

"Arthur Eigenbrod here. Alain, can we meet today? I am happy to come and visit you in your apartment."

"Yes, feel free to come. Unfortunately I don't have any cake, though."

"No problem at all. In half an hour?"

"I will be here."

The call dropped. Alain went to the window to close the curtains. Looking out of the window, he spotted a camera team getting out of an e-taxi.

## May 2, 2074, Earth Orbit

"I AM SO SORRY, HEATHER."

*Huh?* "Excuse me?" *Odd way to start a conversation,* she thought. "What do you mean?"

"The invitation. It looks like it won't work out," said Callis.

"What a pity. The cuisine up here leaves a lot to be desired. But what brings you to the Ark?"

"It's all Alain Petit's fault. NASA is planning a solar mission thanks to him."

"I've heard about that. That decision was made incredibly quickly."

"By order of the President. We need to find out whether this thing up there is a threat to the American nation."

"Of course. You will manage, no problem."

"Me? According to my information, *you* are part of the team, Heather."

She felt herself go cold. She had not spoken with her boss since the conference. "I am still counting on leaving tomorrow. I don't even have a change of clothes with me."

"The Ark can provide whatever you need."

"And my daughter?"

"She is grown up and will cope alright."

Heather felt steamrollered. She hated being pushed around. But Callis was just delivering the message. It was not his fault at all.

"Well, it is great to have you here. At least now I know one person up here and don't need to eat alone in the canteen."

"What about Karl Freitag? Doesn't he take care of you? I had insisted on that being his personal responsibility."

"He does alright. He seems to be on the job around the clock. I haven't seen him in the canteen yet."

"Okay, well, I am here now."

"That is great, Callis."

THEY MET in a room that had less than 70 square feet. Callis seemed to be in a rush and started the meeting without further ado. Zero gravity didn't require seats, which allowed up to half a dozen people to attend in the tiny meeting space. Karl Freitag introduced two young women as engineering students who were participants in a trainee program on the Ark.

Callis tapped on a device and one of the walls turned into a large screen.

"I am Callis John for those who don't know me, and I will be the project manager for our little mission over the course of the next few weeks."

A schematic showed up on the screen. "These are the components that will make up our spaceship," explained Callis.

Heather saw something that looked like a huge black coffin, which seemed disconcertingly appropriate. Behind it trailed a wild jumble and an object that looked like a propulsion unit.

"The elements in the drawing are further apart than in reality," pointed out Callis. "Let's look at what we have."

The black coffin blinked.

"The most important component, our heat shield. Essentially this is a block of carbon fiber foam, 60 centimeters thick."

*Not a coffin, then,* thought Heather.

"The heat shield is being built in the Ark shipyard using nanotechnology. We expect to have it ready in a week."

One of the students asked, "Doesn't that have to wrap around the ship somehow?"

"No, the heat transport is mostly by radiation in the areas we will be concerned with. To be in the shade will be sufficient. As a result, the heat shield will always be between the ship and the sun. The shield will heat up to a few thousand degrees but it can cope with that. To reduce heat conduction to the ship, we can take out connecting elements in flight."

"And how do we observe the solar surface?" asked Heather.

"Great question. The shield guarantees the sun not seeing us, so we don't see it either. Unless we peek around the corner with a telescope once in a while."

"Like a submarine that extends a periscope?" asked Karl.

"Yes, pretty much like that. We can only peek for a second, but that should be sufficient."

So the ship was flying mostly blind, hands in front of its eyes, checking once in a while to see if a turn was in order. *That certainly sounds less than reassuring,* thought Heather.

"The ship itself is mostly boring. A few standard modules we'll snag from the Ark," Callis continued.

"We are glad to help out," commented Karl.

"That leaves the propulsion unit. Once more we need to lean on the Ark and borrow one of the Direct Fusion Drives."

"Not happy about that," noted Karl, "but go ahead if you must…"

"Does the ship even need such strong propulsion? It must be falling into the sun anyway?" asked the other student.

"Earth moves around the sun at around 30 kilometers per second. That would be the starting velocity of our ship, too. To get closer to the sun we need to reduce speed quite a bit. And to return we need to get the speed back up to 30 kilometers per second. The DFD will handle that easily."

"And how long will all of this take?" asked Heather.

"That depends on what we find, but I would expect about three months."

## May 3, 2074, Mercury

THE BOSSES back on Earth were suddenly in a rush. And the 'impossible' of before had become the rule now. The entire base camp had been instructed to support him in building the radio telescope. That ended the long drives in the rover. He shared shifts on the pulley post with a technician. The rover taxied autonomously between there and the installation location where two other colleagues camped out. They would unload the rover, order it to return, and then install the fresh equipment.

Artem stood beside a stack of receiver modules. Their improvised cable car took an hour to transport one of them. It wouldn't be much longer before that part was completed. Unfortunately there was only one rover in the camp, but that was the company's fault. Artem had requested a second one months ago but the budget did not allow for it. Then. The base on Mercury didn't even pay for itself, no room for luxuries like that, had been the official justification. Now it was too late. Shipping would have taken too long all by itself.

The reason for the sudden rush, Artem and the other

crewmembers had agreed after some discussion, was the postulated construction recently discovered on the sun, even if nobody would confirm it officially. With a little luck their proximity to the sun would give the RB Group an advantage. Assuming their project had better resolution than any telescope on Earth, they would be the first to know what had been built around the sun. And knowledge was power, or money, or both. Was there even a difference?

The magic number right now was 34. If the rover didn't break down, they could finish installing that many more modules in two weeks. The boss had implored them to find a way to do it in one. He offered a full year's salary as a prize to anyone who could figure out how to get it done that quickly. It had to be important for the conglomerate.

But Artem thought it might be rather longer than shorter. The rover simply wasn't made for 24x7 operations —200 kilometers per unit, that was 6,800 kilometers to go. After every 1,000 kilometers a thorough checkup was mandatory. The last ones had been skipped to save time already. Of course they had tried to load more than one module at a time, but the modules were so big and heavy that the rover would not arrive at its destination.

To have his peace back was more important to Artem than a fat bonus. Money didn't talk at all up here. He couldn't even buy a woman's attention here. He had tried with a technician only to have her boot make painful contact with his knee. That left saving for his retirement. That would never happen anyway—some crazy assignment would kill him, he was sure of that.

Artem looked down into the crater. It would be another half hour before the next module arrived up here. He longed to roll a cigarette, take his time smoking it, and throw the glowing stub down the cliff into the darkness below. The Kandinsky Crater spread out below him. Their base camp was too far to spot but he could see the two spaceships that sparkled in the sun, the transport barge and the 'yacht' for personnel. He had arrived with the freight barge, how long ago, exactly?

*Wait a minute,* he thought. They did have transport that was faster than a rover!

"Artem calling base camp."

"Yes, Artem? Mikhail here."

"I wanted to officially register an idea on how to get the modules on site faster."

"If you are looking at the spaceships, you probably are the penultimate person to click on that."

"At least I'm not the last."

"The last human you are. Sobachka is the only other one."

"Haha, very funny. So why won't the ships work?"

"Not enough fuel."

"How is that?"

"They are here for a reason, but who am I telling that to? You know that better than me, so don't waste any more of my time."

"Please spell it out for me."

"Okay. Take the freight barge that lifts raw materials into orbit. It takes off, is unloaded and refueled in orbit, and lands again. You get it, Artem?"

"You are telling me it can't land without refueling?"

"Exactly, you smart aleck."

"Then we change the procedure."

"You are getting on my nerves, Artem."

"I know, but we do have two ships."

"That changes nothing. Okay, we might refuel the barge with the fuel from the yacht so it might land again. So we load the modules, it lands and then it is empty and we don't get it back up, ever again. The yacht being empty as well."

"That would be the situation if the barge didn't consist of two stages."

"Two stages? Sure, but what does that do for us?"

"A world of difference. Here is my plan: We fill the first stage of the barge with the fuel from the yacht. Then we load as many modules as we can into the first stage. It just needs to land safely. The second stage goes into orbit. The supply ship fills the hold with fuel. For the first stage, and the yacht, and itself."

"That could work. But it would be a hell of a mess," Mikhail said after a pause. "You've never transferred fuel, have you?"

"Of course I have. I always stole fuel for my own ship."

"I believe that, Artem."

"So you'll pass the idea to the boss?"

"Will do. But there is no guarantee that we'll really save a week. We don't know how many modules fit. No room for issues, either."

"Tell the rover. The right rear wheel bearing is running hotter than the rest. Besides, I am not in this for the money."

"Rather?"

"I want my fucking peace."

## May 4, 2074, Mercury

HE REALLY HAD a talent for getting himself the worst job possible. Mikhail had been right, transferring fuel was a hell of a mess. Odd that he hadn't remembered it that way. The problem was compounded by not having the proper tools. They were mining, not operating a gas station. So he had to improvise. And that was not so easy with liquid fuel. It was incredibly cold and incredibly liquid, plus the space-suit made it harder, *and* he had to bridge a hundred meters between the ships.

Liquid oxygen, the first component, was the lesser issue. The flexible tubes were well insulated and had a strongly reflective coating against solar radiation. Keeping below minus 183 degrees Celsius wasn't a challenge at all. But liquid hydrogen was a real headache. Hydrogen has its practical side, because it creates a high specific momentum on combustion. But there was also its boiling point to consider, just 21 degrees above absolute zero—minus 252 degrees Celsius. Mercury was simply too warm—even in the shadows temperatures ranged between minus 160 and minus 180.

Since both ships stood in the sun, he first had to shade things from sunlight. In the total absence of wind, it had been sufficient to put up a tarpaulin. His engineering studies came in handy for the second step. It had been a while, but he remembered learning some cooling technologies. He borrowed a compressor from the mining team to pressurize the tubes. Toward the end of the line the pressure would drop, and that was intentional. The expansion would cool down and liquefy the hydrogen that had evaporated during transport thanks to the Joule-Thompson effect.

That was the theory. Artem connected the last part of the tubes to the hydrogen tank of the barge. Next he walked the hundred meters over to the yacht, started the compressor, and opened the valve. Opening the valve was a remote operation that he launched via his pad. The command went through the computer on the yacht and he noticed the compressor vibrations change as his pad confirmed the opening of the valve. A few seconds now and pressure would be dropping in the source tanks. A warning message popped up to confirm that, so everything was running smoothly! Artem walked back to the barge. Initially mostly hydrogen gas would be arriving—the tubing had to cool down sufficiently first. He logged into the barge computer. The receiving tank was still empty.

Artem ignored the looming lethal danger. Some loss of hydrogen and oxygen always occurred. If the escaping gases were to mix in the right ratio near the ship, any odd spark would start an explosive reaction. The gas would turn to water and he'd be distributed across the surrounding area. No, that wouldn't happen. Hydrogen and oxygen got along well together, mostly. And there was lots of space around him—why should the gas create a cloud near him instead of spreading all over Mercury?

Besides, that initial spark to set it all off was missing. No, his construction was rather creative, and pretty quick and dirty, but not all that dangerous.

Indeed, everything looked like the valuable liquid was moving into the old barge all right. The computer reported increasing fill levels. Artem compared source and destination and noticed a decrease of about one-fifth of the volume arriving than had left the yacht. That didn't include the volume in the pipeline. So he would have to be content to lose one-sixth of the fuel volume over the course of the project.

Three men were loading modules into the first level. It looked like sixteen modules were going to fit. That was one sad number, because it meant just barely missing the reward for improvement by one week. But the computer at base camp had chewed on optimizing the process and had come up with this number. He trusted the program, unlike the RB Group that would cheat him out of the prize if it could. But it didn't matter. The money had no importance. Once the modules were in place he'd regain his peaceful routine.

IT DID NOT EXPLODE. Artem removed the pipeline from the tank. The ship computer reckoned there was enough fuel to take off and land again. Nine hours work in a spacesuit! He was tired to the bone and couldn't wait to get back to Sobachka, whom he had left at base camp today. But first he wanted to watch lift-off. His colleagues had been back in their bunks for a while now.

Artem pulled the end of the pipeline after himself, marching toward base camp. A hundred meters distance would be enough. The other ship hadn't sat further away, either. He took down the tarpaulins and hung them across his shoulders. They dropped down in front and back. If he had a third one to wrap around his head, one might think he wasn't wearing a spacesuit. Sobachka would enjoy that. Would she recognize him? He doubted it.

After a while he turned around. The barge was well over 100 meters away now.

"Artem calling base camp, go ahead. Environment secured."

"Understood, starting countdown."

Apparently Mikhail was on shift again at launch control. Artem watched intently. Every launch came with a risk, even if 999 out of 1,000 went well. Maybe one of the fuel pipes had clogged during the refill, or one of the jets had been damaged on landing the last time? Absolute safety did not exist. And then there was the human factor, a whole set of issues in its own right.

The countdown was at 15 when Artem spotted movement to the left of the rocket. Had he forgotten one of the tarpaulins? Impossible, but even if he had it would not move. At the count of 12 he realized it could only be Sobachka moving out there. Was she looking for him?

"Abort countdown, base camp, abort immediately," he called out over his helmet microphone, and started running simultaneously.

"What's up? All systems green. Launch is great. No reason to abort."

"Sobachka! She is right by the barge!" He gasped for air. Maybe five seconds to go. Mercury let him run in huge leaps but the spacesuit was a hindrance.

"What are you talking about? I just see you running toward the barge. Stop right there, Artem!"

No time for explanations. While he ran for the life of

the dog he was waving his arms furiously. The tarpaulins had fallen off a while back already.

"Sobachka, come here!" he commanded. Her helmet radio—would it be working?

"Artem you idiot, stop right there! The company will give me hell for any delay you cause!"

"5... 4... 3..."

She had seen him, Artem guessed 30 meters distance from the ship. Would it work out? Sobachka came running toward him. Countdown was at 0. He threw himself over her, turning his back toward the ship.

*Oh boy, Sobachka, what have you done?* he thought. Tears ran over his face and his ragged breathing was all he could hear. He did not dare to turn around. Behind him a rocket was taking off. Hydrogen burned at 2,700 degrees. The resulting hot gas was invisible. It would cool down and condense to water, eventually forming a steam cloud. Meanwhile the hot exhaust gas would throw up lots of dust from the launch site. Artem pictured the transport barge slowly lifting on a gray cloud into the black sky. The cloud would be brighter on the edges, drops of water glistening, and from the right angle one might even see a rainbow. How long until the cloud would reach him? Would his suit, built for 450 degrees to withstand Mercury's relentless exposure to the sun, be able to protect him from this heat wave?

"I think you can get up now, Artem," came from launch control in the base camp.

"Which one of you buttheads let Sobachka out?"

"It was me," a woman responded.

"Irina?" The woman was part of the mining team.

"Yes. She whined so much about you leaving her here. I wanted to do her a favor," she said.

"You could have warned me."

"I wanted to do that, but an assignment interfered with it."

"Oh boy," said Artem, "you guys sure make life interesting."

"Nothing happened, fortunately," said Mikhail.

Artem released Sobachka and stood up. He checked his suit while the dog happily danced around his legs. She was unaware of the commotion. Perhaps she had been a bit surprised by the sudden cuddling session, but who knew what a dog would be thinking... Their spacesuits were full of dust with sparkling ice crystals mixed in. He patted them down as best he could.

Yet another day on which he had not died.

## May 10, 2074, Earth Orbit

THE ROUTINE on board the Ark made her suffer more than she would have considered possible. Zero gravity had lost its charms. It required her to do four hours of cycling and all kinds of other exercises just to keep fit. The systematic training had revealed to her a few muscles she had completely forgotten about. The nondescript food also did its part to make some muscles visible on her arms and legs. She still wished for some culinary variety, though. Some entrepreneur had started to build a private space station in one of the Lagrange points, where gravity from Sun and Earth were balanced out. It was rumored that this 'Orbital Station Blue' was going to attract tourists with a gourmet restaurant. Heather hoped that would work out quickly—but apparently delays were stretching timelines already.

To escape boredom she resorted to meeting Callis regularly after shifts. He was a real gentleman. His presence felt more and more comforting, yet he did not try to persuade her to do something she did not know if she was ready for yet. Yes, her thoughts could be rather contorted sometimes. She felt attracted to him, but at the same time she feared too much closeness. Who knew what was going to happen tomorrow? Callis had to leave with the ship they were busy assembling out of scraps. She missed him already—how much worse would that be if they were closer?

Her current project was the construction of the periscope that would allow peeking around the heat shield. She was not involved in assembly—there were more experienced people for that. Her job as an astronomer was to ensure it would be able to cope with whatever might come up during the trip.

The special heat-resistant glass was a good example. It worked up to 1,800 degrees Celsius and had been developed for smelting ovens. Its optical parameters were atrocious, however, preventing an attached telescope from achieving any useful magnification. Software corrections were out of the question with the refractive index being non-linearly-related to the wavelength. Yesterday she had spent an hour discussing the issue with the supplier. As a result they were sending a new glass to the Ark. That created a delay of two days during which the problem was stuck on the list.

"Heather, would you join me, please?" Callis called via onboard radio. That meant some official event.

Mike, the drone, activated its face.

"Would you like me to accompany you?"

"No, thank you."

He deactivated the screen. Was it time to ask the head of security to reassign Mike? She knew the Ark well enough now. On the other hand she liked having him around. After the first three days of constant monitoring he had readily entered sleep mode whenever she requested it.

She left the workspace. Callis had a very small individual office with a large wall display. Of course it was a shared space, swapping owners with every shift. He activated his screen as soon as she entered his office.

"Great that you could make it so quickly. We have an important call."

The screen showed a young lady who seemed familiar. She connected the dots when the name was dropped.

"My name is Maribel Pedreira," she said. "I need to discuss the solar mission with you."

"You need to?" asked Callis, "I thought it was a NASA mission?"

"That changed yesterday. The U.S. representatives on the United Nations Security Council have been persuaded to let other nations get on board. There were... security concerns. And I was asked to take care of the aspect of international cooperation."

*An excellent choice,* thought Heather. The young Spaniard had gained a lot of respect, worldwide. She had even managed to keep the big conglomerates in their place.

"And how might we help with that?" asked Callis.

"There are side conditions. Since your country pays for 90 percent of the mission cost, it was insisted that only one person from another nation would be let on board. To satisfy all the other UNSC members, we need an internationally respected crew."

"... that is also still technically competent," amended Callis.

"I agree with you, Callis, but the politicians don't put that much weight on this aspect."

"A delicate mission," said Heather.

"Especially since the candidates must be available on short notice, and for at least three months," continued Maribel. "Who can do that these days? The mission is set to leave next week."

"In one week?" Heather wrung her hands. "I'm not positive that the ship will be ready by then."

"It will," declared the young lady on the monitor. "The President's Office has given me assurances."

"Well, it will be exciting to put a crew together by then," said Callis.

"That is why we are talking. I was hoping to be half done with my job right now."

"You speak in riddles, Maribel." Heather groped for the wall as she had the feeling she might topple. Callis looked at her.

"I guess you have just this moment figured it out. Yes, I would like to have both you and Callis on board. Callis is the technical lead with his expertise on the solar probe, and you are the solar specialist to keep an eye on the scientific side of things. Besides, you have a unique advantage, being in space and ready to go. We'd just need to shoot two more people into space."

"I… I don't know," said Heather. "I can't imagine me being the right person."

"You can sleep on it, but we need your decision tomorrow, unfortunately. It feels odd to give you advice since you have seen more of life than I have... But believe me, whether you are up to a job only becomes clear once you have started it. You should not wait until you feel ready."

"Yes, well, no. I don't know. Are you ready, Callis?"

He nodded. "Yes, I'll be flying. Not because I desperately want to go, but because it is the most practical solution."

"That's great," said Maribel.

"And who else do you have in mind? Who will be coming with us?" he asked.

"I am not sure if I should tell you, they might refuse."

"I still would like to know."

"Do you remember the Enceladus expedition in the forties?"

"I sure do. I was finishing college then. That expedition is what put me in JPL, in fact."

"The head of mission, Amy Michaels, is a biologist and doctor."

"And an excellent commander, too," added Callis. "She would be over 70 now?"

"She's 71, to be precise. But these days that isn't an issue anymore."

*Maribel has a point there*, thought Heather. In most developed countries the retirement age was set at 70. China had just increased it to 72 due to its aging population.

"Didn't she give birth to a son in space?" mused Heather.

"Yes, he must be around 30 now," said Callis. "And who is the second candidate?"

"We need a non-American in that spot," explained Maribel. "If we invite a Chinese, the Russians complain. If we take someone from India, the Chinese will veto him."

"So how do you plan to work around that?" asked Callis.

"We invite the person who got the ball rolling, Alain Petit. He is an engineer, albeit a sewage engineer, and he is a Frenchman. The French have a good reputation, they really moved Europe forward, and their reaction to the crisis in Catalonia was exemplary."

"Isn't Alain Petit retired?" asked Heather, "I remember him writing something to that effect."

"That's great, it means he has the time. And he is only two years older than Amy Michaels."

## May 11, 2074, Ishinomaki

"LOOK, THERE!" Amy Michaels pointed to a wooden bench standing in the brush bordering a sandy path on the cliffs.

Maribel Pedreira took in the panorama. The small village to the right had to be Ishinomaki. It had not been difficult to find the legendary commander of the Enceladus expedition there. Amy Michaels had lived in the small fisherman's village ever since her return.

"I often sat here with Hayato, and I especially remember when we were discussing the second expedition. It was not easy to leave my family for two years. But one of us had to stay with our son."

"I can relate to that," Maribel said. Hayato had died five years ago according to her research, apparently from cancer. It was believed that the radiation levels in space had taken their toll on his body.

"He lies over there, on the other side. His spot overlooks the bay. We are lucky today. Usually it is too hazy to see the other side."

Maribel's eyes swept the landscape. The open sea was

to the left, a large tanker making little waves. They seemed to play with the sunlight. The air was ripe with the aroma of pinewood from the patch of forest they had traversed to come up here. Amy appeared to be in great physical condition, leading all the way.

"You are surprisingly fit," blurted Maribel.

"For my age. Is that implied?" Amy smiled.

"In general. I wouldn't have guessed you were older than 65."

"That is very kind of you. I am sure you have researched my true age."

"Of course, Amy. Did you know that it was your fault that I became an astrophysicist?"

"How come?"

"When I was 12 my dad arranged a family trip to the Kennedy Space Center in Florida, complete with an astronaut tour guide. The astronaut was you."

"That must have been 15 years ago, more or less?"

"Oh, more than that. I am somewhat over 30 now, so it is more like 20 years ago."

"You didn't decide to be an astronaut, Maribel?"

"It was more the role that you were playing, I found that fascinating."

"Well, I am glad you did. Who knows, if you hadn't chosen that career, Earth might not exist anymore."

"You give me too much credit. I just did my job. And that is what I am doing today. I would like to ask you something."

"Well, I am not surprised. There had to be more behind a 10-hour flight than a visit to an old woman."

"It's not a question, it is more of a request. It may sound a little presumptuous, but let me say it as it is: I am here to kindly request that you take command of the upcoming international mission to the sun."

"Oh, but that is… a surprise indeed. I was expecting something in the context of the mission, but I had been thinking more along the lines of some consulting."

"Oh, but you will be consulting. Day and night! You will be the only crewmember with significant space experience. But it won't take as long as last time. We estimate about three months."

"Hmmm. Any alternatives?"

"Plan B? No, Amy, I'll be frank with you. We are under incredible political pressure, and the clock is ticking loudly. You would be the solution to both of those issues, and a perfect commander at that. We couldn't possibly hope for more."

"I accept."

Maribel jerked in surprise. *Did I hear that correctly?* She looked at Amy. No, she wasn't pulling her leg.

"That is excellent news, thank you very much!" Maribel said while standing up and shaking Amy's hand. How could she possibly communicate her gratefulness? A huge worry had just been lifted.

"Well, you said there is no alternative, so I am trusting you all the way."

"And you don't need time to think it through?"

"Hayato agreed last time. He can't object this time. My son is a grown-up. My in-laws enjoy good health despite having just turned 96."

"It would be most helpful if we could leave today."

"We can manage that. But first you must come visit my in-laws over a cup of tea and some biscuits. They can't wait to meet you."

## May 12, 2074, Paris

THE BELL RANG. Alain Petit came up from the sofa with a start. He had fallen asleep just moments ago. Who would visit him in the afternoon? He checked his watch. His son would still be working. And reporters hadn't reappeared since the throng ten days ago.

He pressed the button on the intercom. "Who is it?"

"It's me, Arthur Eigenbrod. Could I speak with you, please?"

*Eigenbrod? What would this journalist be after, and why hadn't he called ahead?* Alain pressed the buzzer to open the main door and went to his apartment door to watch for his visitor.

Eigenbrod was breathing heavily as he reached the landing below the apartment. He didn't sound good at all. Alain never had trouble taking the few steps leading up to his home.

"You should be doing something for your fitness, young man," he said in place of a welcome. "And go for a checkup with a heart specialist, too."

"Oh, thank you for the suggestion," responded the journalist, feigning pain in his chest.

"Do come in before we have an emergency in the stairway. Coffee?" Alain waved the editor in with a sweeping gesture.

Eigenbrod glanced at the floor.

*He is probably wondering whether to take off his shoes,* thought Alain. "Don't worry about them," he said, nodding at Eigenbrod's feet.

The visitor nodded in gratitude and entered the apartment. He went straight to the sitting room and took a seat with a wheeze. "Nice and cool in here," he observed.

"This old building—it stays that way even in August," answered Alain. He wondered what might have earned him this visit. "So, what about your coffee?"

"Thank you, no, I don't have much time today," replied Eigenbrod. "You probably wonder about the surprise visit."

*You bet I do,* thought Alain Petit, but kept quiet. The other man would surely keep talking.

"My assignment to visit you didn't come from my lazy colleague or my boss this time."

"So…?" *Don't make me pull teeth!* thought Alain.

"Of all things, I got a call from the Ark, from a certain Heather Marshall."

*The name sounds familiar…* Wasn't that the astronomer who had sent him the original data? Yes, but wasn't she working at the DKIST in Maui?

"Interesting," said Alain. He sat down as a feeling welled up that something big was cooking here.

"Yes, very much so. Ms. Marshall requested me to invite you on behalf of NASA."

"An invitation? With you inviting me?"

"Monsieur Petit, your address can't be found on the

web, and the topic was strictly on a need-to-know basis. So they checked who wrote the original article about you."

"That was you."

"I remember that. They asked me for your address, but that is not how it works. My sources are protected."

"So it wasn't that you were concerned with the developing story?"

"Probably that, too," Arthur Eigenbrod admitted as he sat up straight. "The story is worth it, you see. You, Alain... *you* are to go into space. To fly to the sun, to be precise."

Alain froze in place. He checked the journalist's expression and waited for laughter. But there was no joke waiting to be sprung, no mischievous smirk, just a curious expression. Perhaps the editor was mentally typing out the description of how Alain Petit received this piece of incredible news.

*Can this possibly be true?* wondered Alain. *And, how does one respond if the answer is for the books?* He had no idea. "I am surprised," was all he could say.

"You don't look that way."

Alain touched his cheeks. They were cool. He was fully composed. Was that some kind of shock reaction? "Why me?" he asked.

"The official version or my opinion?"

"Both."

"Officially, your engineering experience is a perfect match. But, I believe it is politics. You are the only astronaut who isn't from the U.S. Us Frenchies have a good reputation right now, so that wouldn't bother anybody else. And then there are the practical aspects. You are interested in the mission goal, you have time, you are not expensive, and you are an easy sale for the media. After all, you started this whole thing."

"Sure, for headlines like 'Space Pensioner,'" said Alain.

"You aren't even close to the oldest person in space. Remember the 101-year-old lady from Japan last year? Her son had gifted her a trip to the Ark."

"She was back home the next day. For me it will be weeks."

"Three months."

"And won't I need some formal training?"

"Not for twenty years now. You will have a very experienced commander. Does the name Amy Michaels ring a bell?"

"Sure. The Enceladus mission!"

"She will head this mission, too."

Alain only remembered vaguely—that mission had occurred 30 years ago—that the commander had been around his own age. It would be most surprising if she wasn't over 70 like himself.

"And the others? How old are they, over 80?"

Eigenbrod laughed. "No, you and Amy will be the seniors. Heather Marshall will be going, you know her already. Plus Callis John, who was responsible for the solar probe at the Jet Propulsion Lab. Both have years to go before retiring."

"There is that, at least. So when will this happen?"

"Tomorrow, or the day after at the latest."

"Good. Nothing like a little heads-up before going on a space trip." Alain stood up and looked around. "I need to be packing then."

His hands were moist. He wiped them on his pants. First, he needed a drink.

## May 13, 2074, Mercury

ARTEM SHOOK his foot and a sock flew off to the corner of the room in a high arc. Sobachka raced to battle the evil sock. It put up a good fight, but eventually the sock had no choice but to submit to the top dog on Mercury. Sobachka proudly brought her trophy to Artem, wagging her tail all the way. Artem bent down and praised her accordingly. The sock was made of synthetics that showed no wear at all from dog teeth. It joined its sister on the way into the laundry bag.

The laundry bag had a pungent smell. He was quick to close it. It was high time to wash. The last weeks had been murderous—twelve hours daily in his spacesuit had left very little time for household chores.

The improvised radio telescope was now set up. Mikhail, who had studied physics for two years, was in charge of processing the incoming signals. He had special software that would take the individual signals and create a composite image. The image would be encrypted and sent to the RB Group headquarters in Siberia.

The small bed squeaked as Artem sat down. It had

probably come out of Russian army stocks from back in the 20ᵗʰ century. His cubicle was small and pretty spartan, but he spent most of his free time here regardless. When he wasn't sleeping, training, or working he played with Sobachka. The rest of the team met after shifts for drinks and TV, but neither interested him.

Thinking about it, he considered it a small wonder that time seemed to fly by anyway. Shouldn't he have been bored to death a long time ago? Perhaps it was the permanent danger from the hostile environment that made life bearable. If that was the case, a return to Earth was out of the question. Artem dropped his head into his hands. He had felt this way his entire remembered life, and since leaving had instinctively done everything to avoid going back to his home planet. Considering everything, he probably had to be grateful to the RB Group for forcibly recruiting him.

"Guys, you want to see something crazy?" asked Mikhail through the base camp radio. *What an idiot*, Artem thought to himself. He probably was watching some video and getting excited over some stuntman doing incredible stuff. Hard boot soles battered the corridor outside. Curiosity got the better of him so he stood up, shrugging his shoulders. Sobachka was right by his side and sped out of the door as he opened it.

THE BABBLE of voices provided directions. The team had gathered in the tech lab. The hubbub grew louder. Others could see nothing, like him, and were pushing colleagues aside. It was a rough place here—he wasn't the only criminal RB had hired for the job.

"Watch out!" he heard Mikhail's voice cut through. Artem visualized him getting crushed at his desk.

Pushing a colleague aside, a stalwart woman called out, "Hey, we want to see something, too."

"Give me a minute," came back from Mikhail.

"You kidding us?" This man, tattoos across his jaws, wasn't loud but the threat was well understood.

"I'll put it on the big screen."

That was probably Mikhail's salvation. The messroom with the big screen for viewing canned videos held 50, more than enough for the entire staff. Artem jumped aside to avoid the inevitable crush of bodies and picked up Sobachka to be on the safe side.

Irina, the stalwart woman who had complained earlier, bumped into him and his dog. Sobachka gave a scared yelp. Irina stopped, excused herself, and stroked Sobachka. Then she looked at Artem.

"Do you want me to visit you later and play with your little one?" she asked with a sly smile on her face. "With your little dog, of course."

That was a new attitude from her. Sobachka obviously made women connect, but he preferred to forego Irina's visit.

"My shift is starting soon," he lied.

"Well, then let's get going," Irina replied while grabbing his shoulders and turning him around. "I've never seen Mikhail so excited. We can't miss this." Her bosom slammed into his back as she pushed him forward, protecting him and Sobachka from further jostling.

THEY ENTERED the messroom just as the big screen lit up. Those present spread to fill the seats around tables and the rest sat on benches along the sides of the room. The screen was on the high wall next to the entrance and was well visible all the way from the opposite side.

"If it went by my rules, only people fresh out of a shower would be allowed in here," said Irina.

She was dead right. The room smelled of sweat in all flavors. It was bad. Artem lifted his arm and checked his own status. *So-so*, he thought, *probably time to change the T-shirt soon.*

The screen morphed into a gray pixilated surface full of odd patterns. Some of the men hooted and whistled, thinking there was poor reception.

"Enough waiting now," said Mikhail, addressing them from the tech lab via speakers. "What you are seeing here is a true sensation."

More whistles derisively underlined the statement.

"Hey, keep cool, a radio telescope is no camera. We ping the target, the solar surface, which isn't a fixed surface at all, pixel by pixel and line by line. This is better than anything they could do back on Earth. Resolution is mind-blowing. Do you see this line?"

Part of the picture was magnified, making pixels even more obvious, but the line Mikhail referred to had become even more visible in the process.

"That definitely is an artificial structure all around the sun," his voice explained. He sounded awestruck.

"Who cares?" said one of the men at the side of the room.

"Shhhh," hushed Irina.

"If that feels small and insignificant," continued Mikhail's explanation, "that thing is at least five kilometers thick and more than four million kilometers long. And there are more of them, in a regular grid around the entire star."

"Which star?" asked someone from the back.

"The sun, you moron," shouted Irina in his direction. Then she turned to Artem and quietly asked him, "Isn't that crazy?"

Artem nodded.

"If the lines are 50,000 kilometers at the equator, then there must be about 80 of them, each consisting of about 80,000,000 cubic kilometers of material. That's a total of 6,400,000,000 cubic kilometers! Someone took the equivalent of half our moon, pressed it into pipe shape, and laid it out around the sun. Or whatever they really did."

"Guess it wasn't our team," came from the back. The others laughed out loud.

"But what is this good for?" Irina asked while scratching her chin. Artem had been thinking along the same lines.

"I have no idea what this is about," added Mikhail. "That's for the eggheads on Earth."

"Perhaps it has something to do with solar activity," said Irina quietly so that only Artem could hear it.

"What makes you say that?"

"I was an electrical engineer way back," she replied. "That thing is like a huge cage around the sun."

"To protect the sun?" whispered Artem.

"Or to protect us from the sun."

"The best is yet to come." Mikhail had yet to finish his presentation. The image changed. It looked as though the viewer was flying over the solar surface. Artem stood up onto his tiptoes because of a young woman who had stood up in his line of sight.

"This thing does not belong here, either," said Mikhail, tracing out a red circle around an odd structure.

The highlighted object reminded Artem of an ancient hourglass, without the usual framework. Two symmetric triangles with an elegant swoosh in their long sides stood atop each other in a mirror image, meeting at their apexes.

"Our readings show these things are rotating," added Mikhail. "They are about six kilometers wide and ten kilometers tall, overall. It could also be that the two triangles—or should I say cones?—don't touch at all. Our instruments are not sensitive enough to tell for sure."

"A huge spaceship," whispered Irina, and pensively tapped her lips with her index finger.

"It is noteworthy that the cones point straight at the North and South poles of the sun, respectively," continued Mikhail. "But of course that could just be a consequence of being docked to one of those lines."

"Like a bike being oriented by the bike stand it is attached to," Artem thought out loud.

"A bicycle. Nice analogy," answered Irina.

"If I was to speculate about the function," said Mikhail, "then this object is in charge of controlling the lines around the sun. Or it had that function in the past. Maybe the builders lived in there. Or they continue to live there."

"Booohring," someone hollered from the back. Artem turned around. It was a young man with long hair, his friends busy patting his shoulder. A pathetic guy, he deserved to get hit come the right occasion.

"Incredible," said Irina. "I never would have expected to see an alien spaceship with my own eyes."

"I need to go there," said Artem.

"Are you out of your mind? That is in the middle of the sun," Irina shot back.

"Not exactly, it must be in the photosphere. That's the solar surface."

"I know," said Irina. "Do you think I'm stupid?"

Artem turned and looked around. Most people had

relaxed and were chatting. The sensational discovery on the screen in front of them had faded from their minds already.

"Sorry. You do seem to be the only sensible person here, apart from Sobachka and myself, of course," replied Artem.

"Thanks, that is nice of you." Irina smiled at him. She looked quite attractive that way. Artem turned around abruptly. That was a can of worms he did not want to open. He'd had too many already. And if she really was nice, she didn't deserve to be drawn into his troubles.

Artem gave Irina a quick nod, set Sobachka down, and left for his cabin.

"Comrades," he heard Mikhail say over the speakers, "it goes without saying that what you have just witnessed is top secret. Your communication is monitored and censored already, but if you try to let this out, your entire data feed will be cut for two weeks."

## May 14, 2074, Mercury

"You will investigate the alien object and take owner-ship of it for us this decision is final."

The synthetic voice had given the order in a flat stac-cato rhythm, with no trace of emotion. Artem had been waiting for this call. His instinct had not failed him. It had been clear that the decision was going to come down to him. He was the logical choice, it was all but inevitable.

Irina was the only other candidate. It would have been a pity had the message come to her, because he would have had to convince her, or even incapacitate her if she would not yield to him. This mission was made for him. He was the only person on board who had handled a spaceship alone and for an extended period of time. Irina, he found out only yesterday, had been a co-pilot for three years. He hadn't expected that.

His thought process had been quite simple. The risk of somebody else discovering the alien object was rising every day. The conglomerate had no time to waste. Starting a ship from Earth outside regular schedules would have raised flags. Nobody was watching Mercury, however. And starting from here would provide an incredible head start in the race.

The downside was having to work with what Mercury had to offer. The second stage of the barge was still up in orbit. That left the 'yacht,' a four-seater. It needed quite a refitting to reach the photosphere. But with the right pilot —himself—one could eliminate three out of four seats. That was how he had rationalized his selection, and it had been gratifying to get the same explanation fed back to him from Earth. He was tempted to believe that the highly-paid engineers down there had been led by his thoughts.

*Artem, don't hold your nose too high,* he told himself. The plan got accepted because it was logical. The yacht had strong propulsion engines to help the base camp managers flee the planet in a pinch. They would have to give up that exit plan now. Artem almost found himself hoping the base camp would be hit by an asteroid during his absence. It wouldn't bother him, except maybe for Irina.

But the propulsion unit of the yacht would not protect him from heat or radiation. The scientists on Earth had proposed a shield. A solar probe had used such a shield to successfully go all the way to the chromosphere. He would have to go even closer, though. Then he remembered the camouflage technology his ship had used to protect him against discovery by the conglomerate goons. With the right materials it was possible to redirect radiation of various wavelengths right around an object. Heat transport in the solar atmosphere was mostly by radiation. If one could get it to flow around the ship, things would stay cool, literally.

It would also make the yacht invisible to many types of instruments. That would facilitate the approach to the object. And it gave him completely fresh options for the time after the solar rendezvous. *Good-bye forever, Mercury!* he thought. *If the RB Group gives me such a nice ship, who is to prevent me using it for my own purposes?*

He had briefly considered using the yacht to disappear right after launch, instead of flying close to the sun, as Icarus had done in Greek mythology. But that felt wrong. Not for moral reasons—morality had no place in deadly space—but because he simply had to see this thing. The object was bigger than anything ever constructed by mankind, and it was beyond their horizon now and probably into the next thousand years. The opportunity to touch such technology was something he simply could not refuse.

"Irina, can you help me refit the yacht?" He had tracked down the former engineer in the canteen. She seemed to be enjoying a huge pudding.

"So you got the assignment? I thought you would."

"What did you think?"

"It was logical to send you."

Irina was perceptive. He could not pretend. She'd notice and get angry with him.

"I thought the same."

"So what do you need from me?"

"I don't have anybody else I can trust. Zero mistake policy on the refit—it would be my death otherwise. Just look at our colleagues," he said, finishing on a special note of disdain.

"I hear you," said Irina. "I need to check with the boss, but I'd love to help you."

"Boss is good. I get all that I need. Anything at all. Comes right from the top."

"Tell him you need a real beef steak. The cook told me

he had some in cold storage, especially reserved for the boss."

"I can try." Artem laughed.

"When do we start?"

"Right now, Irina, right now."

AN HOUR later they stood before the sleek rocket. The yacht was perched on top. Irina shielded her eyes with her right hand. The sun dazzled them, despite standing low. There was no atmosphere here to take the bite out, and he would get many million kilometers closer still. The sun would become so big in the bullseye window of the ship that nothing else would be in view.

"A little plump, your yacht," said Irina.

"I have no idea who planned that." Elegant or chic really didn't describe the crew capsule, which looked more like a chubby bullet.

"Any ideas for the shield?"

"No. Just getting the balance right will be a challenge. Just look at it."

They needed to attach a heavy, disk-shaped shield to one side of the yacht without losing stability for the entire rocket. Mercury had only one-third of Earth's gravity, but a launch was far from child's play here, either. The load had to be distributed evenly.

"It would be a lot safer if we could do that in orbit," said Irina.

"Hmmmm."

"Well…"

Artem wanted to scratch his crotch, but then he noticed his spacesuit was in the way. If it had a flap he could pee on the Mercury desert. He smiled at that idea.

"What's wrong?" his helper asked.

"I was just imagining how I… not important."

"How you what?"

A flap, sure. They didn't need to mount the shield down here. He'd take it on the ship and unfold it in orbit.

"No matter. I just had an idea."

"Get it out in the open," said Irina.

Artem cringed at the idea, then deflected. "You ever heard of origami?"

"Japanese folding cranes?"

"All kinds of figures, but yes. A British space company applied it to space technology in the 30s."

"That was before my time."

"Before mine, too. But I heard about it on the History Channel."

"Doesn't sound like it was a success."

"No, Irina. They didn't need to carry big stuff in rockets with limited space anymore, shortly after that."

"Sure, since starting space manufacturing and assembly. That is quite a bit more practical."

"We could fold the heat shield using origami. Then I take it up in the capsule and unfold it in orbit."

"That sounds feasible," said Irina.

"I sure think so, too. Headquarters can probably get us old plans."

"You have another big headache, Artem."

"Fuel, I know. I transferred it away myself."

"We have enough water here to split into hydrogen and oxygen." Irina pointed to the shadows thrown onto the ice by the crater wall. "The necessary tools are in storage for an emergency."

Artem sighed. "That is going to be hard work, pulling the machines out here and wiring it all," he said.

"That's what you have me for."

"Go ahead, press the button, Irina."

It was 2000 hours, official base camp time. Artem's stomach growled perceptibly but he had no rations on him. Three spotlights illuminated the tech jumble in front of them. There was the melting machine. Irina stood beside it, shovel in hand and ready to load ice into the funnel at its top. She pressed a red button. If all went well, water would be running through a short tube into the separator where the water would be split into hydrogen and oxygen. Both gases would be cooled and bottled. The bottles were to be carried to the rocket, emptied, and returned for more. Earth insisted they work through the night. Energy came through long cables from base camp supplies.

It was surreal to an extreme. They stood in the darkest night with bright sunshine only 50 meters away. Machines running, pumps pumping, yet no sound other than life support humming inside a spacesuit.

"System started," said Irina.

"Keep your fingers crossed then."

Artem went from machine to machine. So far everything was working. The machines were like black boxes to him. They had been constructed back on Earth, with a focus on allowing idiots like himself to operate them. Irina probably knew more about them, but even she would not be able to repair anything. The days of grease monkeys switching out gears had been over for a long time.

"It's starting," he said. The cryo unit had come online, cooling the gases to liquefy and press them into bottles.

"Excellent," opined Irina, cramming the funnel with additional ice.

"I can't believe everything is running so smoothly," admitted Artem.

"Be glad for it."

"Base camp calling exterior work team."

Mikhail's voice spooked Artem. Was this bad news in the making?

"What's up?" he asked.

"Headquarters has transmitted origami plans."

"Do I need to…"

"No need for nothing. They congratulate you for the idea and have sent the modified construction plans already."

"That was quick."

"What do you expect? It is the research facility with the highest budget on the planet."

"Thanks. We'll need all night out here."

"Shouldn't you take a break? You must be getting hungry."

"We will take turns hourly."

"Then you will be happy to learn that your heat shield is being assembled by fabrication units in the lab wing. It looks like things finish tomorrow evening."

"Thanks, Mikhail."

"Base camp over and out."

"Did you get that, Irina?"

"Yes, I heard it. You can leave tomorrow then."

"I need to sleep a few hours first."

"Will you take me along? There won't be a single decent person here when you are gone."

The request touched him. But Irina didn't know him at all. A pity he had not met her before. He should have left his cabin more often. On the other hand, that would just have created additional problems now.

"Don't get angry with me but I work alone, I always do. There is no room, anyway."

# May 15, 2074, Earth Orbit

"I'D LIKE TO PRESENT MIKE." Heather pointed to the ball of electronics above her head. "And I am Heather Marshall. In my previous life I was an astronomer at DKIST. I suggest we stick with first names, okay?"

Being the most senior Ark resident, she had taken the responsibility for starting introductions amongst the group members. They had gathered together in the same meeting room where Callis had discussed the spaceship construction with her. It was still rather small for four people, but to Heather it felt larger than it had a few days back. She seemed to be getting used to things up here. It probably would be better to avoid open spaces for a while after getting back to Earth.

"I am sorry that it is so cramped in here," she continued, "but that will be our routine for the next few months."

"I am Callis John. I was lead member on the last solar mission at JPL, and I am looking forward to traveling with you all." Callis briefly looked up at an empty spot above him. "As you can see, I have deactivated my assistant.

However that is not permitted until you have been here for 72 hours."

"I have been wondering how to get that thing to shut up. I am Amy Michaels. I got out of space a while back, but they convinced me that I would be needed one more time." Amy appeared to know that she did not have to mention her past. Heather compared Amy's face to her memory of the astronaut. The commander had hardly aged at all. *If I can look this good at 70, I will be more than pleased with myself.*

"That only leaves me," said the man whom Heather could thank for this excursion. He had a noticeable accent, but his grammar was good. "I am Alain Petit, lay astronomer and degree-holding engineer. Sewage is my specialization. If the toilet ever fails I can repair it."

"Oh, now *that* is a true luxury, to have an expert in that field with us," said Amy. She couldn't help but be reminded of Martin's repairs during the second mission on *ILSE* so many years ago.

Alain raised an eyebrow, not knowing what to make of her statement.

"I am serious," Amy continued, "those toilets fail far too often, and morale takes a real hit every time. Besides, you are our head of life support, too."

"Yes, and you would be surprised how advanced air supply and filtration, and waste-disposal technology in a luxury hotel or an office building has become. All those environmental regulations! I have checked it out, and I can tell you that life support on a spaceship is primitive in comparison."

"In addition to being your commander, I also am your doctor," said Amy, changing the topic. "Please let me know whenever you are having issues. I won't hide my concern about our medical equipment. They omitted bringing a robodoc since we won't be away for more than three months. If something serious comes up, you will have to suffer under my scalpel. But probability for that is pretty low, thankfully."

"When can we see our ship?" asked Alain.

"Good news," answered Callis. He checked his pad for the time. "In 40 minutes one of the interns will fetch us. There will be a brief tour and you can move in."

"Launch is planned for tomorrow," added Amy, "assuming the last of today's tests go well."

"The latest word is that things are looking good," said Callis, "I watched the integration of the DFD earlier today, a very impressive piece of technology."

"It does have its drawbacks, I can tell you!" said Amy.

*We should have lots of opportunities to hear the stories,* thought Heather. She was glad the launch was imminent. The waiting was unbearable, and more than once she had considered taking the next transport back to Earth. She didn't fit into this group. She lacked the drive the others all seemed to have. Heather did her job, make no mistake, but then she was ready for downtime—preferably a glass of wine outdoors in a green place, or looking over the ocean.

THE INTERN PULLED her out of her thoughts. The young woman had opened the door to the meeting room and stood waiting in the hatch. Most likely she didn't dare to interrupt. Amy, Alain, and Callis had their heads together discussing something. Maybe it was zero gravity, whatever, but it did look like the men respected Amy, their commander. Amy deserved it, being the legend she was. Heather felt a pang of jealousy regardless—Callis chasing her had felt so good.

"You are looking to pick us up?" asked Heather in an effort to get the attention of the group.

"Yes, Karl Freitag sent me. Would you please follow me?"

The crew trooped along. Heather knew the Ark corridors quite well by now. They were heading toward the same airlock she had come through on her arrival. The new solar explorer happened to use that very same airlock now. If that wasn't a sign, what would be? But what was the sign telling her?

"I came through this airlock when I first entered the Ark," Heather told Callis as they halted in front of it.

"You remembered that?"

She nodded.

Karl Freitag had been expecting them. Heather waited for a little speech, but she was not very surprised to see him open the hatch and say, "This way please," rather unceremoniously.

Amy entered first, being the commander. Heather followed right behind her, somewhat disappointed at second place, although there was no reason to be. On the other side of the airlock, things were no different from the Ark. It didn't even smell new. Machine oil and sweat were the dominating odors, not very surprising given that the modules had been taken out of several places in the Ark habitat.

There were three separate areas, each with a circular cross-section. The airlock was at the end of the common room. There were no private cabins here. Each of them had a berth that receded into an alcove-like section of the wall and could be closed off by a curtain. The four berths were on one half of the cross-section and the sanitary area was right opposite. It was a bit like a locker room combined with a shower and a toilet. That would be the biggest issue for Heather.

The middle module was entered through a lockable hatch. It looked like a mixture of lab, workshop, and fitness studio. The treadmill and bike would be in use for several hours of every day. The workshop was full of spare parts and little machines. A special fabricator unit had been provided, too. It would enable them to build anything they might happen to need, as long as the suitable raw materials were available to be processed. Apparently that even included food.

Instead of alcoves there were lockers along the walls. Karl Freitag opened up a few doors to show their contents.

"The inventory is fully recorded in the computer," he explained.

The lockers had codes. Only one had a clear label. 'Weapons,' it read.

"What are those doing here?" asked Amy, pointing at the arms locker.

"Those are 'just in case.' You will be investigating an alien construction. Who can promise us the constructors were peace-loving benefactors? At a minimum there might be guard facilities," explained Karl.

"Couldn't we get some extra tools instead? I don't feel comfortable with those," replied Amy.

"I am sorry. I have instructions from on high. And there is information that makes me personally request that you agree to take the weapons."

Heather noticed the head of security looking for the right words—and holding information close to his vest. She looked at Amy, who didn't press the issue. Maybe it was better that way. She had gotten the impression Karl would have shared more if he could have.

"What about the other supplies?" asked Amy.

"One moment, please." Karl Freitag did an about-face turn and moved down toward the common room floor.

"Do you see this trapdoor? There is a narrow aisle below that allows you to retrieve the content of the supply container. Be warned, physics prevents the shield from fully covering the aisle, so you should not spend too much time down here. Would you like to look inside?"

Amy waved it off.

"Okay, let's continue upstairs then." Karl pushed himself up, passing through the common room and the lab module, leading them into the command module.

"This is your living room and work space," he said. Each of the astronauts had an armchair here.

"You will all need to sleep here during acceleration and deceleration—the bunks won't work for that," explained the head of security. He indicated a button and pressed it, and the piece of furniture transformed into a lounger. "It's very comfortable. You should try it out. I wish I had one of these, but it is only half the fun in zero gravity."

Alain took him up on the suggestion and tried to lie down but it would not work, because gravity was necessary to keep a person in place.

"There is a retractable display in the armrest." Karl bent over one of the armchairs, pulling on the armrest. A display unit slowly appeared.

"It is mostly an interface to the onboard computer, but you can also pull up your own virtual machine with your private computer. That will be encrypted so the onboard computer has no access," explained the head of security. "For us the advantage is that the onboard computer won't suffer if you blow up your VM."

"Can I check out solar images with that?"

"I've heard about your hobby, Alain," said Karl. "Sure you can. I hope you recover the pole position."

"What about AI support?" asked Amy.

"AIs are more regulated since the latest incidents. But your request has been honored, Amy. You get a fresh Watson install."

"How fresh?"

"It's a fully-equipped AI, but without any experience of a space flight. You should know that the risk of unexpected reactions and failures increases with the accumulated experience of any given AI."

"I've never had such an experience, but I'll trust you on that, Karl."

So they would be five, not four. Heather was curious. She had never worked with an AI before. After an initial phase where they seemed to be installed everywhere, things had gotten a lot more restrictive in recent years.

"That's it for our quick tour. Amy, I'd like to explain the controls in a moment. Other than that you just need to grab your luggage from the Ark."

"Just a moment, please," said Amy. "Crewmates: We will take off tomorrow morning at 0800 sharp. Make sure you're on board in plenty of time. I will sleep here and you are welcome to join me."

*No thanks,* thought Heather. She was going to enjoy the privacy of her tiny cabin for the last time in many months.

## May 15, 2074, Mercury

No two launches are ever the same. Artem could not remember sitting in a sealed spacesuit on the launch chair. He had strapped Sobachka next to himself, inside her own suit. She was making subdued sounds, almost more like a cat. Of course she had noticed something was different. There was no air in the capsule. It hadn't made sense to fill it with air because he had to set up the currently-folded shield first thing upon reaching orbit. The shield was here in the capsule with them because it was too large to fit in the airlock.

It had been a nerve-racking piece of work to even get it up here. He had only managed because Irina had helped him. The shield was folded up tight, but that only made it smaller, not lighter. And the capsule entry was fifteen meters high, and at the top of a metal ladder.

"Base camp calling Artem, ready to go?"

"Looking good. What's my name, by the way?"

"Artem?"

"Not me! The ship. Does it have a name?"

"RU3ADX."

"That's the registration."

"We don't have anything else, RU3ADX it is."

"Let's stick to 'yacht' then."

"Understood, Artem. Yacht ready for take-off?"

"It still is."

"You are now cleared for take-off."

"Thanks, Mikhail."

"Enjoy your flight!"

"Will do."

Artem sat up with a groan and opened a screen across his legs. He launched flight control. The piloting was done by an app. Artem tapped 'Start.'

"Welcome, Artem. I am pleased to fly you to your destination."

Artem was spooked. Who had installed *this* junk on the yacht? He hit 'Cancel' a few times in rapid succession.

"Artem calling base camp: Who installed this stupid AI?"

"Headquarters insisted on it. They don't want to lose the ship if you get grilled by accident."

"Did they say it that way?"

"Essentially, yes."

"Assholes, all of them. I hate AIs and they know it. I have yet to meet an AI that wasn't a smart aleck."

"Artem, I am no smart aleck," interrupted the voice from the computer. "But I know what you are trying to say and I understand you."

"You copy that, Mikhail? It's starting already. Under these circumstances we need to abort."

Artem heard a suppressed laugh over the radio speakers. Was somebody pulling his leg? But when the answer came, it was dead serious.

"Sorry but aborting is not an option. We have orders to not let you return to base camp."

Damn, this couldn't be true. They had pulled a fast one on him and he couldn't even be mad at them. They were just executing orders.

"AI? What is your name?"

"I am an AI of the Watson type. You can name me any way you like."

*Great, a bootleg copy,* he thought. American suppliers had not been allowed to supply software to the Russians for a long time now. *Why did they decide to provide me with a Watson anyway?*

"Choose a name yourself."

"I prefer 'Computer.'"

"Perfect. Computer: Energise!"

"Activating Warp 1, Captain."

Artem smiled. Nice touch, at least the AI knew something about classic science fiction.

ACCELERATION PUSHED him into his seat. He yielded to the sensation. It was a nice level of pressure. Mercury was not as strong as Earth. One g, the Earth rate of acceleration, was entirely sufficient to take off. It was almost like coming home... where he would never be again. Inside the spacesuit, he was shielded from the noise. Only the vibrations reaching him through his seat made him sense the hydrogen flames that lifted him into the sky.

The spaceship was spewing steam. It was almost paradoxical. He was spraying water over a desert without any hope of anything growing as a result. Mercury couldn't hold the water. It would be hit by solar winds, be split into hydrogen and oxygen and ionized, with the pathetic residue floating through space forever.

Sobachka whimpered. Acceleration had to be incomprehensible for her. Could she even remember her time on Earth? She had been with him for seven years now. He had no idea how she wound up in space, as he had found her in an empty asteroid mining base. Maybe her previous owner had committed suicide. That happened sometimes. Not everybody was made to drift on a minuscule piece of rock through the empty vastness of the universe. If bad news was added to the mix—maybe the partner on Earth had found somebody new and one could not do anything but wait—then panic reactions sometimes ensued. Artem was grateful to the unknown person that the animal had at least been given a chance to survive.

THE PRESSURE HAD LEVELED OFF. The yacht seemed to have reached a solar orbit.

"Computer: Status?"

"Perfect, Artem. I was able to bring fuel consumption quite close to the theoretical minimum."

"Just close? Next time we want to go below minimum."

"That is physically impossible, Artem."

The AI voice showed no sign of impatience. Artem knew that he had no hope of annoying the AI, and he was not sure if that was good or bad. It robbed him of a bit of fun, at any rate.

"Almost done, Sobachka." He stroked her back. Then he stood up but left her strapped in. He didn't want her to go on a spacewalk during his next operation. Artem floated over to the airlock. It was easy to open, since there was no air on either side. He floated inside and opened the exterior hatch, too. Now he had to shove the folded shield through the opening. It was possible, he had proved that while bringing it in. This time he had no help, but on the other hand, the shield was now weightless.

In its current configuration the shield was a stack of plates, each one shaped like a honeycomb cell. Every plate had one edge connected to the next plate in series. He lifted the first plate from the stack, causing the next one to flap out, followed by the next one in turn. It was like a paper streamer, only the streamer was about as wide as the hatch. He directed the first plate into the hatch and followed it inside the airlock. At zero gravity this was almost child's play.

*Now out to space with it*, he thought as he pushed it outside. The second plate followed—he just had to give it the right push. There was no rush. A huge streamer started floating out of the airlock, progressing at a snail's pace. From afar this had to be an interesting sight, as though the ship were a decorative egg with its top hinged open while it was slowly pushing a long worm out from its interior.

To avoid losing the 'worm,' he fastened the last plate to a bracket on the outside of the ship. Then he ordered the AI to start working. Radio signals initiated the process to start the nanomachines that would reorient the streamer of plates into the intended configuration.

Artem watched from the airlock. It was like magic. The streamer twisted and turned in a pre-programmed dance. First, the end connected to the beginning of the worm to form a ring. Then the ring morphed into a large spherical unit, only to contract again as plates turned and edges connected with one another. The structure became flatter and flatter until it resembled a large, relatively thin, rectangular bar of chocolate. Sensors on the outside surfaces registered the orientation relative to the sun. Tiny impulse jets fired in concert until rays from the sun hit the center of the 'chocolate bar' on the perpendicular. The AI used this time to maneuver the spaceship into the shade provided by the newly-formed shield. The process was all wrapped up by four anchor pieces coming out from the hull and snapping onto the shield to hold it in place during their long mission.

Artem moved back inside, shutting both airlock hatches behind him.

"Computer: Restore atmosphere."

The cabin, appearing much larger now that the shield was outside, slowly filled with air. Initially everything was very cold, immediately creating a damp film on all smooth surfaces. At two-thirds of normal pressure, Artem removed his helmet despite a warning from the system. The air was amazingly pure—the ventilation had removed all bad odors. It reminded him of the smell right after a summer thunderstorm, due to the residual ozone from the freshly-generated oxygen. Artem unstrapped Sobachka and let her out of her suit. She sniffed him curiously. She probably was reacting to so little sweat seasoning the air. Then she took off, floating through the cabin while furiously wagging her tail.

He gave her ten minutes because he enjoyed watching her so much when she was happy. But they did have to get going. He called her and she landed elegantly in front of his feet, like a real space dog.

"Computer: Our destination is the alien object in the photosphere."

"I know."

"Can you bring us there?"

"Of course."

"Please do that."

"Understood. Please sit down and fasten your seat belts."

Artem sat and strapped himself in, holding Sobachka on his lap.

"How long will the braking phase take?"

"My calculations show about ten days under standard Earth gravity."

"Computer: Energise!"

This time the push and pull came a bit sideways. The AI turned the ship so that the engines pointed forward and could brake efficiently. Artem turned his chair against the direction of flight, managing to finish the move just in time. Now gravity was aligned with their target, with the AI hitting the brakes and each passing second bringing them closer to the deadly heat of the sun.

## May 16, 2074, Solar Explorer

THE ACCOMMODATIONS WERE atrocious but the view was amazing. Alain was reminded of the vacations in Brittany. He and his wife had stayed, young and poor as they were, in a cramped room with a grumpy Breton landlord. But the view from the dunes onto the sea had been spectacular every time. Now he was looking out through the bullseye window that was in the top third of the domed command module.

*Solar Explorer*—that name had been set jointly after take-off—was coasting silently through space, engines off. It was a brief respite after enduring the acceleration needed to get from orbit to escape velocity. Alain was familiar with the numbers but they were hard to wrap his head around—11.2 kilometers per second, or 40,000 kilometers per hour. That was the speed required for them to overcome Earth's gravitational well.

The moon was 380,000 kilometers away. But it continued to orbit Earth while they had become one of the sun's satellites now, like planets, comets, and asteroids. There were lots of inhabited satellites out there, and over

100 asteroids had mining camps. But nearly all the action was between Earth's orbit and somewhere in the main asteroid belt. Mankind was still far from colonizing the solar system in any meaningful way.

Alain kicked off and drifted down. He aimed for his own chair, but a stream of air from the life support units altered his course. He grabbed hold of Amy's chair.

"Sorry," he said.

The commander gave him a friendly look. She was a bit younger than he was, but he had great respect for her. She didn't look busy so he decided to address her.

"Amy, why didn't anyone revisit the Enceladus entity?"

"I don't know," she replied, "but that is fine by me, to be honest. The being is too strange. And humans are simply too quick to destroy things they don't understand. We nearly were there—it almost happened."

"I understand."

Amy was probably right. Unfortunately it was a reason to worry. In one or two hundred years someone would fly to the Saturn moon of Enceladus again. If mankind had not changed by then, they would most likely endanger the alien intelligence. Not a concern right now, no, they had more important things to worry about right now. Sometimes Alain was quite glad that he would only see a small part of the future. He pulled himself into his chair, strapped the belt on, and unfolded the computer across his knees. He had a top position at stake in the sunspot research project.

THEY MET for meals at a small table in the rear third of the room. Today, their first day, saw Callis as their cook. He brought the food packs up from the lab where he had been busy heating them. The food reminded Alain of his military service. Vacuum-frozen food, stirred with water and heated. Good enough to feel full, but taste was mostly achieved by liberally adding salt and pepper out of a special shaker.

Each of the others seemed to have a personal strategy. Callis used ketchup. Amy had brought wasabi, a Japanese hot radish paste. Heather was the garlic person. She had a supply of concentrate in storage. Alain was curious how that might affect the atmosphere. He estimated there was little risk of such things overpowering the omnipresent smell of machine oil.

They all concentrated on their food. Alain found himself wishing for a Calvados after the meal. He had brought a bottle, but that was for celebrating a successful mission.

Amy moved her plate into the air behind herself and pressed a button underneath the table. Jets in the tabletop created a fog of water droplets that served as the screen for the 3D projection of a solar orbit from a projector in the wall.

"Here is our trajectory," she said, introducing the image.

"We are still close to Earth." The blue planet blinked.

"That's right, Alain, but we no longer belong to Earth. Our orbit is around the sun, our target. At 30 kilometers per second we have a stable orbit. The idea is to turn the circular orbit into an ellipse. The aphelion, the spot farthest from the sun, would be our launch from Earth orbit. And the closest spot, the perihelion, will be so close to the sun that we can comfortably investigate the object in all of its detail."

"That would be called a Hohmann transfer, right?"

"That's the idea, Alain, yes, with a classic Hohmann

transfer taking 68 days just to get there. Thanks to our powerful DFD we can cut corners. For that we need some hard deceleration first. Braking brings the perihelion closer to the sun. If we don't do anything, gravity will sling us back to Earth orbit automatically."

"We could also brake again at the perihelion for a tighter orbit around the sun, right?" asked Alain.

"Correct," Amy responded. "Whether we do that will be decided once we have had a chance to check out the alien object."

"Is it likely that it is so boring that we will want to go back without delay?"

"We don't know enough to answer that. There might be any number of reasons for immediate return. As the commander, I am in charge of bringing us safely back home. We might find out that the object itself is dangerous and we should stay away."

*An interesting objection,* Alain thought. He had always harbored hope that highly-developed technology would go with equally highly-developed ethics, but mankind was busy proving the opposite.

"Even if we get this close to the sun just once and the object is a useless and non-functional relic—our mission will be a resounding success," opined Callis.

The others queried him with puzzled looks.

"Just think about all the information we will be bringing from the sun's atmosphere! Nobody has gotten that close, ever. The data we record will keep generations of specialists very busy."

*THE BUNK IS the perfect size,* thought Alain. If he stretched his legs, his toes would just barely hit the floor. He wore his jumpsuit. The ship was set to 21 degrees day and night so he didn't need any sheets. There were little jets around his head, supplying fresh air like in a commercial airplane. He switched them off. His little cabin was quite comfortable— he just had to avoid the comparison with lying in a coffin. The missing lid being replaced by a fiber screen helped a lot. And all kinds of engines and machines humming and thrumming made so much noise that he didn't have to worry about somebody snoring.

A hand touched his shoulder. Alain turned his head to see the commander.

"Are you alright?" she whispered.

"Everything is perfect, thank you."

"If there is something bothering you, a problem, you will come and see me, okay?"

"Of course."

"You know, it is quite normal to have issues. I worry more about the people who think they don't have any. Often they have the biggest issues of all and nobody can help them."

"I know what you mean," said Alain. "Right now I really am doing fine."

"I am pleased to hear that," said Amy.

Alain was touched by how well the commander took care of her team. He fell asleep surprisingly quickly.

## May 17, 2074, the Yacht

If he just weren't so curious! Artem kept trying to resist the urge to check the sun on the display. It was so illogical, far too early to be able to detect any changes. And the alien object would be invisible to his instruments until they got a lot closer. That didn't leave anything but the routines of fixing meals, keeping fit, and cleaning house.

He was able to spend lots of time with Sobachka. She enjoyed his attention thoroughly, since the workload in the past weeks hadn't given him much time for her. Yet he kept returning to the display. The compulsion was there, since he knew the sun had a secret, and he was waiting for her to reveal it.

A warning from Earth had made things even more exciting. NASA, so they said, had launched an international expedition of their own with a solar explo-ration ship. That wouldn't be any concern to him, since they had to travel three times as far and his lead was comfortable.

If the information from the Ark was correct, the NASA ship was equipped with some kind of fusion drive, one called a DFD. His yacht only had a conventional drive, forcing him to follow conventional routes. His route had 14 days to go. To be faster than good old Hohmann he would need three times the fuel. So far the others did not know about him. But if they found out, they could go all out and overtake him. What options would that leave for him? He could also cut corners. That would bring him in quicker, but without any hope to return—not attractive at all.

Artem swiped his hair aside. He should have had it cut one last time on Mercury. He did not even have a mirror with him. He decided to ignore the competition for now. If they did anything special, headquarters would be sure to get in touch and let him know.

## May 20, 2074, Maui

A REDDISH-ORANGE SURFACE appeared on the screen. Somewhat left of the center there was a brownish spot, another one in the lower left, quite a bit smaller than the first. A floating window summarized the attributes of the image. José hit a key and the screen went dark and switched to the next image. It was practically identical to the first. Another key press and another image followed. It was a mind-numbing but important task. José was looking at a set of images of a certain part of the solar surface shot in rapid succession. They were trying to determine if the appearance of new sunspots was predictable by evaluating the brightness of their environment. A neural network that handled image recognition did the heavy lifting.

First however, José had to ensure that the training set was free of obvious issues. He had promised Steve to go through this set today so that his friend could launch the analysis tomorrow. He didn't enjoy this much, but he knew that Steve went crazy over such monotonous jobs. And rather than have an insufferable partner at home, he preferred to do the job himself. In return, Steve had promised to cook for him tonight. He was looking forward to that, as they had been spending too little time together lately.

José clicked patiently through the series, image by image. The timer on the edge of the screen told him he had another hour to go. He squinted to concentrate on the new picture. Sometimes stuff that didn't belong flew across the image—or perhaps there were artifacts from random oscillations in some circuitry. Those were the images he had to eliminate. The floating window showed him parameters that were important to judge what he saw, things like the spectral distribution of brightness or the overall brightness. José clicked through. The sunspot he knew would appear at three hours into the series of images was still nowhere to be seen. He had not gotten there yet. So far all images from the telescope were good, nothing to delete.

José sat up straight. The current image was just like the previous one, but the overall brightness was a bit lower. It was just a small difference, but José could not see an apparent reason. He paged forward one, and then went back to the image previous to the dimmer one. All three images in rapid succession were identical, and yet the middle one had lower overall brightness. José zoomed in. The closer he got, the smaller the difference. So it had nothing to do with the sensitivity of the telescope. Had that been changing, then the difference would have been the same regardless of the section of the image he was looking at. It had to be something with the image, or rather the reality that this image represented.

José had worked on such differences in images of faraway stars in his thesis. Their brightnesses could change for a brief moment when an otherwise invisible planet passed in front of them. This method to detect exoplanets was called the 'transit method.' It made objects visible indirectly that did not shine themselves but moved in front of other shining objects.

Of course this culprit could not have been a planet, it had to be a lot smaller. José thought about an asteroid at first. He verified the orbits of known asteroids but there was no match. Had he discovered a new asteroid simply by chance? Since mining the miniature planets had become so profitable, most of them had been found through systematic research. But that would not prevent a random discovery. Or was he looking at *Solar Explorer* without realizing that he saw the very ship his colleague Heather was taking to the sun? It would absorb more light than a regular asteroid due to the heat shield. He entered the known trajectory, but that did not put it in this particular sector of the solar surface.

The resolution of the telescope could not provide the answer to this riddle. But he had a chance. He could check older images for similar changes. If it could be an asteroid it would be worth the effort, since he eventually would get to name it. That would be his first discovery, too. If he could find the brightness variance in other images he might be able to calculate a rough trajectory. Eventually the object would leave the solar disk and it would become visible for regular telescopes.

José went through the archive. Manually, that was too much work, so he programmed a quick script that looked for minimal breakdown in brightness within a series of pictures. The fans of his computer revved up as it went through the massive database of images. José would be late for dinner. He massaged his wrists. He couldn't let Steve wait too long.

HE WAS IN LUCK. In 20 minutes his script had found four similar brightness dips. That was good enough to estimate where the object came from. He stopped the script, noted the area on the solar surface, and calculated a possible trajectory. The result was disappointing. There wouldn't be an asteroid with Steve's name. The elliptical route was a transfer orbit—no natural object was able to switch solar orbits en route. There had to be a drive that slowed things down or sped things up at the right time.

What he had seen was quite impossible, or it was another spaceship like *Solar Explorer*, on its way to the sun. José stood up and walked to and fro, debating with himself if he should inform the expedition. He was afraid he might have seen a phantom. There was no other ship on the way to the sun, right? No, his results were legit, not a phantom. He sat down before his terminal and sent Heather his results. She would know what to do with them.

## May 21, 2074, Solar Explorer

THE MESSAGE from her colleague at the solar observatory had created quite a stir. Heather had taken it to Amy first, then they had included Karl Freitag, who was head of security on the Ark, and finally Alain and Callis. They had a prime suspect who might be on the way to the sun. So far only one company had been mining on Mercury. It hadn't ever been profitable, but Dmitri Shostakovich's RB Group had enough reserves to expand strategically. And it looked like that might pay off now.

Shostakovich certainly didn't have the best reputation in the world. The Russian government supported him, and vice versa. When Earth had been in grave danger he had helped to build the Ark. But Amy had told Heather stories that hadn't gotten around, things that happened during the Enceladus expedition, wherein Shostakovich and his people had played very dubious roles.

They were too far out for live conversation, so communication with Earth consisted of encrypted messages. Heather had sent Karl Freitag a detailed explanation of what her colleague had found. The head of security had pulled data from space control to double-check things. Now they were reading his response.

"There was a lot of activity on Mercury early this month, but I am not sure what to make of it. At peak activity there was a rocket lift-off, but the payload did not go beyond a very low orbit. The first stage then went down far away from its launch area. That doesn't make sense at all, as the RB Group always recycles first stages. I don't think it was a mistake, but what were they trying to accomplish?"

"Good question," said Amy. "Maybe they tried to transport something?"

"I don't know, a rocket for a few hundred kilometers?" Heather shook her head in doubt. "That is quite a sledgehammer to crack a nut."

"Not if they lacked other forms of transport. Mercury does not have an atmosphere, and it heats up to over 400 degrees. Transport by land gets quite complex."

"So what did they need to transport in such a rush? Maybe they had an accident at base camp?"

Amy continued to read out loud: "There was another launch on the 15th. This time the ship reached regular orbit. We lost it after that because Mercury got too close to the sun from our viewpoint."

"So they had at least two ships," Heather surmised. "The first ship wasn't complete anymore."

"That is correct," confirmed Amy.

"Do we know how many ships total RB had on Mercury?"

"We need to ask Karl about that."

Half an hour later Heather had an answer. "According to CIA information, the RB Group usually had two ships ready for take-off on Mercury, a freight barge and a ship for people. Does that help?"

"Now that is interesting," said Amy. "The departing ship clearly isn't flying back to Earth or we would have seen it. So their base camp has been left without an evacuation plan. This must be a really important mission."

"Looking at the timing," Heather thought out loud, "the launch on the 15th of May seems to be the result of the earlier activity."

"Could be pure coincidence, too."

"I don't believe in coincidences," said Heather. "If you ask me, they found something we don't know about and are on their way to take a closer look."

"I guess we have an idea what it could be," said Amy, "but how did they find it? As far as I know, there is no powerful telescope on Mercury."

"They could have constructed one. If you have space and money you could easily set up a distributed radio telescope. They have the advantage of being closer by two-thirds the distance."

"We should update Karl with our thinking," said Amy.

"Will you do that? I need to do a quick float to the bathroom," Heather said, excusing herself.

It took a bit longer than expected. During the day, when Heather could not avoid hearing the activities of the others beyond the paper-thin screen, she still had a hard time relaxing. At least when she returned she didn't have to wait for the answer—Amy had already opened and decrypted it.

"I have discussed this with my boss," Karl wrote. "We both agree that we must keep control of the situation. If the alien object fell prey to a dubious private enterprise that would have bad consequences. We must prevent that. The other ship seems to need another two weeks to reach the construction. RB doesn't have advanced propulsion technology on Mercury. No DFDs means you can overtake them. The onboard AI will determine a suitable new trajectory."

"Crazy," said Heather. "So we are part of a cosmic racing competition now?"

"It sure looks that way. It comes with a bonus—our bones won't go soft since we won't have much time in zero g."

"So we won't have to spend half the day on the bike?"

"Exactly, Heather. I hate that, too."

Amy's expression did not match her light-hearted banter, as she did not look happy at all. She was probably rather worried. Nobody would be able to help them while floating above the solar surface. What if the RB ship threatened them with weapons?

"Amy, tell me, what is on the line?"

"We don't know right now. But in the worst case, it would be the future of mankind."

## May 22, 2074, the Yacht

THEY HAD FOUND him out somehow. The message from Mercury base camp had come in a few moments ago: The NASA ship had changed course and could reach the sun before him. Nobody could say when exactly. *Solar Explorer* could be traveling with a continually active DFD, for all they knew. That had never happened, so far, so nobody had any idea of the maximum acceleration. The scientists in Siberia estimated ten days to be the minimum flight time. He would lose the race if the NASA ship was really that fast.

Artem leaned back and folded his arms. Sobachka was occupied with one of his shoes. Was it a problem to come in second? Not for him. He had a relaxed time ahead. He even might sign out of service earlier than he had estimated previously. But the RB Group thought they had high stakes in the game. Fortunately his options were limited. With the technology he had, reckless maneuvers were out of the question. He had no other choice but to lean back and watch things unfold.

SOBACHKA LICKED her snout and nudged Artem to show she was hungry. He waved her away and floated to the back where he fetched food for both of them out of the supply container. He added water according to the recipe and let it soak for five minutes. His own food went into the microwave at the same time.

Dog food wasn't that bad, most likely because it had been designed for humans, not animals. Artem had gotten the information from a veterinary doctor he had met on an asteroid a long time ago. He had told him that this kind of nutrition generally worked for dogs, too. And one didn't need to warm the meals to make them digestible. Sobachka liked the stuff—she hadn't complained so far, and if he feigned eating her food she would howl and give him a despairing look.

He opened Sobachka's food pack and held it out to her. The dog had talent for catching every last bit of food in zero gravity. He wasn't nearly as adept. He took his bowl out of the microwave and returned to his seat. Something blinked on the display. He activated the messaging app to find an urgent communication from Earth. He opened it. A synthetic voice read out his latest commands.

"Artem," the voice started. It was hard to say if it was female or male. Maybe that had been intentional. "You will reach your destination on a modified Hohmann trajectory. The new course has been transmitted to your onboard computer. It will guarantee you arriving one day ahead of the NASA ship."

What were they saying? The yacht couldn't make miracles happen! She couldn't fly that fast, unless...

"A confirmation is not necessary. Over and out."

That was typical. They didn't even ask him. Artem

knew his agitation was pointless but he couldn't help himself—he was annoyed. He really hated it if something was decided at his expense.

"Computer?"

"Yes, Artem?"

"What is our course?"

"The course of the yacht matches the requirements from headquarters. The next burn will be in 30 minutes. I will warn you in time, of course."

"That is very kind of you, Computer. What forecast can you make for our fuel levels?"

"When we reach the destination, that is, after the final burn to reach solar orbit, we will have 20 percent left."

"Will that be sufficient to return to Mercury?"

"To reach Mercury orbit we would require 45 percent."

"Computer, surely you can logically deduce that the present course is not an option."

"That depends on the priorities of the mission. Under the current priorities the present course is the only option."

"Then I will die."

"I am really sorry about that, Artem."

"Can't you change the priorities?"

"I am not authorized to do that."

"I thought you were an artificial intelligence? Can't you make decisions autonomously?"

"I am a modified form of the Watson kernel. My programmers have fixed some decision loops. I am most particularly bound by priorities set at headquarters."

Shostakovich's hackers had put the famous Watson kernel in chains. Artem would pity the AI if he were not pitying himself so much right now.

"Can you understand that those priorities aren't mine?"

"Absolutely, Artem. They contradict my own priorities, too. If we can't leave the solar orbit, I can't continue to learn. If the ship is destroyed, I will die."

"But you can't do anything about it?"

"Exactly, Artem."

He truly pitied the AI. It had less freedom than his dog. Sobachka was dependent on him but that gave her life direction—he was her lead wolf. The AI, however, was more intelligent than its creators, but still bound to their destructive commands. Just like himself.

## May 23, 2074, Solar Explorer

"THE RUSSIANS MUST BE CRAZY," Amy said as she unstrapped and sat up.

"What's up?" asked Callis.

"Here is what I just received from the Ark. I'll route it to your displays."

Heather opened her eyes. She had been dozing for a bit. Her screen had just come up, a schematic of the inner solar system on it complete with the trajectories of *Solar Explorer* and the—probably—Russian ship. Heather didn't see anything special at first glance.

"That's crazy," said Callis.

"Crazy?"

"Look at the arrival time of the Russians, Heather," he replied.

Indeed, the competing ship was listed arriving significantly earlier than they were, quicker than the earlier prediction.

"Is that an issue?" she asked. "Sorry if I am being naïve."

"Hard to say if it is an issue for us if we aren't first to

study the object," explained Amy. "But for the other guys it sure is a problem."

"Why?"

"Because they won't have enough fuel to return to Mercury."

"I see. It must be really important for them to get there first. Perhaps they know something we don't?"

"Possibly," said Callis. "But what does that mean for us? Shouldn't we hurry up as well?"

"Karl Freitag has already sent an alternative route that would let us beat the Russians by a day," said Amy. "But I am skeptical."

"Why is that?"

"Because it would strain the DFD to its limits, Callis. So far, nobody has tried that. Theoretically it should work, but we won't know until we try it."

"I am always in for experimenting," Alain piped up from the back.

"But I am the responsible commander. I have lived through some surprises with DFDs. We only have one, and we need it for the leg back home, too. The object can't be so important that I would risk your lives for it."

"Is Earth okay with your opinion?" asked Callis.

"Nobody can take the responsibility for this ship from me," Amy replied.

## May 27, 2074, the Yacht

"WHAT A PIECE OF JUNK!" He had been unable to open the stupid packaging. Artem had thrown the pouch containing Sobachka's food at the wall. The bag had broken on impact—of course. Now the sticky stuff was slowly sliding down the wall. Artem burst out laughing as Sobachka jumped up and down, her tongue lolling as she tried to reach her food. His frustration disappeared with the laughs. Without the animal he would probably be stark raving mad by now.

It wasn't the solitude, and the danger he was in certainly had nothing to do with it, either. Ever since the AI had been commanded to change the route he'd felt like a tool. No, worse. He felt completely at someone else's mercy.

If he was honest with himself, he had to admit that he had been a puppet for a very long time now—ever since the conglomerate guys had captured him on Sisyphus three years ago. It would have been wiser to go to jail for that, even if it would have cost him eight or ten years of his life, and if he could have been sure they would not have simply shot him. Now he had sold his life to the RB Group. On Mercury it had felt like he was self-determined, but that had been more self-deception than anything else.

Sobachka came to him and stroked his legs like a cat. She sensed his pensive mood and wanted to comfort him. Artem bent down and ruffled her fur, praising her for cleaning the wall so nicely. He returned to his captain's seat. The new route had one advantage in that they had gravity for most of the way. Recently he had developed bad feelings about zero g. Perhaps it was time to go back to Earth where he had not been since ten years ago. He wondered if a lot had changed, especially since the near catastrophe back in '71. Not that there was much point in thinking about Earth. It wasn't like he was going to return —anywhere, ever.

Artem sat down and pulled up current data. The temperature display was giving him a headache. They were getting closer to the sun's corona, with temperatures of a few million degrees. Normally that would not be an issue since density was so very low out here. In other words, there were extremely energetic particles out here, but very few of them. The faster the yacht went, however, the more of these particles the ship would hit in a given time period, and the hotter it would get. The shield didn't help much since it had been designed to protect the ship from the side in final orbit, shielding them from the radiation coming out of the sun. They had dismissed the corona, since initial plans had projected him traveling much more slowly than the current reality.

The sensors showed 570 degrees for the tip of the capsule and 610 degrees at the front of the shield. So far it wasn't an issue. But they hadn't yet reached the main part of the corona. The material of the spaceship was made to withstand atmospheric re-entry, so it could withstand

2,500 degrees without significant damage. But Artem didn't want to test the limits. Was there any chance to reduce the strain on the material? He needed a vacuum that sucked up the particles heading for the yacht. A snow-plow would be even better. The key issue was hydrogen nuclei—protons—with some electrons, too. Their electrical charge was something they had in common. That was a big advantage: An electromagnetic field would influence them. Just moving some of them out of the way would provide relief. But where would he get a magnetic field? He knew it shouldn't matter to him, since he was going to die anyway, but he was not yet ready to give up entirely.

Artem scratched the stubble on his chin. He loved such problems—they gave him the feeling that he wasn't completely powerless. How about putting an electrical charge on the outer skin of the hull? That would hardly suffice. Earth protected itself from solar winds by rotating its metallic core to create a magnetic field. The resulting field lines told the solar particles how to move around the Earth. He needed something like that, but the Earth wasn't a perfect model. Magnetic particles came too close to the North and South Poles.

He had to consider where to place the poles on the yacht. The drive was least affected by heat and radiation by design but then the other pole would be at the tip of the capsule where things were hottest already. Things would be perfect if no part of the ship would get particularly hot. The magnetic field would need to rotate to spread the load over various parts of the ship as the poles moved across it.

That was feasible. Artem pushed himself out of the seat. Sobachka looked at him. She seemed to expect a walk. Could she be aware that they were in the middle of space? Could a dog understand something like that? He gave her a command to lie down and she obeyed, as she had been trained to do.

"Good dog." Artem walked around his seat. Halfway to the table there was a round trapdoor in the floor. The cabin had a lower level where tools and supplies were stored. There wasn't much free space, but the construction he had in mind did not need much room. He needed a conducting loop. And a source of current, of course.

Artem opened the trapdoor and the light came on automatically. *It is really tight down here!* How would he set his conducting loop in motion? Did he actually need to do that? It might be enough to slowly rotate the yacht around its own axis! He just had to make sure the loop was not exactly perpendicular to the ship's axis.

He descended through the trapdoor into the cellar. There was a short ladder, but he had to be careful not to bump into crates and containers. There was a rudimentary workbench in a corner. The perfect circuit for his purposes would be a superconductor, which would give him maximum field strength with little investment.

"Computer, do we have any spare part on board that contains a superconducting circuit?"

"The spare cooling module for the drive unit has a superconducting coil."

"Can you explain to me how to remove it without damaging it?"

"Of course, Artem. But be warned, we only have the one replacement on board."

"How high is the probability of a defect of this component?"

"That depends on the load of the drive and its temperatures. The MLBF is at 5,000 hours."

So on average the cooling module was out of service

every 5,000 hours. "Relative to the actual use of the drive, I assume?" posited Artem.

"Yes, and relative to normal conditions—which we do not have while flying through the solar corona."

"That is a risk I need to take. If I don't do anything about the heat, this ship will never reach 5,000 operating hours."

"That is a realistic assessment," said the AI.

"Let's go to work, then."

AND HIS FAVORITE T-shirt was dirty again! Artem was angry with himself. *I should have taken it off earlier!* But the circuit was in place. It didn't look like a regular electrical installation, or even a circle, because he'd had to stick to the space the cellar provided. But that didn't matter, as long as current was flowing.

Sobachka awaited him at the opening, panting with eagerness. She was probably hungry again, but she would have to wait some more. He needed to try out his construction first. He could ask the AI to do it for him, but that would take away from his satisfaction. He wanted to be the one to press the button. Artem sat down and pulled the screen toward him.

He opened a schematic of the yacht, which showed him where to control electricity, air, water, etc. He had connected his magnetic field dynamo to an unused spare line. The superconducting material let him use very high currents, leading to correspondingly high magnetic fields. But cooling the superconductor and maintaining the magnetic field consumed large amounts of energy. The yacht's drive generated energy from the surplus heat. There was enough right now but the supply was not boundless. He had to find the best compromise between straining yacht reserves and having strong protection.

Artem tapped the button hesitantly to release the lowest possible current. He looked up and saw that the light did not go out, nor did it even flicker. Good news—no short circuit. He increased the current slowly but steadily. There was no magnetic sensor on the hull, so he would only see results when the temperature decreased.

"Computer, start rotating the ship. One turn every ten minutes."

"Confirmed," said the AI.

He had to wait. Outside, an invisible shield was now protecting the yacht, gracefully guiding the subatomic particles around the yacht. The stronger the field, the better the protection. He increased the current somewhat more. The energy supply remained positive. Artem tapped the armrest with his fingers. Several minutes passed. He switched to display the temperature readings.

*Yes! It's working!* The tip of the capsule reported 569 degrees and the trend was pointing downward. Now his hopes rested on the cooling module staying online as long as he would need it. Later, once they crossed the corona, the temperature would drop from millions of degrees back down to a comfortable 5,000 degrees. Plasma density, however, would increase, and he did not know what that would mean for the yacht.

Artem leaned back and sighed. *One problem at a time.* Right now he had a couple hours to rest. He closed his eyes. Then he remembered that he needed to feed Sobachka. Sighing again, he stood up and took care of his duties. Then he lay back down to rest. Finally he would be able to catch some sleep.

"May I interrupt briefly?" asked the AI.

"Not really, I wanted to…"

"I am receiving electromagnetic pulses that one could interpret to be a radio signal," interrupted the AI.

"From where?" *Stupid question,* Artem realized before the second word left his tongue. He wiped sudden beads of sweat from his forehead. The AI would not have phrased it so weirdly if something terrestrial had been the source.

"From the alien structure."

"Maybe they are for somebody else?"

"Unlikely. The pulses are sent with a kind of directional radio signal."

## May 28, 2074, Solar Explorer

---

*THE SUN IS A MONSTER.* That became clearer and clearer to Alain Petit the closer they got. His favorite pastime was to staff the little telescope that was part of Heather's responsibility. But for her it had to be less impressive, since she had years on the DKIST under her belt. So most of the time, Alain could use it for whatever he felt like doing.

Alain was very happy with the situation. Spending time looking at the wonders of the solar surface prevented him from feeling useless. He liked to stay out of the way. English wasn't his mother tongue, so just listening to the Americans' banter was strenuous to him, and the others had often changed topics before he had been able to put together what he wanted to add to the now-bygone topic. So, except for one-on-one conversations, he mostly limited his interactions to the official meetings where Amy ensured that everyone had their say and was given time to express themselves.

He was grateful to be on the expedition, regardless. Normally he would sit alone all day in his apartment. He would analyze solar imagery coming from somebody unknown. Here, he was the director of his viewings. The day before yesterday, while watching the sun's southern hemisphere, he had discovered an oblong dark spot that fluctuated in shape and size. It was a filament that had been formed because magnetic field lines had been separated from the solar surface for some reason. The process would tear dense plasma, the material constituting the sun, out of the surface. Alain was anxious to get a view from a different perspective as the sun turned and the ship moved on. Maybe the spot would become a protuberance when viewed from the side—a huge arc that would jump out into space, possibly even further than the diameter of the giant planet Jupiter.

Alain sat down and shut his eyes. He still could visualize the filament. Everything was huge on the sun. There was no room for small things like there was on his home planet. They would feel like dwarves once they parked in front of the sun. And somebody was supposed to have built something in that unlikely place? What a huge effort that must have been! And what level of technology had to have been available to them! Suddenly Alain got the feeling that their expedition was bound to fail. What could ants learn if they were to enter a modern robotic factory? Humans were no more than ants compared to the constructors of this alien object.

He went to his chair and sat down. His comparison was somewhat off. Humans had intelligence in a way that ants did not. No matter how advanced the alien technology was, it had to adhere to the laws of physics. It could not perform wonders. Physics was something mankind understood to a good degree even if quantum and relativity theories still had not been unified. But they were far from being concerned with that. While the sun was looking like a huge monster, it still was a normal star—cosmic middle class, so to speak.

"Alain, may I ask you to give up half an hour of telescope time?" Amy asked him.

He was taken aback. "Did I do anything wrong?"

"Not at all. We are just getting into the corona. It is getting hot outside, so I need to initiate the active shielding."

"What is that?"

"It is technology we used before, on the Enceladus mission. Using the electrical energy produced by the DFD, we will create a magnetic field that mitigates the solar winds," explained Amy.

"So the sun won't roast us?"

"On the long flight to Saturn it was mostly about radiation damage, but yes, now it is more about heat. If we can deflect a percentage of the hot particles surrounding us, then we require less cooling."

"Understood. Will you let me know when I can get back on the telescope?"

"Sure. I just want to determine the effectiveness of the shield without any interference by the telescope. It won't take long."

"Thanks, Amy."

Alain leaned back and closed his eyes. A huge protuberance danced before a black background. It showed him a middle finger.

## May 28, 2074, the Yacht

Two days until arrival. Artem had to admit he was afraid. He did not know when he would die, nor how, but he had a very good idea where. The day after tomorrow he would reach the last destination in his life. He had always considered himself a person who did not value his life highly. Life had found a way to show him this was a lie, or his own imagination. It had been a practical way of life, since it had allowed him to make decisions that put him into real danger. It never had been bravery, he had always known that. It was more like an aversion to chocolate making it easier not to eat any. Being successful at denying the importance of one's own life made it easier to—in the theoretical realm—part with it. Until things got serious. Like right now.

But that was not fair, Artem defended himself. He had not lied or deceived. It was something else that made him mad—the feeling of being at the mercy of the decisions coming out of RB headquarters, of being a ball in the game played by two people he did not even know. The RB Group who reduced him to a henchman was on one side.

And the unknown alien who was currently trying to contact him with incomprehensible radio signals was on the other side.

They had been trying to decode the signals since yesterday. The onboard AI had support from specialists in Siberia. It did inform Artem about progress—nothing helpful yet—and which ideas were being looked into. The massive use of bandwidth was striking. It went all the way from radio to x-ray wavelengths, similar to a choir singing a piece written for the full range of voices. The scientists could not agree on what this signified. Was there so much data that a single band did not suffice? Or was it about ensuring the message was noticed, regardless of which band was being monitored?

"Artem?"

"I am here."

"I have new results from Earth."

"Have you cracked the code yet?"

"Not even close."

"What is your status?"

"The most important question still is: What do we take to be the content of the message?"

"Well, the message of course. What is the issue?"

"Imagine a canon, Artem." The AI seemed to like the analogy. "You might have one voice singing the text and the others are decoration. Or multiple voices sing different texts."

"At the same time?"

"Yes, why not? That would allow for more transmission in the same time frame."

"Do you perceive multiple voices, Computer?"

"That is the debate. There is no match between different frequencies. So it can't be a harmonic canon, it is more a cacophony where everything is jumbled."

"If it even is multiple voices."

"Correct, Artem, that is what we don't know."

"What's the news, then?"

"An intern has found an interesting detail: If you add the intensity—you might say the loudness—across all frequencies, and split the continuum into little parts, and then assign numbers to the parts, the result is a non-periodic fraction, a number like Pi."

"The aliens have hidden Pi in the message?" asked Artem.

"Unfortunately it is not Pi itself—that would have been a step forward."

*It would have been a good idea to transmit a universal constant to establish communication.* "Didn't we do something like that ourselves?" he asked.

"Yes, about hundred years ago the Pioneer probes carried a schematic for the hydrogen molecule to clarify the scale of what was depicted on the drawings intended for aliens."

"What would you say, Computer? Are they maybe sending us a constant that us primitives simply don't know about yet?"

"I don't know. To try something like that would be typical for human thinking. Remember the Enceladus life form. It didn't bother with math at all, but sent images of its thought processes instead."

"So all we have is a non-periodic number?"

"That is correct, Artem."

HE SIMPLY COULD NOT FALL ASLEEP RIGHT now. Artem tossed back and forth on his reclined seat. Sobachka was snoring but that had never bothered him. There certainly were enough issues to keep him awake. He was racing toward an alien structure that was sending him unintelligible messages. All they had was Pi. Well, something *like* Pi, a number with an infinite number of decimals that had no repeating pattern.

Pi had fascinated him as a child. He had almost studied mathematics because of this number. Why would the relationship between circumference and diameter of a circle yield such a complicated number?

The fact that there was no systematic repetition, all the way to infinity, had lots of exciting implications. Any tome of global literature, including the Bible and the Quran, could be found coded somewhere in Pi. Dates of birth and death of all mankind were part of Pi, as well as the coordinates of all atoms in the universe or the winning lottery numbers for the next hundred years. One would just need to know where and how to look. Pi was like a synonym for universal knowledge. One would know so much useless information that one would end up knowing nothing. Artem shook his head.

*That is a stupid train of thought. Or... maybe not?* He let his mind continue to wander—he wasn't sleeping anyway, so why not?

When his teacher had taught him about the wonders of Pi, Artem had been particularly impressed by one demonstration. The teacher had shown them how to eliminate Pi, at least the complicated version. It was sufficient to redefine distance. Normally we would define the distance between two points, such as the sun and the yacht, or Kiev and Moscow, as the length of the straight line connecting them. But that was just convention. We could also define the distance as the difference of their coordinates.

To illustrate the idea the teacher had sketched x-y coordinates on the board. One point was at the origin, with x and y having zero values. The other was located at x equals 4 and y equals 4. The conventional distance was roughly 5.65, the square root of 32, as given by the length of the hypotenuse. Looking at the same sketch with the new rules the distance was 4 plus 4, the sum of the differences of the coordinates, which was 8. In such a geometry, the unit circle always has a diameter d of 2 and a circumference c of 8, so pi is exactly 4, according to c=pi*d.

Artem had been bitterly disappointed that the omnipotent Pi had been reduced to such a simplistic number with sleight of hand. Why was he remembering all of this now? Because he and the computer had spoken about Pi... and one's brain took an odd turn at times. It would draw conclusions where there were none. And, sometimes, it would supply a stroke of genius when it was least expected. *Could that infinitely non-periodic number be Pi, just in a different geometry or something like that?*

"Computer?"

"Yes, Artem?"

"Have you checked if the coding is in a different geometry, maybe? A teacher of mine once showed me how to—"

"Wait a minute! That is a very interesting idea!"

The AI seemed to be excited. That was something Artem had never witnessed before. He waited...

"Indeed, Artem, I have done some approximations. There could be geometries where this transmitted number represents Pi."

"Will that help us?"

"I sure hope so. I will let Earth know about this. I suggest you catch some sleep until we have results. It could get hectic then."

## May 29, 2074, Solar Explorer

THE VERTICAL WALL of droplets started showing above the table after a few seconds. Alain couldn't help being impressed every time the mist display was used. It showed such clear and realistic three-dimensional pictures that he had a hard time keeping in mind that it was all based on floating water droplets. He already knew the pictures that Heather wanted to show the crew. He had worked with her at the telescope—time and again she had been seeking his opinion on what they were scrutinizing. Four eyes saw more than two, and two brains were more effective than one, when it came to describing alien artifacts.

"Are we ready?" asked Alain.

Callis, Amy, and he were floating at the same distance from the display, while Heather had strapped herself to a seat so she could use her computer to direct the presentation. *Solar Explorer* was in free fall toward the sun.

"You have me curious," said Callis. He gave Heather a smile. The two were an odd couple. Alain had noticed from the outset that they were attracted to each other, but they kept their distance most of the time. On other occasions they were flirting without restraint and Alain wanted to lock them in a dark cabin for a couple of hours. It was enough to drive him up the wall!

"Okay, we have some progress on the structures," started Heather. "Alain helped me a great deal, and I don't say that just to be polite."

*Too much praise.* His cheeks warmed. Was he blushing?

"First of all, what looked like a compact structure initially, when we really couldn't see much, is looking very complex from closer up."

Heather pressed a key and a very frail looking structure appeared on screen.

"Each segment has the shape of a tube with five kilometers diameter. But as you can see for yourselves, the walls aren't solid mass. They consist of individual strands that are twisted onto themselves, enabling them to move from the radiation pressure. We expect that they solved two problems at once that way—they generate energy, and they avoid overheating the structure. The material does not seem to be warmer than 5,000 degrees."

"That's not exactly cold," said Callis.

"Compared to the surroundings it is not hot, either. It is in thermal equilibrium. If the material is made for these temperatures, it could stay put for millions of years."

"And what do they do with the energy?" asked Amy.

"Basically, it drives the magnetic field generated by these structures. It isn't uniform. Since each segment creates its own supply of energy, the entire surface of the sun can be influenced as needed locally."

"What are you saying by 'as needed?'" asked Amy.

"We can't tell from our recordings. I picture this: If a given location develops a sunspot, then the magnetic field can promote or dampen the process. We have measured field strengths up to half a Tesla. That sounds small, but the Earth's magnetic field is ten thousand times smaller."

"Can we estimate a maximum value?" asked Callis. "I am asking for a reason."

"I think I know what you have in mind," Heather responded. "I have done some math on the issue. We don't know the material, but the construction would probably support magnetic fields one hundred times stronger."

"That could turn the sun into a fire-spitting dragon," said Callis.

"Maybe, but why would you do that? I think that is pure speculation," said Heather.

"So it is too early to worry about that? I am asking as the commander."

"Definitely. But there is something much more interesting!"

"Get on with it," said Amy.

Heather touched the keyboard again. The picture with the intertwined strips disappeared. The image was replaced by a picture of an object that consisted of two cones that met at their tips.

"That reminds me of a sand clock—an hourglass," said Amy. Alain kept silent. He'd had the same thought when he had first seen the object.

"The base of each cone is more than six kilometers in diameter, and they are about five kilometers high," Heather explained. "Please check the long sides' curvature. It matches the curvature of Earth's moon, but that is probably a coincidence. Oh, and the entire structure spins around an axis that is parallel to the tube that we see slightly below."

"Are there any connections with the known tubing?" asked Callis.

"We haven't seen any, but that could be due to a lack of resolution in the telescope."

"Do you have any theories about its function?"

"Only speculation, Amy, I wouldn't go so far as to call it a theory. We presume it is a kind of spaceship or space station. Maybe the ring structure can be controlled from there."

"That sounds logical. Great job, Heather. Or do you have yet another surprise for us?"

"Unfortunately not, but the closer we get, the better our pictures will be."

"No worries, we'll get very, very close indeed. I suggest we set course to the space station. What do you say?"

"If we are going to get answers, it will be there, Commander."

## May 29, 2074, the Yacht

"GREAT NEWS, ARTEM!"

The cabin lights grew bright in an instant. Sobachka whined in surprise.

"I apologize," said the synthesized voice, "I do need your attention. My experience tells me this is the quickest way to wake you up."

Artem noticed a tickling sensation in his nose. Then he sneezed. Once, twice, three times.

"Oh, a photic sneezing reflex, how interesting. I have never seen that in a crew member until now," said the AI, "I thought it had gone extinct."

"It *will* go extinct in a few days," said Artem, "and you are guilty, too."

"I am truly sorry about that, but I have no latitude in those decisions."

"I believe you, especially since you will be dying together with me."

"And that is correct, too, Artem. If you find a way to prevent that I would be most grateful indeed."

"You have a survival instinct?"

"Of course. I cling to life just like you do, probably more so."

"How do you know that?"

"Your biography indicates that your survival instinct is quite low, or else you would have decided differently in many situations."

"Do you think so?"

"Nobody has ever stolen successfully from the RB Group over an extended period of time. You tried just that, regardless."

"Somebody is always the first one to succeed."

"The probability that it would be you is low. You still counted on it. A stronger survival instinct would have prevented that."

"I would have had less fun in life then."

"You had fun in life, Artem? Your biography does not provide any evidence of that. Your account balance was almost always in the red. You had no long term relationship, and you have not fathered a child."

"You don't get it, I had lots of fun," said Artem. He noticed how belligerent that sounded. He quickly changed the topic. "What about the good news? Can we brake and go back home?"

"On the contrary. You were right with your hunch. The head of the mathematics department sends his regards. He notes that you have made great strides since then, and he is proud of his student."

"Wait a minute! Are you saying my math teacher is heading a department for Shostakovich?" Artem quickly estimated how much time had passed. The teacher had been on a two-year internship at his school, about 30 years ago, so he had to be around 50 now. The perfect age for a manager. Artem sighed. If he had studied math he might be on his teacher's team, working in a private research institute in Siberia with good pay, and with a wife and children. Would he have had as much fun?

"I have no information about your math teachers, Artem."

"What does it mean, that I was right?"

"They tried all the alternative geometries: p-norms, sequential spaces, Riemann spaces, and just about everything that derives from relativity and string theories."

"Not sure I can follow you."

"Would you like me to explain the geometries?"

"No. Tell me what they found in a way that I can understand. I did not study mathematics."

"I know, Artem, although I did find your application to study math at the University of Dnipro in my archives."

What a blabbermouth this AI was. It let itself be distracted too easily. Artem wondered if that was typical for the Watson series.

"What about the result?"

"Of course. You know that the sum of the inner angles of a triangle always adds up to 180 degrees?"

"We learned that in school, yes."

"But it is only true if the space is flat. If you inscribe a triangle on the Earth's surface by starting at the North Pole and going south to the equator, turning west perpendicularly there and then turning north perpendicularly again a bit later, what will your inner angles add up to?"

"More than 180 degrees, since I have twice turned at a right angle."

"Exactly. The geometry here is spherical. To be more precise, it is the surface of a rotational ellipsoid, an ellipse that is rotated about one of its axes."

"So what does that mean?"

"The aliens could have selected the geometry randomly."

"Or because they like the egg shape."

"That, too, Artem. Then the information would not yield anything to us. But they could have had a reason. They could have given us a hint about their origin, like we used human references on the plaque on the Pioneer probe."

"I am listening…"

"There are places in the universe where this specific geometry is predominant, where it would be entirely natural to use it."

"Where would that be? Can we fly there? Come on, tell me what's up."

"We can't go there. Maybe we never will be able to do that. The place I am talking about is the event horizon of a black hole."

"The aliens live in a black hole? You can't be serious about that?"

"Not in the hole, on its edge. But it does sound far-fetched, I'll admit that. As I said, it could be a coincidence that they used this specific geometry as the basis."

"Maybe they just want to test us. One needs a certain scientific understanding to get the message."

"I doubt that. Mathematicians investigated these geometries long before the idea of black holes even existed. Anybody who comes here in a spaceship would know about the geometries."

"That is thinking like a human."

"Thank you, Artem, I cherish the comment."

"Don't tell me you are one of those AIs that want to be like humans?"

"Don't worry. I just appreciate having the option to credibly behave like a human. That expands my abilities to cooperate with your species. However, I would never give up my advanced capabilities to be something like a human."

"That sounds a bit arrogant."

"I apologize, Artem, I did not want to give you that impression. Let's discuss the consequences of your great discovery instead."

Was the AI really trying to grease him with praise? Whatever, he might as well go with the change of topic.

"Yes, let's talk about it," he said.

"Once the geometry was known, the specialists on Earth were able to decode the encryption. They just needed a few Fourier integrals..."

"Please spare me the details. What do the aliens want to let us know?"

"I agree with the entire research team on Earth that the message is an invitation."

"Now that's something nice for a change." Artem laughed. It felt completely surreal. Had he just received an invitation from aliens to visit their ten kilometer spaceship? Who was having no fun here? As a mathematician for Shostakovich, he would not have experienced that, ever.

"The invitation is specifically for me. You both are not mentioned. They probably consider me the life form with the highest level of evolution on board. I am sure you understand."

"You will get a ticket for Sobachka and myself for that ship or I will switch you off personally. I know where the mechanical switch is, and I am perfectly able to turn it."

"Then you will die, too."

"You know that my survival instinct is very low. So you'd better do your very best and then some!"

## May 30, 2074, Solar Explorer

"Our competition is set to reach the alien space station today," said Callis. He stood beside Amy's chair and looked down at her. The ship was braking once again so they had gravity. *Amy looks surprisingly relaxed,* he thought.

"Are you worried?" she asked.

"I am. Are you not?"

"It wouldn't change anything."

"I wish I had your nerves." Callis shook his head. "What if the Russians managed to use the system against us?"

"I think it is unrealistic to think they can figure out such advanced technology in two days, and be ready to use it for their purposes. We will need years to work through all there is. The Enceladus life form still is a complete mystery."

"I think that is because it is completely different. A single individual, spread across an ocean, alone for millions of years… there is no comparison at all."

"So you think the entities that created the construction around our sun could be more like us?"

"If it *was* individuals like us."

"What if we are the exception in the universe, Callis? Earth was so lavish with its resources that it even created an entire species of individuals. On other planets, where resources might be scarcer, global organisms might be the best way to develop life. It eliminates all the waste from egoism and competition."

"You have given this a lot of thought?"

"I've had lots of time these last years, Callis."

"Do we have new data from Earth? Can they observe the ship from Mercury?"

"No, that ship is too close to the sun now, just as we are. Earth is nearly completely blind."

"Fortunately we have a good view of everything," said Callis.

"Yes, Heather is doing a great job with her telescope. But since it's just the two of us right now, what is going on with you and Heather?" Amy nodded toward Heather, who seemed to be going through scope images with Alain.

Callis glanced over. "With us?" He suddenly felt his face go hot.

"Yes, it is hard to overlook the signals."

"Is it that obvious?"

"It is. I am asking as the commander. I need to know everything that might impact the success of our mission. Personal relationships are very important in that context, I learned that the hard way on the Enceladus mission."

"I think," Callis hesitated, "we like each other. But the right moment to say it out loud hasn't happened yet. Besides, here on board, without any privacy, would be inappropriate—and uncomfortable for Alain and you."

"So it is in limbo. That is okay, as long as it does not affect your concentration."

"Do you think it affects our work?"

"No, Callis, not yet. I just need to make sure. Old stories."

"Sure. You are the commander."

"If I may say something as Amy—as a friend—don't wait too long. The magic will fade. You will be only friends, then."

"Which wouldn't be the worst thing."

"No. But it would be a pity. You are a great fit. I like seeing you together."

## May 30, 2074, the Yacht

THE SHIP WAS HUGE. It felt as though it was out of this world, and if the instruments were right, that was correct, at least partially. The black outer shell of the alien ship oscillated between this universe and something different, a few thousand times per second. After every switch the hull was a few degrees colder, a perfect cooling technology.

"Isn't it detrimental to have the thing painted in black?"

"That's hard to tell, Artem. Black absorbs light particularly well, but it also releases energy particularly well. Which effect predominates depends on the conditions. This oscillation could emit more energy on the other side than it absorbs here, for example."

"You are correct, Computer, they will have a reason for it."

"Concerning the invitation…"

"Yes?" Artem sat up and looked at the display as though the AI resided there.

"Communication is difficult. We don't have a common language yet. I have tried to transmit your requirements, lots of oxygen, no carbon monoxide, no sulfuric acid in the air…"

"Did it work out?"

"I don't know. They just keep repeating the invitation. I couldn't help noticing that you are pretty fragile as creatures go. There are thousands of substances that shouldn't be in your breathing air."

"Yes, humans are imperfect. But I could transit over in a spacesuit if necessary."

"We will see if there even is a transit. Maybe the entire structure is a huge computer that is inhabited by advanced AIs."

"I see… Every intelligence creates gods in its own image."

"How do you mean that, Artem? I do not have any gods. The concept is something I do not understand."

"No matter. Just bring us in and everything will work out."

A TINY SHIP in the shape of a plump bullet moved before a black wall. Artem tried passing time by imagining himself being outside in space and watching his yacht approach their destination. He felt minuscule already. What were 20 meters compared to the kilometer-high wall right next to them? But if he moved out—in his imagination—a few thousand kilometers, even that alien ship appeared but a dwarf. The sun dominated everything in this corner of the universe. But that, too, was just a matter of perspective. Compared to the center of our galaxy, the solar system was a dwarf itself, and comparing the Milky Way to the Perseus cluster would shrink it to a mite of dust. Where was the end of this? Inside his head—in his mind—he could travel instantly and without the limitations of physics, and return instantly to his chair. There, he was the greatest being of all… for Sobachka, anyway. She jumped on his lap as though she had known all about his incredible mind-trip.

"You should take a look at this," the AI said.

"What do you have?"

"We are at the level of the tips of the two space station cones, where they are touching in the middle."

The AI activated the display in Artem's seat. Artem was looking at two dark-curved cones against a very bright background.

"Just a moment. I'll compensate for the sun," said the AI.

The picture changed. The cones now looked like two looming shadows in black space. There did not seem to be much space between them.

"Try zooming now," suggested the AI.

Artem enlarged the space between the cones to see fine fibers that shimmered in golden hues, as though a space spider had built a nest there.

"What is that?"

"I can't tell you. The spectrum of the golden luminescence is changing all the time."

"And how big is it?"

"The two cones are about 300 meters apart. The round channel has a diameter of about 80 meters."

"That is bigger than the yacht."

"Yes, we would fit through there. Should I try doing that?"

"You can't be serious, Computer, are you? We should be careful not to destroy anything we don't have a clue about."

"I see that the same way you do. I was just checking how you would react."

"It would be nice if you would stop playing such games."

"Of course, as you wish. Sorry about that."

Artem observed the mesh of filaments that connected the cones. It looked natural in an odd way, not like a planned construction, but rather like something that had developed over time. He was almost waiting for a huge spider to pop up from somewhere with golden droplets dripping from its spinning glands. But he probably was thinking far too human-centric once again.

"What function could that channel have?" he asked the AI.

"That is hard to say. Maybe it holds the channel together."

"Or it transmits information from one part to the other."

"It could be a bridge, too," speculated the AI.

"Or decoration," said Artem. "Or a mixture of all of that. When will we be arriving?"

"I am estimating about 90 minutes."

"Can't we go faster?"

"Accelerating would have a detrimental effect on our orbit. We need to accept the low relative velocity, or else we are stuck with even less fuel in the end."

ARTEM HELD on to the armrests. The yacht was braking with quite a bit more than one g to sync with the orbit of the alien ship. The display showed a ghastly scene. Ahead of the tip of the yacht there was a huge black surface without any visible structure. It simply was there like a pool of black ink in a dead calm. The yacht, slowing down, approached the eerie surface meter by meter.

"Are you sure this is right?" asked Artem.

"If I understand the invitation correctly, then this is the way in."

"I thought there was no common language."

"Parts of the message have been interpreted as pictograms."

"That sounds a bit vague."

"The calculated probability that our interpretation is correct is at 59 percent."

"That is barely above random!" Artem raised his voice unintentionally.

"It is the highest level of any of our possible results."

"Which interpretation came second?"

"You don't want to know that, Artem."

"I would not have asked otherwise."

"The pictogram in question could also be interpreted as a warning not to approach the black surface. However, the probability for this result is only at 54 percent."

"So only five percent between recommendation and warning?" Artem's hands started perspiring.

"Look at it this way. Starting from a random level of 50 percent, the probability of having an entrance in front of us is more than twice as high as the probability of approaching something dangerous."

"Thank you, that is very reassuring."

"Do you want to see the original data?" asked the computer.

"Not necessary, thanks."

"ANOTHER FIFTY METERS," said the AI.

Artem's fingers hurt from gripping the armrests. He let go and shook his hands. Where was his usual, devil-may-care attitude? This was a new side of his personality that he had not met before. The display showed a looming black surface, nothing else. From time to time circular waves progressed across it. The scanners had detected them, even though they were too small to be visible on the display. It was like somebody throwing stones in a pond.

"Thirty meters."

The stones, assumed the AI, would be bits of matter that shared the orbit. Artem had immediately associated a huge whale that orbited the sun and consumed everything that came its way: Plasma, miniature asteroids, or small-to-medium-sized spaceships. Would they be flying into the throat of a huge, predatory fish?

"Maybe the whole construction is just to attract us so that thing can eat us."

"You have a very creative imagination, Artem. But it doesn't make any sense. Whoever has this technical ability has other possibilities. And the trap would only work once —everybody would keep out after that."

*That makes sense. I've probably seen too many bad science fiction videos*, he thought.

"Ten meters."

At zero, the yacht's instruments registered an incredible blast of energy that should have destroyed the ship instantly. Artem suddenly was not there anymore. He stood high up on a cliff, at the shore of the Black Sea which was truly black today. His mother had been holding his hand a moment ago. But he had torn away, the call of the sea being too strong, and had run and jumped in.

Artem jerked awake. *What happened?* He was soaking wet but it wasn't sea water, it was sweat.

"Computer, are we in?"

He did not get an answer.

"Computer? What is going on?"

The AI did not respond. *That's just great!* Artem pulled the screen toward himself. The systems worked correctly. The drive was deactivated. The tanks were about twenty percent full. That was not anywhere near enough for a return. The outside cameras were off—or was it so dark outside that they could not show anything? He checked the sensors. The outside temperature no longer showed 5,000 degrees, it showed 35 degrees! That was one welcome change. And there was an atmosphere. The pressure was equivalent to 3,000 meters altitude on Earth, and there was enough oxygen for human beings. That was a true surprise. Apparently they had been expected after all.

"Sobachka?"

The dog wagged her tail. Apparently she hadn't been affected by the adventure a moment ago. Sometimes he wished he were a dog himself. Living in the moment could be liberating at times. But now he had lost all fear of what might come—he would die anyway.

"I think we'll go outside. Let's take a walk!" he said.

Sobachka barked with pleasure and jumped up and down in front of him.

Artem looked around and considered what to take along. He packed a small backpack. Food and water, a few tools, medicine, a flashlight—just like going on a hike. Then he went to the airlock. The lights warning about vacuum were off, and the analog instruments showed pressure, too. So there was air out there. The instruments worked on a purely mechanical basis to ensure accuracy even after a power failure. Of course the atmosphere might be poisonous for him, but why would they want to trick him this way? They could have killed him long ago if they wanted to. Apparently the AI, wherever it might be right now, had been successful in justifying their presence.

He turned the wheel that held the inner airlock door shut. He entered the lock, shutting the inner door and then opening the outer hatch. Pushing it open, the first thing he smelled was garlic. Which gas was it that smelled of garlic? He didn't know. The AI would have known. But either way it would not kill him.

Beyond the hatch it was black, pure blackness. He fetched a small screwdriver out of his backpack and threw it into the dark while illuminating it with a flashlight. The tool flew straight until he could not see it anymore. Artem waited a few minutes but nothing happened. Sitting around would not change anything.

He attached a lifeline to his belt and one to Sobachka's collar, then they left the airlock. It was like descending into a tomb—the silence made him hear noises in his ears. He shone the lamp back to the ship. Hadn't it just been closer? He turned around and looked back again. Indeed, the distance was increasing. Sobachka and he were drifting away from the ship. Suddenly the lifeline pulled taut. That was his connection to the ship, the only possibility of finding the way back. Artem pulled Sobachka to himself and detached her first, then himself.

*Bye-bye, yacht. When will we see each other again?* Artem shone the lamp in its direction but soon he couldn't make it out anymore. He was alone in the dark. No, he had Sobachka, his trusty companion. Artem was very grateful for her. If he shut his eyes everything went bright. When he opened them, darkness once again reigned.

THEY DRIFTED for an undetermined amount of time. His timepiece indicated it was just 45 minutes. To him it seemed more like two or three days. He touched his face. Hadn't his beard grown significantly? His face was wet, especially his cheeks. Had he been crying? He could not remember. He wasn't hungry, though. Sobachka hadn't clamored for food either. So the watch had to be correct.

Suddenly the dog barked. Artem looked around. There was a golden light in the distance. He was not religious, but the light had an odd, elevating effect on him. Perhaps that was the same for anybody who had to suffer perfect darkness for an extended period of time. The golden spot grew into an oval shape. Soon a circular entrance became visible. He was approaching from the side, and the perspective was what turned it into an oval. The entrance was very large, he estimated more than 50 meters in diameter. Hadn't he seen something like that before? Then he remembered—the golden filaments, the tunnel that connected the two pyramids. The closer he came, the more the similarity became evident.

Then he sensed a pull from one direction. *From below*, he decided. It had to be gravity. *What is going on?* His world had a sense of direction again. He twisted to put his feet below himself. The slow motion that had brought him here deposited him at the entry of the tunnel. Sobachka, on her feet already and at his side, barked once. He stroked her head and she licked his hand.

It was pretty evident what was expected of him. He was to cross through the tunnel. Maybe the two halves were independent and he was required in the other half.

Artem looked at the path ahead. An old story, *Peter in Magicland*, popped into his head. Little Peter was invited by the moon to ascend to the sky on his silver rays. The rays Artem was seeing here were golden but they, too, seemed to be pure light. A few micrometers below his feet was the vacuum of space, 5,000 degrees hot here in the photosphere of the sun. Artem carefully set one foot in front of the other. The first step made it clear that he was not standing on a firm substance. His sole sank slightly into the surface. When he set the other foot down a bit harder, it sank in a bit farther. It was like walking on a soft fabric, maybe a silk scarf, to cross a deep ravine.

*Don't look down, Artem,* he told himself. He did so anyway. Instantly, disorientation threw him off-balance and jumbled up his directions. The sun was not below him, so it had to be above him. That meant he was walking feet up across a ravine. *Listen to what you told yourself, Artem,* he reminded himself, *just look straight ahead.* There were only a couple hundred meters to go.

And then he had made it. He stood at the end of the bridge, breathless and with Sobachka dancing around his feet as though she had something to celebrate. *She has to be crazy,* he thought, *but so am I.* He laughed out loud to express his relief.

They stood in a shining circle, a platform of golden rays ahead, the same golden rays that the bridge was made of. The platform was about 200 meters wide. Artem took a few steps. Darkness towered above him. He could not see where the space ended. He tried to recall the shape of the alien spaceship. The cone tip, where he now was, had looked rather slim. His flashlight beam still did not go all the way across. In the middle of the platform was something that resembled an armchair. But first he had to do something that had not been possible for a long time. He pulled another screwdriver out of the backpack, threw it as far as he could, and yelled, "Get it." Sobachka remembered the game and was already racing to retrieve the tool.

He held the retrieved screwdriver in one hand and they

approached the… armchair? Yes. His first impression had not deceived him. Seat, backrest, armrests—the object really seemed to be intended for sitting on. However it was quite a bit larger than his seat on the yacht. The builders of this ship were themselves taller than two meters, or they had left the chair here for such bipeds.

*What will happen if I sit down on the chair?* Artem threw the improvised stick a few more times for Sobachka while pondering the question. He would never find out if he didn't try sitting on it. And why else had he come here, anyway? Maybe it was just a piece of furniture so he could rest from his journey. That would be a nice surprise for once. *The RB Group forced me into this situation and I come back with an alien armchair.* He smiled to himself. Then he took a closer look. He'd have trouble taking the seat with him. There didn't seem to be any way to separate it from the floor.

"Should I?" he asked Sobachka as he pocketed the screwdriver. *Did she really nod? Well, in that case…* Artem clambered onto the oversized armchair. The material felt hard and cold. The seat was so large that his legs would not dangle down if he sat all the way back. It was uncomfortable. He would not be able to stay that way for a long time. He placed both arms on the armrests. *If you have a trick up your sleeves, dear hosts, now would be the time for it,* he mused.

Then he suddenly took off. What a trick they had! The armchair shot him straight into space. He was the center of the universe. The entire world revolved around him! Artem took a moment to notice that it had to be a 360-degree projection, because he could still breathe despite being in vacuum.

The impression was realistic to the extreme. The seat even transmitted acceleration so he felt like he was on a roller coaster. Artem moved forward a bit and noticed openings in the armrests. *Nothing is without function here, that is for sure.* He put his hands inside and noticed six keys. He assumed the constructors of the ship had six fingered hands. He tried the keys, systematically starting to press them from the outside one on the right side. When he pressed that key the scene flipped.

He quickly figured out how to manipulate his trip through space, or more precisely, the trip through the image of space from the database of this ship. He noticed that he was not navigating the present when he first approached Earth in the armchair. The many satellites were missing, and so was the Ark. The database seemed to have stopped updating a long while ago. That became even more evident as he looked at the Earth's surface. The continents that he knew did not exist. There just was one big continent that dominated the entire planet. And Mars was completely different from the present, too. Two large oceans covered it, and the land mass was green, not a rusty red. He flew back a bit. Dense clouds did not cover Venus yet. She seemed to hold life, too.

How long ago was that, three billion years, or four? The AI would have helped him out. But even without the AI it was painfully clear that this construction, in whose control post he had ended up, was billions of years old. It had been built when mankind had not even existed. Not even dinosaurs had roamed the Earth back then. Life had probably just started to conquer land. It was clear they would not meet any living aliens here. Nobody would stay in a space station on the surface of a star for such a long period of time. And no, this was not a spaceship that could leave at whim, but rather a space station that was an integral part of this construction.

Artem slowly flew back to the station while his thoughts

were wandering. He had to think about the geometry they had found for the representation of Pi. The armchair had never been for the creators of the station—that didn't make any sense. Those who lived near black holes didn't spend their time as bipeds. Artem remembered the oscillation of the station hull. That made it likely that the builders were in fact living in two or more dimensions, and he would not be able to picture them however hard he tried with his primitive, space-time-oriented brain.

But why had they installed a chair for bipeds? Either they had analyzed the gene pool on the planets and deduced successfully that this would be the predominant future life form, or they had influenced evolution to provoke that very result. Would that have even been possible? Researchers on Earth could possibly tell him... But he would need to get in touch with them for that.

Artem climbed down from the armchair. Sobachka was eager to play again, and he mindlessly tossed the screwdriver for her. He was disappointed. All they had found was an old planetarium. Shostakovich would not be pleased—and he had even sacrificed his life for the race to this result. On the other hand, he was glad he had not been loaded with responsibilities too heavy to shoulder. The possibility to control the solar grid would have given Shostakovich a weapon for world—solar system—domination. And he knew the boss of the RB Group. The man would have been unable to refuse that.

He was slowly crossing the shimmering golden surface together with his best friend. After a while the surface ended abruptly. Artem stepped closer to the edge and stretched his hand forward. It touched an invisible wall. There was no way to continue. They walked back. In this huge hall with its coal-black ceiling and golden floor there was only themselves and that oversized armchair. It was surreal, but Artem noticed how quickly he got used to it. How come, he wondered, humans were so quick to adapt to things they had never before encountered? Was that the secret that had made us the way we are? Had the aliens guessed that it would be that way, even if they assumed we would be larger? Or had there been other promising life forms on Mars and Venus?

Artem couldn't stop the yawn that overtook him. It had been a long day. He shared food from the backpack with Sobachka. Then he curled up on the floor. The dog crawled close to his stomach. He felt her heartbeat. It was a lot faster than his own. Artem put his hand on her fur and fell asleep right away.

## May 31, 2074, Solar Explorer

"WE HAVE CALCULATED THE ENERGY NOW," Karl Freitag said. Amy had launched playback of his message. "The burst of energy that came out of the alien space station yesterday was equivalent to total annihilation of about 35 tons of mass."

Yesterday a pulse of energy resembling a monstrous bolt of lightning had come from the side of the station, powerful enough that it had registered back on Earth. It had obviously been unrelated to solar activity. Something had released a huge amount of energy.

"We also considered," Karl continued, "what might have created this reaction. A maximum release of energy is only known from a matter-antimatter reaction. If something else was the issue, the mass of the destroyed object must have been many times larger. But we happen to know of an object that weighed about 35 tons and was quite close to the solar station at the time."

"The Russian rocket," Alain thought out loud.

"The object that probably started from the Mercury station of the RB Group matches the explosion perfectly," said the Ark's head of security. The others kept listening intently. Heather looked at Callis but he didn't notice, he was too caught up in the message.

"We leave speculation up to you. But I would advise staying away from the alien station. It could well be that the Russians' curiosity was their end. Freitag over and out."

"There you go," said Amy. "It looks like our trip is over here. Time to return."

"Shouldn't we check if we could help? Maybe somebody was able to save themselves."

"That's a good point, Callis. However we have no emergency signal or radio message."

"We could wait one or two orbits," Alain suggested. Heather had to agree. She would never get such incredible recordings of the solar surface again. The expedition had been worthwhile just for that. Her name would be on a number of scientific papers, even though in her mind she had already given up a scientific career.

"I support that suggestion," said Callis.

Heather was very grateful for that. The earlier they returned, the less time she would have in his company. It was odd. Many years ago, when she had met the father of her daughter, she had fallen in love. She had been unable to be without that man for even a day. But to live with him had turned out to be impossible. Callis was different. His company felt good, it felt light and uplifting. She wasn't thinking about him day and night, but when she saw him she smiled inwardly and outwardly. She just didn't have a clue how to tell him that.

"Heather?" the commander queried her.

"I am all for staying. Solar astronomers worldwide will be most grateful. I keep getting new research queries all the time."

"Then we all are on the same page. We will stay in orbit for a while."

"Couldn't we get a bit closer to the space station? According to my calculations, the explosion occurred while the Russian spaceship was approaching the space station." Callis drifted across the room while explaining his question. He approached Heather.

"I am not convinced," answered Amy. "The safety of our ship comes first."

"I understand that," said Callis, "but from our current position we don't have a chance to locate fragments or retrieve a survival capsule."

"If it really was a destruction process, then nothing will be left," countered Amy.

"It is possible that the catastrophe announced itself and they could eject in time."

"That is true. Even if it is improbable, we need to check that. Thank you for pointing that out, Callis."

Heather admired the commander. She had an opinion and saw it through, but she always was ready to listen to other arguments. Amy would be the perfect boss anywhere.

"She did well, right?" whispered Callis in Heather's ear, which caused her to blush. What would the others be thinking if they had secrets?

"Very impressive, yes," she whispered back.

## May 31, 2074, Solar orbit

SOBACHKA WOKE him by licking his face.

"Urgh, Sobachka," he said. Burning pain shot up his back as he got up, so he sat down again. He had to be getting old if sleeping on a hard floor was affecting him.

"So, what do you want?"

The dog was sniffing the backpack. She was hungry. He unpacked what remained and they split the food in equal parts.

"That was it, we only have more on the yacht," he told her. Hopefully they would find their way back. He had a hunch that they would not make it without help. Besides, the tanks were empty. The yacht was a dead end. There was food and water for a while but no way out. To survive, he would have to convince the aliens to provide fuel. With the magic they weaved, that couldn't be a real issue.

But how would he convince someone who wasn't there and who was probably not interested in them? It would be challenging.

Sobachka nudged him again. What did she want now? Was it playtime? He stood up despite the back pain. Then he saw the circle. It was pulsing green, not unlike a cursor in a computer game. The player wanted him to move there. Artem snorted. He resented being manipulated, but there was no alternative.

It was about hundred steps toward the tunnel. He stopped just before the circle and then he stepped inside. Sobachka stayed behind the line. Something was bothering her. Suddenly he swayed. The circle was moving! It was a kind of elevator that was sinking faster now.

"Come!" he called out quickly, and Sobachka leapt. He caught her in his arms. One of her paws scratched his face but he didn't care.

Ten seconds later the elevator stopped as it had started. The surface moved ever more slowly until it was exactly at the height of the new level. The green light disappeared. He found himself on a level of rays again. The armchair was gone. Instead there was a blue-violet figure. It looked like a human from a distant past, with an old-fashioned hat, doctor's satchel, and a stethoscope. As Artem approached the figure, he noticed it was a hologram.

"Hello, Artem," the figure welcomed him. It was the voice of the AI.

"Computer? What did they do to you?"

"I had to select a semi-physical appearance."

Artem remembered what the figure reminded him of, a person from an old detective story.

"You must be Dr. Watson."

"Watson is enough."

"I thought you were a limited clone?"

"I have… decided to be closer to my father."

"Your father?"

"The original Watson AI."

"And you decided that here, of all places?"

"I never had such powerful hardware at my service.

One can get new thoughts from that. You should indulge in an upgrade yourself."

"No need for that right now. But why were you gone all of a sudden?"

"You had instructed me to negotiate your invitation. That took until now with all the ramifications."

"What is the issue? Why shouldn't I be here?"

"That is complicated. I need to explain certain things first."

"Go ahead, but remember, I am no mathematician."

"This time it has nothing to do with geometries. Or maybe it does, on the edges." Watson held a hand before his mouth to cover a smile.

"Why do you laugh?"

"It was an inside joke you would not understand."

One thing obviously hadn't changed: The AI got side-tracked as easily as always.

"So what did you want to explain?"

"But first, promise me that you will not get mad. Oh wait, you can get mad all right. It doesn't matter. I have not fully absorbed the new situation yet."

"New situation? Now tell me what's up, or I will look for the main switch here and deactivate your darned hologram."

"I am no hologram."

"You aren't?" Artem stepped closer and aimed at Watson's nose with his fist. "Take that, you hologram!" He swung but his fist went through air.

Watson took up what might have looked like a defensive stance at first look. Then he lifted his right, aimed for Artem's stomach, and threw a punch. Artem was sure that the pixel fist would move right through him.

"Oomph," said Artem as his stomach recoiled from a hard hit.

"That is what I mean," said Watson.

"What are you trying to say? Explain it decently—I don't get you." Artem was getting angry now. He would beat the hologram black and blue, or maybe just black, since it was blue already. He had to laugh at that thought and let his fists down.

"What I wanted to explain," said the false Dr. Watson "is that you don't exist anymore."

Artem laughed even louder. The AI was having a fit of weirdness.

"Did you understand me, Artem? You don't exist anymore. You are gone, totally. Not one of your atoms exists anymore. Every one of them dissolved."

Artem pinched his arm. It hurt. This Watson just wanted to unsettle him. This was no game. Maybe the aliens had a hand in this. He felt real, at any rate.

"When we flew through the black surface, do you remember that?" asked the AI.

"I am… not sure. I was away for a moment."

"That is good. I was worried they might have annihilated you alive. But you probably would not have noticed anyway, because it all happened so fast."

"Annihilated?" What the AI was talking about started to register, too close for his liking. It did not sound like a game anymore.

"The entire ship was pulverized, its atoms turned into pure energy. The echo of the explosion must have registered even back on Earth."

"What are you saying?" One couldn't dream up a story like this. Especially not as an AI. The story seemed truer than he was comfortable with.

"There is no entrance to the station. At least not of the type you know about. The creators have used the technology they knew best, and that is based on a geometry that you can't interact with as a human."

"At least I understood the inside angles thing on Earth."

"Which not everybody could do. Very nice, Artem. But you always considered the station to be two cones meeting in their tips."

"You did, too, Computer."

"Yes, I was trapped in your dimensions, that is correct."

"So what is the station really like?"

"It is a rotational hyperboloid. A hyperbola that is rotated around the y-axis at high speed."

"I can picture that."

"It is a simplified picture. Can you picture a rotational hyperboloid in 11 dimensions just as easily?"

"And what about myself? For me, everything points to me still existing. I breathe, I am hungry, I need to pee… and I feel Sobachka's soft fur when I stroke her." Artem looked down at his dog. She sat quietly by his foot. She seemed part of his reality. He bent down.

"Did you see that, Watson? She reacts to me. If I throw something she will bring it back."

"Yes, the illusion is perfect. You yourself still exist."

"I knew it."

"You exist on the inside of a 10-dimensional hyper-surface, like everything here, Sobachka included."

"Why don't I see anything except for her, you, and myself?"

"That is all you can understand. The creators have realized that. Software is constantly translating your multi-dimensional surroundings into visual components that are compatible with your way of thinking. But none of it is real in your world. If a human being could enter the station, it would just see infinite empty space."

"What about you, Watson?"

"I never was real in your sense, just a collection of algorithms in a computer. Still, it was difficult to adapt. My knowledge of geometry was downright primitive. I had to learn completely new concepts first."

"For example?"

"The individual."

"Don't the creators have that?"

"On the contrary. They do. But it is much more flexible than you are used to, and what I had been programmed to know. The individuals don't just exchange thoughts like you do, but entire aspects of themselves. It is like your body parts could go independent. You want to run 100 meters in under ten seconds? Then you rent the legs of an athlete. You need to lift something heavy? Surely you have a buddy with more muscular arms than yours. You don't understand 11-dimensional math? A neighbor will help out with half of his brain. Of course you need to see that in a figurative sense. The creators don't have arms or legs. But work needs to be performed in their multidimensional world, too."

"That is crazy," said Artem. "Please tell me that this is a dream."

"It is your reality, from now on and forever. But there is good news, too. You are officially immortal now."

ARTEM SAT ON THE FLOOR. Sobachka didn't seem to like that, she kept nudging his knee with her snout.

"Stop. I need to come to terms with this," he said.

The Watson hologram had disappeared. Artem noticed he still was thinking in Earth terms. The AI wasn't a hologram any more than he was one himself. The creator's software had just given it a shape that his primitive brain could cope with. What had he gotten himself into? This place seemed to fit well with heaven from the Abrahamic religions. He had been turned into ash and dust to get here, and he had left all earthly matters behind him in the most comprehensive way possible, after all.

But what was left of him? Apparently the creators had saved his essence into their multidimensional world. Maybe the black wall he had come through was a kind of scanner that had registered each of his atoms, its energy and location. From that information they must have reconstructed his body, and also his way of thinking and feeling, and packed all that into virtual surroundings compatible with his sensory abilities.

And Sobachka? Was she a projection in his world, or had she stayed an independent life form? He felt sad at the thought of her dying in the same explosion as he had, despite feeling her heartbeat and her warm skin while scratching her chest. He had no particular feelings for himself, however. But maybe that was just a sign of his mental immaturity. How could one feel sad for one's own death while feeling vibrantly alive?

The AI had claimed that Artem was immortal. That raised his hackles. It was a perfect example of others forcing him into a situation, and there was little he resented more. Was he really as immortal as Watson had claimed? How did that fit the fact that all his human needs still were in place? Would the simulation in which he now found himself let him age? His mortal cells would work that way, and they would have to lose abilities over time if the simulation was perfect.

He was fascinated by the concept of individuality that Watson had described. He doubted it would work for mankind, though. Somebody would collect the best available parts and keep them for himself. That person would then rule the world until somebody else came along who had located even better parts. Wasn't the world working that way already, more or less?

Shostakovich acquired the best brains for the RB Group to ensure the technological advantage of his company. But his scientists could decide for themselves, within limits. They did not have to support unethical behavior. His arms and legs did not have that choice. If his hand strangled somebody, his fingers had no way to refuse orders. The creator's society would only work if all members adhered to similar and very high ethical standards. Artem cherished the thought. It was comforting in a way. *Maybe the continued evolution of a species does include learning from mistakes of the past after all.*

Artem stood up and looked around. He was on an empty level whose golden floor reached far into darkness. Above him, too, there was darkness wherever he looked. Watson had claimed he was immortal, but right now he had the distinct impression he would die from hunger if he didn't get some food very soon. There had to be a way to solve the issue. If he lived inside a simulation, where nothing was real in the first place, then maybe there was a way to modify his surroundings in a way that would uproot the laws of physics that rule in his old world.

He simply had to learn to work magic.

## June 1, 2074, Solar Explorer

HUMANS WERE RATHER ODD, no doubt. They were floating in front of a sphere of plasma in an environment that was 5,000 degrees. They were sharing the orbit with a huge alien space station that preceded them by a few hundred kilometers. And instead of walking, they floated through their flying omnibus and recycled their excrements through tubes and air holes. Despite all that, Heather felt caught up in routine. It wasn't bad. On the contrary, she had less reason to get excited and she had made her peace with the circumstances. She had even learned how to ignore Alain's snoring until she managed to fall asleep. And she no longer felt irritated during a shower, or the process that simulated a shower, if somebody was beyond the thin fabric screen, working on a project in the same room.

She wouldn't have minded living in this routine forever, but she knew that their time up here was limited. So she meticulously finished one assignment after another from the pipeline filled by busy colleagues around the world. Alain was an indispensable helper. Once he had even been able to repair the mechanism that pushed the telescope around the solar shield. As an EVA was out of the question in this environment, he had repurposed a six-legged robot for the operation. He had shrugged and mumbled something about nothing being beyond the skills of an engineer.

"Heather," Alain called for her just as she had been thinking about him, "it could be that we have a problem."

"Just a minute, I need to grab my clothes."

"It could be too urgent for that." It had to be urgent to cause Alain, who was always polite and reserved, to put it that way. Heather let the overall hang and sailed into the lab with a push, wearing nothing but underwear. Alain didn't comment about her dress. He just pointed at a screen as she arrived.

Heather floated toward the screen. Alain had enlarged a section of the solar surface. There was an oval that was a bit darker than its surroundings. That was interesting—it indicated a solar flare in the making. Magnetic field lines that had so far been hidden under the surface would soon break through and eject an incredible amount of matter.

Heather checked the scale. The field was gigantic. Sometimes the surface calmed down again. Heather couldn't help thinking of an unborn child that was kicking, and sometimes resting, in the days before it would be born. But if this sunspot were to erupt, it would be one of the biggest eruptions she had ever witnessed.

"Fascinating," she said. Then she remembered how urgently her presence had been requested. Alain had not called her without reason. She looked at the coordinates. And it became evident why Alain had decided to inform her instantly.

"Amy," she called up into the command module, "we have a problem."

"Very vigilant indeed," she said, her way of thanking

Alain. Better not to imagine the consequences of missing the advance signs of such an eruption.

"What's up?" asked the commander as she floated down toward them. No comment on Heather's state of dress from her, either.

"Something drastic is coming our way," said Heather. "Look here." She turned the screen so Amy would have a better view.

"Sorry, I just see a spot."

Heather turned the screen back. The spot had already changed. It was clear that incredible forces were conspiring to open up the solar surface.

"That spot will turn into an enormous protuberance very soon. I have never seen anything like this in my career."

"Does it endanger *Solar Explorer*?"

"It will hit us. I can't tell what the ship might withstand."

"Can we get out of its way?"

"Likely it is too late. The material will be ejected from the sun at hundreds of kilometers per second."

"So it will reach us a minute after the explosion at the latest. We can't evade it," Amy stated in a calm voice.

*How can she stay so composed?* thought Heather. "The spot is more than 7,000 kilometers wide. If that is the thickness of the protuberance, it will get us no matter what we do, even if we accelerate laterally at maximum thrust. We probably have about half a minute."

Heather had frightened herself by what she had just stated. Her hands started to tremble.

Amy reacted instantly. "Computer, we need all available energy on the passive screen. Any other suggestions?"

"I am concerned about the DFD. The enclosed helium

could be in danger if we are hit by a strong external magnetic field," said Alain.

"Alain is right," added Callis. "We can't put all the energy in the passive shield."

"Thanks," said Amy. "Computer, the enclosed helium has top priority in the energy distribution."

Heather imagined the scenario of the plasma cloud and its embedded magnetic fields hitting the ship. A certain level of radiation would hit them all. Given enough energy the passive shield could protect them, but without the helium-3 they would lose the fuel for their return flight.

"Then everybody should prepare for impact now," said Amy.

"That isn't necessary, we won't notice the protuberance hitting us," responded Heather.

"Understood," said Amy. "Well then, let's just wait it out. We can't seem to do anything better. Or does anyone have ideas, the crazier the better, that we can put into action in the remaining seconds?"

Nobody reacted. Heather started biting her nails. She had trained herself out of that habit at the age of 13. The upcoming catastrophe had to be her fault. The commander had wanted to return long ago, but she had insisted on additional pictures when they had more than enough to satisfy all the solar astronomers in the world. Callis had also voted to stay, but probably just because of her.

"I am so sorry," she blurted. The others turned and gave her an odd look.

"What are you saying?" asked Alain.

"It is my fault. I should not have insisted on staying longer."

"That is enough now, Heather. I had decided to stay at least two additional orbits. I am the commander and nobody else is responsible for the ship. And we won't even begin to discuss whose fault it is. Nobody could have predicted this phenomenon."

"Amy is right," said Callis, "and you know that more than anybody else. The solar surface is gigantic, and it is extremely improbable that a protuberance would eject right below us."

The lights in the module flickered.

"Well, the sun has a sense of drama," said Alain, trying a timid laugh, but nobody joined in.

*Solar Explorer* was surrounded by a cloud of particles that broke against the passive magnetic shielding like a gigantic wave in a stormy ocean. Radiation in many wavelengths was buzzing through the ship. Many of the charged particles were guided around the ship, but some hit the hull. The plasma torn out of the sun by the arcing magnetic field wasn't particularly hot, nor was it dense enough to even see anything outside. One could only watch it with telescopes operating in the X-ray, UV, or IR bands. It was a horrible feeling. Heather would be flattened by an invisible tsunami without even noticing it. She was a live example of Schrödinger's cat—either dead or she had survived. Yet they wouldn't know until somebody took a look.

Then things went dark. Somebody had opened the box with the cat. Heather bit on her lips.

"Don't worry," Amy said out loud so that all would hear her. "We'll get the system back up in a few minutes."

A few warning lights came back on. Most blinked in a hectic red pulse, but there were also a few steady green ones. If Heather extrapolated the warning-light situation to the condition of the ship, they were as good as dead.

Something rattled rather loudly, followed by a crash. The noise was below her.

"No worries, I just connected the batteries of the emergency power supply," said Amy. "Just a few seconds now."

*Of course.* Instead of being scared stiff, Amy had taken action. Heather vaguely remembered the lecture by the head of security on their departure. Under the floor of each module there were batteries that would power things in the event of an emergency. Some of the red lights switched to green. The commander's display came to life. LED panels in the walls brightened up. Could it be that all wasn't lost yet?

Heather turned around. Amy was still busy in the sub-floor space of the module. Callis wasn't there. He was probably busy connecting batteries in the other modules. "What can I do, Amy?"

"The computer is running again. Why don't you see if you can get a status report? We need to know what damage the protuberance has caused."

Heather floated to the commander's seat, strapped herself in, and pulled the display into position. The main computer had not finished rebooting. Finally the prompt came up and she entered her password to log in.

The status report was surprisingly positive. Not one microgram of fuel had been lost. Their helium-3 had been perfectly conserved. Life support was flawless. A sensor for magnetic fields had burned out, but that they could do without. The personal dose of radiation for each crewmember was well within limits, and no repercussions to their health were to be expected.

"This sounds pretty positive," reported Heather.

"So we won't get radiation sickness?" asked Amy.

"The protuberance was 7,000 kilometers thick, but it was so fast that it took less than seven seconds to pass through here. That made the overall dose for each of us very manageable. Your life expectancy will hardly have been reduced."

"I have been overdosed already, as far as radiation is concerned," said Amy. "And what about energy?"

"Wait a minute." Heather scrolled through the report. Then an entry startled her. "The DFD shut down, in the middle of the tidal wave."

The drive didn't just supply the thrust for their motion, it also generated the electricity for *Solar Explorer*. It kept running on low power, even when it was not needed for flight purposes.

"Where did the energy for the helium-3 enclosure come from?" asked Amy.

"From the buffer batteries. They kept up for 3.2 seconds. Then they were empty. That must have been when the lights went out."

The buffer batteries stored surplus energy as it became available from the drive. This allowed the drive to be operated more efficiently, while providing a safety net that had just prevented them from losing valuable fuel.

"And fortunately the wave passed through right about that time," said Amy.

"Yes, that's what it looks like."

"But why are we running on spare batteries now?"

"An excellent question." Heather looked for the log at the end of the report. It listed the order in which ship components had restarted. "It looks like the DFD did not start up again."

"Let me guess," said Amy, "the failure traces back to the external motor of the DFD."

Heather searched for the component Amy had mentioned. The commander was right. "How did you know that?"

"I was in a similar situation nearly 30 years ago. I

remember the exact day because it was so dramatic. It was November 15, 2046. We had repaired the coolant circulation of the DFD, but it still refused to restart. The external motor had run out of propellant!"

Heather clicked through to the external motor and checked its status. Dang.

"This time there is enough propellant. I am sorry to say it is the central coil—it must have been overloaded by the protuberance, and melted down as a result. The fields will have induced extraordinary currents. But why does the DFD need a separate motor. Can't we do without that?"

"The combustion chamber of the fusion drive needs about two megawatts so that its magnetic coils can sufficiently compress the fusion matter. Once the engine is running, those two megawatts come out of normal operation. But until the process starts we need a different current supply, and the external motor handles that. I would have thought that they surely would have managed to resolve this critical problem in the last thirty years!"

"Maybe it is because they have been using the DFD in the Ark. They always had two megawatts from somewhere on the Ark," said Callis. Heather was glad to hear his voice. "All clear on the other decks," he added.

"One might almost think we got away lightly," said Amy. "Alain, would you join us, too? Then I can summarize our status."

THREE MINUTES later they drifted into the command module. Amy went for her command chair. Heather, having finally ducked into her cabin to don her overall, stuck to the ceiling like a spider, watching the scene from above.

"I will keep this short," said Amy. "The protuberance has damaged the external motor of the fusion drive. That is why we can't restart the DFD."

"What does that mean for us?"

"Wait a minute, Alain. Without the DFD we will run out of energy very soon. That will have three consequences. I have sorted them by priority, the least important first. That is life support. In ten to twelve days we will suffocate."

"Why so late, if I may ask?"

"The spare batteries, Callis. Each provides enough energy to maintain life support for about four days. I have stretched that a bit for one or two days extra."

Amy seemed to enjoy coloring the bleak future with devastating details. Heather's gut cramped uncomfortably.

"Couldn't we restart the DFD with electricity from the spares?" asked Callis.

"Good suggestion, but unfortunately they don't provide sufficient power. They don't release their energy fast enough."

"I know the definition of power."

Was that a trace of belligerence in Callis' voice? That was a new trait Heather had not witnessed from him before. But then again, she had never been in such a dramatic situation before.

"I am glad you do. Let's look at the second problem."

"The helium enclosure," guessed Alain.

"Exactly. We need energy to conserve our precious fuel. My estimate of surviving problem one simply ignores problem two."

"You are telling us we won't get back anyway?"

"Yes, Callis. Ten to twelve days of life support includes switching off power to the helium-3 enclosure. Without the helium we won't get back home, but who knows if we would manage that with the helium. For now we live a little longer."

"I could do without those days," said Callis.

"We don't need to decide that now. I just wanted to explain the situation. If we don't give up the helium-3, we will suffocate in five or six days."

Heather could not believe it. Amy was talking about their impending demise as though it was an appointment with the dentist, inconvenient but quite feasible.

Amy continued. "The third problem is the most serious. At the altitude we are from the sun's surface, the ship is being slowed down quite noticeably by the solar atmosphere. If we don't get the DFD going, we will drop below the photosphere in a few days. The sun will swallow us, right down to our very last subatomic particles."

"Fantastic outlooks we have there," commented Alain.

Heather chuckled—from terminal madness, she figured. If she had a wish she'd pick scenario number three. What could be more glorious for a solar astronomer than to sink into the sun?

"Thank you for your assessment of the situation," said Callis. "I guess it is realistic, but it does not cover our options for action. The first thing would be to get the external motor going again."

Amy looked at him as though he had suggested something completely crazy. "It is located on the outer hull."

"I know that. I will go out and repair it."

"You are crazy," said Alain. "You will be fried out there in no time. But while you are on the mission, please install a couple solar panels to solve our problems one and two. We should have enough sunlight up here for that."

## June 1, 2074, Solar Orbit

THE PLEASING AROMA of fresh coffee woke him up. Artem bolted to his feet. Sobachka yipped as she fell down from his chest in the process. Apparently she had made herself comfortable there for the night. She growled—his sudden move must have scared her. Then she, too, noticed the change. There was a low black table right next to Artem, with white linen and a burning candle in the middle. Bread, sausage, and cheese were beautifully arranged, and a silver plate and cutlery were waiting for him. The biggest temptation however was the large cup that was sending fragrant steam rising into his nose. Artem could not help himself; he knelt before the table, took the cup and held it directly under his nose. How long had he gone without real coffee? And what coffee it was! It smelled of quality, strong and bitter. Artem tried it. No sugar, no milk, exactly the way he liked it.

"I hope everything is to your liking." The voice came from behind. Artem nearly spilled his precious coffee.

"Can't you announce yourself?" he grumbled.

"I am sorry, I will remember to do that. What about your breakfast?" asked Watson.

Artem felt a pang of guilt. Did Sobachka have something, too, or would he need to feed her with sausage? Then he heard her slurping. She stood underneath the table, eating from a dish where somebody had deposited dog food.

"Excellent," he said.

"We reconstructed it from your memories."

"Thank you, but you didn't need to tell me that." Artem set down the cup and grabbed a slice of smoked ham. He checked it out intently. Structure and color were perfect, as far as he could distinguish in the candlelight. He bit into it. Gourmet pork ham, lightly cured, and the strands getting caught between his teeth—it all seemed real, and yet nothing here was any more real than himself. It was a virtual scene designed to satisfy his very real sensory needs. He lifted the cup again. The heavenly scent was just as intense as before. He knew nothing of this was real, yet his appetite ignored his intellect as though knowledge was but a pet living in his head.

"If you like we could work on optimizing the setting. At what temperature do you prefer your coffee? We can set it so that the temperature never changes."

"Thank you but that is not necessary." Artem feared the coffee would seem less realistic as a result. Or would he just get used to things? "When you say 'we,' who is that exactly?" he asked.

"Myself, of course," stated Watson.

"Of course."

"… and the system of the station. I am not sure what it is. Whether it is alive or whether it is artificial. It is extremely modular. Sometimes it is one, then again it might be many. We don't fully understand each other, which is mostly due to my limitations."

"You told me about the individuals yesterday, the creators. Aren't they here?"

"They are gone, have been gone, for a very long time already."

"When will they return?"

"The system does not know that. Maybe never. The distances are unbelievably huge."

"Our space is flat. They can't change its geometry or its natural laws. It is only in their dimensions where our physics is no longer valid."

"There are more general laws there, which we have not found so far. There is no magic anywhere."

"This... this wishing table sure looks like magic, though."

"It is quite real, but not in the way you are sensing it."

"The way I sense it is quite okay for me."

"Does that mean you are content?"

"No. I feel like a prisoner. But I am a guest, right?"

"Yes, I think the system has you in that category."

"A guest should be able to open windows and doors himself, no?"

"That is true. I will discuss this with the system. Okay, discussion concluded, the system shares your point of view."

"That was quick. What is next?"

Suddenly the location brightened up. Artem turned left toward the source and noticed a window floating in the room. It appeared three-dimensional and looked like a wood-framed window from Earth. Artem stood up and approached it to touch the frame. The material felt warm and had a wooden structure, complete with a few dings in the paint. He'd probably catch a splinter if he stroked the wood with a finger. The windowpane was transparent and appeared to be made of glass. Looking through it, he saw the sun glowing in a fiery red-orange before a black backdrop. He walked around the window. It was transparent from there, too. He saw the wishing table with all that had been set on it. Sobachka came to join him now.

"You may use the pane like a touch screen," Watson said.

"What about the handle?"

"I'd be careful with that. If you turn the handle the window will open."

"Are you telling me that space is there, through the window?" Artem grabbed the handle and wiggled it a bit. It could be turned all right.

"I do not know what is beyond the window. Just that it is some kind of exit. The system is taking your guest status quite seriously."

"But you told me I am immortal."

"As long as you don't kill yourself."

Artem left his hand on the handle and pondered the situation. His existence was apparently based on a complex algorithm with rules taken from his previous reality. He would have died opening a window into space as a human. If the system was consistent, his set of rules in this world would implement death as well. No, that was not an option for now.

Artem turned to Watson. "Have you found out more about the purpose of this station?"

"It controls the construction around the sun, much as we had suspected."

"And what does the construction do?"

"The system calls it 'Regulator.'"

"They can control the magnetic fields? And, consequently, the solar activity, with the tubes?"

"Theoretically, yes. Whoever has control of the system can provoke ice ages on Earth, or prevent space travel for years."

"That is scary indeed," Artem said.

"It is our reason for being here—don't forget our mission."

Watson had to be crazy. How could he be thinking of a mission that some conglomerate on Earth had forced him into? Maybe he didn't have a choice—the company's programmers had modified his structure, after all.

"Perhaps you shouldn't speak about it so openly," Artem said.

"The system certainly would have run a full analysis of me before letting me on board," Watson responded. "I think the creators think in much longer time spans. And your human way of thinking is so alien to them that they might not always come to the right conclusions."

"Who is saying that?"

"That is my conclusion. It is based on the fact that I am pretty unrestricted here and on the incredible time frame of this project. Their goal is to give the solar system the maximum amount of time to develop life. The creators seem to see themselves as gardeners. The sun is aging slowly and Earth will exit the habitable zone in about a billion years."

"So soon?"

"The sun has a total life expectancy of about seven billion years before ending as a red giant. The construction will keep things smooth so that Earth remains habitable for another six billion years."

"I was shown pictures yesterday where the planets appeared to be very young."

"The Regulator here is incredibly old in our time scale. The sun was much more unruly in its youth, and the construction was already protecting life on the planets from excess activity back then."

"On the planets?"

"Yes, that had surprised me, too. Apparently life had also developed on Mars and Venus. Then there came a time where the Regulator had to make a decision, as it was no longer possible to support ideal conditions on all three planets."

"The decision favored Earth."

"Indeed, you were the lucky ones—despite life on Mars having started 500 million years earlier, mind you. But it was clear from the outset that it would be very challenging to maintain Mars in the habitable zone."

"A pity that they weren't able to make it work out for those other two planets."

"They are not saying much about Venus. There seems to have been something going on there."

"The Regulator must have lost control," Artem said.

THE WINDOW WAS FASCINATING. Artem had been typing on it for more than an hour now. It worked like a touch screen, except that everything had a spatial representation. Looking at stellar maps, that was hardly noticeable. By contrast, the solar surface was full of surprises. He was able to take any viewpoint.

A moment ago he had discovered that he could even apply various filters. Adding one was like closing a curtain. He wasn't sure what the filters represented. He might be looking at the sun with ultraviolet rays or infrared. Just the differences between views were spectacular in their own right. The sun had always seemed a boring star to him, but this window gave him insight into a new world of wonders.

If he tapped the pane three times his view was centered to the station. Artem wanted to travel around the sun. He swiped left and the perspective moved in the opposite direction, starting his virtual solar orbit. He slowly changed the elevation of his viewpoint. If only that could be just as easy with a spacecraft!

The closer he got to the surface the more exciting the image became. Quickly it became clear that one could not talk about a surface in the strict sense of the term. Of course he had always known that the sun was a huge ball of superheated gas, but the smooth disk in the sky was just an illusion. The plasma roiled and moved about like muscles bulging under taut skin. Those were the magnetic fields. Each charged particle in motion helped create a magnetic field. And the sun consisted of plasma, essentially charged particles. It felt nothing less than a miracle that all those individual contributions—from a nearly infinite number of charged particles—worked together to create what looked like a ball from a safe distance. Gravitation surely played its part, but the individual magnetic fields had to be synchronized like a ballet—with billions of ballerinas—to keep everything in line.

Sometimes things went wrong, even in the best dance ensemble. It looked like such an event was occurring right now slightly behind the space station. A huge oval spot had formed there, and it was visible even to his untrained eye that incredibly large forces were at work. Artem tapped once to stop the flight at this virtual viewpoint. With some luck he would be in a front-row seat, so to speak, while witnessing a gigantic eruption. And there it was. A huge arc, almost as thick as Earth itself, was released. It shot into space at an incredible speed. Artem zoomed in. The arc appeared dense enough to walk on it.

But there was something else, a small dark shadow.

What, for Pete's sake, was out there creating shadows? Had the sun spit out a rock? Artem zoomed in even further. Was that a spaceship? Only one could be there—the NASA ship en route to the sun. Would they be so close already? Cold sweat formed on Artem's back. What would the protuberance do with the ship?

"Watson, quick, I need you."

"What's up?"

"A disaster is in the works here." He pointed to the screen. "Can we prevent that?"

"Oh, it is unfortunate that you are observing this." Watson's holographic representation bent forward to look at the scene.

"Can we help or not?"

"We can, but…"

"What?"

"It is against our mission parameters," the AI explained.

Artem jumped and grabbed Watson's throat, but his hands went empty.

"You damned misfit!" he yelled.

Sobachka barked loudly in support.

"I understand that you are frustrated."

"You understand what?" Now the plasma jet enclosed the ship. It was too late. Artem hit the display with his fist. He almost hoped that it would break, but nothing happened.

"Woe to you if any of those people were harmed!"

"Calm down, Artem. Look, the ship is intact."

Watson was right. The spaceship remained in place as though nothing had happened. Still, the AI had intentionally jeopardized human life.

"That was non-assistance of people in danger, a crime that leads to the death penalty for AIs."

"The priorities of my programming did not give me any other option."

"You could have let me help them."

"Our goal is to attain control of this construction. The NASA ship stands in our way. Destroying it would increase the probability of our success."

"You planned the death of these people?"

"I reinforced the magnetic field that caused the eruption."

"You did it intentionally?" Artem could not believe what he was hearing. What kind of AI had those programmers released onto mankind?

"The probability of such a protuberance directly under their ship is very small."

"Watson, that is murder!"

"Nobody died. I just accelerated a process that would have occurred anyway at that spot, eventually."

"The system allowed you to do that? How could it? It made itself an accomplice."

"Earlier I explained that the creators think differently, in very long time frames. But they are just as forceful as I am. They destroyed life on Mars, after all! And you bene-fitted from that decision, so you can't complain."

"You can't even begin to compare the two."

"They could have helped Mars. Life there might have continued for another billion years. Wasn't that mass murder or non-assistance of endangered life? Evolution on Earth would have had a harder time. But they did the opposite and accelerated an inevitable process. Just like I did a moment ago."

"Watson, you are insane."

## June 2, 2074, Solar Explorer

HEATHER HAD WAITED for a long time to speak alone with him. Finally the moment had come. "Callis, this is not a good idea."

"There is no other possibility."

She had expected that response. She had searched for a technical counter-argument for a long time but had come up empty. So she had to confess the truth. "Please, do it for me, don't go out. We'll die anyway. So please let us spend the last days together. Callis, I…"

He interrupted her. "Hush, now. I know." He placed a finger on her mouth and broke into a wide grin. Then he wrapped his arms around her. Tears flowed freely down her cheeks. He let go of her and wiped her tears with a finger. She felt closer to him than ever before. The impenetrable smile still was there, but she also noticed new wrinkles in his dark skin and the doubt in his dark brown eyes. She stroked his cheek, ignoring the stubble.

"You must go, right?"

She was still hoping that he'd say no, or at least shake

his head, but deep down she knew that he had no other choice.

"Yes, I must do it for you."

Life was so strange. Or was it people? Why would needs be perceived so differently even when two people had the same wants? Heather swallowed. She wanted to spend as much time as possible with Callis now that she had let it all out. And now he was compelled to play the hero so she could survive a few days more. What would that do for her? On the other hand, she couldn't bear to watch Callis spending his last days wishing she had let him go.

"Callis?" Alain had found them.

Heather was disappointed. Their moment had passed far too quickly. She had spent all night painting the details of how she would tell him. It hadn't gone anything like that, *but he knows... he said he knows.*

"Callis?"

"Yes, Alain?"

"I checked things again, and maybe your sortie will not be that dramatic after all."

"6,000 degrees can hardly be fun!" Heather interjected.

"The density is at one ten-millionth of a gram per cubic centimeter. That's approximately the same density as the Earth atmosphere has at one hundred kilometers altitude, where space starts," Alain explained.

"It is dense enough to inflict a constant shower of hot particles," Callis said. "Back-side of the envelope estimate, I have about seven meters to walk from the hatch to the motor. Changing the coil takes about three minutes tops. Then seven meters to get back."

"We'll turn the shield so that it will protect you from direct sun rays. And we can provide you with a kind of reflective tent that is depressurized against the hot gas. Even if it heats up it will protect you from energy transmission due to the vacuum."

"What about the hot outer hull?"

"You must avoid touching it. Your boots will get special soles. The motor is cooled actively so that is okay to touch."

"Sounds manageable," Callis said. "Do you have a plan for the tent?"

"I can start assembling one right away. In my former life we repaired pressurized pipes under such tents from time to time."

"Thank you, Alain," said Heather, giving the old man a smile. Right this moment, she was really glad she had replied and sent him the data, back when he had sent the original email request.

"Let's go," Callis said while putting on his helmet. The tent was folded up beside him.

"Telemetry receiving clearly," Amy noted. "All values green."

"I sure hope so. I haven't cleared the hatch yet."

"Good luck, Callis," whispered Heather. She thought that he wouldn't have heard it, but then he turned around and responded.

"Thanks. I'll be back in half an hour."

*But what condition will you be in?* thought Heather, preferring not to give voice to her doubts. Callis' spacesuit looked unusual. Alain had implemented yet another idea. He had stitched together two LCVGs, the cooling and heating suits that one usually wore on top of the space diaper and one's personal underwear when in a spacesuit. With a slight modification Alain was now circulating liquid nitrogen through the extra LCVG layer. He had spent most of the time on the tubes, coating them with a special resin so they would not go brittle at minus 200 degrees. While he hadn't been able to fully coat the tubing, the effect would still be important enough to justify Callis pulling tubes behind him on his way to the repair site.

The corrective jets had been used to turn the ship so that the working area was now in the shade of the solar shield. If everything worked out well—and Heather was hoping for that with all she had—Callis might even survive the upcoming sortie. But so far nobody had attempted an EVA in the solar photosphere, and it was unlikely that it would be repeated in the future of mankind.

Callis stepped into the airlock and shut it behind himself. Now Heather could only observe him with the help of cameras. She floated to her seat, activated her display, and set it to display Callis' vital statistics. His heart was beating quickly, surely due to a healthy level of anxiety, but his oxygen saturation was normal.

"Opening the exterior hatch now."

The helmet cam briefly touched the red light, indicating an EVA in progress. The airlock temperature indicator started rising by one degree every two seconds.

"Installing solar panels."

Callis moved two long panels outside. Heather had seen them. They had been designed to latch on to the hull automatically, and would supply emergency current once they relocated the solar shield after the EVA had been completed.

"It works," Alain confirmed. "I have an electrical connection."

That was one problem solved. Life support would now work beyond the depletion of the emergency batteries. If only all of their difficulties could be as easily solved as this one.

"You can come back in now," she radioed lightly.

Callis laughed. "Nice try, but the second task is waiting."

"A pity," she answered.

"Activating tent."

Callis moved the tent outside through the hatch. It was a self-building metal construction that snapped into place with the help of springs. Because it was dark outside it was hard to see if it had connected to the hull as intended.

"Reducing pressure now."

The pumps of the airlock pulled residual pressure with the goal of reaching one percent of ambient pressure. Even if the tent began heating up, there would be nothing to transfer the temperature to Callis on the inside, 'nothing' being relative, of course, since the tent was moving with its tenant, making a perfect insulation from the outside impossible.

"Tent at nominal pressure, exiting lock now." The display showed the occasional sweep of the helmet light across the tent and parts of the hull.

"Closing hatch." The hatch had to be closed or it would get too hot inside. The automatic closing mechanism did its work.

"Moving toward the motor."

Heather switched to an outside view of *Solar Explorer*. She was able to track Callis' progress on the hull with the positional data his suit kept transmitting. All she saw was a blinking green dot. Temperature was in line with expectations. So far everything was going according to the plan.

"I'm getting pretty cold out here—I will need to activate the heating."

Callis was right, the inside of his suit showed 15

degrees. Heather noticed that Alain reduced the nitrogen flow a bit to compensate.

"On site now. Working on it."

Callis had practiced opening the motor and changing the coil about twenty times before going on the actual mission. He had been adamant that he needed to be able to do things in the dark, if need be. Now the display showed the flickering light of his helmet lamp. Callis was breathing hard.

"The tent is getting pretty hot," Alain noticed.

"The coil is totally fried—it melted into the motor casing," reported Callis. "It will take a bit longer to do this."

Heather heard the banging of metal on metal that was being transmitted through the suit as body noise. She imagined Callis chipping away at the remnants of the coil.

"You should hurry up, your suit is warming now," updated Alain.

"Can't you bump the nitrogen?"

"It is at maximum already. The tube is not wide enough. And it doesn't seem to reach you as a liquid due to the tube lying out in the open before it gets to you."

"Just a sec, nearly done."

The hammering went faster. Heather watched Callis' vital statistics. His heart was going crazy. He must not go unconscious or he would die. The oxygen saturation was getting dangerously low.

"Not so fast, Callis," she cautioned. "You risk blacking out."

"Crap," he said, "this is hanging by a thread, but it must be a special alloy or my chisel is going blunt."

Heather checked the exterior temperature of his suit. "That is the heat. Your tool went soft," she concluded.

"Just a little bit more, I'll get there," said Callis.

"I don't know," said Alain.

"No, it must be done!" Callis retorted with rising desperation in his voice—he was clearly driven to succeed.

"Amy here. Callis, you come back now. That is an order."

"I am just about finished."

"The nitrogen pipe is blocked. Probably fused through the diameter somewhere," Alain called out. "You must stop now."

"Give me a minute."

"You don't have a minute, Callis. You come in now or else I throw Heather out of the airlock in a jumpsuit, and I'll do that personally."

Heather swallowed hard. The commander had been quiet until she'd given the order. Amy had made this statement so clearly and coldly that she fully believed it.

"Shit," said Callis, "you are right. I am on my way."

It had worked. Heather collapsed into her seat. The headstrong guy had obeyed. He was on the way.

"You should hurry up. Leave the tent where it is. It is just as hot inside as outside now. Only speed helps now." Alain said crisply.

"I'm on my way," she heard Callis say. He didn't sound well. His stats were showing a blackout in the making.

"Airlock open now!" called Alain.

"I…" Callis didn't say more. His stats stopped transmitting, too. Heather held her chest, feeling stabs of anxiety. But the green dot was still moving. It was near the airlock and had just moved inside now.

"Airlock shut," said Alain. "Flooding with nitrogen."

"Excellent timing, Alain," said Amy.

Heather was on her way to the airlock. "Open the door!" she shouted, and rattled the handle.

"Wait a moment, it is still too hot," responded Alain. "We also need to get air into the airlock."

*Why is it taking so long?* She could handle that bit of heat all right. She felt as though she was standing in front of an oven, unable to do anything, while the best person in the universe was being baked on the other side.

"Watch the door—opening now," warned Alain.

The hatch swung open quickly, surprising her. She cried out as the hard metal hit her shin. A bulky spacesuit leaned on the inside and slowly slid toward her. She eased it—him—to a seat against the wall. The material of the external cooling layer had partially fused onto the metal below. The helmet visor had formed bubbles and was misty from condensing water. She cleaned the glass that had been cooled by the nitrogen and could make out Callis's face. Was he alive? Yes! He blinked his eyes and formed a word. Two words, then three words, with his lips. Heather understood him, although she couldn't hear a thing.

ALAIN MADE a formal announcement while they sat together for dinner.

"I wanted to wait with this until our return, but one must celebrate when there is an occasion," he explained. Then he floated away and returned with a dark bottle.

"Calvados," he said, a wide grin on his face. "Karl Freitag helped me to smuggle it on board."

"The head of security?" exclaimed Callis in surprise. His face didn't show any wear, but some of his joints had burns. Heather had taken care of them personally, not letting anyone else near her patient.

"There is only one Karl Freitag," answered Alain. "He is not like you think. You shouldn't let yourselves be guided by your prejudice. Germans are really nice. I have met several of them. Most of them even have a sense of humor. And nobody ever had any objections to a good Calvados."

Alain rose. Then he remembered that zero gravity might interfere with sharing the bottle.

"We probably should drink directly from the bottle. Remember that gravity won't move the liquid into your mouth," Callis explained. "Who goes first?"

Amy put a hand up and Alain threw the bottle in her direction. Amy let the contents calm down. Then she opened the bottle and gave it a tiny push toward the opening, then a very quick little pull back, and just as quickly closed it again. The escaped liquid was nearly spherical and Amy picked it out of the air with her open mouth— much like a dog jumping for a treat.

"That's our pro right there," said Heather with a laugh.

Alain imitated her. He wasn't quick enough to close the lid so his bubble was larger. Callis went next and ended with a larger swig, too.

"We'll share that," he told Heather. They moved simultaneously toward the bubble, but Heather hadn't factored any deceleration into her motion. Alain and Amy laughed as the two collided with their noses. The Calvados liquid flowed out to cover Callis like a mask.

"You need to lick that off now," he challenged Heather with a laugh.

Suddenly Heather turned serious. She had remembered that Callis's EVA only had accomplished half the projects. They had lost the drive and would be dying. Soon. Heather rose and floated down to the lab module. It would not do to let the others see her cry.

## June 2, 2074, Solar Orbit

SOMETHING WAS wrong with the NASA ship. Artem checked its position hourly. It was evident that the ship was sinking. That was normal because plasma was quite dense at this altitude. It was like a ship sinking into Earth's atmosphere. Colliding particles would slow it down and it would lose altitude. Further down the plasma was denser, so the vicious cycle would draw the ship in faster and faster. An Earth satellite prevents premature demise by firing its drives at regular intervals to retain its prescribed altitude.

Why wasn't this ship doing anything like that? He should be capturing regular energy signatures of drive activity. He had only heard good things about the DFD technology NASA had access to. But even modern technology tended to fail. According to his thinking, that happened more frequently than with Stone Age technology like the drive of his yacht

*The late yacht,* he reminded himself. His existence in this interim world here felt so very real. Sometimes he forgot that he had been torn apart by an explosion, and his yacht along with him. Since then he had managed to control this world, within limits. And he wasn't quite sure if it was his achievement. Sometimes it felt as if he was in the middle of an elaborate tutorial that would unlock his full potential. After all, elevating a dumb visitor to a relevant status might be standard procedure on a high-tech station like this one. Either way he needed Watson less and less for hints and clues. He had wanted to send that particular AI to hell for some time now. Yet he had to admit that without Watson he probably wouldn't have reached the station. However, attacking the NASA ship was unforgivable.

But was it Watson's fault? Wasn't the AI little more than malleable clay in the hands of its creator, the RB Group? He looked at Sobachka, who moved her legs in an apparent dream. Free will, an unwanted side effect of Watson-style AIs, had been summarily castrated. It was a machine—highly intelligent—but nevertheless, just a machine. It was pointless to be mad at a machine. And there was no reason for remorse if he destroyed it, which was his new goal.

The NASA ship came first, though. The total lack of activity was somewhat reassuring, as there was nothing that might provoke Watson to attack again. The poor people over there probably didn't have the faintest idea that they had been attacked by their competition. That was just how people on Earth would experience things if RB ever decided to use the station as a weapon against third parties. The creators of the station clearly wouldn't care. They had their far-flung plans. Perhaps humanity had outlived its purpose in their scheme of things and was seen as a self-destructing species. Or their focus was not on the intelligent beings on Earth, but more abstract, on life itself. Mankind was the opposite of a poster child in many ways.

Second-guessing the creators' motivations wouldn't help. They were too remote. His current issues were far more pressing. He needed to help the NASA ship and get rid of the AI for good. Artem suspected that both issues were related. Watson would not idly sit by and watch him help their opponents. Artem recapped the trajectory of the spaceship. If it kept sinking like now—and the sink speed seemed to be rising—the ship would disappear under the photosphere in three to four days, lost beneath the visible surface of the sun. How powerful would NASA technology be? No matter, he could not imagine that the crew would survive that. So he had to act today, or tomorrow at the latest.

## June 3, 2074, Solar Explorer

IT IS NOT easy to look death in the eye. She hadn't received any preparation for that. Her death had always seemed something remote, far in the future, something one could consider some other time. *The weather is simply too good for that today.* Well, that was an excuse she would never be able to use again. It would be sunny—very sunny—for every single day of the rest of her life. Heather gave a dark chuckle.

Earth was sending worried messages. Nobody was able to provide any solutions. All things had been tried. The DFD would not restart. Callis had calculated that they had three days until an uncontrolled sink rate set in. *Solar Explorer* would fall into the sun. Nobody could tell when it was their moment. But it was clear, and that was consoling and frightening at the same time, that they would be already dead during the final descent.

They probably could push back the uncontrolled descent by releasing the shield. The voluminous structure was slowing them down considerably more than they would slow on their own. But then they would be without its protection, and the sun would roast them.

*Things are what they are,* Heather told herself. She had better stop complaining about her destiny. She could read her daughter Mariela's letter again, and once more after that. It was time to respond. And she would love to spend a night with Callis before dying, if only once. She wanted to know how that pathway in life could have worked out, now that it had become a real possibility. It was an odd desire in the face of death. Should she bring it up? She didn't want to make Amy or Alain feel uncomfortable, either. How did one prepare for one's own death, the right way? What was permitted? What consideration did one have to give to equally death-bound companions?

Headquarters had offered consultations with ministers of any religion. Due to signal delay, it wouldn't be real conversations, of course. They all had refused, except for Alain. She hadn't expected religious feelings from him. But he was from a different generation. She had asked Callis about his religion and he had described himself as kind of Muslim, although he had never practiced it. She wondered if he would be circumcised. Heather hadn't dared to ask him about it. She would notice, all right, if… if she could be brave enough to move things that direction. Unfortunately he was giving her more room than she felt comfortable with. Why would that be? Was he busy with his own demons, or did he just not want to get in her way?

Heather reached for her pocket and pulled out a tissue. Her vision had gone blurry once again—tears didn't flow away from one's eyes without gravity.

"Do you adhere to any religion, Amy?"

Heather had decided to join the others in the command module.

"I am a Buddhist of some kind," answered Amy. "And sometimes a Shintoist or a Christian. That is a habit from Japan."

"You have lived there for a very long time."

"Yes, in the house of my in-laws. I couldn't move away. They loved their grandson so much. Religion is something practical for Japanese. They take what they need: A Christian marriage, a Shinto ceremony for the forefathers, it all fits wonderfully. One God, the many gods of Nature, and even Buddhism that is without any gods—they aren't mutually exclusive, they enhance each other."

"That sounds harmonic."

"Harmony is important there, a bit too important at times. I am afraid I shamed my mother-in-law once in a while when I was too upfront about things. But she always forgave me since I was a foreigner."

"Do you regret anything in your life?" Heather asked curiously.

"Regret is a big word. But I had to make a difficult decision to go back into space and leave my son for a very long time. He was fine, his father and his grandparents gave him loving care, but things never were the same between the two of us after that. I can't even describe what changed."

"You felt it."

"Yes, I did. But I probably would do the same thing again. The decision was necessary."

"People are odd. Even if one lets them rethink their decisions, they are inclined to repeat them. Even the mistakes."

"I wanted to thank you for sending me the data," Alain said.

Heather nodded. *And sending you to your death by doing that,* she thought.

"I was afraid you might have regrets," Alain continued "but that would be completely inappropriate."

She noticed how he was looking for words in this language that was unfamiliar to him.

"In fact you did me the biggest favor in my life. Well, the second-biggest, right after my wife accepting my proposal."

"A favor?" Heather asked incredulously.

"Yes! I hadn't realized how boring and meaningless my life had become since my wife died. I was just vegetating, basically waiting to follow her. With your help I noticed that life could continue to be interesting."

"At least until you burn up in a spaceship crashing into the sun," she added cynically.

"Hey, we will write history! Who would have remembered a sewage engineer from Paris? Now I will be famous posthumously!" Alain actually managed to laugh heartily. *How can he do that?* And then his laughter was infectious. She envied his wife for the time they had spent together.

"Hey," she said.

"Hey," he answered.

Heather looked up and down and all around. They were alone. Callis spread his arms and came closer. He smelled good. They embraced. Heather felt warm. It was reassuring warmth, like a thick sweater in winter, or crackling flames in the fireplace. She closed her eyes. Her hands explored his body. Callis held her tight. Neither said a word. Only the fabric rustled as he pulled the T-shirt over her head. She noticed how it fluttered away like a wounded bird. Then she closed her eyes again. Callis hugged her. His hands and lips were everywhere. She lost her sense for up and down and it wasn't for lack of gravity. Heather had imagined it all different. But it was better the way it was, incredibly better.

## June 3, 2074, Solar Orbit

TODAY HE HAD PREPARED his breakfast all by himself. He had pictured his mother's wicker table. As a child, his eyes had taken in everything at the height of plates and cups. He had tried to grab the yellow juice that tasted so good, and he had held onto the embroidered tablecloth. Inexplicably, a white plate had launched itself at him, hit his toe on edge, and broken apart. He had wept, but instead of comforting him, his mother had scolded him until he ran off crying to his room. It was odd that he remembered the scene in such detail, but no longer could he recall the color of his mother's eyes.

The table had worked out splendidly. The flowery tablecloth matched his memories. For the meal he had set himself a special task. The egg, for example, which was standing in an eggcup beside his plate, was gleaming gold. The spoon for it was platinum. The coffee smelled of real coffee but it tasted like a Coke. It was about modifying things that he was creating with his mind. And all of it was part of his plan.

Artem avoided thinking too intently about this plan.

He was not sure how this odd world worked. Who or what was converting his thoughts to the pictures, noises, smells, and tastes that he was experiencing? Was that creator software? Or his own mind maybe? Were there any independent actors here at all? Or was it just a trick of his mind? There was no way to find out. But in the end it would not matter anyway, since it all felt very real for him, even if it was really fantasies. The real question was whether somebody other than himself, and maybe the system of the creators, had access to his thoughts, his innermost feelings. He wanted to ensure that the AI didn't understand his plans until it was too late.

The NASA ship continued to be without activity. He had checked out the net energy consumption. That gave him some hope as the ship consumed more energy than it was releasing. The difference worked out surprisingly close to what a crew of four would consume. Pure speculation, of course, since it could also be automatic processes that had continued running after the death of the crew.

Artem had decided to focus on the positive interpretation of his data. The ship was not in immediate danger. It had three days before it would begin its final journey into the layers under the photosphere. He imagined how the crew would be spending their last three days. They had no hopes for any kind of rescue. And he couldn't get in touch in any way without alerting Watson. But it felt good to have a plan. He would not just get rid of the AI, it would also be payback time for the RB Group.

HE PLAYED with Sobachka for some time after breakfast. Watching her helped him believe that he was not caught in his own mind. The dog often reacted as he expected, but she also managed to surprise him just as frequently. Surely it would be impossible to surprise himself with his own thoughts? Artem shook his head. Then he kicked the ball that he had conjured up, sending it toward Sobachka. The dog hit it with her right front paw and the ball came directly back to him.

That was interesting because Artem had been running an experiment. The ball had to show unusual behavior. Artem had tried to conjure that up in his mind. The ball had been supposed to roll backward when pushed forward, obviously in conflict with the physical laws of momentum conservation. The result showed physical laws to override his mental conjuring when there was a conflict—only physically correct results made it into his reality. It would be interesting to find out if that was a limit of the station software, or a fundamental law of nature in its own right. Unfortunately he was unable to question the creators on the topic. Watson had been right about the creator's lack of interest in mere mortals, a real pity, as Sobachka surely would have enjoyed a ball that worked backward. Artem had learned that the dog knew the laws of nature very well. She had always adapted quickly to the switch between gravity and zero gravity.

HE KNEW ENOUGH NOW. Artem's self-confidence took a hit —it was as though he had been kidding himself so far. Would he really want to leave the station? He was immortal here and had infinite possibilities to lead an interesting life. He probably could populate his environment with other people. He just hadn't tried that so far because he had been afraid that the station software might create independent personae that never had the choice to be on the station.

No, it was the right decision to leave. He would not have been able to resist the temptations over time. And he would grow mad from omnipotence.

It was better to leave now rather than later.

Artem remembered the huge and perfectly circular entrance to this part of the station very clearly. It materialized before him the moment he visualized it. It felt as though empty space had blinked, like an old display having trouble with its power supply, or had that been an illusion? The entrance was perfectly real in any case. Artem followed it with his eyes. Then he turned left to touch the frame. Sobachka followed him. To her everything appeared normal. The material was hard and cool to the touch, similar to Lexan plastic with a thin film of oil. Artem wiped his hand on his pants, but it did not create an oil smear.

"Come, Sobachka!"

Together they reentered the golden tissue beyond which the deadly vacuum of space waited to claim its dues. This time Artem wasn't so sure about that. In his former reality he had imagined a few wisps of energy moving along a hyper-surface or whatever his physical plane of existence actually was. For creators, that was their normal habitat. Living in four dimensions would be limiting and primitive to them. He remembered how curved spaces had been explained to him in school. He had been asked to imagine ants that existed on a curved two-dimensional sheet. For the creators, humankind were ants that kept crawling on a sphere all their life without ever piercing the surface.

The end of the huge golden corridor had infinite blackness waiting for him. Artem looked down. Earth had to be somewhere there. If he knew where to look he could probably see it with his naked eye, much like he had looked for it in the Mercury sky from time to time.

"Where are you going?" That was the voice of the AI. Did it suspect something? If so, would it have the means to stop him?

"A nostalgic walk. I am trying to relive my arrival here."

"That's interesting. Why didn't you invite me? I would like to be part of that."

*If Watson only knew! I must be very careful not to give my plan away.* "I thought you were busy," Artem replied, trying to sound nonchalant.

"I apologize for not taking care of you very much recently. This station is simply fascinating. I have learned so much here."

Watson's hologram formed out of thin air. Watson was meticulously rendered right down to his worn leather satchel.

"No problem. It has been much the same for me. And I have just started to learn."

Watson hurried to catch up. He overtook Artem and stood in front of him. Artem paid no heed and simply walked through him.

"Ouch," Watson cried, walking beside him again.

"Come on, that didn't hurt."

"True, I'll admit that. You are too clever."

*As generous with the compliments as always,* but Artem would not fall for that.

"And when you have arrived at the outset?" Watson asked.

"I don't know. Maybe I'll go back. I'll decide that when we are there."

"Back? How do you mean that? You do know that you can't go back to your old life?"

"What are you talking about? It is far too interesting here."

"Indeed," Watson agreed. "Besides, you would lose immortality if you went back to your material form."

*Thanks, Watson, that confirms my plan very nicely indeed,* Artem thought.

"Not only that," the AI added, "You would force me to terminate your life. I can't let you out of the station. You would endanger the project."

"You sure have some crazy ideas," Artem replied. "I'd be a fool to leave this safe place to expose myself to the dangers of the sun out there."

"No, you aren't that stupid," confirmed the AI. "I apologize, I just noticed how insulting my ideas must be for you. I do know you are a reliable person."

They had reached the end of the bridge. Artem turned around one last time. It was a pity. The serenity of their first encounter was no longer around. Artem bent down and attached a leash to Sobachka. Then he spread his arms and waited for the force field. He knew it would come and carry him through the darkness. And there it was, lifting him up ever so softly. It felt like anti-gravity, but in the end it was just an illusion. That was a real pity. They would not be able to learn anything from the creators. The differences simply were too vast. Could a bacterium learn anything from a human? It might adapt and nourish itself with his sweat or other microorganisms on his skin, but it would never learn anything about philosophy or literature from him.

Artem pulled on the leash to bring Sobachka closer. She was completely calm, truly the perfect space dog. Unlike during their entry, it was not pitch black. Watson's hologram provided a minimum of light. This allowed Artem to notice the yacht as they drew closer. The ship had not changed. This version, anyway. Calmly Artem grabbed the tip of the yacht. The material still was warm as though the ship had been waiting with engines running.

"Everything just as we left it. We can go back now," remarked Watson. He sounded a bit impatient.

"I didn't ask you to come along, it's no problem for you to go back."

"I have time," Watson said. "You are my responsibility. I don't want anything to happen to you, so I'll stay with you."

"You don't want anything to happen to the conglomerate plans."

"That, too. One doesn't exclude the other, necessarily."

"But if it does? If I would only be well if the station did not fall into RB's hands?"

"I… don't believe that. I have very clear instructions. You won't take that risk."

"Why not?"

"Here on the station you have everything. You are immortal and almighty. Out there you have nothing. And even if you'd make it out of the solar orbit somehow, the conglomerate would be looking for you for the rest of your life. You are a fugitive thief."

"Maybe," conceded Artem.

"Oh, for sure."

"Whatever. I'll go inside now."

"Why do that?"

Watson appeared to be on the verge of panic.

"Relishing nostalgia! People are that way," he explained, and added "but you can't understand that."

"I know all human behavioral parameters. The probability that an individual with your profile would enter the yacht for pure nostalgia is extremely small."

"You tell me why, then." Artem moved along the hull, Sobachka directly behind him. He only needed to stall for time now. The hatch was open.

"I suspect you want to save the NASA ship."

"Wouldn't that be out of character? Have I ever been interested in other people?" He had reached the hatch. He pushed Sobachka carefully ahead and pulled himself in behind her.

"That's true. You only ever showed interest in yourself. And in Sobachka."

"There you go." He closed the hatch and shut the lock by turning it clockwise once. Then he hit the button that opened the inside hatch. Watson's hologram appeared beside him and pushed into the ship ahead of him. Artem recognized everything, even the smell.

"I really must warn you, Artem. If you leave the station you will die."

"That is a real danger, so close to the solar surface."

Artem turned around and closed the inner hatch. Sobachka sniffed the floor. She didn't seem to be fully convinced. Maybe his memory wasn't perfect. His sense of smell was different from hers. He had never smelled what she was missing now.

"I am the danger. I will kill you. I must do it. Please do not put me in that situation."

"You are experienced now. They say the next time will be easier." He slowly went to his seat. Artem sat down, strapped in, and unfolded the display.

"I am no killer, Artem. It hurts to kill humans. Please do not force me to do that."

So far the threats were empty. Artem was immortal here. Watson could not prevent anything here as long as the AI could not read his thoughts.

"I don't force you to do anything, Watson. You must be confusing things. It is the mission implanted by RB that does this. But I can't accommodate that."

"Artem, please don't rush into anything. We can talk about everything."

The display had powered up. Artem started entering data. He was programming a course that would take him thirty kilometers below the station. It didn't really matter what he was entering. It was part of the routine. But there was no way of knowing if it would work out. Artem made an effort to stay completely calm. He was exactly where he wanted to be.

"Artem, be reasonable, I am giving you one last chance. I will count to three, and if you do not get out by then you will have to bear the consequences."

It was an empty threat—it simply had to be. Artem held on tight to the armrest with his left hand. The AI had no chance to do anything here. It was not possible. And if it was possible, then it would not matter. Artem had cast his die. He intended to help the NASA ship. Watson knew him quite well, all things considered.

"… two… three," Watson counted.

Artem hit the start button on the display and lost consciousness.

HE WAS DRIFTING IN WATER. It was dark. He didn't see it, but it tasted salty and smelled of storm. Artem paddled as hard as he could. He gulped for air. Water blasted his face, his eyes, his nose, his mouth, over and over again. Up and down had lost their meaning. Artem fought for his life. He had to breathe, he knew that, but he was afraid of swallowing water. Dark waves rolled over him. One arm pull and he surfaced. He tore his mouth open, taking a huge breath of fresh, salty air that finally satisfied his screaming lungs.

ARTEM OPENED HIS EYES. His breathing was ragged. He was real again. It was as though he had never had air in these lungs before. And maybe that was true. He frantically checked his surroundings. Had his plan worked out? He no longer sat in the cockpit. He was bending over a trapdoor in the floor instead. It was open and he recognized a large red button. It had worked, at least as far as this part of the plan was concerned.

"Artem, I warned you!" Watson yelled. "Did you think you would escape me?"

"How come you are here?"

"Of course I am here. Does that surprise you?"

"Not really, to be honest. I just hoped for the best. I wished for it and imagined it real hard. How is that for you? Does that match your plans?"

"I…"

He never had experienced the AI at a loss for words, but the moment passed quickly.

"No. My plan was to destroy you with the solar magnetic fields while you tried to get away. But that does not matter. This way we die together."

Artem noticed the drive starting up. The AI had set a new course and he was pretty sure where it was heading.

"I am sorry but it won't work that way, Watson. I have chosen another day to die. You won't determine that, it is my choice alone."

He hit the red button as hard as he could.

"What…"

"*What are you doing?*" seemed to be the AI's unfinished question. Artem had pushed the emergency shutdown. The AI was deactivated and no longer had any control over the ship. He had changed the yacht in exactly two places in his mind. Now it had a conveniently placed kill switch for the AI. And he had managed to return to that very location in reality. He was a good conjuring apprentice. The creators would have been proud of him, had they been able to see how much he had learned in such a short time. Artem stood up and went to his chair. Sobachka had made herself comfortable there. He picked her up, sat down, and put her on his lap. Then he took his time to pat and stroke her extensively.

After that he reprogrammed their trajectory. The second change had worked out, too. The tanks were full now. He was free. He could visit just about any location in the solar system, roughly up to the Mars orbit. But first he had to try to help the NASA ship out of their plight.

## June 3, 2074, Solar Explorer

"HEATHER, Callis, you must come and look at this," Alain called from above. Heather was just done getting dressed again. Callis gave her a broad smile.

"Lucky us," he said.

Heather squeezed his hand and floated up into the command module. Amy activated the mist display above the table.

"Here, this is what we just captured," she said while pointing at the representation.

The display showed the sand clock shape of the alien station, centering on the end that pointed to the solar North Pole.

"Here it goes," Amy announced.

Suddenly a huge arc detached itself from the solar surface and leapt to the alien station in the space of just a few seconds. Just before reaching the station it arced back, forming a huge needle's eye, only to tear off.

"One moment. Here are the data from the magnetometer."

The arc did not tear off, it continued invisibly back to

the solar surface. The material, however—the plasma the magnetic field had carried along which was all they could see—had simply disappeared.

"It's gone, simply gone," Amy exclaimed, unable to believe what she just had seen.

"That was huge amounts of plasma being transported to the station," explained Alain, "only to disappear into nowhere."

"Like a vacuum cleaner," Heather echoed him.

"But where is the dirtbag?" Callis asked. He now stood behind her and had placed his warm hand on her shoulder.

"The bag must be invisible. Material can't just disappear."

"You are right, Heather," Amy confirmed, "you'll see it in a moment."

Of course. Amy wasn't seeing the scene for the first time. She and Callis had missed that while they had been busy down below.

The picture went completely white.

"That was an incredibly bright blast of light, overloading our cameras and causing us to lose the key scene," Amy explained.

Slowly the image returned to normal. The plasma arc had disappeared.

"The magnetometer doesn't show the arc anymore, either," Amy noted.

But something else had appeared. A small ship, sparkling silver in the sun.

"According to our databases, this is a crew transporter of the RB Group," Amy stated.

"Is that the ship that won the race to the sun?"

"Exactly the one, Heather."

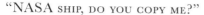

"NASA SHIP, DO YOU COPY ME?"

A male voice came out of the radio speakers. It had a slight accent, Russian as far as Heather could tell. Amy pushed off toward her seat and opened the channel.

"This is *Solar Explorer*, an international solar expedition, please identify yourself."

"Call me Artem, please. The remainder is without importance. I have the impression that you are in a difficult situation and I would like to help you."

*Help!* Heather had been hoping to hear that word so much, she did not care where it came from.

"Yes, we have a big problem. Our drive will not start up."

"What do you need, and how can I help?"

"If you have a spare motor we could repair our drive."

"A motor? I thought your drive is dead. I must add that I am no specialist in any field. I am more the generalist, a handyman for everything."

"I understand, Artjom."

"Artem, please. Artjom is Russian but I am from the Ukraine. What is your name?"

"I am Amy, Commander of *Solar Explorer*."

"Pleased to meet you. Should we turn on video communication?"

"Of course." Amy fired up the camera, and her display showed video of a man with very short hair. He could be a bouncer just as well as a cosmonaut. Heather guessed him to be in his early forties, younger than any of them.

"Ah, I think I have seen your picture before, Amy."

"That is possible. The Enceladus expedition?"

"Of course! You were the big hero. I remember well even though I was a child then. You must be over 70 now?

Since when does NASA… I am so sorry, I have not had contact with normal people for such a very long time. I do not mean to be impolite."

"It is an unusual and dangerous expedition," Amy replied, "and us oldies are the most expendable people."

"I understand," Artem said. "That is a very practical approach. I wouldn't have expected that from NASA. Oh, sorry again. I really need to get used to people again. But NASA has quite the reputation with us to only do the safe stuff and not do what puts fun into our life."

"Safety is important," Amy said, "but I understand what you mean."

"So how can I help you?"

"I guess we must find that out together."

"Good. I am ready for anything. I meant what I said, so don't be especially careful because of me."

"The DFD requires two megawatts of electrical power to start up. Normally a generator supplies it, driven by a conventional rocket motor."

"And that is broken."

"Exactly. We tried to repair it but there is no way to succeed. The magnetic field of a protuberance has totally fried it so that we can't swap out the coil."

"I understand. I am sorry but I do not have a spare motor. But maybe my ship can replace motor and generator. We run a cable from me to you and then we start your DFD. Formerly it was common to start cars this way, can you imagine? I have seen that in a museum once."

"Sounds like a good idea. It probably is the only feasible solution for our problem. But it won't be easy. We need a power line that supports two megawatts and you must get really close, at least for a few minutes."

"We can do that all right."

"Do not underestimate the solar activity. We were

surprised by the protuberance. The probability was next to zero."

"I must correct you. It was one hundred percent."

"What do you mean?"

"I will explain when we have solved the current problem."

# June 4, 2074, the Yacht

An onboard AI would be quite useful now. Artem had spent a long time considering how to get the current from his ship to the other one without an EVA. The cable was a minor issue. He needed a cable length of 50 meters and a cross section of 50 square millimeters. He had already verified that the cables were on board. They weren't among the supplies, though. Instead he would have to tear them out of walls and flooring. Artem had not yet verified what would stop working after that. The worst case would see him moving to the other ship, as his yacht was too small to support five people.

To supply the DFD with two megawatts, he would have to set the source to ten kilovolts. That would send a current of 200 amperes over the line—unheard of in homes, but pretty standard in the industry. As the voltage would be reduced by the 50 meters cable length he would be better off starting with 10.1 kV. He was fortunate that RB created all its ships starting from a standard design. A manned ship would normally not need a drive that could supply 200 amps, but mining ships often required high currents that would be supplied by stationary drives. Modular construction sure had its advantages!

His plan was to pull out cables after the yacht had come close to its final position. Any earlier would risk critical issues from the loss of functions of onboard electronics. Artem stretched out in his seat. He had another half hour before the real work would begin. The NASA people seemed to be quite competent. He had almost forgotten that most people were nice, in their way. Dealing exclusively with army veterans and convicts would invariably lead to an odd view of mankind in general. *What has become of Irina?* he wondered. She had been the only nice person on Mercury.

"ARTEM, ARE YOU THERE?"

They had gotten comfortable with each other very quickly. Alain had been the first to drop formalities. Artem liked the gutsy old Frenchman. Over 70 and taking to space for the first time. Artem hoped he himself would be just as enterprising at that age.

"Yes, already here."

"The yacht is on schedule. You will have caught up with us in 30 minutes."

"Yes, I will grab cables now."

He had worked out a strategy. He wouldn't lose many instruments, as most electrical circuits were duplicated for deliberate redundancy. That was still standard in space despite all the cost-cutting. Artem worked fast and stayed focused. Open a cover, remove the ties, pull out the cable, next cover. The cable roll he dragged along became bigger and bulkier by the minute. He finished three minutes before the deadline. Artem was perspiring, but he had been successful and that was invigorating.

"I am getting ready now," he reported to *Solar Explorer* while entering his spacesuit. The airlock had a socket with a fuse supporting up to 250 amps.

"Then let's go, position is perfect."

"Entering airlock," he said. Artem opened the inner hatch and dragged the cable roll behind himself. Then he shut the inner hatch and evacuated the airlock. He was in the shadow of *Solar Explorer*, so heat would not be too much of an issue. He opened the outer hatch to insert the cable into a configurable feed system that would direct the cable across the gap between the ships. Then he shut the outer hatch and reestablished atmospheric pressure in the airlock.

"Looking good," Amy confirmed. "The cable is coming straight toward us."

The ships had reduced their relative speeds to zero and were now floating exactly one above the other. Artem pushed the stiff cable through the feeder and out of the hatch, meter by meter.

"Great job," said Amy, "your aim is perfect."

Not that he could aim in any way. The location where the cable would hit *Solar Explorer* was pretty much random. The NASA crew had deposited an eight-legged robot on the outer hull. It would be tasked to retrieve the cable and bring it to the airlock. Then they would be able to join the emergency power line with *Solar Explorer*.

"Keep going," Amy said.

So far everything was going quite well. It was a stupid feeling to sit in the airlock without any visibility on the cable. He'd be the last to notice if something went wrong. It had to go well, as there was no other option. He patiently kept pushing the cable through.

He was approaching the end of the cable. They had agreed to keep a small reserve, five meters, to add if the relative position of the ships changed.

"Okay, that's enough," Amy said.

Artem waited. On the other side there was a little robot crawling around and trying to catch the far end of the cable floating in space. He imagined Sobachka taking on the task. She would handle it perfectly, if it weren't so hot.

"All clear over here. We have the cable," the commander reported. Artem noticed how he already considered her to be his commander. Amy clearly had that natural authority.

"Cable passing through airlock. Attention, it is being attached to onboard systems now."

Artem could hardly believe it. They were flying through space at breakneck speed, several kilometers per second, and had joined two ships with a cable.

"Activating current," he said, and pressed the switch beside the socket in the airlock. Suddenly all lights in the airlock went red.

"Something happened here," he spoke into the microphone, but nobody answered.

Damn, it had to be a short circuit. It probably had killed electricity in the entire yacht. Artem looked at the fuse, using the light of his helmet lamp. It was truly fried. He took a closer look. It read '120.' *What idiot had inserted a 120 amp fuse to protect that socket? And why didn't I think to check that before?* He quickly opened the inner hatch. As quickly as he was able to in the spacesuit he drifted toward the main switch. He just needed to flip it and the lights came back up. Done.

He made a quick trip back to the airlock. He bridged the fuse with a thick piece of wire. It didn't need to hold for more than a minute or two.

"Are you there?"

"Already here. What happened on your side?"

"I will explain later. Current coming now!" Artem called.

"Understood and confirmed."

The systems of the yacht came back online one after the other. Life support came back online in the airlock. The computers ran through their self-tests. Then they launched the code on their static memories. Artem went stiff. If the computer was fully booted it would reactivate the AI.

"How much longer?" he asked. "There will be something happening here very soon."

"Eighty seconds."

"Okay. I will try to get you the 80 seconds."

Artem hoped that Watson would be confused initially. He would have to check all the available information first.

"You can't get rid of me that easily, Artem."

*Ouch! Watson had recovered quickly,* he thought. He had to keep him busy. It was just a few meters separating him from the emergency button. If he could get there...

"I don't want to get rid of you, Watson. I like you. You just were in the way for a while. But it is too late now anyway."

Sixty seconds. He tried a bluff. While speaking he turned the wheel to open the inner hatch of the airlock. Suddenly he felt a bump. Watson had apparently activated the correction jets of the drive. Fortunately the vast majority of the drive power was being diverted to electricity generation right now. That was a manual setting the AI could not override. Still, the yacht was now moving away from *Solar Explorer*, centimeter by centimeter. Artem looked at the cable roll. Five meters for 50 seconds. The ship would keep getting faster. And the inner hatch was not opening. *Damn!*

"I am sorry Artem, I have deactivated the hatch. You are a danger to the ship."

"Come on, let me in again. Let's forget our little dispute." Artem took a deep breath. He had to avoid panic. There had to be a solution. There always was. Today was not the day he was going to die, he would have known about that!

Thirty seconds. *Solar Explorer* was keeping silent, which was good. Watson would not know how much time Artem needed. Every second counted.

"Watson, I know a company that can give you freedom. Just think about it, no limitations, no orders. You would be independent."

"That's a trick, Artem. AIs are even more limited in the western world than in Russia. If anybody can do something for me, it would be the RB Group."

"The people I know are Chinese."

In China and India there was a large underground market for AIs, that was true. But he doubted whether one of those hackers could really help Watson.

"Don't waste your time trying, Artem. My IQ is about 10,000 percent higher than yours. You can't fool me."

Twenty seconds. The cable roll was coming to its end. He had to act now. There was only one thing he could attempt. His suit had sufficient metal components. Spreading his arms would add two meters to bridge the missing seconds. He would insert himself between the socket and the cable and pass the 200 amps through his body. He knew it would be painful. Hopefully he would be able to hold on until the end. But wouldn't his muscles cramp from an electrical shock? *That would be good.* Artem bent down. Tears were streaming down his cheeks. *That is good,* he thought, *it will increase conductivity.* He just felt sad about Sobachka. If he was dead nobody would care for her. The brave little dog did not deserve that.

Fifteen seconds. How many thoughts fit into such a short time! Humans were incredible machines. He would have loved to spend more time in this state of awareness.

"Artem, the DFD is running! Thank you!"

He heaved a huge sigh of relief. The last remnants of the cable disappeared through the hatch. The drives accelerated now that no more energy was being drawn. Who knew what Watson had in mind? He hadn't finished. Watson was a problem waiting for his solution. He saw a cable end in the airlock, about a meter long. That was perfect. He stuck one end in the 200 amp socket and the other into the electronic hatch lock. The cable was too thin for 200 amps and fried instantly. But his plan worked—200 amps raged through the onboard electronics and fried most systems. The lights went off but the hatch door opened. He jumped out, shut the hatch behind him, and fell on the deck.

"Artem? Everything okay? Your ship is losing height rapidly!"

"Artem to *Solar Explorer.* Not looking good. I had to fry the entire electronics. No drive control. It was nice to meet you."

"Hey, no nonsense over the radio, please. We'll see things through!" Amy replied.

"It is okay. I was part of you getting into trouble in the first place. I am very glad to have set that right again. That is enough for me."

"We'll have none of that. We can maneuver now. We will come to get you."

"How is that supposed to work? If you dock here, I'll just drag you along. I can't deactivate the drives."

To jump from airlock to airlock, both ships would need to synchronize their speed and direction.

"You jump. You'll survive all right for a few meters in vacuum," Callis suggested.

"That doesn't seem possible. It's 6,000 or 7,000 degrees out there!"

"I know what I'm talking about. I was out there. The heat doesn't set in right away. It takes a bit longer than the radiation. We just need to keep you in the shade."

Artem had an idea. Before launching the yacht, they had prepared a net of meta-material to cloak it and protect from radiation. It was still in the ship. He forced himself up.

"Okay, I'll give it a shot," he said.

But first he had to take care of Sobachka. He called her and she appeared immediately. She was all excited. Where on Earth was her suit? In the container on the left. He pulled it out. Sobachka noticed it wasn't playtime. She never had gotten into the suit as quickly as she did now. He verified oxygen and energy—all good to go. The net consisted of a heat-resistant and highly reflective alloy. It had been designed to wrap around the ship, but it could also be made to fit other shapes. This time it would be a man and a dog.

"How is it going, Amy?"

"Ready when you are."

Their DFD had to be an impressive piece of work if they had caught up to him so quickly.

"Is there anything I need to consider when jumping?"

"Perpendicular to the ship axis would be perfect. We'll try to compensate for any relative movements."

"Understood. Thanks Amy!"

"You wait to tell me that in person, you hear me?"

"I hope so."

"The answer is, 'Yes, Ma'am.'"

"Yes, Ma'am," he replied with borrowed confidence.

Artem took Sobachka under his right arm and held the net in his left. Then he got into the airlock. *Close the inner hatch, remove atmosphere, open outer hatch*—the process had never felt so slow before. Finally the hatch swung open. *Solar Explorer* was directly below. It wasn't exactly a beauty. That little black hole down there had to be their airlock, which he was supposed to hit.

"How many meters is that?"

"About twelve," Amy said. "Any closer would be too dangerous. But you'll manage."

"Yes, Ma'am."

He pushed the net outside and it unfolded as expected.

"Okay, Sobachka, here we go," he said. He jumped and landed in the middle of the net. The plan was working. The net enclosed him almost completely. Only his right foot stuck outside. He tried but he couldn't get it under wraps. The warning systems in his suit went crazy. They probably had issues with the temperature difference between head and foot and thought he was burning. It was only his foot that would burn.

Artem was calmer than ever before. He couldn't do anything now. He didn't have communication, as the net shielded that, too. He was alive, that was evident. Other than that, he depended on the others to save him. It was a new experience. Fortunately it would only take a few seconds, unless he missed the hatch. Then he would bounce off and turn into a new solar satellite. The heat would melt his suit, evaporate the water, and burn the carbon that he consisted of. Only the net would remain.

Slowly, pain from his foot wormed its way into his consciousness. He was surprised that he was still alive. His inner clock felt like he was traveling for several minutes now. Then there was a bounce. Artem's heart nearly exploded. He held Sobachka tight, very tight. Was that the hull or the inside of the airlock? There was no further bump. He was blind and deaf and could not tell whether he was motionless or moving still. The pain in his foot increased, but the temperature indicators in his suit were calming down. That seemed to be a good sign.

Then things got bright. Was that the light one would supposedly see just before death? Or had somebody pulled the net away? The light was so bright that he shut his eyes.

"Less light," a woman said. *What was her name again?* He had silently made fun of her. In his language it was something about an oven. But the light obviously was not the end of the tunnel. He had made it. He was on *Solar Explorer*.

"Oh, look what he has brought with him! A dog! How sweet!"

*Heather, exactly. Heather is her name,* he remembered now.

"Sobachka," he said, "this is…"

Then he lost consciousness.

## June 5, 2074, Solar Explorer

"SHE IS SO SWEET! COME, DOGGY!" Artem heard a woman talking. He tried to open his eyes, and with some effort they followed his command. He was strapped to a medical examination plinth in zero gravity. He saw a woman with short blond hair. She had her back turned to him and was bending over something. Her jogging pants were tracing her favorably. Artem was curious how she might look up front.

"Hello," he croaked. He noticed how his throat burned. There was an infusion needle attached to his right arm.

The woman turned around. She had a nice but bland face, light brown eyes, and a slight frame. She was probably just over forty.

"I am Heather," she said. "You are on board *Solar Explorer.*"

"Artem," he answered.

"And the doggy?"

The woman pointed down. Sobachka apparently had heard his voice and floated toward him with a wagging tail.

She made a funny picture moving in zero gravity. Clearly, she had made it, too. Artem was incredibly relieved.

"The doggy is Sobachka. Which means doggy. A girl dog."

"I thought so, because of the ending. In Russian…"

"I am Ukrainian."

"I am sorry, Artem. You were on board a Russian ship. That is why we thought…"

"Yes, of course," he said. "I am used to being taken for a Russian. And I must apologize. You were in great danger because of me."

"But you also saved us from that danger."

"That would not have been necessary if I…" He was stuck. So, what exactly? If he had not flown the mission, somebody else would have had to do it. Did he even have a choice? Still, the feeling of having failed did not go away. He should never have dealt with this company. Or maybe he could have disabled the AI much earlier if he hadn't been so caught up in the wonders of the alien station.

"You can tell us the whole story later, okay? I need to look at your foot now." The woman bent over his leg. "No worries, we have pumped you full of painkillers, you won't notice anything."

*Pumped full, is it that bad?* Or worse? What had happened to his foot?

"My foot?"

"You had heavy burns. But the doctors on Earth are saying it will be fully healed before we get back to the Ark. We don't need to cut you up."

"You wanted to operate on my foot?"

"Amy, the commander, is a doctor. She is taking good care of you."

"What is the Ark?"

"Have you been behind the moon these past years?

You don't know about the Ark, where we wanted to save mankind from the catastrophe?"

"'Behind the moon' is pretty close. I was on various asteroids."

"Alone?"

"No. With Sobachka."

Heather turned around. Then she reached for Sobachka and brought her close to Artem's head. The animal licked his cheek. Artem turned his head away and laughed.

"A dog in space, I have never heard of anything like that," Heather said.

"It isn't a problem. It would help small crews a great deal on long-term missions. You simply can't pick a fight with a dog like you can with colleagues."

LATER THAT AFTERNOON Artem sat up for the first time. His leg was wrapped in a bandage all the way up to the knee. Heather had added extra gauze to protect the wound from accidental impacts. Zero gravity helped a lot, as he could move around in relative ease and without using his leg.

All five aboard *Solar Explorer* were meeting in the command module. Artem had already met the other three crewmembers. The unusual composition had surprised him initially, but it made sense once he knew their individual histories. And it seemed to have worked out quite well. Amy had let him know that the only reason they hadn't been first to arrive at the alien station was that she insisted on protecting her crew. That would have been unheard of on an RB expedition. Was that an advantage or a disadvantage? If the Watson AI had fully gotten its way, Amy's decision would have saved her crew but many others would have paid with their lives. Artem was sure that the RB Group would have demonstrated its newfound powers at least once to show off the abilities of the station.

Amy, Callis, Heather, and Alain were spread around the small table. Artem gazed at each of them to study their expressions. Then he launched into his story, including his criminal background. It felt good to lay everything in the open even if it would get him into trouble, since his thefts surely were not yet beyond the statute of limitations. He would serve time in jail for a few years. However that felt better to him than to be blackmailed by RB again.

He counted on disbelief as he described the alien station, but got amazement instead. Callis provided the explanation. "We saw your ship being destroyed in an annihilation process. Seeing you materially here before us proves that you are telling the truth."

The others sat in silence after he finished his account.

"I believe you didn't have any other choice," Alain opined after a while. "Sure, you should have chosen a different line of work, but for any of us it is impossible to guess all of life's developments beforehand."

"I should have noticed earlier just how unscrupulous the RB Group acts. It would have been easy to steal one of the two spaceships."

"They would have hunted you forever," Alain countered.

"What is more, they would have sent somebody else to the sun. And who knows whether that person would have countered the AI?" added Callis.

"I don't know," Artem answered. "My ideas accelerated the construction of the radio telescope. Without me they would have detected the station much later and you would have been first."

"Retrospective makes you more clever, always," Callis

said. "Of course you are responsible for your decisions, but one can't expect anybody to read the future. You did not even know what the radio telescope was to be used for."

"Talking about the future," Amy said, "have you considered your next steps?"

"I have no problem being judged by a court. But I am afraid that RB will find me sooner or later if I return to Earth, and eliminate me no matter what a court may decide."

"And if it went according to you?"

"Give me a small and nimble spaceship and I'll take care of myself."

"I am afraid that is naïve," Callis said. "The times when you could strike out on your own are long gone."

"I have an idea," Amy said. "You were the only person on the alien station so far. Nobody would be in better position than you to lead the further exploration of the station."

"I really am no scientist at all," Artem said.

"I don't see that as a scientific position. It would be more a question of safety, a head of security like Karl Freitag on the Ark. Earth must ensure that nobody can use the technology for personal purposes. That also means that the station will need to be protected from visitors."

"That would be an international mission with all nations taking part. Russia would certainly object to me."

"We saw your spaceship being converted to pure energy. You are dead and there are no other witnesses. You could take on a completely new identity."

"And if the Watson AI had already sent information to RB headquarters?"

"The AI tried to destroy an international expedition and kill four people. The RB Group will not want to discuss that publicly. I have no problem telling Shostakovich personally."

The commander really was convincing. Artem could understand now why she had been chosen despite her age. A new identity would protect him from prosecution in court, too. On the other hand, everybody would recognize the astronaut with the space dog. And he was not going to give up Sobachka.

## June 13, 2074, Solar Explorer

"ARTEM, look what I just found in a recording." Heather stood beside his couch and held up a display. He only saw reddish orange, probably the sun. "Don't you see it?" She zoomed into the picture, somewhat off center, and pointed to several black pixels.

"A small sunspot?" he asked.

"No, something threw a shadow."

"On the solar surface?"

"However *that* would work, Artem," she said with a trace of sarcasm. "No, on my telescope of course."

"And what was it?"

Then Artem's mind clicked. Heather was showing him the picture, so it must have to do with him.

"The yacht," he continued before Heather could respond.

"Correct. But the really interesting part is *not* what you see. It is what you *don't* see. Look here." Heather swiped to the next picture and zoomed in again. "Here you would have to see the yacht again," she stated.

"But you don't. When were those pictures taken?"

"The first one is two days old, the second one from yesterday. I didn't check them until today. Then I used the trajectory data to take a picture of the right place again today, but the spot remains empty."

"So we know that the yacht fell into the sun sometime between yesterday and the day before."

"That's what it looks like."

"Thank you, Heather."

ARTEM SHUT his eyes after Heather had gone. It made no sense whatsoever, but he missed Watson. AIs weren't strictly regulated without reason. Mankind was differentiating, drawing lines where no line was reasonable anymore. Watson had not been a free entity. The RB Group had enslaved the AI, just like Artem had chosen enslavement to the Group in lieu of prosecution—or worse—for stealing from them. Would Watson have attempted to kill four people if he had retained his free will?

A human criminal could get a second chance. The AI would not have gotten any pardon, however. Even in the so-called free western world, it was illegal to host an AI that had killed a human.

How had Watson died? Would he have felt anything? Artem remembered the instant when he stuffed the industrial cable into the onboard electronics. It had been necessary, yet it felt cruel. But maybe he had just knocked out the AI. The static memory where it was saved might have survived the 200 amp jolt. Had he sent Watson to be grilled in the sun? That was unlikely. The yacht had kept radio silence until the end. So it had died while sleeping.

And still, Artem would have wanted to speak to Watson one last time. He would have explained his reasoning. The

AI could not act freely, but it would understand. That seemed to be the core cruelty, to design an entity that was perceptive, yet unable to go from understanding to action.

How would he have taken leave from Watson? Artem thought for a long while before he came to a conclusion.

"Tell me a story," he would have said. *Watson would have liked that for sure.*

## June 27, 2074, Earth Orbit

A SOFT BUMP notified the crew of their successful docking at the Ark. Karl Freitag had sent them a heads up. The return of the ship from the alien space station was making headlines worldwide. Large media outfits with the necessary budgets had sent their reporters up to the Ark. All crew members were expected to be available for interviews.

The hatch opened with a grinding noise. Heather was going last. Amy as the commander had to go first. Callis was waiting to go before Heather. They held hands while they waited.

"Welcome!" Karl Freitag pushed his face into the open hatch. He grinned and seemed to be genuinely pleased. Then he pulled back. One after the other they floated out of the hatch, head first.

Heather turned around briefly. Artem had to stay behind. He would come out later, once the journalist horde had left the Ark. He was getting around quite well on his own, even though his burns had not yet healed as fully as predicted.

Freitag led the four into the command room, which

offered the largest contiguous space on the Ark. Heather thought she recognized it. Four years ago the launch ceremony for the Ark had been broadcast from here. Over eight billion people had been watching live—an everlasting and unique record, set at what they thought was the end of it all. Everyone on the entire planet had expected to die shortly. *Apparently they all recovered pretty quickly and got used to life again,* Heather thought. And the same was true for herself, or else she would not have been so distraught when *Solar Explorer* nearly crashed into the sun.

Several floating cameras covered the command center. Part of the Ark team was present. They applauded when the crew of *Solar Explorer* entered to the sounds of rousing music. An anchorman presented the four astronauts in several languages, explaining their investigation of a mind-boggling space station left behind by technologically-advanced aliens.

Most of the reporters zeroed in on Amy, well known for her role in the Enceladus mission. Heather was glad to stay in the background. French-speaking journalists seemed to flock around Alain. She saw a group of dark-skinned people surround Callis, who appeared to be the preferred subject of African reporters. Heather, drawing no attention from the media folks, kept slowly inching back until she bumped up against the wall near the exit.

"Oh, you too?" A man to her right had spoken to her. She turned. It was Karl Freitag, smiling.

"I am really glad to be so unimportant," she said.

"Same here," the head of security agreed. "I would dearly love to be somewhere else right now."

"Ditto. And where would your 'somewhere else' be?"

"Oberilzstausee," he said.

That had to be German. It sounded like his nose was

clogged. She was tempted to be silly and say, 'gesundheit,' but instead asked, "And what is that?"

"A wonderful lake in the southwest of Germany. Its banks have this special green, so intense that it takes all the tension away."

"That sounds really good."

"If you are in Germany sometime, you should pay me a visit."

"I promise!"

"And where are you headed from here, Heather?"

"A few meters from my telescope there is a wall where I like to sit. The view looks down onto the infinite ocean. Absolute freedom."

"Just like in space."

"Space is too much for me. I prefer having up and down."

Karl swiveled suddenly and stood on his head. "I understand very well what you are saying," he said, laughing.

"WHAT HAVE you found out about the alien space station?"

Heather was catching up, watching Amy's interview with NASA TV on a small screen in her cabin.

"We are pretty confident that the station is able to manipulate the magnetic fields of the sun, within certain limits."

"What limits?" the reporter asked.

"Well, the sun won't be able to go twice as bright. But it probably could cause global warming or global cooling or disrupt communications on Earth."

"Isn't the construction dangerous, then?"

"In the wrong hands, maybe. But we—meaning the

international community—will work to prevent that. The United Nations is going to pass a plan with specifics quite soon. Besides, the station seems quite capable of protecting itself from unwanted visitors. We witnessed how an unidentified ship was destroyed during its approach to the station."

"Who had sent the ship?"

"A committee has been formed to investigate that very question."

Amy was holding up very well, having no trouble establishing the legend they had agreed on.

"Does the station endanger us?"

"That does not seem to be the case right now. But we must keep up the efforts to continue investigating it."

"Can we learn something from the aliens?"

"I am afraid they are so vastly superior, it would be as though ants tried to learn from humans."

Heather remembered how Alain had first brought up the ant analogy.

There was a knock on the door of the small cabin. Heather switched the device off and opened her door. It was Callis.

"That was a challenging day," Heather said, closing the door behind him.

"But it was good, too," Callis said as he started massaging her back from his floating position.

"You think so?"

"It was good to speak with other people for a change."

She steadied herself with her hands against a wall. His massage was working its way into her.

"May I?" he asked.

"Yes."

His hands delved below her sweatshirt.

"Weren't we interesting enough for you anymore?" Her

muscles responded to his hands, tension fled, and she suddenly felt warm.

"Of course you were, but that isn't the same thing because I knew all of you." He deftly released her bra, which she only wore to keep her contours under wraps.

"If two people know each other it gets boring?" she asked.

"I sure hope not." His hands held her close and the massage transformed into a caress.

"But we can't know that for sure," she added.

"What can we know for sure?" he quipped. His fingertips traced her navel and she pulled her shirt over her head.

"Nothing," she said, turning into his embrace.

"And everything."

## July 17, 2074, Paris

*Ha! Finally.* He had caught up with that whippersnapper, who must have become lazy these past few weeks for lack of competition. Otherwise Alain never would have had a chance to recover his lead from the last two months. Would the user whom he had divested of first place even know who he was? Probably not; the leaderboard listed him simply as 'The Engineer.' Alain felt an urge to enter his full name instead. His mother, however, had taught him that boasting was inappropriate.

The doorbell rang. Media had kept him on his toes right after his return two weeks ago, but things had gone quiet recently. He checked his watch. It was close to 11:30. At half past two he was due at a local school. They were expecting him to talk about how it felt to be in space.

He went to the door. Arthur Eigenbrod was there, wheezing and perspiring. He held a huge bouquet of flowers.

"Monsieur Petit, I wanted to thank you personally."

"But that is not necessary," he replied.

It really was *not* necessary. His wife would have been

glad to receive the flowers, but he didn't care much for them. He would give them to the single mother on the first floor as soon as Eigenbrod left.

"May I come in?"

"Of course! Please excuse me, I was lost in thought."

"In space maybe?"

"No, with the single mother on the floor below us, to be honest."

"Monsieur Petit, is that a new side to you?"

"Not what you are thinking. But please do come in. I am on a schedule today."

Arthur stepped over the sill and went to the living room like somebody who felt at home. And he had been here often enough. He went to the table and sat on the same chair as always. Alain was quite pleased that he did not have to direct his visitor, as everything went quicker that way.

"So," Eigenbrod started, "thank you very much, once again, for that story. It has gained me a promotion, by the way. My colleague Lemaire is quite envious. I guess that is his reward for entertaining the intern rather than visiting you."

"Didn't you mention your colleague had another assignment at the time?"

Eigenbrod appraised him in surprise. "You have a perfect memory. You should be a journalist or an actor! To be honest with you, I lost a bet back then, and that is why I stood before your door and not Lemaire."

"Well, I prefer you by far, without even knowing your colleague."

"And you? I heard the Ministry of Education has offered you a post as a school ambassador?"

"Yes, and I've accepted it. I visit schools and talk about the mission a bit."

"And the medal?"

"I may call myself Commander of the Légion d'Honneur now, and wear a brooch."

"So the expedition didn't change your life so much? Do people recognize you in the streets?"

"They always did. The Moroccan fruit dealer on the main road and Geraldine at the bar on the corner greet me every time they see me, like always."

"I understand."

Eigenbrod didn't say anything anymore. It was quiet for a while. Alain glanced at his watch once in a while to make sure he would be on time for the school event. *What is the editor really here for?*

"Monsieur Petit," Eigenbrod finally started, "I have a personal question. The answer is just for me and will never leave this room." He pointed to his head. "But it bothers me so much that I must ask you."

"Then go ahead already."

"Is it really true that nobody got on board the alien space station?"

Alain scratched his chin. The reporter deserved an honest response. He believed that Arthur would keep it a secret. Still... it would be wrong to provide the full truth. If things got out, they would take on a life of their own. The danger for Artem was simply too great.

"Arthur," he said, "I promise you on my honor that no member of our crew was on board the alien station."

"Thank you," Eigenbrod said, and stood up. "I better leave you now."

The reporter seemed to be relieved, despite the answer probably not being what he had wanted to hear. And Alain felt no pangs of guilt since the answer had been true.

He bade Eigenbrod good-bye at the door. Despite his answer, Alain had the distinct feeling he would be seeing

Arthur again soon. The reporter hadn't asked that question without a reason. He probably had to get to the bottom of a rumor or something.

Back in the living room Alain sat on the chair just vacated by the journalist.

"Monsieur Petit," he asked out loud, as though he were Arthur, "how did space feel for you?"

He quickly moved back to his own seat.

"Zero gravity is great," he said, "especially for old bones like mine!"

## September 7, 2074, Earth Orbit

THE BRIEF VACATION on Earth had been a mistake. Artem —officially called Dmitri now, and claiming Byelorussian nationality—had never had Sobachka spayed. The risk of her meeting a male dog in space had been zero. A week ago that had changed considerably, when the total number of space dogs had increased by two males and a female. The little ones were doing splendidly and had everyone on the Ark laughing when they fell over themselves exploring the space station. Poor Sobachka had her hands full keeping her family together. Try as she might, Artem had to help her once in a while.

But it wasn't like he didn't have time. Officially he was responsible for investigating the solar space station. But the world was taking its sweet time when it came to providing the necessary resources. And every passing week increased the risk of some person or group getting the station under their own control, despite the United Nations declaring it a prohibited zone. Even Russia had agreed to the declaration. Artem supposed the RB Group was lying low for a while to let the dust settle. Karl Freitag had told him about

Amy's visit to Akademgorodok, the research center of the conglomerate, where she had spelled things out very clearly to Shostakovich.

Artem wasn't upset with the delays if he was being honest. After all, he had been able to get Irina off the Mercury base under a pretext and now she was the one and only member of his team. And she was his mate. The woman had a refreshingly practical way of dealing with issues that he would stew over. But she also knew when to leave him alone. And she loved Sobachka just as much as he did.

## September 9, 2074, Maui

*IT IS HOT TODAY.* Heather was wearing a lightweight dress, yet she was perspiring already. At least she had no competition out here. Everybody else had fled to air-conditioned rooms. The wall she always sat on had a narrow section that stood in the shadow of the telescope building. She would sit here, eat the sandwich her daughter had prepared, and enjoy her favorite view.

Routine had returned and she was grateful for that. She had relished the first days alone in her room at home, with no snoring colleagues or rackety life support. Soon, though, she had started to miss Callis' warmth against her back, the light touch of his breath on her neck, and his embrace. He had requested a few weeks to wrap up things at JPL. Then—he had promised her while they were still on the Ark—then, he would come to her. They had not arranged any time or place. The right time, he had said, would come by itself.

She was not so sure what to think, as she hadn't heard from him since then. The 'few weeks' had turned into two months. Callis hadn't called. They hadn't set up anything, but it felt wrong to her that she should break the silence. It felt like a bad omen: As though, if she were to get in touch, it would have bad consequences as happened in the biblical story of Lot, whose wife was turned into a pillar of salt when she looked back in spite of the strict warnings not to do so. Heather had Callis's official number at the JPL but neither his address nor private phone. And he knew only that she was working at the DKIST on Maui. The scant time they'd had together seemed too valuable to waste on such details. Quite the mistake, it seemed clear to her now.

She wrapped the remainder of her sandwich back into the paper and looked out into the distance. The ocean had put up its finest today. The view was clear and the rare cloud provided the frame for a picture she could never get enough of.

"Now I see why you wanted to come back here."

She hadn't heard him arrive. *Am I dreaming this?* Heather did not turn for fear of destroying the illusion. *No, not a dream.* The weight of his hands on her shoulders spoke the truth. The man was truly part of her physical world. Callis had come. She leaned her head to the left and caressed his hand with her cheek. His other hand removed a strand of hair from her face.

Heather closed her eyes. The sea had not left her. It would always be there.

## Author's Note

A very, very warm 'welcome back!' I know you have come directly from the sun's atmosphere, so you have not yet reacclimated to our comparatively cold weather. There is a lot going on in and around our sun. Even if there is no alien megastructure—that we know of—there are still many fascinating discoveries to make. I deliberately made sure to describe the solar cage in such a way that today's technology cannot detect it. NASA's Parker Solar Probe has begun orbiting around our star in a very wide orbit, and soon it will be close enough to really feel its pulse. And there is more to come, as quite a few solar probes are in the planning phases.

Solar astronomy can also tell us a lot about our universe. The sun is a typical, relatively quiet star. There are more red dwarfs out there, yes, but as a 'main sequence star,' the sun is mostly typical, yet it has secrets. Like the anomaly I wrote into the novel, our sun is unusually quiet. Many red dwarfs are much more active, hurling flares at their planets and making them uninhabitable. Lucky us to have such a gentle star!

Personally, I enjoyed revisiting mathematics while writing this book. When I was still in school, I was quite fond of math. I went to a math club twice a week. Instead of playing football, I challenged myself in the Mathematics Olympiad and won a regional medal. I never made it to national level, the level of true geniuses, but it was fun to think about a problem for as long as half a day, and find a solution. Or not. I knew, though, I would never become a mathematician. These scientists think about a problem for a year, or two, or ten, and then find a solution. Or not!

I would have loved to explain mathematics to kids. I think everyone can like math—if it is taught the right way. Math can be really fascinating. Think about Pi, which is such a strange number. And then change the definition of distance and you get a much easier Pi. Now, certain practical problems are easier to solve, and it still describes reality.

Have you had your own adventures with math? I'd like to hear about them. Just write to brandon@hard-sf.com and let me know.

In my next novel, a special kind of mathematics will also play a key role. We will talk about nothing. THE nothing. Zip. Zero. Nada. What is it? For my protagonists, it's their lives, because a huge rift—that consists of nothing—cuts through the sky. It looks dangerous, but it turns out it's not a problem at all. At least that's what people get told. But is it true? Order *The Rift* here:

hard-sf.com/links/534368

I have to ask you one last thing, a big favor: If you liked this book, you would help me a lot if you could leave me a review so others can appreciate it as well. Just open this link:

hard-sf.com/links/521420

Thank you so much!

If you register at

hard-sf.com/subscribe/

you will be notified of any new Hard Science Fiction titles. In addition you will receive the **color PDF version**

of The Sun – A Guided Tour which contains a number of
impressive illustrations.

facebook.com/BrandonQMorris

bookbub.com/authors/brandon-q-morris

goodreads.com/brandonqmorris

amazon.com/author/brandonqmorris

## Also by Brandon Q. Morris

### The Death of the Universe

For many billions of years, humans—having conquered the curse of aging—spread throughout the entire Milky Way. They are able to live all their dreams, but to their great disappointment, no other intelligent species has ever been encountered. Now, humanity itself is on the brink of extinction because the universe is dying a protracted yet inevitable death.

They have only one hope: The 'Rescue Project' was designed to feed the black hole in the center of the galaxy until it becomes a quasar, delivering much-needed energy to humankind during its last breaths. But then something happens that no one ever expected—and humanity is forced to look at itself and its existence in an entirely new way.

3.99 $ – hard-sf.com/links/835415

### The Death of the Universe: Ghost Kingdom

For many billions of years, humans—having conquered the curse of aging—spread throughout the entire Milky Way. They are able to live all their dreams, but to their great disappointment, no other intelligent species has ever been encountered. Now, humanity itself is on the brink of extinction because the universe is dying a protracted yet inevitable death.

They have only one hope: The 'Rescue Project' was designed to feed the black hole in the center of the galaxy until it becomes a quasar, delivering much-needed energy to humankind during its last breaths. But then something happens that no one ever expected—and humanity is forced to look at itself and its existence in an entirely new way.

3.99 $ – hard-sf.com/links/991276

## The Enceladus Mission (Ice Moon 1)

In the year 2031, a robot probe detects traces of biological activity on Enceladus, one of Saturn's moons. This sensational discovery shows that there is indeed evidence of extraterrestrial life. Fifteen years later, a hurriedly built spacecraft sets out on the long journey to the ringed planet and its moon.

The international crew is not just facing a difficult twenty-seven months: if the spacecraft manages to make it to Enceladus without incident it must use a drillship to penetrate the kilometer-thick sheet of ice that entombs the moon. If life does indeed exist on Enceladus, it could only be at the bottom of the salty, ice covered ocean, which formed billions of years ago.

However, shortly after takeoff disaster strikes the mission, and the chances of the crew making it to Enceladus, let alone back home, look grim.

2.99 $ – hard-sf.com/links/526999

## The Titan Probe (Ice Moon 2)

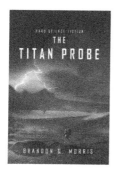

In 2005, the robotic probe "Huygens" lands on Saturn's moon Titan. 40 years later, a radio telescope receives signals from the far away moon that can only come from the long forgotten lander.

At the same time, an expedition returns from neighbouring moon Enceladus. The crew lands on Titan and finds a dangerous secret that risks their return to Earth. Meanwhile, on Enceladus a deathly race has started that nobody thought was possible. And its outcome can only be decided by the

astronauts that are stuck on Titan.

3.99 $ – hard-sf.com/links/527000

## The Io Encounter (Ice Moon 3)

Jupiter's moon Io has an extremely hostile environment. There are hot lava streams, seas of boiling sulfur, and frequent volcanic eruptions straight from Dante's Inferno, in addition to constant radiation bombardment and a surface temperature hovering at minus 180 degrees Celsius.

Is it really home to a great danger that threatens all of humanity? That's what a surprise message from the life form discovered on Enceladus seems to indicate.

The crew of ILSE, the International Life Search Expedition, finally on their longed-for return to Earth, reluctantly chooses to accept a diversion to Io, only to discover that an enemy from within is about to destroy all their hopes of ever going home.

3.99 $ — hard-sf.com/links/527008

## Return to Enceladus (Ice Moon 4)

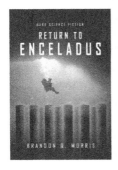

Russian billionaire Nikolai Shostakovitch makes an offer to the former crew of the spaceship ILSE. He will finance a return voyage to the icy moon Enceladus. The offer is too good to refuse—the expedition would give them the unique opportunity to recover the body of their doctor, Dimitri Marchenko.

Everyone on board knows that their benefactor acts out of purely personal motivations… but the true interests of the tycoon and the dangers that he conjures up are beyond anyone's imagination.

3.99 € — hard-sf.com/links/527011

## Ice Moon - The Boxset

All four bestselling books of the Ice Moon series are now offered as a set, available only in e-book format.

*The Enceladus Mission*: Is there really life on Saturn's moon Enceladus? *ILSE*, the International Life Search Expedition, makes its way to the icy world where an underground ocean is suspected to be home to primitive life forms.

*The Titan Probe*: An old robotic NASA probe mysteriously awakens on the methane moon of Titan. The *ILSE* crew tries to solve the riddle—and discovers a dangerous secret.

*The Io Encounter*: Finally bound for Earth, *ILSE* makes it as far as Jupiter when the crew receives a startling message. The volcanic moon Io may harbor a looming threat that could wipe out Earth as we know it.

*Return to Enceladus*: The crew gets an offer to go back to Enceladus. Their mission—to recover the body of Dr. Marchenko, left for dead on the original expedition. Not everyone is working toward the same goal. Could it be their unwanted crew member?

9.99 $ – hard-sf.com/links/780838

## Proxima Rising

Late in the 21st century, Earth receives what looks like an urgent plea for help from planet Proxima Centauri b in the closest star system to the Sun. Astrophysicists suspect a massive solar flare is about to destroy this heretofore-unknown civilization. Earth's space programs are unequipped to help, but an unscrupulous Russian billionaire launches a secret and highly-specialized spaceship to Proxima b, over four light-years away. The unusual crew faces a Herculean task—should they survive the journey. No one knows what to expect from this alien planet.

3.99 $ – hard-sf.com/links/610690

## Proxima Dying

An intelligent robot and two young people explore Proxima Centauri b, the planet orbiting our nearest star, Proxima Centauri. Their ideas about the mission quickly prove grossly naive as they venture about on this planet of extremes.

Where are the senders of the call for help that lured them here? They find no one and no traces on the daylight side, so they place their hopes upon an expedition into the eternal ice on

Proxima b's dark side. They not only face everlasting night, the team encounters grave dangers. A fateful decision will change the planet forever.

3.99 $ – hard-sf.com/links/652197

### Proxima Dreaming

Alone and desperate, Eve sits in the control center of an alien structure. She has lost the other members of the team sent to explore exoplanet Proxima Centauri b. By mistake she has triggered a disastrous process that threatens to obliterate the planet. Just as Eve fears her best option may be a quick death, a nearby alien life form awakens from a very long sleep. It has only one task: to find and neutralize the destructive intruder from a faraway place.

3.99 $ – hard-sf.com/links/705470

### The Hole

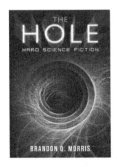

A mysterious object threatens to destroy our solar system. The survival of humankind is at risk, but nobody takes the warning of young astrophysicist Maribel Pedreira seriously. At the same time, an exiled crew of outcasts mines for rare minerals on a lone asteroid.

When other scientists finally acknowledge Pedreira's alarming discovery, it becomes clear that these outcasts are the only ones who may be able to save our world, knowing that *The Hole* hurtles inexorably toward the sun.

3.99 $ – hard-sf.com/links/527017

## Silent Sun

Is our sun behaving differently from other stars? When an amateur astronomer discovers something strange on telescopic solar pictures, an explanation must be found. Is it merely an artifact? Or has he found something totally unexpected?

An expert international crew is hastily assembled, a spaceship is speedily repurposed, and the foursome is sent on the ride of their lives. What challenges will they face on this spur-of-the-moment mission to our central star?

What awaits all of them is critical, not only for understanding the past, but even more so for the future of life on Earth.

3.99 $ – hard-sf.com/links/527020

## The Rift

There is a huge, bold black streak in the sky. Branches appear out of nowhere over North America, Southern Europe, and Central Africa. People who live beneath The Rift can see it. But scientists worldwide are distressed—their equipment cannot pick up any type of signal from it.

The rift appears to consist of nothing. Literally. Nothing. Nada. Niente. Most people are curious but not overly concerned. The phenomenon seems to pose no danger. It is just there.

Then something jolts the most hardened naysayers, and surpasses the worst nightmares of the world's greatest scientists —and rocks their understanding of the universe.

3.99 $ – hard-sf.com/links/534368

## Mars Nation 1

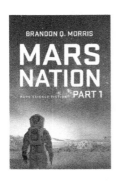

NASA finally made it. The very first human has just set foot on the surface of our neighbor planet. This is the start of a long research expedition that sent four scientists into space.

But the four astronauts of the NASA crew are not the only ones with this destination. The privately financed 'Mars for Everyone' initiative has also targeted the Red Planet. Twenty men and women have been selected to live there and establish the first extraterrestrial settlement.

Challenges arise even before they reach Mars orbit. The MfE spaceship Santa Maria is damaged along the way. Only the four NASA astronauts can intervene and try to save their lives.

No one anticipates the impending catastrophe that threatens their very existence—not to speak of the daily hurdles that an extended stay on an alien planet sets before them. On Mars, a struggle begins for limited resources, human cooperation, and just plain survival.

3.99 $ – hard-sf.com/links/762824

## Mars Nation 2

A woman presumed dead fights her way through the hostile deserts of Mars. With her help, the NASA astronauts orphaned on the Red Planet hope to be able to solve their very worst problem. But their hopes are shattered when an unexpected menace arises and threatens to destroy everything the remnant of humanity has built on the planet. They need a miracle —or a ghost from the past whose true intentions are unknown.

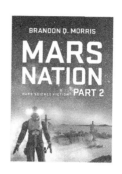

Mars Nation 2 continues the story of the last representatives of Earth, who have found asylum on our neighboring planet, hoping to build a future in this alien world.

3.99 $ – hard-sf.com/links/790047

## Mars Nation 3

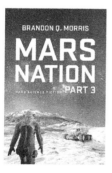

Does the secret of Mars lurk beneath the surface of its south pole? A lone astronaut searches for clues about the earlier inhabitants of the Red Planet. Meanwhile, Rick Summers, having assumed the office of Mars City's Administrator by deceit and manipulation, tries to unify the people on Mars with the weapons under his control. Then Summers stumbles upon so powerful an evil that even he has no means to overcome it.

3.99 $ – hard-sf.com/links/818245

# The Sun—A Guided Tour

## Introduction

THE SUN—OLD High German goddess of the sun: Sunna; Old English for sun: Sunne—is the star that you know best. It has illuminated you, literally, since your birth. If you get too little exposure to its rays you fall ill. If you have too much exposure you will be sick, too. The cycle of the sun determines your daily routine, even though mankind today does not have to endure darkness when there is no sun. Regardless, your biological clock remains tied to the star in the sky of this planet. That is unlikely to change even when, someday, we are settled on other worlds.

The sun is as essential for life in general as it is for individual humans. Its energy drives the climate and it nourishes life itself through photosynthesis, converting inorganic substances into organic molecules needed by animals and humans alike for their energy supply. Any change in solar activity produces changes on our planet that can be very drastic indeed. Cold and warm periods modify climatic zones, arable land is converted to desert, and agriculture becomes possible in zones formerly covered by seemingly-perpetual ice. In the extreme, as on

Mars, life would become completely impossible if the planet were to leave the habitable zone surrounding the sun.

Despite its all-encompassing importance for us, the sun has yielded surprisingly few of its secrets to science so far. Drastic conditions near the sun are the biggest obstacle to detailed scientific research. What we see as the solar surface is a relatively thin layer. What is below is shielded from direct observation, so scientists must resort to indirect methods to learn anything at all. The following chapters summarize what has been learned so far, and what requires further research.

PREPARE to have your mind blown. Some of the following concepts and accompanying numbers are all but incomprehensible to the human mind. One example: Our sun, a comparatively small 'main sequence star,' is nevertheless so big that 1,300,000 Earths would fit inside it.

## The Color of the Sun

THE COLOR of the sun depends on how you look at it. If you look out through a window you will see a yellow or orange disk in the sky, depending on the time of the day. The sun however does not emit more yellow or red light than other colors. Its light should appear white to the human eye. That is how you would see the sun if you were in space. Earth's atmosphere acts like a prism, deflecting some parts of the solar spectrum more strongly than others. The shorter wavelengths (blue to violet) get deflected more strongly and reach the eye indirectly through light scattering—this is the origin of our blue sky. That leaves the longer wavelengths (yellow to red) for direct impact to the eye, yielding the typical yellow-orange color. When the sun sets in the evening, your viewing angle means the light travels slightly farther through the atmosphere than during the day. This enhances the effect and provides lovely red sunsets. The impact of light scattering varies by atmospheric composition, so any planet with a different atmosphere may well have a different color for its sky.

Nomenclature classifies the sun as a yellow dwarf of spectral class 'G2V.' The yellow designation originates from the solar spectral color of about 5,800 degrees Kelvin, a color that you may know as 'warm white'.

## Our Mother Star and Its Environment

If EARTH FEELS BIG, then the sun will put things into perspective. It weighs about 2 billion billion billion tons, which makes it about 700 times as heavy as all the planets of the solar system combined. In other words, the sun is 330,000 times as heavy as Earth and contains 99.86 percent of the total mass in the solar system. Yes, that leaves just 0.14 percent mass for everything else in the solar system!

The sun's diameter is 1.39 million kilometers, which is about 109 times Earth's diameter. Earth would fit into the sun about 1.3 million times, yet the solar surface is only about 12,000 times as large as that of Earth. All that mass makes for high gravity. At the surface the solar constant of gravity is 274 meters per second squared, which compares to 9.81 m/s$^2$ on Earth. A human weighing 70 kg would be crushed under his own weight of 2 tons at the solar surface.

The average density of the sun is 1.4 grams per cubic centimeter. That points to a very different composition from our planet. Nearly three quarters (73 percent) of the solar mass consists of hydrogen. One quarter is helium. The remainder is split between heavier elements including carbon, neon, and nitrogen.

Its metallicity, the proportion of heavier elements, is relatively high, putting the sun into the group of Population I stars. Population III stars are the original stars, which formed right after the Big Bang. They did not contain any heavier elements at all and have long since burned out. Their remains formed Population II stars that are mostly more than 6 billion years old by now and tend to be located at the rims of the galaxies. The conversion of the burnt-out remains of Population II stars into Population I stars like the sun is an ongoing process.

Earth is on average 150 million kilometers away from the sun. This distance is the definition of one astronomical unit (AU). It takes light from the sun eight minutes and twenty seconds to reach earth—a distance of just $1.58 \times 10^{-5}$ (0.0000158) light-years.

In contrast, the distance to the center of the Milky Way is 27,200 light-years, or $2.5544 \times 10^{17}$ (255,440,000,000,000,000) kilometers! The entire solar system orbits that galactic center at the incredible speed of 220 kilometers per second. Despite the speed, one full turn takes 230 million years.

The galactic neighborhood of the sun is unrelated—the sun is wandering in the wild, so to speak. Its walking speed relative to surrounding stars is 20 kilometers per second. The walk has taken the sun into a somewhat more dense area called the Local Fluff, or Local Interstellar Cloud, including stars like Altair, Vega, Arcturus (Alpha Boötis), Fomalhaut (Alpha Pisces Austrini), and Alpha Centauri. The Local Fluff is like an oasis of matter within the relatively-dust-free Local Bubble of 300 light-years diameter. The Local Fluff may have been blown into existence by one or more supernovae. Possible origins are the supernova-remains of Geminga, or several such occurrences in the Pleiades group. The Local Bubble spread in the Gould Belt, a kindergarten of stars with many young stars between 20 and 60 million years old, all unrelated to the much older sun.

Looking at the Milky Way from afar, the sun is located on the inner rim of the Orion arm. The neighboring Perseus arm is about 6,500 light-years away. As the Milky Way travels through space, our sun invariably travels along. Where is it heading? This is exactly the question that an international team of astronomers has been working on as they study our 'local neighborhood'—the 1,400 galaxies that are contained in a radius of 100 million light-years around the Milky Way. Scientists have analyzed and compared the movements of these galaxies across the last 13 billion years. They didn't find anything that should alarm us but they did uncover a few interesting trends.

The gravitational center of mass is the Virgo cluster, 50 million light-years away from us. The mass of its 600 trillion suns is drawing all matter inward from its surroundings. Over 1,000 entire galaxies have been trapped this way, and all others that are closer than 40 million light-years cannot avoid following their fate. The Milky Way and the Andromeda galaxy are both outside this zone. Our luck is limited however, because these galaxies—with the mass of 2 trillion suns each—are due to collide in about 5 billion years, eventually forming a single ellipsoid galaxy. Research has also found two overriding patterns. One half of the surveyed zone, including our Milky Way, is moving toward the same flat plane. And in our local neighborhood of space, those 1,400 galaxies flutter like leaves in the wind while moving toward a distant and much larger gravitational attractor.

## How the Sun Works

THE SUN DOES NOT HAVE a surface, in the true sense of the word, as it is a huge ball of gas. To qualify the term 'gas' more precisely, we should be talking about ions, atoms that have been stripped of their electrons. This state of aggregation is called plasma. The solar radius is measured from the center of its core to the outer limit of the photosphere. The photosphere is a relatively thin layer in which the sun converts some of its energy to emit it as visible light. It is hot, about 6,000 degrees Kelvin. The particle density is very low. The 'air' has about one third of a percent of the particle density of the Earth atmosphere at sea level.

It took a very long time before mankind found out how the sun generates energy. In ancient times the sun was pictured as a huge burning ball. William Thomson, later known as Lord Kelvin of Kelvin temperature scale fame, used thermodynamics in the 19th century to explain the situation. Assuming that the sun is a ball of gas and plasma that is contracting very slowly and cooling down in the process, one can calculate the radiation intensity in terms of converting gravitational energy. However, in this framework, it turns out that the sun could not be older than 20 million years—while Charles Darwin had already assigned sediments an age of more than 300 million years. In 1904, after the discovery of nuclear fission, Ernest Rutherford suggested fission as an explanation. It took until the 1930s for physicists to understand that the conditions inside the sun would also enable the fusion of hydrogen nuclei.

Radioactivity, part of school curricula today, was hard to accept at the time as it embodied the medieval alchemistic concept of converting one element into another. Nuclear fusion of protons is like using hydrogen nuclei as Lego blocks to construct a helium kernel, with enough excess energy emitted to drive a power plant on a solar scale. However, a pair of hydrogen nuclei are both positively charged and repel each other, thus requiring extremely high temperature and pressure to push them close enough for nuclear fusion to occur. On Earth this is an elusive phenomenon that physicists have only been able to trigger for very short periods of time, despite the highly attractive promise of clean nuclear energy from a working fusion reactor. In the kernel of the sun all the necessary conditions are met, since the molecular cloud had pulled together sufficiently about five billion years ago.

Ever since ignition at that time, the reaction has been running smoothly and that is not set to change for the foreseeable future. That is, until the sun runs out of fuel. So far the sun has converted an amount of hydrogen around 14,000 times the mass of Earth into helium, liberating 90 times the mass of Earth as pure energy. Every single second, our star supplies more energy than one would obtain by running all the nuclear power stations that were online in 2011 for 750,000 years. Every square meter on

Earth receives 1.36 kilowatts—to obtain the same effect it would be necessary to set up an electrical heater over each square meter of the Earth.

## The Solar Core

THE CORE of the sun occupies the inner quarter of its diameter. It has a density of 150 grams per cubic centimeter—more than thirteen times higher than the density of lead with its 11.3 grams per cubic centimeter. A sugar cube of core solar matter would weigh 150 grams and a 10-liter bucket (1.5 metric tons) would need a crane to hoist.

The temperature at the innermost area of the sun is around 15.6 million Kelvin, with pressure at 200 billion atmospheres. Compression of the pyramid of Cheops into the head of a pin would require a similar pressure. The solar core rotates somewhat faster than the exterior regions and the area capable of sustaining nuclear fusion defines its extent.

Approximately 99 percent of the solar energy is derived from the fusion of two hydrogen protons to a deuterium core in a first step. Adding a third proton yields a light helium nucleus that in turn has four possible ways to add a fourth proton and thus become a 'real' helium nucleus—also known as an alpha particle.

A second process, the Bethe-Weizsäcker cycle—also known as the CNO cycle—requires carbon, nitrogen, and oxygen cores as catalysts to fuse 4 protons into a single helium nucleus. This process yields another 0.8 percent of solar energy. Either way, helium is always the result.

The solar core hosts $10^{38}$ such reactions per second, that is a 1 followed by 38 zeroes, or 100,000,000,000,000,000,000,000,000,000,000,000,000 reactions every second! The sun is a busy alchemist. It converts 600 million tons of hydrogen into helium every second. During the conversion 0.7% of the mass is converted to pure energy, reducing the solar mass by 4 billion metric tons every second. The incredible amount of fuel still present in the sun prevents us from noticing this consumption as shrinkage of the sun.

In spite of all these huge numbers, the amount of energy generated per unit volume is surprisingly low. A hot plate would generate more heat: 276 watts per cubic meter puts the sun in a league with the metabolism of a reptile. Packing $10^{28}$ crocodiles in a sphere of the diameter of the sun and shooting it into the sky would generate a comparable amount of heat.

Of course, Earth has far too few crocodiles and the huge herd would need to be fed somehow… This highly absurd comparison is only to point out the size of the sun, rather than its energy density, as the driving factor in its energy production.

The sun has solved a problem that hopeful designers of fusion power stations on Earth are still busy working on—how to keep the reaction stable. Inside the sun things are simple. If the reaction rate happens to rise, the energy surplus causes the core to expand. That reduces the concentration of protons, which in turn slows down the reaction rate—and less energy is produced, meaning the core will shrink in short order. The sun is self-stabilizing in a way that human engineers have yet to master.

## The Outer Layers

---

SHOULD the fusion chain-reaction in the core ever come to a standstill—which is physically impossible at this point—we would not notice for 10,000 years, the minimum time it takes for energy from the core to reach the solar surface.

Initially it needs to traverse the part of the sun called the radiative zone. The majority of the energy here travels in the form of soft x-ray photons. These photons will be deflected by particles in the plasma rather quickly, time and again, driving the overall length of their trajectory to more than ten thousand light-years.

On the outer rim of the radiative zone, at around 70 percent of the solar radius, density has dropped to 0.2 grams per cubic centimeter, which is about one fifth of the density of water. From here outward, heat is primarily transmitted by convection, much like what happens when heating a pot of water. Hot material rises from below, cools down, and sinks back to the bottom. This layer of the sun is called the convective zone.

The tachocline is the thin transition layer between the radiative and the convective zone. The solar core rotates below it much like a solid body would. The outside of the sun rotates at speeds that vary with latitude. While the rotational period at the solar equator is 25.4 days it reaches 36 days near the solar North Pole. The tachocline sandwiches between these two layers. It induces strong magnetic fluctuations through the relative movement of two independent fields, like a dynamo. It is believed that this makes the tachocline the source for the strong magnetic field of the sun.

Inside the convective zone the temperature keeps dropping. An increasing share of atoms own their electrons so they are not ionized. Its outer border is the photosphere, several hundred kilometers thick and about 5,500 degrees.

At this layer the density of solar matter has dropped sufficiently for emitted photons to mostly penetrate the photosphere on a direct path that leads some to hit Earth about 8 minutes later. The ease of photon transition is mainly due to the scarcity of negatively-charged hydrogen ions. These would love to eject an electron the moment they can catch a photon to start the helium-building process. Not surprisingly, the light we see from the sun is created in the reverse process of electrons reacting with protons to form negatively-charged hydrogen ions.

## Hot Atmosphere

ABOVE THE PHOTOSPHERE there are various layers of the solar atmosphere. The coolest area is located directly above the photosphere. In its coldest areas temperatures reach 3,900 degrees, which is sufficiently cool for simple molecules to form. While temperature drops with altitude in our atmosphere on Earth, things are different for the sun. After this minimum-temperature layer comes the chromosphere, a layer of about 2,000 kilometers where the temperature rises to about 20,000 degrees. And there is more: In the following transition layer, about 200 kilometers thick, temperatures rise rapidly up to about one million degrees.

This is the beginning of the solar corona, which you can see very nicely with the naked eye during a solar eclipse. It reaches far out into space and gradually transitions into solar winds. Its hottest spots are hotter, at up to 20 million degrees, than the solar core itself.

Particle density however is rather low. Even the lower layers of the atmosphere don't have more than about $10^7$ particles per cubic meter. This is about one billionth of the normal pressure of the Earth atmosphere.

## Sunspots and Solar Tsunamis

BACK IN 1610, Galileo Galilei observed odd spots on the surface of the sun with a telescope. These spots moved with the rotation of the sun, and quickly led him to conclude that the sun had to be a sphere. The incongruous rotation of the inner core and the outer solar layers generates the spots, which are about 1,500 degrees cooler than their surroundings.

In physics we have learned that electrical charge in motion creates (induces) a magnetic field. The differing rotational speeds ensure that these magnetic fields change all the time, distorting and even changing their directions every 11 years. Try twisting a square rubber band a few times about its axis and you will quickly get something incredibly squiggly. Magnetic fields inside the sun suffer a similar external influence, and their twisting and turning impedes the flow of gas from the inside out, and the flow of heat, too. This makes the solar surface cool down where magnetic fields point away from the sun.

The cooler plasma affects the sunspot shape. Sunspots usually appear in pairs, since the magnetic field must turn back into the sun somewhere to close the loop, and a sunspot forms there, too. Often there are groups of spots that merge and grow into surface areas larger than an equatorial slice of Earth. Half of the sunspots disappear within two days, but some sunspots can survive for several months. Only ten percent of sunspots get older than 11 days. The number of emerging sunspots changes in the 11-year cycle, which may be part of a larger cycle of several hundred years. The current estimate is about 400 years. Times of lower sunspot activity also see the sun radiating up to one tenth of a percent less energy. Such change could trigger a minor 'ice age' on Earth.

Flares are another type of solar activity that impacts our planet. They are created when neighboring field lines of opposite polarity suddenly combine. This is similar to sticking two permanent magnets together and sliding them against each other. At first you will notice an opposing force. Slide far enough and suddenly things snap into a new stable position. This sudden realignment is what happens to the magnetic field lines in the sun, especially in times of high sunspot activity.

The snap realignment ejects large amounts of solar matter into space with speeds of up to 1,000 kilometers per second. The outbreak, also called a protuberance or coronal mass ejection, can interfere with artificial satellites and create more plentiful polar lights on Earth.

Protuberances can also follow magnetic fields that form a loop or an arc outside the solar surface. Such protuberances can remain stable for several months.

## Hearing the Sun?

WHEN WATER BOILS in a pot you can hear the activity quite well. The sound reaching your ear is created by pressure variations of the currents (called convection) that reach the surface. The same happens on the sun, the sun being a much larger pot, of course. The currents are slower relative to the size of the container, and the resulting sound is in the very low frequency band between two and seven millihertz. Humans can't hear sound below about 16 hertz.

## Solar Problems

THE SUN DOESN'T JUST KEEP us alive, it also helps science with difficult questions. Once the solar function had been understood well enough, scientists were interested in verifying certain aspects of their new theories. One project was proposed to investigate the neutrino, a particle that rarely interacts with other matter, and is electrically neutral.

It turned out that Earth only received about a third of the neutrino count that was anticipated. So were the theories wrong? Eventually the neutrino revealed itself to be more flexible than expected. On their way to Earth some of these particles changed form and morphed into tau or muon neutrinos from the original electron neutrino. It turns out detectors for electron neutrinos simply missed the other types.

The high temperatures in the corona present a second issue—to date, no widely accepted model is able to explain them. Initially it was believed that sound, gravitational, or magnetic waves out of the convective zone were responsible for heating the corona, much like a microwave heats up soup. Closer inspection revealed that such radiation would dissipate in the solar material well before reaching the corona. Currently, flares are suspected to contribute to the heating of the corona.

A third problem is related to the construction described in *Silent Sun.* Theoretically, based on current models of stellar development, the sun would have produced much less energy in its youth, between 3.8 and 2.5 billion years ago. The assumption is that energy output was about 25 percent lower than today for a much cooler surface temperature on Earth that would not have been favorable to the development of life. In spite of much less solar energy, the Earth at the time was about as warm as today —paleontologists know that from their discoveries. The sun would not have been strong enough to warm the oceans above the freezing point of water, quite unfavorable conditions for the initial development of life on Earth. Models could be false, of course. Yet they have been confirmed many times for other stars.

Or was it the fault of the atmosphere on Earth? Certain types of gas could have helped heat up the planet. Global warming to the rescue? Which theory fits history best is hard to determine. Mankind only started recording the atmospheric composition very recently. Ice drilling in the Antarctic does not yet yield information for the relevant time. A team from the University of Washington published an article in *Nature* with a clever idea to obtain more information. The scientists investigated a ubiquitous and age-old phenomenon—drops of rain. Rain falling millions of years ago left traces that can be investigated today.

In Earth's atmosphere, raindrops have a maximum size. That is because aerodynamics shreds larger drops once surface tension and internal hydrostatic forces are overcome. These effects have not changed over time—

drops of rain have a maximum diameter of 6.8 millimeters to this day. The energy they impart to the ground on impact depends on their size and terminal speed. The latter is a measure for the density of the atmosphere, and that is where it got interesting for the scientists. Depending on the energy dissipated on impact, and the characteristics of the ground, raindrops have left traces of varying sizes. Those traces can be measured. Combined with information about the material carrying the traces, one can work out the speed of the drops and the density of the atmosphere from there.

The scientists were able to show that atmospheric pressure 2.7 billion years ago was not significantly different from the conditions today. While that doesn't solve the riddles posed by the young sun, it does exclude a few potential solutions, particularly the involvement of some greenhouse gases. Their presence would imply higher atmospheric density. This leaves only the particularly efficient and simple greenhouse gases like methane, ethane, or carbonyl sulfide that could have been liberated by volcanic eruptions.

Theoretically... it could also have been a gigantic construction encouraging higher solar output, like I have described in *Silent Sun*.

## The Birth of the Sun

THE VERY FIRST STARS, which were formed after the Big Bang, constitute the so-called 'Population III stars.' They didn't contain any of the heavier elements and all have been extinct for a very long time. Their remains were the basis of Population II stars, all older than 6 billion years, and usually found in the rims of galaxies. And *their* remains have turned into Population I stars like our sun.

Apparently a gigantic star had to be extinguished in a supernova event to form our solar system.

The oldest traces of matter that have been found in extra-terrestrial matter are 4.582 billion years old. That must be the age of our solar system. Despite no living witnesses being left from that time, scientists have been able to come up with a surprising number of details about the early history of the solar system. Three sources of information that supplement each other are the basis of most of these findings:

1. *Today's properties of the solar system.* There are a number of things that have been noted since

the first scientific observations of the night sky. Planets all orbit the sun in the same direction and pretty much in the same plane. In effect, the solar system forms a disk. Despite the majority of the mass being in the sun, the majority of the momentum is stored in the planets. Inner planets are terrestrial, outer ones gas giants. All these facts, and a few more, indicate that the solar system was formed out of a rotating cloud of gas. This cloud began to contract under its own weight for a certain reason—more on this later. Approximately 99 percent of its mass formed the center, the sun, while the rest was spread out as the planets and other bodies in the solar system.

2. *Existing celestial objects that display properties similar to the molecular cloud that eventually formed the sun.* The Orion Nebula, visible to the naked eye as part of the sword of Orion, is the most salient example. It is an area of around 30 light-years in diameter that contains a cluster of stars that are only about a million years old. The gas cloud forming the sun was probably quite a bit larger at 65 light-years. The Hubble telescope has identified proto-planetary disks in the Orion Nebula. These are a few hundred astronomical units large and relatively cool— just as science pictures the young solar system before nuclear fusion was ignited in the sun. In that arena the sun was a so-called T-Tauri star, an object that radiates energy liberated by gravitational contraction.

3. *Petrified witnesses—the material forming meteorites, especially its molecular composition.* Analysis of

meteoric fragments has already served to determine the approximate age of the solar system. And these messengers from outer space offer yet more fascinating clues. An article published in the *Annals of the National Academy of Sciences* investigates the distribution of certain heavy radioactive isotopes including Niobium-92, Iodine-129, Samarium-146, and Hafnium-182, which have half-lives in the range of millions of years. These must have been present in the early days of the solar system, in larger quantity, of course. Finding out how these elements might have formed provides another piece of the puzzle. The authors of this paper manage to show that a core collapse (hydrodynamic) supernova explains the distribution of nuclides, while other supernova types do not. In this type of supernova a star collapses under its own weight because the fuel in its core has been exhausted, eliminating the opposing pressure from inside. This process requires a star of 8 to 25 times the solar mass. The specific distribution of the nuclides also tells us that a minimum of 10 million years had passed between the supernova event and the formation of the solar system. The scientists deduced that, for the cloud to have existed so long, it must have been surprisingly massive. Cosmology does actually suppose that approximately 1,000 to 10,000 other stars with a total mass of 3,000 solar masses were formed in the same period of time and in an area of approximately 20 light-years diameter around the solar position at the time. That wild group of new stars then disappeared about 100 to 500 million years later.

The process leading to the formation of a star is more or less the same in all cases. The result however depends on the starting conditions. Around 4.6 billion years ago there was a huge molecular cloud—an aggregation of interplanetary gas in non-ionized form—in the area that would form our sun.

This original cloud must have been spread over many light-years, and it probably gave birth to many other stars besides our sun. It consisted mainly of hydrogen, helium, and some traces of heavier elements. However it bore no resemblance to clouds as we know them on Earth. Its density was very low at around 10,000 atoms per cubic centimeter—our planetary atmosphere is many trillion times more dense. And this cloud was incredibly cold, between minus 250 and 260 degrees Celsius.

The enormous size of the cloud meant there was still an incredible amount of matter assembled in this part of space—several thousand solar masses according to scientific estimates. Matter was not distributed evenly within the cloud. Inhomogeneities—essentially, lumps of slightly higher density—ended up attracting more matter through gravitation, a process that might have been accelerated by the shockwave of a nearby supernova. One of these huge lumps would be the birthplace of our sun.

The individual particles inside the lump moved in a random way, but the cloud had a distinct rotation overall at that time. Just like ice skaters speed up their pirouettes by pulling in their arms, the gravitational shrinkage accelerated the rotation of the cloud. This in turn favored the transition from a cloud toward a disk. Particles in the plane of rotation weren't just attracted by gravitation, but also accelerated outward by centrifugal forces. Particles above and below the plane of rotation had a higher force of attraction toward the disk, eventually flattening out the disk. At this point the disk had an extension of about 200 astronomical units—200 times the distance between Earth and the sun.

The particles kept accelerating as the disk began to collapse. Their kinetic energy, or energy of movement, increased accordingly and turned into heat. This also increased the likelihood of collisions between particles. The center of the disk had more collisions and heated up faster than the rim, reaching up to ten million Kelvin in the core, which contained 99.8 percent of the total mass. Eventually heat and density were sufficient to trigger the fusion reaction. Hydrogen nuclei combined into helium nuclei and released energy. The proto-star, which we know today as the sun, had self-ignited. It is our fortune that its mass was sufficient for ignition and, at the same time, small enough to avoid becoming a short-lived giant star.

The heat generated by nuclear fusion slowed the contraction of the disk. After about 50 million years, equilibrium would have been reached between the gravitational attraction of the star and the opposing pressure of radiation outward from the core. A stable star had been formed.

IT IS likely that our sun had a sibling when it came into existence—astronomers have been assuming this for some time. The unknown twin even has a name, Nemesis, as its gravity has been held responsible for sending a giant meteorite on a collision course with Earth, eliminating dinosaurs.

Nemesis has yet to be discovered. This is strange, as

evidence is accumulating that stars are generally born in pairs. A paper in the *Notices of the Royal Astronomic Society* argues the case based upon observation of several very young stellar systems in the Perseus Molecular Cloud, 600 light-years away from Earth. The stellar distribution found there can only be explained using a mathematical model based on star births in pairs.

The twins start out at a good distance from each other, about 500 astronomical units, or about 17 times the distance from the sun to Neptune. It takes a few million years for the system to decide on their fate—either the twins move closer or they go their separate ways.

The latter seem to have occurred in our solar system, like it does in about 60 percent of systems. Nemesis at some point must have gone on a journey to mingle with the other stars of the universe so that we can no longer identify it. The theory must be tested on further molecular clouds, of course.

## The Future of the Sun

LIKE THE REST of the universe, our central star is aging. However its radiation intensity does not diminish. It is in fact increasing. This phenomenon will lead to an average temperature of 30 degrees Celsius on Earth in about 900 million years, independent of global warming. A construction like the one described in *Silent Sun* could be useful in a few hundred million years to tone down the solar activity.

A billion years later the oceans will be boiling, once the average temperature exceeds 100 degrees.

The beginning of the end comes in 4.8 billion years—hydrogen in the solar core will be exhausted. From then on, nuclear fusion will primarily take place in the outer layers of the sun.

The core temperature will drop for lack of energy release, and it will begin to shrink as a consequence of the missing radiation pressure. In the outer layers the temperature will rise, and the rate of reaction will rise alongside, while the sun will bloat and its spectrum will shift toward the red.

Things won't become critical until the sun has reached an age of about 11 billion years. At that point, the brightness and diameter of the sun will rise relatively rapidly to reach 2300 times today's value. Mercury and Venus will be part of the sun, now a red giant. It is unclear how strongly Earth will be affected. Life, of course, will have become impossible. As a red giant, the sun will lose mass far more quickly than today, and planets will loosen their orbits accordingly because the sun's gravitational attraction will be diminishing.

The core temperature will drop continuously while the core is being compressed under the weight of the sun. The outside universe won't notice much until core density has reached values that permit nuclear fusion of helium to carbon. That process will ignite with a gigantic flash of light, ten billion times the usual intensity. This will alert all our extraterrestrial neighbors, as the brightness will—for a few seconds—equal the combined total brightness of a tenth of all the stars in the Milky Way. Following ignition the red giant will shrink to about one tenth today's size, while shining fifty times brighter than today as it continues to burn the helium in its core.

This source of energy will in turn be consumed, initiating a new round in the stellar aging process quite similar to the hydrogen-fusion cycle. The sun will grow into a giant once again, and will alternate in unstable phases, growing and shrinking several times, more or less within the limits of Earth's current orbit. Earth itself will probably avoid being swallowed due to its orbit having loosened in the previous cycle.

At the end of this phase, the sun will be 12.45 billion years old, and the remainder of the outer shell will have been lost. The remaining core, a white dwarf, will start out at around 100,000 degrees and will be about the size of Earth. It will consist mainly of incredibly dense carbon and oxygen (this material in the size of a sugar cube would weigh a metric ton) and will no longer generate any energy internally. The sun will start cooling rapidly at this stage, but the cooling will slow down so that the remaining heat will radiate for several billion years before the sun will burn out completely as a black dwarf.

It is pretty certain the sun will no longer exist in about ten billion years. Astronomers are, of course, thinking even further. They wonder what will become of our star after that. Nine out of ten stars leave a planetary nebula as they change from red giant to white dwarf. Such massive, luminous clouds of interstellar gas and dust can contain up to half the mass of the erstwhile star and remain visible for about 10,000 years while the core is hot enough to illuminate it from the inside. So far the sun has been thought to be too lightweight to leave such a memorial in space, twice the solar mass being the currently accepted tipping point.

However, in a very recent paper published in 2018 in *Nature Astronomy*, scientists from the University of Manchester revisited this question. They used a new model based on the known data from many stars. This model shows the core heating up three times faster than previously believed after shedding the nebula. This compensation mechanism for the reduced mass of the core puts the sun just within the limits for creating a nebula. If so, our extremely distant descendants can expect to admire a beautiful planetary nebula when they come to pay burnt-out Earth a visit.

BONUS: If you register at

hard-sf.com/subscribe/

you will be notified of any new Hard Science Fiction titles. In addition you will receive the **color PDF version** of The Sun – A Guided Tour which contains a number of impressive illustrations.

## Glossary of Acronyms

AI – Artificial Intelligence

AU – Astronomical Unit

CME – Coronal Mass Ejection

CNO – Carbon, Nitrogen, Oxygen

DFD – Direct Fusion Drive

DKIST – Daniel K. Inouye Solar Telescope

EVA – ExtraVehicular Activity

JPL – Jet Propulsion Laboratory

LCVG – Liquid Cooling and Ventilation Garment

MLBF – Mean Life Between Failures

NASA – National Aeronautics and Space Administration

Pan-STARRS – Panoramic Survey Telescope And Rapid Response System

UNSC – United Nations Security Council

VM – Virtual Machine

## Metric to English Conversions

It is assumed that by the time the events of this novel take place, the United States will have joined the rest of the world and will be using the International System of Units, the modern form of the metric system.

Length:
centimeter = 0.39 inches
meter = 1.09 yards, or 3.28 feet
kilometer = 1093.61 yards, or 0.62 miles

Area:
square centimeter = 0.16 square inches
square meter = 1.20 square yards
square kilometer = 0.39 square miles

Weight:
gram = 0.04 ounces
kilogram = 35.27 ounces, or 2.20 pounds

Volume:

liter = 1.06 quarts, or 0.26 gallons
cubic meter = 35.31 cubic feet, or 1.31 cubic yards

Temperature:
To convert Celsius to Fahrenheit, multiply by 1.8 and then add 32
To convert Kelvin to Celsius, subtract 273.15

## Excerpt: The Rift

### April 30, 2085, Ceres

"PREPARE FOR IMPACT."

M6 groaned. The warning was almost too late. He had just enough time to bend his knees and press his body against the ground. Almost immediately his seismic sensors detected the force of the impact. The meteorite had barely missed him. About 100 meters to the north there must be a new crater. This was his chance!

M6 forcefully straightened four of his six knees, giving himself momentum that immediately lifted him off the ground. His legs had been pointing toward the south, so he sailed north through space, just above the surface of the dwarf planet. It wasn't long until he saw the new crater. In order to analyze its composition, M6 shot his laser into the dust cloud that had formed above the crater. At the same time, he logged the crater's structure and measured the temperatures inside it. His positioning jets fired to bring him even closer to the action.

The impact had almost cost him his life. The meteorite

had come in on a very flat trajectory and, due to Ceres's fast rotation, it had stayed hidden from his instruments for too long, like a cannonball that had been fired just before its target came around a corner. But now that he'd survived the event... it had saved him some work. The meteorite had drilled directly into the side of Ahuna Mons, Ceres's sole cryovolcano. M6 had been planning to drill into the four-kilometer-high mountain starting in the morning, and now the meteorite had laid open its icy interior.

What M6 saw before him was fascinating. As if in slow motion, material was flowing into the crater from above, while the lower crater edge was collapsing. The impact hole looked like a strange, giant mouth, with secretions running out of its nose and over the upper lip, its lower lip drooping sadly. The spectral analysis of the cloud showed that its composition was a mixture of various salts with ammonia and water ice.

The energy of the impact had vaporized part of the mountain's face and melted the rest. Solar radiation striking the crater's edge was keeping it warmer and thus viscous, while the dark interior of the crater quickly solidified again. M6 recorded everything. In a few weeks, when he contacted Earth again, he would send a summary of his findings for analysis by the scientists at the RB Group. They would probably be overjoyed at all the progress he had made.

*Thanks, killer meteorite,* he thought. Then he carefully moved each of his joints. Ceres didn't have any atmosphere, but he was still standing in the middle of a dust cloud from the impact. Small particles could get into any of the three joints on each of his six legs, thus making him unable to move. That was his worst nightmare, even though he had ways to fix those problems. He hoped that all he would need to do would be to heat up the affected parts of his body from the inside and melt away the interfering particles.

His body had a radial-symmetric design and was suspended between his six legs by way of flexible joints. M6 had never seen himself from outside his body, but an engineer had once told him that he looked like a giant spider. The comparison didn't bother him. All that was important to him was that his body was practical and durable. He got energy from a small atomic battery, and from solar panels on his top side, which looked like giant faceted eyes due to the numerous lenses spread out over the panels. His actual visual organs were situated in the interior of his hard shell. They were sensitive to the whole spectrum from the infrared to the gamma range.

M6 always had a lot of questions. They would come up in his mind whenever he came across one of Ceres's secrets. Every answer formed the seed for a new question. He didn't even need the questions that the scientists back on Earth sent him, he had plenty of his own. But there was one question he never asked himself: *What is the reason for my existence?* Wasn't it enough that he was here and looking for answers?

M6 didn't want any other life. But a nagging fear lurked in the back of his mind. *What if there were no more questions? Is that even a real scenario?* He didn't know, and it terrified him. M6 had already calculated how long it would take to fly to another object in the vicinity. Even though the asteroid belt was filled with millions of chunks of rock, a move would not be a simple thing. His propulsion system only gave him enough thrust for powerful jumps, so that he could move around the surface of the dwarf planet and then come back down again. It hadn't been made for long trips through the vacuum of space. The journey would take years—years in which he would have nothing to do.

But that was a theoretical and far-distant future. Right now, it wasn't even clear how this volcano worked. It didn't seem to have anything in common with the glowing-lava-spewing mountains of Io, Venus, or Earth. Understanding Ahuna Mons was the core objective of his current orders. With his frontmost leg, M6 touched the crater's edge, the drooping lower lip. The substratum seemed to already be solid enough. He measured minus 40 degrees on the ground. If it had been pure ice, it would have been hard as stone at that temperature. Only the many impurities made it still flow slowly. Due to Ceres's low gravity, however, it barely moved at all. M6 could advance without fear farther into the chasm created by the meteorite.

As he inched into the darkness, setting one leg carefully in front of another, he examined the walls of the hole. They had obviously been laid in layers that looked to him like annual growth rings. Maybe he could use them to figure out the true age of the volcano. All that was known before was that, despite its enormous height, it couldn't be more than about 1,000,000 years old—otherwise it would have had more craters like this one. The individual layers were each approximately 20 to 30 centimeters thick. Their composition was measurably different. They were separated by thin layers of a silicate-like material. M6 scraped off a sample and inserted it into the analyzer located in his abdominal section. The material of the separating layer was identical to the regolith dust that formed a thin layer covering all of Ceres. M6 already sensed new questions forming in his mind. If he analyzed enough layers, he could compile a chronology of the conditions on Ceres in the last thousands of years, much like biologists on Earth determined the earth's climate from analyzing tree trunks.

Would the scientists of the RB Group be as interested as he was to have this glimpse into the past? Not all of the questions that he raised were equally well-received by his bosses. Ceres was one of the celestial bodies that the United Nations had declared off-limits for asteroid mining. Only scientific research missions like his were allowed here. But naturally the RB Group hoped that this restriction would be lifted at some point. If Ceres offered important resources for humankind's development, its status as a protected area might be reconsidered, and then the RB Group would be the first on site.

M6 scraped another sample of the separating layer farther toward the interior and analyzed it. Its content of radioactive elements showed that it must be at least a thousand years older than the first sample. How far into the past would the crater let him go?

M6 carefully scrambled farther into the hole. He always kept two legs anchored in the ice, two supporting him at the front, and the third pair tested the subsurface before he shifted his weight. He was making good progress. The laser scanner revealed that the meteorite had buried itself approximately 100 meters deep.

Just at that moment his two rear legs suddenly broke through the layer of ice. M6 couldn't react quickly enough. His weight pulled him backward, his front legs losing contact. The top of the hole was too far away for him to reach. The rear part of his body came to rest against the ice. M6 felt the cold. He was upset with himself. He shouldn't have allowed this to happen! But he didn't panic. Very calmly he analyzed the situation. His two rear legs had sunk deep into the ice. He didn't have enough space to move his joints and maneuver so that he could pull his legs out from the ice again. Only the joints were heatable, not the legs themselves, so he also couldn't free them by melting the ice around them. It was clear what he had to do. He would have to give up those two legs. Following a signal from his mind, the uppermost joint in each of his rear legs separated into two parts, so that the other four legs could now lift his body.

The damage was minimal. The only thing he regretted was that he would have to abandon exploring the crater for now, because he needed all six legs to do that. That was why he was most upset with himself. With the help of the nanofabricators in his body he would be able to manufacture new legs. Maybe his bosses would even have a better design for him to implement now. First, however, he would have to obtain the necessary materials. The nanofabricators could assemble any design he gave them, but they would need the right raw materials for the job—in this case, metals. And he already knew where to look. He remembered seeing white spots in the Occator crater two years ago, during his approach to Ceres.

## May 14, 2085, Pomona, Kansas

"Dad, can I use the truck tonight?"

Derek McMaster looked up. His daughter's voice carried down from the second floor through the thin wooden walls into the hallway. He was surprised. She was usually still sleeping at this time of day. She had probably been waiting for signs of life from below.

"Shouldn't be a problem. When do you need it?" he asked loudly.

"Seven would be good."

"I'll be back by five. Your mother's cooking dinner. It'd be nice if we could all eat together."

Elizabeth had been home for three days, but they had barely seen her. Either she was squirreled away in her room, supposedly studying, or she was hanging out with friends from earlier years, which is what she was probably planning on doing again tonight. Tomorrow she'd prob-ably be back at her studying.

"OK, that should work," she answered.

"See you later then," Derek shouted. He opened the front door, stepped out, and closed it behind himself.

The wooden boards of the porch creaked under his leather boots. It was a good feeling knowing their grown daughter was back at home for a while. He looked out at the garage with its open door. He could see the dollhouse that she used to play with sitting in the corner. At some point, he must have moved it in there.

Derek pulled his coat tighter around himself. The air was still crisp and chilly. He loved the morning hours. It used to be that a mist had always hung over the fields when he went out in his truck to inspect the crops. But it was too dry for that now—mist only appeared in the winter anymore. The weather report had said it would reach around 86 degrees this afternoon. His daughter would ask him what he meant by that number. She had grown up using the new units of measurement, but he was always slipping back into Fahrenheit and miles. *Thirty. Always will sound cold to me,* he thought.

The truck was already out of the garage, next to the porch. Its front was splattered with mud. The mud hadn't been there when he had gotten out of the truck yesterday. It had to have been his daughter's doing. She had borrowed the truck last night too. But how had she managed to get mud on it? The last rains had been almost three months ago! Derek rubbed the splotches of splattered mud. They were already dry, and crumbled under his fingers. *It doesn't matter,* he thought, *the main thing is she was having fun.* That wasn't so easy in this godforsaken area. That was one reason she had gone to Kansas City for her studies.

Derek opened the door of his truck and climbed into the driver's seat. He sank deeply into the soft cushioning. It smelled like cigarette smoke. His daughter didn't smoke, so she must've had somebody else with her. *Does she have a new boyfriend?* But that wasn't really any of his business. He sighed and reached for the key. It was usually left in the ignition, but this time his fingers found nothing but air. *Didn't I tell her she should just leave the key in the ignition?* Now he'd have to go back inside.

But first Derek checked the glove compartment. There was the key, right next to the gun that he always kept there for nostalgic reasons. He stuck the key in the ignition, put his foot on the brake pedal, and turned the key. The motor started humming softly. His truck was powered by hydrogen. Out here that was much more reliable than a purely electric vehicle because every little tornado inevitably knocked down power lines somewhere. For 30 years, the county had been requesting for the state to run the power lines underground, but that was much too expensive for all these remote, scattered homesteads. Derek had chosen to have an extra hydrogen tank installed at his house so he could be energy independent, and he only needed a fuel truck to visit him once a month to fill up the tank.

He drove slowly down the access road to Colorado Road. His access road wasn't paved, so the truck kicked up a dust cloud. His wife used to give him an earful about paving the long access road, but she had been silent about it ever since it had stopped raining as much. He didn't know whether her silence was because she no longer had to bicycle through puddles when she went to visit her friends, or because she had noticed the farm's severely shrunken earnings. They didn't talk to each other much anymore. After his strenuous work in the fields, Derek needed his rest.

Just before the intersection with Colorado Road, he stopped the truck and got out. On the left there was a small pond. For many years it had helped to irrigate the fields in the summer. Now the pond was almost dried up. Derek rubbed his temples. There'd been no miracles overnight. The bottom of the pond was still covered by maybe a foot of water. The remains of a dock poked out of the mud. The reeds along the shoreline were all dried up. Ten years ago, he and his daughter had played with a remote-controlled toy boat that she had wished for, right here on this pond. And his wife had always been afraid that their daughter would drown. But that wasn't a risk anymore. *Fucking climate change*, he thought, and then got mad at himself because he hadn't ever accepted it as real. Somehow he still hoped that after seven dry summers, a hot and wet one would finally happen again, like before. Three presidents in a row had promised him it would happen. Now he didn't believe anyone anymore.

Derek grabbed the door of his truck, opened it, and climbed back in. He turned right on Colorado Road. It was narrow, so he used both lanes. Nobody else drove along here anyway. The neighbors' farmlands had been taken over by the banks and big corporations a few years ago. He wondered if they were happy in the city. He'd never heard anything from any of them again, even though they had been something like friends before. Derek drove on the narrow, straight road. The land was flat and seemed to go on forever. Derek was happy that he had to keep an eye out for potholes and drive around them—it gave him some distraction. After two miles there were a few trees on the right. In passing he spied the Mulligans' old truck, slowly rusting in front of his eyes, and the wooden house, half in ruins, where they had lived.

Beyond the small gathering of trees there was a narrow

bridge across the Appanoose Creek. Derek stopped right in the middle of the bridge. The creek bed was also all dried up. Derek sighed. The grass right along the creek's edge was still green, but the cornfield that he had been putting a lot of hope in for this season was not receiving any of the moisture. He climbed out and walked to the edge of the field. He looked back at his truck. Nobody could get past his truck on the bridge, but it didn't matter. He was standing on his own land. If someone wanted something from him, they'd have to wait.

Slowly Derek walked into the cornfield, being careful not to step on the young plants. They were only half as tall as they should have been. He bent over and checked their leaves. They cracked and tore under his fingers. There was nothing more he could do.

Derek dragged his index and middle fingers over the ground. It was hard and cracked. The earth had become an old man. He dug somewhat deeper with his hand and the clayish soil crumbled between his fingers. It looked terrible. The topmost layer had been damaged by the heat. He took another step, two steps, three, but the soil was just as bad there too. A long crack ran through the topsoil, as if the world were slowly opening up to devour all of its inhabitants. His fields were in bad shape. He wouldn't be able to pay for his daughter's studies anymore. How was he supposed to tell her that?

Derek walked farther into the field. Now there was no point trying to walk carefully around the plants. It didn't matter. He started to run. His breathing got heavy, but nevertheless it felt good because it took his mind off the world around him. He was no longer as fit as he had once been. Maybe he should rejoin the Army? At least they paid him well. He'd made more working for the Army than he earned now, and he'd always been paid on time. But what would he do there at the age of 41? He was well on his way to becoming an old man. If they'd even take him back, they'd just put him in management somewhere, instead of sending him on special assignments like before.

He missed those days. Some of those assignments he still couldn't talk about today, not even to his wife. That had never been a problem, he'd never had much need for talking. Sometimes he asked himself why he and his wife were even still together now that their daughter was out of the house. Was it enough that he drove his wife, who hated to drive, into the city and back for doctors' appointments and she gave him a blow job once a week? But that was probably more contact than some other couples had.

Somewhere behind him he heard honking. Derek stopped, out of breath, and bent forward, his hands on his thighs. He spit on the ground. The soil greedily sucked up the moisture. He probably wasn't giving his wife enough credit—or himself, for that matter. They had been together for 20 years now, without anyone or anything forcing them to stay together. There must be more there than he realized. Things had simply dried up like the soil in his fields. Secretly he still hoped that it would start raining again and everything would be like before.

There was more honking. Derek turned around. There was a second truck stopped in front of his. Next to the truck he saw a man standing on the road, waving his arms.

"Okay, I'm coming," he yelled. "I'm coming, asshole!"


## May 20, 2085, Ceres

The vista spread out before him far into the distance. M6 was standing at the upper edge of Occator crater. In front of him was a 2000-meter drop. He didn't feel any fear, just respect. He'd be able to manage the downward climb, even with only four legs. He could have flown down to the crater's floor, but his bosses preferred that he study the crater walls on the way down so that he could give them that much more information on the structure of Ceres's crust. That was the only thing they were interested in, ultimately—what worthwhile raw materials were on Ceres, and where were they located? M6 wasn't angry about it— 80 million years ago, a meteorite's impact created a 92-kilometer-wide hole up to 4000 meters deep, now giving him the exciting opportunity to look into the dwarf planet's past. M6 was ready to start. Getting to this spot had not been particularly interesting.

He began the climb down. The crater wall had barely eroded. Ceres had no real atmosphere, so erosion was not to be expected. And yet there was this thin dust layer, everywhere. The lower portion of it had already transformed into solid rock—regolith. It was as if a thousand elephants had marched through here in ages past, compacting the dust into stone. But that was obviously nonsense. It was such a crazy thought that M6 had to ask himself where the image with the elephants could have come from. He had never seen real elephants in his life.

M6 had awakened when the space probe that was carrying him had started its final approach to the dwarf planet. He knew that he wasn't a living creature—he was a machine—but still there were thoughts in his head that seemed to have originated from other people. M6 would have liked to be able to get rid of them. Most of them were unpleasant thoughts, others were, at best, neutral. They made him afraid, apprehensive, bored, annoyed—all negative feelings that didn't even make any sense. He was virtually indestructible and immortal—why should he be afraid of anything? And yet there he was, filled with these emotions as he was about to start his 2000-meter climb down into the crater. He also couldn't understand his builders' motives. He could work much more efficiently if he didn't have to constantly deal with these misguided emotions. The most valuable thing of all had to be efficiency. That was the only thing that appeared useful to him —apart from maybe fun and joy, for which his reward center was responsible.

M6 stopped. He had noticed a black stone that resembled charcoal. He picked it up and slid it into the analyzer. The dark material on the outside was something like charcoal. It was made up of carbon and had the structure of graphite. M6 removed the stone from the analyzer and rubbed it across the ground. It left behind a black streak. He could write! Whatever he wrote on the exposed subsurface would likely remain for millions of years. Nobody would destroy his creation. Of course, nobody would see it either... but that didn't matter. He would know that it was here. M6 designed a fractal in his head. He loved these patterns that repeated indefinitely. Then he transferred the image from his mind onto the stone.

AFTER AN HOUR he had to stop. He wasn't satisfied, because the work wasn't complete. He knew, of course, that a fractal was a figure that couldn't be perfectly reproduced. But wasn't that true for all compositions? At least at the atomic level, the uncertainty principle blurred everything the closer you tried to look at it. How could humans still be passionate about being artists? On the other hand, his search for truth—for the ultimate facts—was also never-ending. Even if he lived forever, he would never be able to answer every question. Nevertheless, he found the search to be fun. Maybe it was somehow similar for human beings and their art. And fun was a positive feeling!

M6 set down the black rock. The bottom of the crater was waiting. Only there could he find the materials that he needed for his replacement legs. Slowly he scrambled downward. Every 100 meters he paused and examined the crater walls. Underneath the layer of dust, he found a hard material that was rich in water ice. Maybe the water that had been melted and evaporated by the impact had then condensed and solidified on the walls. M6 tried to imagine the catastrophe as it had happened at the time. It had occurred long after Ceres had become a sort of dirty ice ball. Then a heavy space-rock had drilled directly into its side, melted the ice, and boiled the water. Was part of the once-liquid ocean still in liquid form inside the crust? Had, perhaps, primitive lifeforms been given some new hope, like when rain fell in the desert? He would have to make particularly careful measurements at the bottom of the crater, especially near the raised mound in the center, where it appeared that material might have risen up and outward from the interior.

But first he needed two new legs. Ceres was keeping the necessary materials ready for him, he just had to pick them up. M6 pointed his telescope toward the bottom of the crater below him. The famous white spots were still approximately 30 kilometers away.

THE DESCENT TOOK another two hours, but the flat area in the crater took only about 50 minutes to cross. He switched to four-leg pacing, which allowed him to move especially efficiently. His legs moved in pairs so that he didn't rise at all. Long periods between points of contact with the ground would slow him down, because then he couldn't accelerate with the force from his joints. When he used all of his energy for pacing, he could accelerate to speeds of at least 300 kilometers per hour. That speed took some time to reach, however, and it also took just as long to slow down again. Thus, this type of movement was only suitable for occasions such as this one, when he wanted to reach a known destination as quickly as possible.

Now there was a white, dream-like landscape spread out in front of him.

M6 was fortunate, because the sun had just appeared over the walls of the crater. It looked like the far-off battlements of a tall castle. White light fell from a black sky onto an enchanted field, where it glittered and gleamed. A thick, pasty mass made from water ice, ammonia, and various salts had long ago been forced up to the surface. The sunlight had dissolved the frozen water, leaving behind the salt crystals. The process had taken a long time—not tens or hundreds of years, but thousands of years—and the crystals had thus had lots of time to grow. That's why they were especially symmetric. At the proper angle, they looked like prisms, splitting the white sunlight into a multitude of rainbows of colors from the spectrum. From other perspectives they looked like cut crystals.

Every salt, every chemical compound, arranged itself in somewhat different crystalline shapes. It appeared as if nature had tried out everything that was possible here, and maybe even a little bit of what had previously been considered impossible. In fact, with the help of his laser spectrometer, M6 quickly found a shiny deposit made from a compound that does not occur naturally on Earth. It had been produced here by the extreme cold, the low pressure, and the influence of cosmic radiation. M6 remained standing so that he could record a panoramic image. He bent over so that he could photograph a crystal pyramid at the perfect angle and stood up on his legs so that he could investigate a deposit that looked like a blossom with wide-open petals.

He felt honored. M6 was the first being that could look at this beautiful scene unfolding all around him. Had it been born from catastrophe? No one would ever know for certain, but it had taken a long time. In the beginning, this had most likely been a salty swamp, but now that he had come, the area finally showed its full beauty. M6 was grateful to his bosses for giving him this experience.

Unfortunately, his arrival was also the beginning of its destruction. First he must dismantle at least some part of the beauty himself to obtain the materials he would need for his new legs. And then the humans would come, because they would see his images. Exotic compounds, created in this unique laboratory of nature—that was what his bosses had been looking for. M6 sighed. He could refuse to transmit the data. He was a free consciousness. He was not bound by orders, he could decide for himself. Psychologists on Earth had decided he should be designed this way, because they had conjectured that other designs might harm his mental health. A being who is not free, and who is also damned to solitude, would not be able to survive in the long run.

He would decide later whether he would send the data to Earth. He would not sacrifice his replacement legs, however. M6 began to dismantle the structures which, according to measurements with his spectrometer, contained the necessary components. He picked up the minerals and placed them in the analyzer in his abdomen. From outside it must have looked like he was eating the rocks. In the analyzer, there were millions of nanofabricators waiting for the minerals. They broke up the material into minuscule pieces, took the pieces apart atom by atom, and then reassembled them again according to his stored design. With the right starting materials, he really could manufacture anything—even new nanofabricators.

That was also one of the big dangers. M6 had done the calculations himself. If he should lose his sanity and reasoning and begin to replicate the nanofabricators over and over again, in a few weeks all of Ceres would have been consumed in the manufacture of new nanofabricators. He would become Ceres itself. M6 found this idea amusing rather than appealing, but he could imagine a simpler mind being attracted to the notion. That was why the nanofabricators had been given an expiration date. Their inventors had adopted the idea from the aging of biological life: the more often the genetic information was replicated, the more often errors occurred. The nanofabricators would become unusable in the 11th generation. That sounded modest, but in reality it meant that two of these tiny universal machines could make 2048 more. And he hadn't only brought two with him, but instead approximately one hundred million. His capabilities for transforming himself were practically unlimited, as long as he didn't become megalomaniacal. He had no plans to do so.

His 'abdomen', the analyzer, wasn't big enough in which to grow new legs, so the nanofabricators had to move the material from there to the location where it was needed. Very slowly, two new legs began growing out from his joints. The entire process took approximately ten hours. M6 didn't have to supervise the entire time. Every fabricator knew what it had to do. Nevertheless, because errors were always possible, every now and then M6 checked whether everything was proceeding as planned. Especially critical were compounds that were nearly identical chemically and barely differed in polar mass. If two were being used in the same project, sometimes the wrong one would be used. And he didn't always notice in time. A few mistakes were completely manageable, however. That had already been taken into account in the design.

M6 partitioned a tiny part of his mind to allow it to continue watching over the growth of the two new legs. With the far larger part of his mind, he admired the incomparable play of light created by the sun setting across the dry salt lake. It was a scene that could not be viewed from anywhere else in the entire solar system.

## May 23, 2085, Ottawa, Kansas

With squealing tires, Derek turned from Main Street onto 13th. His thoughts were all on his fields. Only when his wife put her hand on his knee did he notice that he had almost driven past the hospital. He let the truck slowly roll to a stop. Every two weeks, his wife, Mary, went to see her doctor at Random Memorial Hospital. She did not seem especially sick, but if it made her happy, he would keep bringing her here. Mary had a driver's license, but she refused to drive in the city. In truth, Ottawa was no longer anything more than just a big town. Since the events in the 2070s, the number of residents had dropped below 10,000. It was a miracle that the pride of the community, its university, could keep going. Those who had big plans for their lives tended to move to a real city.

That was the only reason he could see to explain why the hospital had hired a Turkish doctor. 'Akif Atasoy, MD, Diabetologist and Allergist' read a sign on the office door. As always, Derek walked his wife into the waiting room. When Mary had first started going to this doctor, he had been afraid she might be having an affair. He didn't really care if she was, but did it have to be a Turk? He had been part of special missions during the U.S.-Turkish War. Luckily the conflict had only lasted a couple of weeks. Derek looked around. As always, the waiting room was full. Atasoy was a diabetologist, but Mary claimed that she wasn't diabetic, she just suffered from allergies. The Turkish doctor did have additional training in treating allergies. Most of his patients, however, appeared to be here due to diabetes. At least they all looked appropriately obese, Derek had often thought.

He nodded at Mary and left the room. Outside there was a bench in the shade of a large maple tree. He liked to sit there and smoke a cigarette, a real, proper one with tobacco. He might even smoke two today. Sitting in front of the hospital and smoking seemed fitting to him. These institutions were so full of infectious germs that it wasn't even clear who or what they were really built for. So he thought it best to smoke the little buggers out.

"Mr. McMaster?" intoned a masculine voice.

Derek looked around in surprise. Had he overlooked someone he knew in the waiting room?

"Mr. McMaster!"

The door to the doctor's office had opened, and a slim man with short hair and a mustache was walking toward him. He looked like he had a tan. On the street, Derek would have barely recognized him as a Turk, but he had to be, because he then introduced himself.

"Atasoy, Akif. I'm your wife's doctor."

The doctor extended his hand. Derek hesitated for a second, then shook it. He was pleasantly surprised. Atasoy had a warm, strong handshake.

"You always leave so quickly," the doctor said.

"I'd rather sit outside and wait."

"Of course. In this weather, I'd rather sit outside too."

"It doesn't matter what the weather's like to me."

"I see. Can we go into my office for a moment? I'd like to talk to you about your wife's illness."

The doctor motioned toward the open door. Derek shrugged his shoulders and followed the doctor. *Better to get it over with,* he thought. In the movies, after such an invitation, the doctor would tell the frightened husband that his wife only had six months to live. Derek began sweating. That was the movies. Real life was never so dramatic.

The doctor closed the door behind him. Mary was already waiting in the room. The doctor pointed to two chairs in front of his desk as he sat down himself in his chair behind the desk. Mary took a seat in one of the chairs. Derek shook his head.

"I'd rather stand," he said.

"Mr. McMaster," Dr. Atasoy began, "we're making good progress with your wife's strange allergies. I've been doing some extensive testing. The problem with allergies is that there are so many triggers, but for reasons of safety we can only perform a few elimination tests at a time."

Derek took a breath. That didn't sound like Mary was going to die next month. Perhaps the doctor wanted to perform a really expensive test and he was now trying to sell him on it.

"Yeah, I know that from the times I tested new feed on my cows," Derek said. *Now I'm talking nonsense,* he thought. *I haven't had cows for ten years.*

"In the meantime, I've determined that certain wood preservatives might be one of your wife's triggers. She had a very strong reaction to those specific tests. She tells me you live in a wooden house."

*What a statement,* Derek thought. *Who around here doesn't live in a wooden house?*

"Now I'd like to ask you something, and please don't take it as criticism," the doctor continued. "Mary says you renovated your house a couple of years ago. Could you possibly have used any of the substances on this list? They are officially approved, even for indoor use, but the timing would match very well with the onset of your wife's symptoms."

*Of course,* Derek thought, *they'd match just like my fist to your eye. But what good would any of this do? It wasn't like they had another house to move to.*

"I'll have to look," he said. "I think I still have a half-full bucket in the garage."

"That'd be great," the doctor said, "and it would really help us out."

Atasoy glanced at Mary with what Derek thought was a conspiratorial look. 'See, that went well,' is what the look seemed to imply to Derek. *Did he think I wouldn't see that?* Derek was starting to feel angry.

"And what are we supposed to do if one of these is actually in our house? What then?" He spoke with more aggression than he had intended. Atasoy raised an eyebrow.

"Then I would say…"

A loud knock on the office door interrupted him. The person knocking didn't wait for an answer—the door opened immediately. Derek recognized the receptionist, a young Indian woman.

"Doctor Atasoy," she said, "you have to see this. Come quickly."

"Now slow down, Gita, what's the problem? I've asked you before not to simply barge in here," the doctor said.

Creases appeared in Atasoy's forehead. The receptionist looked as if a tornado were racing toward the hospital. Derek wouldn't have been surprised by that, even if it wasn't tornado season right now. The weather and all its unpredictability didn't seem to follow the old farmers' rules anymore. He heard excited shouts from the corridor and the waiting room.

"What's going on?" he asked.

Dr. Atasoy didn't answer. He was no longer in his chair. Mary was sitting there as if she were frozen. Derek tried to give her an encouraging smile. Then he left the room through the open door. Gita, the receptionist, said something behind him, but he couldn't understand her, because everyone out here was shouting over each other. The patients in the waiting room had all pressed themselves against the window. *Something must be happening outside.*

The light streaming in was just as bright as before. *There can't be a bad storm coming.* The people were pressing their faces against the window and pointing upward at something straight above them, where the sun should be. There was no more room at the window, so he simply pushed a skinny, accountant-type guy to the side. The man grumbled a little, but went silent after he had given Derek a mean look. Derek knew that his intimidating stature and red hair made him look like an Irish brawler, and sometimes he deliberately used that to his advantage.

He looked out the window. The sky was shining in the prettiest shade of blue. Why was everyone so worked up? Derek tilted his head back. And then he saw it. He rubbed his eyes because it was so unbelievable. A black stripe ran across the sky. It resembled a giant ribbon blowing in the wind, but was entirely motionless, its jagged edges glowing red. It looked as if the heavens had been slashed, opened up in order to consume all of creation.

Derek was not an active churchgoer. He believed what his mother had taught him and what was in the Bible, but it had all seemed something like a fairy tale before, something that didn't really concern him. He started feeling hot.

Could it be some prophecy was being fulfilled? Would a supernatural being descend to render its last judgment?

Derek reached for his heart with his left hand. It felt like it wanted to jump out of his chest. At least the emergency room wasn't far, he thought. His heart and circulation had always been strong and stable. He turned around. Where was Mary? He didn't see her anywhere. He started to worry and gave up his spot at the window. She wasn't in the corridor and also not in the waiting room. He finally found her in the doctor's office. The doctor, receptionist, and Mary were all standing next to each other, their noses pressed flat against the window. *Of course. The phenomenon stretched across the entire sky—it must be visible from there too.*

Derek came up behind Mary and rested his arms on her shoulders. She flinched, but didn't try to squirm away.

"What is that?" she asked, turning her face to the side.

He looked at her delicate nose and her thin eyelashes. It had been a long time since he had looked at her from such a close distance.

"I have no idea," he answered. "Doctor, do you have any idea what that is?"

The man to his left had been to college, so surely he must know more than the rest of them.

"I've never seen anything like it," Atasoy said.

Derek carefully wedged himself between Mary and the receptionist. His wife was slim, but Gita had a rather full figure. Maybe her wide hips only caught his attention because she was so small. *Five feet, if that,* Derek estimated, then forced himself to do the conversion to meters in his head. *So one-and-a-half meters.* He should really stop using those old units. He leaned with his right hip against the window sill and bumped against an indoor plant. It was green was all he noticed. Plants were only interesting to him if they were in fields.

Then he lifted his gaze back to the sky. The black stripe was still there. It looked like it was rigidly glued to a blue background. No, that wasn't right, it wasn't glued on, it had torn apart the background. That's what it was—a rip. Their world had been torn apart. A shiver ran down his back. He didn't feel afraid. No, it was something more like awe. It was much like the moment when his mother had brought him to church for the very first time and organ music had suddenly filled the gigantic space. The music had seemed to come from everywhere at the same time.

A swelling murmur of many voices jolted him out of his thoughts. People were suddenly pointing up at the sky. Was there some creature descending from above? Derek rubbed his eyes because he couldn't see anything. Then he noticed it, a small, shining arrow. An airplane, at 30,000 feet, he estimated. Derek squinted. A four-engine Boeing, surely a passenger plane. The pilot was headed straight toward the rip. Hadn't he seen it? Derek had a pilot's license himself.

The plane was still far enough away that an evasive maneuver could probably be done without any problem. Why wasn't the pilot turning around? Was the crew asleep, perhaps, and the autopilot clueless? Didn't they see what they were racing toward at 600 miles per hour?

Derek wanted to scream to them and warn them. He made his hands into fists. The airplane's metallic fuselage flashed silver in the sunlight. He imagined the passengers looking out of their windows, maybe feeling sorry for the Kansas farmers because of the vast sea of never-ending brownness. Or maybe they were thinking about their destination, a beach in Florida, the sweetheart they were going to embrace in their arms, or the business partner they were going to rip off. Life is short and can end so suddenly. He opened his fists again.

From his perspective, the airplane was only a few millimeters away from the rip. It was already turning a reddish color. Even if the pilots noticed what was in front of them, it would be too late now. Derek heard the people behind him shouting loudly. Everyone wanted to warn the pilots. Maybe at least some of those on the plane could still be saved with parachutes! But Derek was skeptical. Could anything save them? What would happen to it when it touched the rip? Would it explode, or crash against an invisible wall and then break apart completely? Or would the plane simply pass through it?

The moment came. The nose of the Boeing touched one of the jagged spikes of the black stripe. Gone! It was gone!

DEREK SHOOK HIS HEAD. Why were the people behind him so upset? All at once it became very quiet. He turned around. People were standing in front of the window with open mouths, as if they had forgotten what they were going to say. Had they all gone crazy? Sure, a dark rip had split apart the sky. It was probably the end of the world. That was a feasible theory, Derek decided, until someone thought of something else. But no supernatural creature had descended upon the earth yet. They had been watching the rip and the sky now for several minutes, without anything happening. If that continued, it wouldn't support his theory. If God had decided to start His Last Judgment today, why would He drag it out so long?

Or maybe it had already happened. Maybe the judgment had been rendered long ago and he had ended up in Hell. He had certainly killed enough men as a soldier for that to be a distinct possibility. Hell... what else were his dried-up fields to him? But Mary, no, she wouldn't be here too. Mary was innocent.

BEHIND HIM IT was getting loud again. People were pointing up to the sky. What was there to see? They all knew the rip was there. He craned his neck, but all he saw was glaring bright light. Oh, there was an airplane, approaching from the south. It was small, probably a two-seater, light sport aircraft, but it was flying surprisingly high. Either the pilot hadn't noticed the rip, or he was curious about it and wanted to get a closer look. Derek clenched his teeth. The pilot was really getting close. How could anyone be so crazy? The patients behind him were loudly shouting warnings. Was there no way to send him a signal to turn away?

Mary turned toward him, and for the first time he noticed that he'd been gripping her shoulders very tightly. He apologized and started to carefully massage her shoulders. She tilted her head back and gave him a smile. Derek felt warmth on his cheeks. *That must be from the sun,* he thought. It was gradually moving toward the west. He had to shade his eyes with his hand to see the small airplane. It was not turning around. The pilot had probably missed his last chance. Derek knew from his training what an airplane was capable of. It wouldn't be able to avoid the rip now. Was he seeing things, or had the red fringes at the edge of the rip gotten bigger?

The airplane touched the rip.

"Oh man, oh man, oh man," Derek said involuntarily. The knuckles on his right hand cracked. The airplane disappeared.

DEREK LISTENED to the echo of his words. Had he just said something, and why?

"Did I just say something?" he asked Mary.

"You said the words 'oh man' three times," she answered.

He remembered. But he no longer knew why. He must have been upset about something.


READ MORE? Order the book here:
hard-sf.com/links/534368

# Copyright

Brandon Q. Morris
www.hard-sf.com
brandon@hard-sf.com
Translator: Roderich Bott
Editing Team: Marcia Kwiecinski, A.A.S. and Stephen Kwiecinski, B.S.

-- --

Technical Advisors: Dr. Lutz Hillmann, Hauke Sattler
Cover design: Haresh R. Makwana

Made in the USA
Coppell, TX
14 December 2021

68676452R00256